CORPORATE TORSOS NEED NOT APPLY

JR POMERANTZ

1

ALICE BURST INTO THE HOSPITAL

Alice burst into the hospital room as soon as the flood-safety airlock allowed. "This is ridiculous," she said. Now she faced the safety dais, a massive pyramid. "And so is this." She used the handrails to heave herself up the steep slope and scrambled to the bed.

"Every room has ten points of safety," the hospital flood-safety manager's recording chirped in her ear.

Ten points of *profit* was more like it.

"Noodle." Her mother's voice was upbeat for someone walled in by her sick bed's safety bars. "You got here fast. Have a seat. You must be exhausted."

Alice collapsed into the lone chair next to the bed. Now she was face-to-surgical tube — a tube full of pink fluid draining into a hideous contraption next to the bed. She examined the other end, where it connected to her mom, tube in skin, bubbling beige goop around the edges. A wave of nausea crashed in Alice's stomach.

"How do you feel? Is the tube stuff supposed to be that color? What did the doctor say? Did they get the tumor?"

Alice couldn't get all her questions out fast enough. Time to face the facts that had dragged her away from college.

"Oh, it's fine." Alice's mom tapped the tube. "Perfectly normal. Doctor says."

Time to face the past week's events: her mom's diabetes, her mom's unchecked blood sugar, her mom's flu, her mom's car accident, her mom's lung tumor. Her mom's mortality, come to call. "Hi, Alice," her mom's tumor was saying. "Oh, were you happy there at school? Perfect. Let's take that away from you, shall we? Come back to Nu Jersey now. It's time to suffer in your flood-threatened hellhole again."

Alice looked at her mom. Really took in the whole scene. Flipped up her monoculous and stared with both eyes.

She was the portrait of health. If you blocked out the tube and the goop, she could have been lounging in a spa.

You don't think your mom's going to be conscious after major lung surgery. You don't think your mom's going to be talking up a storm after major lung surgery. And you really don't think your mom's going to look like she entered a senior beauty pageant for the bedridden.

After major lung surgery.

It had been three months, the longest they'd ever been separated. Who was this new person? Gray hair dyed brown and shiny, *styled*, even. When was the last time Alice saw her mom's hair styled? Oh, yeah: *never*. Flattened under a lousy, hospital-issued headset so cheap, it didn't even have a monoculous. How would her mom watch clips? It didn't look like it was bothering her. Cheeks rosy, eyes bright.

"Perfectly normal? With a tube sticking out of you? On this stupid pyramid? I should have come yesterday."

"Oh, Noodle. It's for safety. The surgery went well. I'm going to be fine."

"How long do you have to stay here?" How was she talking and breathing with a tube sticking out of her lung?

"You didn't have to come, you know."

This whole disaster wouldn't have happened if I hadn't left you, Alice didn't say. Guilt flushed her face, searing her cheeks worse than the low-grade fever her headset signaled.

"The car did all the work. You know. All you have to do is program it and touch the wheel every three minutes. Then you sit there and wait. Anyway, I had to come. You can't drive yourself home after lung surgery."

"Yes, I can. The car does all the work."

A monitor in the distance screeched the flat line of a motionless heart.

It could have been her, flatlining. Any moment, it could still *be* her. Her mom was all she had. Alice couldn't imagine losing her.

"I'm glad you're here." She patted Alice's hand.

"Me too."

"Take off your headpiece and let me get a good look at you."

Pre-flooders always treated headsets like a silly accessory, not like a life preserver. Before the Flood, people didn't even wear headsets. They didn't need a locating device, a network that knew where you were at all times. In case of flood. No LINC back then to tell the network where you were when the water came crashing in. To tell you what to do, which way to go. To raise your safety dais higher. Close your airlock. Pump out the water. Pump in the oxygen.

Alice, like the rest of her peers, had been trained to keep the headset on at all times. She checked her monoculous for a non-existent message. Pinched her nose, which had gone cold. Shifted in the uncomfortable chair.

"Take off my headpiece," Alice repeated. Held her breath, as if the Flood was happening. Fought against the years of training, the disaster nursery rhymes.

Take off the LINC and you're gonna sink.

Was she afraid? Yes.

Did she have courage? Not really.

But she'd do anything for her mom.

Pre-flooders treated the Flood like an isolated incident. Data point of one. Eighteen years ago.

Flood babies and post-Floods knew better. It could happen again at any time. Best to stay panicked. It was good for the reflexes. Wasn't there a rhyme about that, too?

Alice flipped up the monoculous and removed her earpiece, slipping the headset off her head.

"There you are." Alice's mom touched her cheek. Her hand felt strong. Warm.

"How was the lung surgery? I wish I could have been here."

"Unless you're a doctor, you don't have to do much. Lie down and wait," her mom said.

"When are they going to release you? Tomorrow, you think?"

"Oh, sweetie. I don't know. They haven't said."

Alice needed to check for parking drones. She got up, popped her headset back on, descended the dais, and snuck a peek out the window. Just the hazy sky out there. No drones in sight. She ascended once more.

She'd only stopped once on the way up from Tampa, to use the bathroom. Forgot to plan it, she was so worried. Forgot to announce it ahead of time via LINC. You'd think the LINC could do it all by itself, without the additional administrative step.

Nope.

When she returned to the car, a parking drone was ticketing her junker right in front of her.

Unscheduled stopping. A thousand cryptos.

The drone whooshed off before she could curse or cry. Now she couldn't sustain any more financial accidents. All the money she had was borrowed, and there wasn't any more coming.

And her mom wasn't working.

Alice hadn't worked before, hadn't spent enough time at college yet to know how to do much of anything worth pay.

"Did they use the doctor-assisted robot arm to cut you open?"

"Oh, sure. I saw it before I went under. Big, ugly metal arm." Mom shifted and her mattress pad crackled under the weight. Still sturdy. Her body didn't look any different, except for the tube. "It was better-looking than my doctor."

Alice grinned.

"How's school?"

"Fine. Tampa Island is a lot different from Nu Jersey. They have a different attitude." She hadn't realized how much school meant to her until she had to leave it. She skirted the rusty metal box on the other end of her mom's lung tube. Resumed her seat. Bounced her leg.

"Are you happy there?" Mom looked through the dirty lens of Alice's monoculous and into Alice's heart, racing with unanswered questions.

Why did we stay in Nu Jersey after the Flood? Why didn't we leave?

"Sure. It's okay. I like it so far." Alice turned her head so Mom couldn't see her free eye well with tears. "But that's not what's important right now. Why didn't you call me at school when you got sick?"

"There was nothing you could do. It started a few weeks ago. I went to the doctor. Just the flu, they said. Gave me some pills, but that only ruined my insulin."

The big metal box at the end of the tube beeped. Alice jumped up.

"What is this thing?" Whatever it was, it was rusted. Nu Jersey hospitals still hadn't replaced all the medical equipment that had weathered the Flood.

"I don't know," her mom said. "But if a contraption that was underwater eighteen years ago still works and it's the only thing available, who am I to be picky? I'm an old woman. They ought to save the good stuff for the babies."

"I should call the nurse." Alice paced to the end of the safety dais and back.

"Now, Noodle, don't you worry. Sit back down. They'll come if there's a problem."

"Are you sure?"

"Positive. Come sit down." Alice sat herself back in the chair, couldn't stop bouncing her leg. She had this electric feeling running all through her body. Stress, probably. But she knew stress. This felt different. Maybe this was extreme stress. Recurring stress. Ruin-your-whole-life stress.

"Did you say, your insulin stopped working?"

"Right. They downgraded my hours at work last month. I was

spending more time at home. You know how damp our old place gets. I got the flu. They gave me some pills. My insulin stopped working. Then my pump was worthless."

Alice's mom wasn't eligible for a fake pancreas. Too old by the time it had hit the market. Didn't make the cut.

"Why didn't you call me?"

"And then I had the accident. A diabetic meltdown, they called it. Pretty dramatic if you ask me. Nothing melted. I don't remember anything. Guess I blacked out while I was driving. The medic said I took it off auto and tried to drive it myself."

Alice was holding her breath again. It slipped from her now, became a heavy sigh.

"They say I crashed the car immediately." Her mom laughed.

The laugh of another misfortune, of resigning herself to her fate. The laugh of life after the Flood. The laugh of putting all your effort into your child while retaining nothing for yourself.

Alice got up and resumed pacing the length of the dais plateau.

"Is it totaled?"

"Only a little fender bender. We auto-stopped right away, apparently."

"But not before you crashed."

"No," her mom laughed again, "not before I crashed."

"I haven't slept or eaten since I got the news at school. I was so worried. They piped it into my headset on Tuesday during bioanthropology class. The message wasn't from you though, it was from the hospital."

"I didn't want them to contact you. I didn't want you to worry."

Alice shuffled down the pyramid to look out the lone flood-proof window again. One drone, distant. Didn't look like a parking drone.

"Too bad. I'm worried."

"You didn't drop out of school, did you?"

"No." Alice's voice betrayed her as usual, advertised the lie with a squeak. Mom didn't probe.

"Good," was all she said.

Maybe they had hit a place in life where they simply lied to each other out of convenience and ignored it out of courtesy. Adulthood: That's what it was called.

"A car accident was the best thing for me," she said. "Those paramedics had no choice but to send me through the CAT scan, and that's when they found this golf ball." Alice's mom pointed to the spot where the tube entered her lung.

"Luckiest car accident ever. A golf ball?" Alice's mind tried to imagine how any of this was good.

"Yep. That's the size of my tumor. Cancer, the doctor said. Ninety-nine percent certain. Had to come out."

The pink liquid in its plastic tube slowed, reversed, headed back into the lung.

"Is it supposed to be doing this?"

"Yes, yes. The doctor explained everything." Mom's headset went askew from her violent nodding. Alice straightened it and smoothed her mom's hair.

"What did you do to your hair?" Alice asked.

"How was it crossing the levee?" her mom countered. Alice decided to accept a sick woman's deflection, but it was too weird, the hair. Did the hospital do it?

"Fine, no problem." Alice tweaked her own nose and sniffed. The eastern seaboard toll had gone up, actually. Way up. Way way way way way way up. She'd only been able to afford the trip because school had let her keep some loan cryptos upon withdrawal.

"Were there lots of cars on the road?"

"No."

"Noodle, did you start after dark?" Anger crept into her mother's voice at Alice's safety violation, but they were interrupted by the airlock's violent gasp. Alice jumped. Life in Nu Jersey was stupid — you spent most of your time locking and unlocking all the safety doors as if the next floodwaters were hovering above the building, waiting to crush you.

And what if they were? Airlocked patients were supposed to rise out of their hospital beds and remove their own lung tubes while waiting for the waters to subside? Alice longed to get back to Florida.

Beautiful Tampa island. It was obvious Nu Jersey had never recovered from one little devastating tsunami, eighteen years ago. The only thing waiting to crush Alice now was debt.

A nurse pushed a small cart ahead of her, hitting the button to close the safety door and repressurize the airlock.

"Hold," she called. Alice slid her foot into the foothold under the chair. The nurse hit the safety dais button next to the door, and they braced for descent. Nothing happened. She hit it again. Didn't budge.

"At least we're safely in the air instead of down there in the Flood zone," her mom said.

"I wonder why it isn't working," Alice said.

The nurse's face said she wasn't interested in looking on the bright side or examining the intricacies of flood-tech engineering. She sighed and pushed the cart up the safety dais, sweating. In post-flood Nu Jersey, it was all uphill, all the time.

"Hey," Alice said. "I think there's a problem with this tube. It looks like the pink gunk is getting backed up."

The nurse paused to catch her breath and then burst into action. One gloved hand reached into her pocket, pulled out a stick of gum, and popped it into her mouth.

Not a medical procedure.

"Impossible," she said.

"But I just saw it. Could you tell me how the surgery went?"

"That's confidential. Now please step into the hallway."

"What do you mean? Mom, tell her she can tell me what's going on —"

The nurse looked at Alice like *she* was the tumor. It killed Alice's words in her throat. How was she ever going to protect her mom from Nu Jersey health care?

"You go on, Noodle." Mom waved her out. Her tone was even, matter of fact. "I'll be alright. We'll talk later."

Bright eyes. Too bright. Did they have her on some experimental drugs? Either she was on drugs, or surgery really agreed with her. Maybe both.

"Alright," Alice said, resigned. "I'll go check out the food options. But I'm coming right back."

She descended the dais and left the room, then lurked in the hallway, trying to hear through the airlock. Finally, the nurse came out.

"Your mother's fine. The surgery was a success. She needs rest, that's all."

This medical warden took a moment to stare Alice down before flipping her monoculous up and stalking off.

Alice wasn't so sure.

2

SENATOR SAM HURST SCREAMED

Senator Sam Hurst screamed into Bob's ear. "Did you hear me? He's dead!"

Who was dead?

Bob had either blacked out from stress or fallen back to sleep. He peeled his head up from the pillow, adjusted his headset, clicked his monoculous into place.

Sam (D-NY) had reversed his monoculous view so Bob saw what he did: Senator Tom Fletch.

Tom had his head down on the table at their usual Regency suite, a congressional clubhouse for scheming and whoring.

Bob bolted upright. "What? He's *dead*?" His voice occupied a special place between a whisper and a shriek. "Get the other senators," he said, swallowing the bile in the back of his throat. It was always back there. This wasn't *special occasion* bile. "I'm coming."

Either viewing the corpse of a key senator in his cabal or sitting up too quickly was too much for Bob's insides, and his acid reflux won its way into his mouth.

"You better get here before Fletch Senior does." Sam's tone was half threat, half plea. He disconnected without waiting for Bob to respond.

Bob ran a panic marathon around his condo. Spit into the sink. Zapped half his face with his laser razor. Put his plastishirt on. Zapped another quarter of his face. Threw on his buoysocks. Ripped open the door. Slammed it shut. Found some pants. Cursed the slow elevator. Hurled himself into his car. Screamed, *Central Nu Jersey Regency Premiere*. And sat there, waiting for the car to spring into action, sweating and shaking and swearing.

Bob forgot to override flood safety settings, so his car paused at The Flood Memorial, a holographic re-enactment in the center of downtown Trenton.

There was no way to override: It was mandatory.

Twenty-nine seconds ticked by. He watched them go in his monoculous.

Bob punched the roof of his car and let out a guttural scream. The car continued after the necessary time period and arrived at the hotel, steering him toward the valet parking as usual.

Bob yelled, "No, don't. DON'T. Park in the lot, PARK IN THE PARKING LOT. *THE PARKING LOT!*"

The car steered him to just outside the lot and shut itself off. "You've arrived at your destination," it announced. It was an older model.

On the topic of older models: Fletch Senior. Was he here already?

Bob slipped into the Regency through a side entrance and swiveled his head in all directions. Nobody in sight. No camera crews, no cops, no lurkers from *LINCNewsNow!* Nobody knew about Tom yet. They could fix this.

He took the flood-proof elevator to the tenth floor and tapped on the usual door.

It opened, just a sliver.

"Who is it?" Sam whispered from the other side.

Bob crammed his body through the crack and tumbled into the room, falling to the floor. He picked himself up.

There he was: Senator Tom Fletch. Dead. Seated at the head of their usual planning table. Face down in a pile of beige powder the size of a delivery drone.

"Hi, Bob." Gina's primary talent, besides the hooking, was snapping her chewing gum rapid fire, and she did it now, right in Bob's face, staccato blasts.

"What happened?" Bob could count on her, anyway. She was one of the gang's regular prostitutes. More consistent and trustworthy than his colleagues.

"I dunno. I didn't talk to him today. You know he only does chitchat with the boss. She said it was time to party, the usual, get there now, like two-minutes-ago now. So Cindi and I came on by. And he's like this. I guess he made a mistake."

Bob sat down hard on the minibar. "I guess he made a mistake," he echoed.

He ran to the hallway bathroom and dry-heaved. Came back. His insides were a tornado of fire, spitting battery acid up into his esophagus.

Bob sat down again next to Tom. Still dead. He went through his options, as if staring at them through his monoculous:

> Quit
> Leave town
> Kill self
> Deal with it

Only three of the eleven had shown up so far, and were lounging around the room, useless, looking lost. They'd been like that ever since their fathers selected them to run the Northeast Corridor of the United States of America, as far as Bob knew.

"Sam? Where are the others?" Sam didn't answer, slumped over at the table. Wouldn't make eye contact. Kept on staring vacantly out the window. Or was he looking at something in his monoculous? "What are you doing? Are you watching a clip? We've only got Virginia and Massachusetts."

He scooted his chair closer to the drug pile, Bob noted.

"And Rhode Peninsula," Rhode Peninsula called from the adjacent bedroom.

"You can call us by our names, you know. We're not just states," Massachusetts said.

"You're *just states* to me," Bob shot back. "States that formed a bloc we controlled, until one of you royally screwed us all. The most irritating, irresponsible states ever."

Bob sighed and hung his head. Blew out the invisible candle, low and slow, like in the therapy clips. He peered into the bedroom, where Rhode Peninsula held a laser razor in one hand, his monoculous in the other. The senator squinted into his device, repeated a tip on beard trimming, and poorly mimicked the advice with his razor-holding hand. He zapped part of his goatee off. A whole chunk of it, gone.

"Goddamn it!" Bob yelled. "What the hell are you doing? Put that down, for *Flood's* sake. No, don't. Now you have to zap the other half off."

Something rustled behind Bob. He whirled around. Sam scooped a fistful of mystery drug off the table. Their eyes locked. Sam bolted for the master bath, trailing powder across the suite. Bob was a second too late: Sam waved the door shut just in time.

"Sam. Sam, come out here." Bob's voice sounded like his own father's. He pounded on the door.

"No," Sam said with firm and irrational resolve, like the toddler Bob didn't have. How could anybody reproduce around here, even if they did have a willing partner, when there were all these sixty-to-ninety-year-old children to watch? "I can have this. I *can*."

Bob sighed and gave up. So many battles lost in one single day. He turned back to the table. To Tom.

Virginia sat at the table next to Tom, picking his teeth. He prodded Tom's lifeless hand with a magnetic etcher from the hotel-provided stationary set.

"Man, cut it out."

"He doesn't mind," Virginia shrugged. "He's dead."

Rhode Peninsula emerged from the bedroom, newly shorn and red-chinned from the laser razor.

"Why'd you have to mess with your dumb beard in the first

place?" Bob said, his voice becoming a whine. "Now you look different. We need to act normal."

"I think it makes me look more distinguished."

"I think it makes you look like an actual vagina," Virginia said. "I think you *have* a vagina and you *look* like a vagina."

"I think you can go fuck yourself," Rhode Peninsula said. He poked at the coffee maker with no result, then raised his hand and tilted his head to connect to room service. Bob leapt over and swatted his headset off his head before he could connect.

"Not now!" Bob shouted. He pointed his thumb at Tom, like Tom's corpse was driving and Bob needed to hitch a ride.

"I'll be over here in the bedroom if anybody needs me," Gina called over her shoulder.

Bob needed to hitch a ride, alright. The room was getting a smell.

"Sure, Gina. Thanks," he said.

"Sam, are you taking a dump in there?" Rhode Peninsula called.

Bob crossed to the bathroom door and pounded on it until Sam responded.

"No," he said through the door. "I'm not. Stop knocking. I'm busy. Use the other bathrooms. I'm powering up so I can think us out of this mess."

"You think it's such a great idea to do a bunch of drugs that already killed a man today?"

Sam didn't answer. Maybe he was already dead.

"Yeah, yeah. Sure you are." Bob glanced at Tom again and wished he were dead too. All these years of political positioning, of getting these guys into power, of keeping them there despite their ineptness and creeping decrepitude. All ruined by the only one who was kind of a friend.

Not a real friend, though. Those didn't exist in politics, or in post-Flood America.

"I need coffee." Rhode Peninsula's whining touched a nerve deep down in Bob's fatigued brain.

"I need you to shut up," he spat back. "How is it you don't know how to use the coffee maker? How many times have you been in this room?"

"I don't know, but I don't." Rhode Peninsula looked so desperate Bob felt guilty. How did that work, exactly? *He* was useless, and *Bob* felt bad.

"Fine. I'll do it," Bob said for what must have been the *heptillionth* time during his press-secretary career. Working for the Illuminati *sucked*. He plopped into the chair next to Tom's corpse.

Sam emerged from the bathroom and sat down next to Bob. Side-eyed the drug, nosebleed in progress. "We need to talk."

"Not now," Bob said, rubbing his temples. "Wipe your nose."

Sam was on top of Bob in an instant, superhuman. He seized Bob by the jacket and dragged him across the suite, shoving him through the doorway of the master bathroom and waving the door closed.

Press secretaries never got any respect.

"You smell awful," Bob said. "You're so, so swampy. It's making me —" Bob gagged.

"You listen to me," Sam snarled. "Fletch Senior could knock on this door any minute, or the other door, any door, I don't know which door he's going to knock on, and I'll be goddamned if we don't have a plan when he does." He was flush with sweat, too close, moistening the air near Bob's face and clogging his nose. Bob tore himself free.

Tom's dad. That shriveled old ballsack.

"I'm not afraid of—"

"You should be." The senator licked his lips over and over in rapid succession.

"I'm handling it." If not for the Post-Flood Government Reduction Act, Bob would have had twice as many senators on his hands. What a nightmare. Then again, he wouldn't have lost coverage for an entire state with one drug overdose. "We've got an hour. Maybe more."

"Once Tom's LINC reports him dead to Fletch Senior, we're finished," Sam squeaked. "He probably already knows."

The delicate positioning of eleven powerful *politicorp* families laid to waste, thanks to the mastermind's idiot son, Senator Tom Fletch II (R-NJ).

"Great, thanks. I definitely couldn't have figured that out on my own. Drugs are making you super sharp today. Try not to die in here." Bob escaped the bathroom, waving the door shut behind him. He needed to think. Sam could flip out alone.

He headed over to the main room's bar, hit the button on the coffee maker and paced, waiting for it to print.

Rhode Peninsula crept in and stole it as soon as it was finished.

"Hey! Give it back." Bob gave a commanding look, never effective. Rhode Peninsula simply stared back at him and raised the cup of coffee.

"Stop it. Give it here."

Rhode Peninsula put the cup to his lips. Took a good, long slurp.

Bob sighed and hit the print button on the coffee maker again, resuming his wait.

"What's your problem, Bob?" Rhode Peninsula sat down hard on the bar couch. Its flotation-device cushion farted. He giggled.

"My problem? My problem is I've got a body to deal with here, not to mention the drugs and whores you guys always keep around. That's my problem."

"Nah, buddy. Steve can take care of it. I can connect him in right now. And Gina doesn't talk. She knows when to open her mouth and when to keep it shut. Don't kill her."

"Don't kill me, Bob," Gina called from the bedroom.

"I'm not, Gina. I'm not."

Bob peeked out the lone window of the Regency's priciest suite. He and the gang owned this region. No camera crews. No spy drones. Publicity wouldn't be an issue.

"Write the press release like you always do," Rhode Peninsula said. "Tom was jogging. He had a heart attack. Super sad. Congress is really sad. Put all the flags at half mast."

Bob drained his coffee in one go and swallowed his bio-cup whole. He missed the cup material of his youth. Was it paper back then? Now he couldn't remember. You didn't have to eat it when you finished using it, he knew that much. He hit print, waited five seconds, gulped and ate the next cup of coffee.

"The problem isn't the press release, Dave. The problem is this person-sized hole we now have in our secret society." Bob sat down and tapped his headset, drafted the announcement, fingers flying on the virtual keyboard in front of him. Queued it up in the LINC→News™ national and northeast corridor editions. His hand hovered above the *send* button on his monoculous.

"Guys, who's gonna replace him?"

"I dunno." Rhode Peninsula shrugged.

Sam jogged in. His nosebleed had run from lip to chin and down to collar by now. "An outsider? No. Fletch Senior always says *no outsiders*. What if he tells people about us? Some turncoat runs to the *LINC Times*, we gotta kill him. Or discredit him—"

"Maybe," Rhode Peninsula said, "we should discredit, *then* kill him?"

"What about Tom 's corporation?" Bob cut in.

"How about this?" Rhode Peninsula stood up and puffed out his chest, ready to self-congratulate. "We find someone who *looks* like Tom and brainwash him to think he *is* Tom. How many people know what Tom looked like, anyway?"

"I'll tell you what. I'll tell you what. I'll tell you what."

"Fucking stop it, Sam, you're saying everything three times again, just like the last time. Saturday." Rhode Peninsula slapped Sam across the face, then rubbed the crusted blood remnants on Sam's shirt.

"Thanks," Sam said. "This gets a little rough in the second hour." He wiped the rest of the blood on his face off with the tails of his shirt, then pulled it over his head and handed it to Bob.

"I need a new one," he said. "And I'll tell you all what. Tom's dad is gonna show up and murder us because we let this happen. This ruins the Project. This ruins the Project good."

"Fletch Senior is so old." Rhode Peninsula wandered closer to the table to check out the powder pile. "I don't even know if he's mobile anymore."

"Oh he's mobile, alright. I saw him two weeks ago and I don't wanna see him again," Sam said. "Ever." He opened his eyes as wide as he could. "That old monster isn't gonna cry any tears over his boy, I don't think. He'll be too busy murdering *you*." Sam stabbed the air near Bob's forehead with a two-finger anti-salute. "So you better figure something out."

Bob got up and looked outside. Still no activity in the parking lot, no drones in the skyway. Only Trenton Bay out there, placid to the point of stagnation. Bob drew the curtain closed.

The suite door slid open. Unannounced. No buzz at the door. No identity announcement in his headset. A man walked in. An actual stranger walked through the hotel room's unguarded door.

Bob dropped the cup of coffee he had just printed. All the senators looked up.

A new witness? Bob would have to murder him. His first political murder. How would he even kill anybody? Could he use a laser razor? He'd never murdered anybody before. Could he? No. Not immediately anyway. Maybe over time? Also no. He ran to position himself between the man and the body, but it was too late.

"There's no use hiding Tom Fletch's corpse from me, Bob." The stranger's face was too chiseled.

"Who the hell are you?" Bob shivered under his plastishirt, though he wasn't cold.

"I'm Eric Smith." His hair was too combed. And his chin: too defined.

"Never heard of you." Eric Smith hadn't left one-fourth of his facial hair on his un-panicked face.

"Tom Fletch Senior sent me. I'm in charge now."

Bob vomited two cups of hotel coffee and partially digested biocups onto the table, where they mixed with the pile of mystery drug, bubbled and fizzed.

3

ALICE HEADED TWO FLOORS DOWN

lice needed to kill an hour or two before she checked on her mom's progress for the *gazillionth* time, so she headed two floors down to investigate the cafeteria. The hospital was a maze. Every so often a cluster of LED lights was out, making it a dim maze, too. She waited for her food while two employees behind the counter argued over the amount of noodles to give her. Nu Jersey was an easy ten years behind the rest of the country. At school, machines dispensed the noodles. And the machines didn't short you.

She sat at a table alone and shoved noodles into her mouth. Was this bland garbage what her mom had in mind when she had given her the nickname Noodle?

Alice wasn't even interested in scrolling headset clips today to see what was going on at school. When would she be back? It was hard to say. Her stomach turned itself inside out. She couldn't get away from the smell of antiseptic. Even her noodles smelled like they had been sanitized, but Alice couldn't remember the last time she'd eaten. She shoved more disinfected noodles into her mouth, over and over, even though she wasn't hungry.

When she got back to her mother's room, the airlock wouldn't open. Alice waved and waved, but got no response. Was everything in this stupid hospital broken? She made a fist, pounded on the sensor. The grunting and cursing sounded distant, but it was definitely coming from her.

The nurse swooped in.

"I need you to come with me," she said matter-of-factly to the floor in front of Alice. Flecks of pink fluid splattered the length of her uniform.

"What happened?"

The nurse didn't answer. Instead, she turned and walked briskly down the hallway. Alice stared at the nurse's back until her feet began moving underneath her, almost on their own, her mind both frantic *and* somehow turned off at the same time. The hallway opened into a holding area.

"Wait here," the nurse said. Her commitment to providing no information riled up Alice's stomach acid.

No windows. All the waiting room residents were either busy on their LINCs or horrifically wounded. Alice sat until she had to stand. She stood until she had to pace. She paced until she was ready to scream.

And she was really, really ready to scream.

She'd resolved to bolt and try her mom's airlock again when a drone wheeled in and stopped in front of her. Its interface screen creaked open. Not a well-oiled machine.

GREETINGS, **designated kin. Please list pre-existing conditions of Patient 8766**.

WHY DIDN'T they have this on file? And why did they have to refer to her mom as a number? But she knew the answer. She knew all the answers, almost by heart. Safety was the only thing they'd given her any information on. It was mandatory. The hospital's safety officer had told her during the briefing: The number is the LINC location. Being located means safety, **In Case Of Flood.**

Anyway, *focus*. List her mom's pre-existing conditions. Okay, she could do this. Her palms began to sweat.

Daughter. It was the only pre-existing condition she could recall. Alice's mom has a pre-existing daughter. She wanted to scream-cry this fact out loud to the room.

Why couldn't she focus? Time to remember all the things her mom had survived.

Across the room, a little boy bled from the side of his head and screamed. Alice leaned closer and saw the cause. An eating utensil, lodged in his temple. Standard-issue metal spork. How does that sort of thing happen? No, don't think about the spork. Focus.

She scrambled through her worried brain to find the right information and pecked a few sentences into the touchscreen.

Born and raised in upstate Nu York

Childhood car accident

Ruptured spleen from a childhood car accident

Life without a spleen

A burst of static in Alice's earpiece made her jump. But she had no time to waste on headset problems. She ignored it.

Lost half a thyroid to thyroid carcinoma

Moving to Nu Jersey

Living in Nu Jersey

Caesarean section of a premature baby

Gestational diabetes

The Flood

Ovarian cysts; simultaneous suspicion of endometrial cancer [ruled out]

The static interrupted her again, louder this time. Was it picking up another signal? She tapped the earpiece. Sometimes a little banging corrected a minor glitch. The thing was old, anyway. Probably needed replacing. It stopped buzzing.

Last week:

Diabetic ketoacidosis

Car accident

Golf-ball–sized lung tumor

Lung surgery

Pink fluid in lung tube

She was done. She hit the button, replaced the stylus. The medical drone creaked away, wheeled itself down the hall. She chewed her nails ragged. Where was the nurse?

The low roar in her headset returned, and it got louder and higher in pitch. Then her earpiece shocked her right inside the ear canal. Alice yanked it off.

She had her fingers in her ear and her headset around her neck, looking here and there for any sign of what was going on. She noticed the spork-child's mother yanked her own headset off, too. Then a new nurse edged into her periphery.

"I finished the list," Alice breathed a little easier. She didn't know what she'd done to incite the other nurse's icy stare of possible judgement, but she wanted to stay out of its path. "Of my mom's pre-existing conditions? It wheeled itself somewhere."

"I'm sorry," the nurse addressed her apology to the air above Alice's left shoulder.

She didn't sound sorry.

"You don't have to apologize. The other nurse was just kinda..."

Wait. What was she sorry about?

The nurse was holding her headset and rubbing her ear, too. But this wasn't an apology. This was something else.

"What happened? What's going on?" Alice asked.

"I don't know. Solar flare?"

"No, with my mom. What's going on with my mom? When I got back, the airlock was closed."

"Like I said, there was nothing we could do." The nurse's tone was neutral. She put on her headset and tapped her monoculous. "It's working fine now."

"What do you mean? Nothing you could do about what? Where's my mom?" Alice stood. The noodles in her stomach rolled and tumbled and threatened to surface. She gulped down a mouthful of bile.

"Put on your headset," the nurse said. She didn't look at Alice, she stared past her. "It'll tell you everything you need to know."

Alice turned around to see what the nurse was looking at, but there was nothing there, only the empty hall. When she turned back around, the nurse was gone.

Alice put on her headset.

WE'RE SORRY. Patient 8766 is deceased due to infection.

ALICE FLIPPED her monoculous up and down. The words remained, hovering in space. She got up.

She couldn't breathe. Her heart beat hard and her chest hurt. Involuntarily, she sat back down, gripped so tight her fingertips turned white.

"No."

Alice stared through the text until she stood up and bolted out of the holding room. She had to find her mother.

This must be a mistake, a glitch in the system.

She stumbled through hallway after hallway until she found somebody sitting behind a counter.

"I need help."

The man stared into his monoculous for so long it was hard to tell if he'd heard her.

Alice rapped on the counter. "Can you help me?"

He tapped off the clip on his headset and looked up. "What's your customer number?"

"Customer number? I don't know. I don't have one. They said my mom died."

"When?"

"Five minutes ago. It's got to be a mistake. I was just with her and she was fine." Alice's chest was so tight she couldn't take in a full breath.

"It should say a number. The patient number. Corresponds with her secure location. You know, in case—" He lifted his arm and swooped it down onto the counter like an animated diagram of the Flood.

"Oh." Alice tapped her monoculous. "Here, it's here. I've got it. She's number 8766."

"You said she's dead, right?" The man waved his hand back and forth, peering through his monoculous and manipulating a database only he could see. "Not what I'm showing here."

Alice leaned over to try to catch a glimpse of his monoculous view, but it was impossible. This low-tech death factory didn't even have upLINC monitors.

"I didn't say she's dead. I said that's what the nurse said. But she's wrong. There must have been some mistake. She didn't even look sick. She looked...great."

"Don't have to look sick to be sick. Didn't look like it was going to flood before the Flood, did it?"

Alice didn't get a chance to argue, because the sound in her earpiece rose from a low static to a shrieking metallic whine until it was so loud she had to tear off her headset. When she looked up, the clerk was holding his, too, and tugging on his ear.

"Second time today, and I haven't taken this thing off in five years," he said. "Never experienced anything like it. You?"

"No, but about my mom — you're saying she's not dead?"

"This is no good. Look at us, off the grid. What if the flood comes? You and I would be goners. How are we gonna survive if we can't even keep our own emergency placement system online?" He looked around as if the floodwaters were going to rush in at any moment and then shoved on his headset.

"Patient 8766. Got it right here. Still active."

"What?"

"Doesn't say she's inactive. Says online. Put your headset on."

Alice did. "But they told me she died."

The man paused for a moment. "Oh, yep. Changed over now. Deceased."

"What? Does it say *how*?"

"Oops. Would you look at that? Says alive now."

Alice banged her fist on the counter in frustration. "Which is it? Is she alive or dead?"

"Hard to say for sure. I'll buzz her headset. Maybe they moved her without telling you."

"The nurse told me my mom was dead." Alice held up one hand, trying to think back to just minutes ago. She struggled to remember what had happened earlier, clutched her forehead as if she could somehow extract the info. Why was it so hard? "Wait. Actually, that's not true. She told me to look at my headset, and the headset said she was dead. Maybe it was a mistake. Are you saying my mom is still alive?"

The man shrugged. "Looks like it. Oh wait, here we are. Rolled over. Status says deceased."

Alice stifled a scream. "Which one *is it*?"

He frowned, rubbing the back of his neck. "Hold on. Alive. Definitely says alive now. Right here." He tapped empty space. "Alive."

"Please tell me you can help me find her. *Please*."

"I've got the headset location right here. Let's go take a look."

"Oh, thank you so much." Relief eased the pain crushing Alice's chest and stomach and ability to think. "I'm so glad I found you. You're the only person in this hospital who's been helpful. Uh, what department is this?"

"Billing. Says here you owe 72,000 cryptos. Let me unhook myself here and we'll go get this all figured out." Billing unlatched his ankle bracelet, let himself out of his cubicle, and started down the hall with Alice behind him. Alice put that unthinkable amount of money out of her head, so she could focus on finding her mom. Two horrific clerical errors on the same day. What were the odds?

Me and mom'll have a good laugh about this later.

"Did it say she'd been moved to another room?"

"Didn't say, but our patient database connects to the LINC so we can recover the intake headset. We'll find her."

Alice turned the corner and slammed right into a man. His shirt

brushed her cheek in the collision, and she was shocked to feel —
was that cloth? Who ever wore clothes that weren't flood-proof?

Unheard of. Hazardous.

"Excuse me," the cloth-clothed, clearly insane man said. His voice
was as slippery as the plastishirt he wasn't wearing.

He paused there in the hallway, probably waiting for an apology,
but she didn't have the time or the energy for manners. She brushed
past.

Billing hadn't noticed. He was down the hallway, talking about
billing. Alice ran to catch up.

"Costs fifteen thousand cryptos if we don't get our headset back.
We'll find your mom's headset. And your mom."

"Do mistakes like this happen a lot?"

"Sure." His monoculous eye drifted to a vacant place. Maybe he
was still watching clips. "Accidents happen all the time."

"I'm not talking about an accident, I'm talking about a mistake.
Like, they told me she was dead but she's really alive."

"Seventh floor." Billing read from his monoculous. "Looks like
we've got a hit."

He jabbed the elevator button. They waited for it to depressurize.
Hurry up and wait. Something her mother always said.

The paint near the ceiling was flaked away, revealing a waterline
beneath that meant every patient on the first floor would have
drowned.

"Great safety features in this hospital," Billing straightened
himself up tall, as if he had designed it himself. "Safety dais in every
room. Airlocks. Pressurized elevators. Best place to be in a flood."

"I wouldn't know." Alice didn't want to say something rude to the
only person in the hospital willing to help her, but nothing in this
hospital worked right. "I've never been in another." And her mother
was missing, misfiled in their great, great safety system.

The lights got too bright. She couldn't hear Billing anymore. Her
breath quickened, vision tunneled. Her mom had to be alive.

The LED closest to Alice winked out. She propped herself up
against the wall.

"You alright?" A tap on the shoulder.

Alice roused herself, squeezed her fists, breathed in slow and deep until her vision came back.

The elevator doors were open.

Billing was inside already, hand outstretched, tap-tap-tapping her on the shoulder. "Hey, are you alright?"

"Long day." She got in.

Next week would be a better week. She and her mom would eat noodle cups together, discuss how to pay for the hospital fees. Plan for Alice to get back to school. They would put this behind them, laugh about it. Maybe she could convince her mom to move out of Nu Jersey. It was sunny next week, in her imagination, even though she'd never seen a Nu Jersey day without a haze.

The elevator's climate control function was broken. It was too hot, suffocating. Billing's forehead dripped sweat, mirroring Alice's own. A ticking sound in the wall like a buried clock got louder as the elevator slowed.

Alice smoothed the bunching in her plastishirt.

"Thanks for this," she said. He was reuniting her with her mother. The least she could do was show her appreciation.

"All in a day's work," he said.

Were they misplacing patients every single day?

Their elevator leveled into its chute and re-pressurized. Alice imagined her mom in a new room, one with a working safety dais. Smiling. *I'm fine, Noodle. They moved my room. What's all the fuss about?*

Alice tipped her head to one side, then the other, as if advancing a five-second clip in her headset. Her neck had been pinched since she got the news. She kneaded the painful knot with one hand. Everything was going to be fine.

"Right this way," Billing said. Alice followed him so closely that a drop of his sweat spattered her cheek.

"Oh," he said, stopping abruptly a few seconds later. "We're here." He reached out to wave the door open.

There was no airlock on this one. It didn't need to be flood proofed.

The sign said it all.

MORGUE

DON'T PANIC. It's a mistake. An elaborate mistake.

Alice's body tingled. Her stomach fluttered.

She followed him in. It was so cold she could see her breath. There wasn't much of it, because she couldn't breathe anymore. It was going to be okay. They'd find her Mom's misplaced headset in here.

Alice knew she wasn't dead.

And then, there she was.

Lone body on a metal table. White plastic sheet up to the neck. Mom.

Alice crumpled to the ground. Beadlets of sweat sprang up on her body and froze. It was so cold. The room closed in.

"No," Alice said, warmth of her exhaled denial condensed around her. "No. No. No."

Billing came over and helped her up, propped her on a vacant table.

"This is a mistake," she said. "She was fine. This hospital made a mistake."

Alice searched her mother's face for a flicker of life. Billing approached the body and pulled off the hospital's headset.

"That confirms it," he said. "I dunno why the LINC has been so testy today. Maybe it deserves a break after eighteen years. Must have been this little guy having a malfunction." He rattled the headset and then tapped his own monoculous. "It's correct now. Deceased. Patient 8766."

Alice's breath came hard and shallow, rasping like the short static bursts of the LINC.

"Look at this," Billing said. He picked up a fancy-looking plant lying atop the sheet. "It's a flower. Is this real? You never see these anymore. I don't even think it's a *fauxlower*."

Alice couldn't respond. She needed to get out.

"It doesn't smell like mushrooms," he mused, twirling its stem. "It's like a rose, from the pre-Flood days. I don't know how they did it. Haven't seen one of these in ages." Billing held it out to her. Alice shook her head. She couldn't stop shaking her head. She reached out and took the flower with a numb and trembling hand. She didn't want it.

She wanted her mom.

"You wanna settle up your bill?"

"Not now." Alice's mind was blank and her voice was blank and her life was blank.

"Okay, up to you. They'll put it through your LINC. Usually give ya thirty days. Hey, I'm sorry about your mom."

Alice didn't respond. She backed out of the morgue on auto-pilot. Didn't speak to anybody. Slipped unnoticed into and out of the elevator. Wandered through hallway after hallway until she found the exit. She collapsed into the front seat of her car.

There on the windshield, her latest parking ticket flapped in the breeze.

Why were there plenty of drones to issue parking tickets but none to save her mother's life?

It was a long drive home, but the car did all the work.

4

THE DRIVE BACK TO THE OFFICE

The drive back to the office was as silent and uncomfortable as the rest of Bob's time with Eric. He got a headache. Then a nosebleed. Nerves, not drugs. Now he had his own buoysock stuffed up a nostril. It acted as more of a plug than an absorptive.The sun was strong once the haze had burned off, and Bob sweated into his nose sock, too.

Eric and the new guy looked fine.

Of *course* they did.

He couldn't stand to be around this new newcomer worshipping this old newcomer while he, the oldcomer, suffered disrespect and neglect. He'd been trying to get just a shred of respect since the Flood, and it had only taken a few days with Eric Smith to wipe it all out. Now he was the has-been of his own stupid secret society.

They pulled into headquarters. The inverted glass pyramid was extra blinding. Eric and the actor adopted a breakneck pace across the parking lot, forcing Bob into a trot. He squinted into the building beyond. He caught his jacket on the emergency backup sensor for the automatic door at the main entrance. When he tore himself free, the whole panel came loose and shattered on the ground.

"I'll have it fixed," he called ahead to two people who weren't listening. Didn't even turn to see where he was or if he needed help.

The new congressman, already busy working on trustworthy hand movements per Eric's instructions, pointed at a potted plastic ficus with an open hand, then gestured with a closed fist, thumb up, at the lobby's virtual LINC Secretary.

He mouthed the lines Bob had sent to his LINC at Eric's instruction: old speeches of Tom's, to get in the right frame of mind.

BOB BROKE his silent pout in the elevator, after Tom 2 was safely sequestered in his new office. "How can we do this without a real election? How can we have a replacement senator from Nu Jersey? People are going to notice it's not Tom. People are going to notice we've got this actor instead of a real politician. People are going to notice us! You and me! They're going to say, who the hell are these guys and what are they doing installing senators?"

Bob's neck was reflected in the elevator, itchy red patches burning angry while Eric leaned against the elevator panel, chiseled out of granite. Staring through him. Saying not one word.

The elevator clicked into its chute and depressurized. Eric stayed silent, so Bob bolted. He swooped past Eleanor. She issued her characteristic salute: eye roll with snort.

"Eleanor, continue to hold all my LINC connects." Bob avoided eye contact.

"I don't think so, Bob." Eleanor was the worst executive assistant ever born. She hit the headset call transfer and was probably eating her noodle cup in a café down the street before Bob could rage against her insubordination. Her vacant chair was still pivoting with the force of her escape.

Bob's monoculous lit up immediately and bile crept up into his esophagus. He would have slammed his office door shut if he could figure out how to take it off autosensor mode. If any assistant had been out there to hear it.

"Bob?" It was Sam Hurst (D-NY). How long had it been since Sam had called about Tom's death? Forever. It had been forever since this coup began.

It was two days ago.

"Hi, Sam. What now? Somebody else die?"

"I saw your article in *The Time* this morning. I was surprised. I didn't know Fletch Industries was ready to push out the phase four LINC gear. I thought they'd need more time. Aren't they trying to find a replacement for Tom on the board?"

"What article? Break it down for me, Sam. I'm super busy these days; I can't keep up with everything." Bob sifted through a LINC search for something pornographic to take his mind off his troubles. He filtered a series of five-second clips about a powerful balding male being sexually respected by his secretary.

"I thought you were still running all the Science Bureau releases. Dad thought maybe you ran this one a little early; we aren't going to get the legislation passed until next week, if we even can without Tom. If people get the information early, they could oppose it, organize against us. I don't know if Fletch Industries is ready. Who's down there now? Tom Senior?"

Big Tom? Running Fletch Industries? That old sandbag wasn't even around on the regular. Legislation? Bob's head spun. He stopped scrolling his porn search.

"Oh, look, Eleanor's pounding on my door. She's saying there's an important connect, coming through in five. I gotta go, Sam. Send me the article, would you?" Bob nodded the connect closed. His hands shook.

Headsets Cause Eye Cancer: *A Time LINC Op-Ed*

LAST WEEK, U.S. Science Bureau head Dr. Art Huntington™ released conclusive evidence from a decade-long, double-blind randomized control trial suggesting phase three iterations of LINC devices are having a negative effect on vision in the United States.

. . .

STUDIES HAVE SHOWN use does not have to be prolonged to result in astigmatism, myopia, and worsening of pre-existing eye conditions. Today in Congress, the House Ways and Means Committee introduced legislation to subsidize a healthier future: high-resolution, LINC-capable headsets for all American families — those in the critically flood-threatened Northeast Corridor and beyond.

AMERICANS DESERVE access to safety without suffering a decline in optic capacity.

BOB'S MIND RACED. It must have been Eric. Initiating the new LINC network way before it was ready. Creating the press release. Taking over completely. Then messing it all up. Pretty-boy Eric, screwing up the master plan. Where had he *come* from? Bob couldn't wait to rub this mistake in his stupid handsome face. He was way off schedule. They weren't supposed to deploy for months.

He stood up, clicked off his alternate LINC projection monitor, set it in his fish tank. The robot fish investigated it. They were as real as TUNAPHARM©. Which was to say, not at all.

"Who's running the show now?"

Bob's robot fish didn't know. And neither did he.

ERIC BURST IN. "MEETING TIME." He dragged Bob down to the conference room.

"I saw your press release," Bob said to the back of Eric's head. "A little premature, don't you think? The headsets aren't even ready."

"Oh, they're ready," Eric responded, his voice acidic with self confidence.

All the senators were in the boardroom, seated except for Massachusetts. He'd won a sloth in an exotic animal gambling event last week and carried it around everywhere like a baby, despite several accidents with its claws. Either it smelled or he did. Hell, could have been one of the others. Bob's stomach turned over. He took a seat next to Sam.

"Hey, Bob. I think that thing's taking a crap. It's not sanitary."

"Who is this guy? Eric. Do you know? Am I being replaced?"

"A really slow crap."

Nobody in this cabal had any focus.

"Let's get right down to it. Phase four of the LINC network will help target our constituents and reach them in ways never before possible. We're casting a wider net, securing a larger number of people than ever before. Gentlemen, you can consider this special election won."

Eric Smith's perfect hair waved slightly in the frigid breeze of the air conditioning. He beamed.

Bob scowled.

"A long time ago, before the Flood, America was quite a different place than it is today."

"Yeah, we know Eric. We were there," Bob griped.

Eric was strutting about like a pigeon after the Flood, proud to peck at Bob's corpse. He clapped his hand down on Bob's shoulder. Bob tried to pretend his wince was a twitch.

"There was no Bureau of Science to disseminate important information to the American people. The government was a mass of frenzied, opposing forces, neutralizing each other and getting virtually nothing done. Governance was a joke. Didn't exist."

This stranger. Lecturing us about our own jobs.

"Luckily, a group of 11 men, 11 politicians — senators of the great United States of America — saw the folly in these ways of non-cooperation. They had a vision, a collective vision of a new form of government — a body composed of men who shut up and worked together to creatively solve problems. These men created a coalition, a secret union among their 11 states to stand and liberate their country from the paralysis of dissent. They even coalesced the people around it. By engineering a flood."

Bob's head spun. *What did he say? Engineered a flood? What's that supposed to mean?*

"They passed this new enlightened system down to their sons, who in turn left the inheritance to their sons, creating stability and personal profit for generations and generations. Until a crop of 11 came who were a bunch of fumbling idiots. And they very nearly ruined the whole thing." Eric spread his arms wide as if to embrace them all.

Tears pricked the backs of Bob's eyes — they always surfaced at the slightest hint of conflict or insult. A weather drone floated past their boardroom window. He wanted to turn to look at it, or anything at all.

"I'm here to make sure you don't ruin the Project after thousands of years of planning—"

Eric leaned across the boardroom table until Bob could smell his lack of bad breath and peer into the barely apparent pores of his flawless skin.

"—and you *will* help me. Got that, everybody? Bob?"

This guy was insane. And the way the gang was sitting there, doing nothing? Already in his pocket. Took him how many days? Bob had worked at it for more than a decade. Could great skin and hair and teeth and minimally visible pores get you anything in this miserable world?

Bob choked back his acid reflux.

"I told you it was shitting." Sam pointed at the sloth's emergent feces. "It was really slow.

5

ALICE STOOD IN THE PARKING LOT

A lice stood in the parking lot, staring past the text on her monoculous at her childhood home.
Her mother's condominium.
Now hers.
No mother included, anymore.

GREETINGS, next of kin. We're sorry to inform you Patient 8766 is deceased. Please make the necessary arrangements within 19.5 HOURS. [Ref. no. 7677]

IT WAS A CHOICE CONDO: sector-one property. Alice didn't want it. She edged closer, retina-scanned inside. Stood inside the doorway.

The pressure and the pain shoved up against the backs of her eyes, threatened to push out her tears.

Your mother's dead face

one time, ten times, a hundred, a thousand.

And wasn't it something else under your fear and disbelief?

Aren't you relieved?

Relieved like the people who stopped running from the Flood, like a victim who runs ten miles with a meniscus tear and a broken ankle.

And suddenly, you stop running.

And the tsunami gets you.

Doesn't some part of giving up hope feel *good*? After the run and the pain, before the water hits, don't you feel the cool relief of surrender?

Alice forced herself up the stairs and wandered around the condo. Paused to look out her mom's kitchen window. It was the same mushroom landscaping from her childhood. Well, her childhood after the Flood. Before the Flood, it had been a field of grass. This was a rumor. She was too young to remember.

Her kitchen window now. She didn't want it at all. She wanted her mom back.

She tested the handle of the emergency flood hatch overhead, created a shower of dust. A little rusty. Alice couldn't recall when they'd installed it. She'd been excited to start kindergarten soon after, she remembered that much. Her education had been delayed a year due to the Flood.

Now that her mother wasn't around to verify things from her childhood or stories about the old days before the Flood, it was like she didn't have a past.

Alice took off her plasti-pants. She tapped the faucet on and it shot out the minimum amount of water needed to wipe them down with a damp, rotten-smelling cloth she found in the sink, the hospital smell now replaced by a mildew smell. Both better and worse, somehow.

She was starting to do the same for her plasti-shirt when her monoculous flashed another funeral home advertisement in its right periphery. One ad or another had been fluttering wildly up there ever since she set foot in the hospital. No way to turn off the LINC. No way to turn off either the emergency location services or the concurrent advertisements. First hospice ads, then coffin ads. Later on, grief counselor ads. Who could afford that?

The countdown had been in her monoculous since the death notice, five and a half hours ago: only another eighteen and a half hours to handle the burial. How? Alice had no idea. She jerked her head to center the ad in her monoculous and connected to Tiramisu Funeral Homes.

"Tiramisu." Alice jumped at the sound and the image. *What was that?*

"Hello?"

"Hold please—"

"Okay." A pause, a few moments of silence.

"And we're back."

The image stabilized. It was a body. Mr. Tiramisu's monoculous faced a corpse.

"Oh, um. Hello. Your monoculous settings are pointed the wrong way. I...I can see what you're seeing." Alice dropped her voice low so she would sound more like an adult. If he knew she was young and filled with grief, not to mention terrified and ignorant about these things, he'd bankrupt her for sure.

"Oh, so they are." He tapped his lens, but nothing happened.

"Are you, uh, Mr. Tiramisu?" *Don't say uh. Adults never hesitated. They plunged forward, even when they didn't know anything. This was all part of being an adult.*

Mr. Tiramisu's face clicked into view. Alice preferred the corpse. It had a less predatory expression on its face.

If only she'd had another year or two to figure out how life worked, there in the safety of college, with a mom alive back at home.

"I am. Have you ever had tiramisu?"

Oh, great. A vocabulary quiz.

"Uh, no."

"Tiramisu was a delicious dessert from the old days."

He spoke as if he knew exactly what her age and status was, and when he looked at Alice he was seeing one giant crypto symbol where a person should be.

"When my daddy started the business, he wanted people to associate us with something nice and tasty, like tiramisu. I'm Albert.

You can call me Al. Says here your mom died. Please accept my warmest condolences."

Al had a bit of goop on his brow and another miscellaneous chunk on his upper lip that made Alice distrust the burial process.

"Thank you, Al."

If she disconnected and did nothing, would the hospital deliver her mom to the door? Could she keep her in the house, for free? Sounded like a crime.

"What can I do for you and your mom, then?" Al coughed for ten full seconds, sniffed for five. Alice watched the countdown tick by in her monoculous. "Want the suburban flood-proof special? Only the best for a special lady who is now dead, I am sorry to say—"

"I—I don't know. I can't afford much. I only have a few cryptos—" Alice raced to flick through her profile settings to ensure her net worth wasn't displayed. She forced her face and shoulders to remain placid, twirled her fingers out of monoculous range of view, and snuck glances out of the corner of her eye to check her account balance. She hoped Al's multi-tasking made him oblivious.

Deception: she was mastering it. She was becoming an adult.

"Alice, look. It says here your name is Alice. Can I call you Alice?"

"Yes?"

"I'm Al and you're Alice." He chuckled. Was he laughing because he was about to extract all the money she had left? Hard to say.

"Right." Alice blew the air out of her mouth like she could blow away these circumstances. Really, she was struggling to breathe.

"If we still put our dead people right into the ground, down there in any old spot, without any planning, when the floods come around again, we'll see them floating right down the street."

Was Al holding a saw?

"Happened the last time. They say we could flood again at any time, I saw it the other day on the LINCfeed."

"Uh, what do you recommend?" Alice sat down. She was too overwhelmed to cry.

"Two hundred cryptos for post-hospital handling." Al's apparently faulty monoculous had reverted back to its outward-facing view.

Yes, it was a saw in Al's hand. Yes, he was sawing a corpse's arm off while they LINCed. "We only take eastern seaboard currencies. That's what you've got, right?"

Al now raked the saw across the young man's sternum.

"Five hundred cryptos for flood-proofing the burial plot," Al got himself caught and had to yank his saw out from under a rib. There was a popping noise and the man's blood spattered onto Al's monoculous.

Alice swiped her bank account into view. It was going to spatter its last cryptos into Al. Half her cryptocurrency and nearly all her credit was from the Florida co-op at college.

She'd lose a third of her purchasing capacity when she transferred it to a northeast corridor market.

"Hey, listen," Al said. "I get it. No matter how much you miss your loved one at the beginning of the burial process, in the end you're annoyed with the cost of burying them. No good. Lucky for you, you called Tiramisu. We'll get you through this on the cheap."

"Great," Alice said.

"We gotta put some chemicals in there. So she can't, you know, float. Then safely into the ground, nice and easy, at a designated flood-proof location. We can put a little pillow in there too. Your choice. Or her choice, if she left you any notes about this sort of thing?"

"No," Alice said. "We weren't expecting this."

"Sure. Who is? Only a little surgery, you figure. I'll be back at work the next day, you think. Bing bam boom." Al shrugged. She heard his bone saw clatter to the ground. He ignored it, so she did too. "Doesn't work out that way. We'll help your mom rest in peace. Don't you worry about it. I'll LINC you the info in a few minutes."

Alice wasn't sure resting in peace was still an option. Civilization had taken a nice and easy thing like dying and turned it into a big fiasco.

She disconnected. The funeral ads disappeared, but a new notice popped into Alice's line of sight.

MORTGAGE PAYMENT DUE. Acct 10628F3965H

Thank you for your timely payment.

Nu Jersey Mortgage Corporation

THE AFTERNOON of the funeral was the stickiest of autumn days since Alice had returned to Nu Jersey. Trenton Cemetery was suffocating, a wet wool blanket of a place. It smelled like sewage and dead sea creatures out there, as if the Flood had happened yesterday.

A small forklift creaked itself forward, inch by inch. Her mother's body tumbled out and hit the bottom of her waterproof, reinforced concrete pod with a meaty thud.

Alice winced, shifted in her chair next to the burial plot, and looked away too late to miss a glimpse of her mom's body tumbling in.

The crane operator climbed out. It was Al. He opened a small briefcase and donned a clergyman's robe. He cleared his throat.

"It has been twenty years since the Flood. Let this be a reminder that every day we get here on Earth is a precious gift from God. Every single day, every hour, every minute. Our Lord and master can take this time from us at any...time, with a—"

Her mom had always said it'd been nineteen years since the Flood. For some reason, nobody ever knew the exact date.

Al jostled his headset, wobbling his head left and right. "— botched surgery," he read. "Or another flood. Will it happen again today? Tomorrow? What about next week, or the week after?"

Alice rolled her eyes. Al was her funeral home customer service liaison, her mom's embalmer, her burial crew, and now her minister. Soon he would be her flood-proof burial plot certification inspector. Sure, she'd gotten the daily special for this rushed, one-person-audience funeral, but did it have to be this—

"In accordance with the safety procedures of Nu Jersey state, county, municipality, and town post-Flood burial procedure codes five dot twenty three dash fourteen, subcode section four oh six dot three dot four, I hereby certify this burial plot. Reference number one seventy-six seventy-seven."

A drone whizzed overhead, nearly clipping the top of Alice's head. It hovered a moment over her mom's plot.

Property of the State of NJ

it said on its belly.

Unlawful tampering is prohibited.

Click. The drone soared away.

"I now pronounce patient eight-seven-six-six buried. Let us bow our heads."

Those were the magic words. The burial countdown disappeared from Alice's monoculous. She exhaled the stress of funeral compliance.

"That will be three hundred cryptos," Al said.

Alice inhaled the stress of debt on top of grief, and there was no room left in her for anything else.

She stood up and kicked her plastic chair. It fell over. She picked it back up. *Chair falling over* might cost extra.

"I'm sorry for your loss," Al said, though his eyes beamed. Probably looking at her cryptos in his back account. "Amen."

"Wait," Alice said. She'd turned to leave, now she paused. Whirled around on Al. "What do you mean, botched surgery? Who told you that?"

"Hmmm. You must have."

"No, I didn't. Did it say so in your headset? On the death certificate?"

"I have to get going. Burials all day, you know. Sorry about your mom." Al scurried back into his funeral forklift and motored away. Alice easily passed him on foot back to her car. She wanted to give him an unkind look but worried it could result in another hidden charge.

She rode home, numb, and scanned into the condo, waving the front door closed and sinking to her knees. Screamed. Crawled halfway up the steps. Collapsed. Slammed her fists down on her newly-owned condo stairs over and over. It all came out now, the tears and the snot and the sobs and the saliva.

Another static shriek from her LINC shocked her ear canal. She flung it off onto the landing.

"Who shat in your emergency flood hatch?"

Alice froze where she knelt. Her heart stopped and her breathing stopped. She wiped away a thick string of drool hanging off her chin, then looked up in the direction of the voice.

On the condo steps, a foot above Alice's headset, floated Alice's mom.

6

BOB EMERGED FROM HIS OFFICE

B ob emerged from his office, half-erect penis flagging under his plastikhakis. After he'd dunked his monitor in the fish tank, he'd cheered up enough to search for balding-pornography-star clips on his headset but couldn't get as excited as required to settle his anger through masturbation.

He had to deal with the problem at its root cause: Eric Smith.

But first, he had to talk to his assistant, Eleanor. And that was a problem in and of itself. She'd gotten so hostile.

Eleanor, I hate you, Bob said via his pointed gaze. *You've never redirected my headset to intercept my calls on a single occasion when I've asked you to. Find me a replacement for yourself. And a new monitor. Mine fell in the fish tank.*

Eleanor glanced up before Bob could open his mouth. "I see you looking at me, you sicko. I won't stand for this! I'm not coming in anymore. And if you stop my pay, I'm going to tell everybody about the time you came out of your office with your *miniscule* cock hanging out your pants."

Bob took a step back and pulled at the small side hairs on his head. How many people could Eleanor possibly know?

"What do you mean 'everybody,' Eleanor?"

"Your politician friends always coming around in here, my friends and family, LINC*cast, six social networking sites, LINC→News!™——"

"Okay, okay, you still get your pay." Bob sighed. "But can you order me a monitor before you go?"

"No. Everybody knows you don't look at anything on your monitor except porn. It's waterproof. Take it the hell out of that fake-fish tank and put it back on your desk, you nitwit."

Eleanor reared up from her desk. Shoved her company-issued headset monitor into her bag. Grabbed a bunch of magnetic etchers and a stapler, stuffed those in there too, and stormed out.

At least she was gone.

Eleanor stormed back in, took her ergonomic back cushion off her chair, and stormed out again with even more vigor. Why had she never applied that energy to her job? In the clips secretaries were for sex, not for getting yelled at. Now he had to pay this one to stay home and keep her mouth shut about him occasionally coming out of his office with his manhood out. Like he was abnormal.

Bob lingered by Eleanor's vacant desk. Distant footfalls echoed down the hallway. He'd heard strange noises more and more lately: Previously dormant parts of the building had people in them now. Since Tom. Since Eric. People Bob didn't know.

The footsteps grew louder.

Eric Smith was a threat, and it certainly wasn't acceptable for him to be encroaching on Bob's territory with these fake news articles. Fake news was Bob's domain.

Two men turned the corner and started down the hallway. Strangers. Coming toward him. Wearing lab coats, swishing with their approach. They nodded in Bob's general direction.

A region in Bob's stomach reserved for anxiety expanded its reach.

7

ALICE ROLLED OUT OF HER CHILDHOOD

A lice rolled out of her childhood bed and stubbed her toe on a box of newsplastics littering the floor — an inheritance of worthless memorabilia.

She'd passed out crying again, her headset askew but strapped on and humming.

An important message vibrated in her ear canal. She straightened her monoculous and waved the text into view.

Notification of the past-due mortgage. Again.

Alice limped into the hallway and peered around the corner of the kitchen. Refills for the SnackAttack where she had left them. Crates of artifacts from before the Flood where her mother had left them. Solids became debris when a flood hit. Illegal.

But all *real* objects. No image of a mom-ghost. No paranormal high-pitched whine in her LINC.

There had been two more encounters this week. A few days ago, Alice had been in the middle of eating her breakfast noodle cup when there it was.

There *she* was?

By the time Alice had finished choking on her noodles, it was gone.

Then, another appearance during her weekly shower yesterday evening. Alice saw her mother's image flicker in through a crack in the plastic shower door. Her hand slipped when she raced to hurl open the door, then her feet slipped, and all at once she was in a sudsy heap.

When she looked up, the apparition was gone.

No sound had accompanied her mother's image. It had faded in and out silently. Like turning on a LINC projector. But it wasn't in Alice's monoculous, that was for sure. She had torn it off both times to see if the image remained.

It did. It was either in her head...or real.

NEED A JOB? Are you a cut above the rest? Want to make twice the cryptos in half the time?

THE AD in her left periphery blinked next to the mortgage reminders. Maybe the mortgage company had bumped it her way? She read the instructions: an old-fashioned in-person interview. Why they wouldn't LINC it out, Alice couldn't figure. Her interviewers must have been old, from before the Flood. But hey, she wasn't in a position to turn down an antiquated face-to-face judging.

It was time to be a cut above the rest. Whatever that meant.

"IT SAYS HERE you were recently in school, studying urban, pre-Flood anthropology and archaeoagriculture. Any reason in particular you abandoned your scholarly path?"

Alice's interviewer, a wisp of a man, leaned in over the desk. He had a doorstopper of a nose rivaling Alice's own George Washington-esque profile.

My mom is dead. Don't say that.

Alice took a deep breath. "I wanted to understand what life was like before the Flood. Before they invented cellular agriculture. There were lots of different foods, right? I was interested in why things are the way they are nowadays."

"But you're not interested anymore." The man scribbled a few things down on a piece of plastic with an old magnetic etcher. "Now you want to sell knives." Alice studied his face carefully for sarcasm, but he was speaking without a trace of irony.

"What? Oh, I mean, yeah. I realized the past doesn't matter. All I care about is...knives. Selling knives." Alice shifted in her chair. *Don't blow this, Alice.*

The flood cuff was way too tight. Her ankle flesh ballooned up around it, and she couldn't wiggle her foot. For an instant she saw her mom's arm at the hospital, compressed in a blood pressure cuff that failed to save her life. *Focus. Get this job.*

"And you're done with your paleoagriculture career? Whatever *that* is."

Alice leaned in. "*Archaeo*agriculture. The theory is this. Mankind was addicted to the analgesic effects of cereals and domesticated animal milks. Civilization is based on the manufacture and abuse of those painkillers. But now, with noodle cup—" Before she could finish, the man had turned his back on her and begun rattling his show knives. Alice finally understood his facial expression. It said, *I'm not going to hire you, I'm going to mock your studies,* and *I'm going to try to sell you a knife.*

The man twirled back around toward her, display suitcase in hand. "I don't think this job is for you. You don't seem to have what it takes. But are you in the market for a do-it-all kitchen knife?"

Dead mom, no cryptos, mortgage due, about to be thrown into the street. No friends, no family, and the only job interview I can get is a man shitting all over my college education, which lasted all of three months?

And I don't have what it takes?

"Can't say that I am," Alice said.

Alice took a box of matches out of her bag. She'd been using them to ignite her mom's elderly stove and cook noodle cups when the SnackAttack was depleted.

"We've got a few other demo objects in here," the man said, rattling the drawers of his desk open and closed. "Check this baby out!" He held up a vegetable slicer. Alice's foot tingled, totally asleep.

Crack! The salesman snapped through the faux vegetables. Some plastic composite he swept into the trash. They didn't even look biodegradable. Safety violation. Who the hell had access to fresh vegetables these days, anyway?

Alice imagined herself using knives to cut noodles or SnackAttack offerings. That's what everybody was eating, her included. Not vegetables.

Crack! The salesman hacked through a fake broccoli floret with too much force. Alice's heart cracked, too. Nothing made any sense. She couldn't even get a job selling a useless product?

Alice struck a match and held it up to the plastic notes on the edge of the man's mahogany desk. She didn't want to leave any trace of herself behind.

It wasn't real mahogany, the desk. A plastic composite with red dust glued on. It blackened and warped, but there was no satisfying ignition. The notes only bubbled a little at the edge until her match extinguished.

Plastics.

Her knife salesman sniffed the air, glancing up from his knife set and demonstration vegetables.

"What are you doing? Are you crazy?" His voice warbled and cracked.

Well, was she? Was grief the same as mental illness? How were you supposed to know which one you were experiencing, if you didn't have enough cryptos to afford healthcare?

He had security shoo her outside.

She stood there for a moment and breathed. Contemplated the Nu Jersey haze.

"Need a job?" A man on the corner with an overly sculpted face handed her an advertisement. Alice reached out and took the ad chip. Nothing to lose.

Her fingers brushed his sleeve. A cloth jacket? Couldn't be. Nobody wore cloth anymore. Alice wanted to touch his sleeve again but settled for a side glance. Did she know him from somewhere? Must be grief talking. She didn't know anybody from anywhere. She was alone. She bumped the ad chip up against her headset.

COME WORK FOR MARKET RESEARCH, Inc.!

"I'LL CONSIDER IT," she said. But the man was already gone.

———————

ALICE ARRIVED home to discover an unmarked box on her doorstep. She nudged it with her foot.

A message popped up on her monoculous.

Greetings, citizen! You have been issued a new LINC headset. Your current headset, I89000 LINC smart interface XP, is known to cause untreatable eye problems. Other assorted health consequences may include headaches and fibromyalgia. The old LINC network system will be phased out within 12 hours.

Please discard your current interface and activate your replacement within 8 hours.

A 1,200 crypto penalty applies in case of compliance failure.

LINC phase four.

For the health and wellness of all Americans!

Alice tossed her old headset in the recycling bin, unpacked the new headset, and turned it on. Eye problems were all she needed on top of everything else.

There was a new message awaiting her on the new headset.

GREETINGS MORTGAGE HOLDER [REF. NJ2628Jf41_+b]:

. . .

YOUR PAYMENTS ARE NOW 60 days delinquent. Kindly pay within 15 days or your property will be repurposed.

THANK you for being a loyal Nu Jersey Mortgage Corporation customer!

8

THE MORNING AFTER TOM'S DEATH

The morning after Tom's death, Bob slumped over his desk as usual. Pushed his collection of chewed-off fingernails together to form a lumpy pyramid. Pictured a pile of powder in its place.

Pictured snorting it all while he got a blowjob of his own, his heart exploding at the climax. Ejaculate and heart juice everywhere.

The hooker covered in semen and bits of Bob's aorta, immediately regretful she didn't get a chance to know this vibrant, middle-aged man.

Bob peered down at his partial erection.

COLLEGE-STUDENT-BOB SAT on the edge of his bed in a dilapidated dormitory room, his view either the cinderblock wall or the slush-covered streets of Ithaca, Nu York. He had no motivation to read about political philosophy. What a dumb, boring topic that had turned out to be. Instead, he headed to the bathroom, took a leak, sought out a ripe pimple and squeezed until it oozed, examined his hairline in the mirror.

"It's not receding," he said to nobody. "That doesn't happen to teenagers." The free genetic trait printout that came with your high school diploma hadn't mentioned it. "Baldness isn't even in my haplogroup."

The dormitory door slammed open, crashing into the cinderblock wall. Bob tore out of the bathroom, pimple still bleeding, to stand face to face with the boy version of a man he and the American public would come to know as Senator Tom Fletch (R-NJ).

"Who are you?"

"I'm Tommy Fletch. My dad owns Fletch Industries. Were you talking to somebody in here? I heard voices."

"No. I think you're hallucinating."

"No way! I'm totally in reality right now. I am pretty high, though. I'm your new roommate."

"What? It's the middle of spring semester. Did you just get here?"

Tommy Fletch perched himself on the edge of the bed, right on Bob's staring spot, and plopped a designer duffle on top of Bob's political texts. Then this newcomer pulled out a vacuum-sealed plastic bag and held it up in front of Bob's face.

"Nah. I got here in the fall. My dad got me a house to live in, but I sold it a couple months ago for 300 pounds of this Black Haze Purple Snow."

"Marijuana?"

"Best marijuana this far from Carolina. Thought I'd sell enough to buy another house before he found out, but then we smoked most of it."

"I thought Carolina was underwater. Bummer about your house."

"I heard Rhode Island isn't even an island anymore. Bummer? Not really, bro! It was worth it. But now I've got to live here in these *shitacular* dorms as punishment from my dad. What happened to your eye? It looks all busted."

Bob had been working first shift at the bagel shop that morning when possibility presented itself. The kitchen door swung open, so he leaned in. Hadn't proven injury enough to get paid time off, much less a settlement. Net failure. Maybe next time. Hopefully next time.

"Nothing," he said. "Bagel accident."

Tommy located some tiny pieces of paper. Bob hadn't seen paper since before the Flood.

He set Bob's e-reader on his knee, and broke the vacuum seal on his designer weed. "Are you a political science major, too?"

Bob twisted his lips into what he hoped looked like a wry grin, a smugness to mirror his new and confident associate. "Fuck yeah, I am."

The leisure class used curse words, didn't they?

Tommy knocked on the particleboard ladder attached to their dormitory bunk beds. "Is this even plastic? This shit is rustic! Can I take the top bunk?" He rattled his bag of weed. "I think it's gonna be better for my smoking. I can't believe our dads are paying millions of cryptos for this prison camp!" Bob marveled at the way Tommy's luscious head of hair bobbed when he spoke.

"Right." He fingered his pimple. His dad paid nothing. The Flood-impacted scholarship paid his way.

"Hey. Do you know how to spell and write or whatever?" Tommy shook his expensive marijuana out onto the face of Bob's e-reader.

"Uh, nobody does anymore. The computer does it for you."

Tommy scraped his premium weed around in a professional-looking way until he seemed satisfied with the results. So much dexterity. So much weed. Bob didn't have enough cryptos to afford a drug hobby. He'd never even tried it.

Bob continued, "I heard they're updating the emergency flood network on our phones, with, like, a retina computer, too. Our phones are gonna be attached to our faces."

"Heh, that's funny. Smart*face*! You know, I think my dad's company won that contract. I'm gonna be rich! Just kidding—we're already rich. You know what? Can I take both these beds? This lower one is good for rolling but I want to go upstairs to this other bed to smoke. It'll look more spacious, right? We can get you a cot."

"I don't want to sleep on a cot."

"No, hear me out. It'll be an intensely comfortable designer cot."

"I don't think — that's not going to work for me. I'd prefer to sleep in my bed."

"Okay, guy. Not a big deal. I'd rather you didn't, but this is your room, too. What classes are you taking? Maybe we can share the burden on reports and reading assignments." Tommy lit the end of his massive joint and introduced what would become a three-and-a-half-year reek of bubble gum, trees, and chemical vats to their room. Without waiting for a response, he continued, "Are you in a frat?"

"Not a frat. Well, kinda. More of a gang. It's complicated."

Here Bob was, in college through the lottery of Flood victimhood, face to face with a man whose easy, wealthy life he craved.

Pot smoke filled the room. Bob stole jealous glances at Tom out of the corner of his eye. If you'd asked Bob then whether he thought this new relationship would culminate in a ritualistic serpent murder and launch his career, he would have said, you've got to be *high*.

———————

"OPEN CASTING CALL!" Eric burst into Bob's office and yelled right into his face.

One of the things Bob hated most about Eric was his barging in at key moments, like when Bob was discovering a dead, drug-overdosed colleague and contemplating what to do in order to hold a loose, stupid cabal of power together.

Hair firmly planted on his scalp.

Palms not perpetually clammy.

No nervous tic below his left eye, or above his right.

Words smooth and polished.

Suit tailored at the waist, no bulging or wrinkling. And made of cloth — how crazy *was* he?

"Casting call?" Bob mumbled into his lapel. Eric had interrupted his neck exercises, his morning mewing session. Eric's chin definition was absurd. Bob had been working on strengthening his chin line for eight years, but it was still a shapeless lump.

"This is how we're going to replace Tom: *an actor*." Eric paced back and forth in front of Bob's desk.

Had Fletch Senior hired Eric without telling Bob? What a shriveled old sack of dust. Where was he nowadays, anyway? Probably getting his organs pickled upstate. He was too evil to die. He'd turn up eventually, hissing orders as usual, for sure.

"An actor?" Bob flipped his monoculous up, cut his morning inspiration clip short. He heaved himself to his feet and waved the door shut. Nobody needed to hear this, including him.

Eric quit his strutting to perch on the edge of Bob's desk like a shitty flood vulture.

"You didn't even know Fletch was into MCAT, did you?"

"I've been busy. Working." Bob crossed the room to fiddle with the screen on his SnackAttack, pretended to review the options. No recent menu updates. He wasn't hungry anyway. He was nauseous. He wanted to sit back down at his desk, but it was too close to Eric.

"*MCAT*, Bob. Ever hear of it? No? Meow-meow?"

Eric was saying foreign words and bizarre acronyms over and over again for no reason.

"Mephedrone, Bob. Tom was addicted to *meph*. The Senator of Nu Jersey was addicted to a cheap street drug. And you had no idea? Unbelievable. That's how far out of the loop you are."

How did *he* know how far out of the loop he was, when Bob didn't even know himself?

Eric brushed an invisible speck off his own spotless lapel, straightened a shiny pin that was either the American flag or a sideways noodle cup.

It was time to get the old Lasik re-upped.

Bob hadn't seen drugs since back in college. While he had been busting his ass trying to develop this stupid little bloc of *politicorporate* power, ordered around by eleven old men and their even more elderly fathers, day in and day out, these guys were busy screwing up and not telling him about it. Tom had apparently graduated from marijuana to something weirder. Meph? And he didn't even use responsibly.

Now they were stuck with this outsider, Eric Smith. Thanks, Tom.

Bob sighed. Maybe he really was out of the loop.

Eric clapped his hands together to startle Bob. "We'll host a commercial audition. Best actor gets the role."

Hyper-intelligent, charismatic, nice-suit-owning, full-head-of-hair-having, perfect-attention-commanding Eric Smith. Solving all our problems with *acting.*

"A commercial audition? For what?"

"For a new senator. Role goes to the best actor who turns up to sell—"

Bob lost his balance out of nowhere, over nothing, and hit the SnackAttack screen in an attempt to stay upright. An animation of a fish popped up. His monoculous flashed.

SnackAttack Thank you for choosing TUNAPHARM© brand iodized fauxfish!

The SnackAttack dropped a cracker out of its lone orifice and dumped a blob of sim-tuna on it.

"Tuna," Eric said.

THE NEXT MORNING, Bob heaved open the doors to the rental studio, expecting a torrent of talent to inundate them with acting genius.

All that hit them was the sleepy haze of the Delaware River. And the director.

"He's gonna bolt." Eric shoved a can of tuna fish into Bob's clammy hand. "And our tuna fish has his eye on the door, too. Go volunteer to run through the lines."

"What? Why me?"

"I have to scan the talent."

Bob tossed the tuna onto the prop table. It bounced off and rolled away.

"TAKE SEVEN, TUNAPHARM© tuna fish commercial!" The director crouched down next to him to scream right into Bob's face. His directorial tie mopped the plywood stage.

Bob's life was spinning out of control. Down on all fours, against the wishes of his kneecaps, quads, and many other body parts, he nibbled on the toe of a tall man dressed like a tuna fish.

"Mmmmmm," Bob read from a popup LINC monitor, propped up on a makeshift tripod of delivery drones. If they didn't get those drones in the air within the hour, there'd be additional charges. He drew his lips over his teeth and gummed the boney top of the tuna fish actor's foot.

The actor yelped.

"Cut! What the hell is wrong with you?" The director swatted Bob in the face and it was his turn to yelp. "Don't eat this guy's fucking leg! You hear me?"

"Yes," Bob's shocked himself with the sound of his own voice. It didn't have the disgust in it he'd expected, no more than if he'd been eating sim-tuna. "I was—"

"Shut it! Take eight!"

Bob went back to gumming the man's leg. Why was he even doing this? Tom Fletch Senior. That was why. He'd sent Eric to spy, Bob was sure of it. If Bob didn't comply with orders, who knew what would happen to him?

"Now the ankle!" The director screamed again, smacking a clipboard on the side of his leg. This guy was serious about his tuna-fish commercial talent-scouting effort. Eric had hired him after only a brief LINC search, but he was the real commercial-directing deal: bullhorn for extra-loud yelling. Clipboard for hitting things, people. Tuna-hawking self-importance oozing out of every orifice.

Bob moved his mouth up to the tuna-fish actor's ankle. The actor was not in full faux-tuna regalia, just a fiberglass fish head and a pair of swimming trunks.

Although it would have been better to *not* be chewing on a man's ankle, he wouldn't have enjoyed eating TUNAPHARM©, either. Sim-tuna was sim-*garbage*. Give him noodle cup any day. He peered into the stranger's leg hairs at his own bubbling saliva.

"Don't nibble! No more nibbling! Gnaw! I want you to gnaw,

goddamit! Are you afraid to gnaw?" The director slammed his clipboard against the improvised props table for emphasis. Fake cans of fake tuna rattled.

Bob gnawed. Fletch Senior was probably watching this somehow, too. That evil old Flood weasel.

"Now the line! Say your line!"

Bob raised his head. A thick string of saliva connected his mouth and the man's leg.

"TUNAPHARM!© No tuna was harmed in the making of this tuna," Bob read.

Eric Smith appraised him from the back of the studio.

BY THE END of the day, they had the next senator of Nu Jersey. Bob picked a man's leg hair out of his teeth with his pinky nail and hauled the studio door down until the magnetic lock clicked into place. His monoculous confirmed it.

Thank you for renting Floodway Studios! Your deposit has been refunded.

It was awful out here, had to be sector-five, or even worse. Maybe no sector at all. The sleeve of his plastisuit jacket caught on the door handle as he turned away, and he nearly tore it off trying to break free. Plasticlothes didn't feel like the safety measure they used to be. Last year's exposé revealed an excessive number of headset images of drowning victims dredged out of lakes, rivers, ponds, streams, plasticlothes intact. Bob had had to edge them out of the LINC→News!™ clips with a flurry of Science Bureau releases. Campaign contributions demanded.

Everybody was still wearing them. Better safe than sorry. Everybody except Eric Smith. His clothes were made of cloth. Since when did anybody in America wear that? Where did Fletch Senior find this monster?

Bob turned back toward Eric and the future senator from Nu Jersey, formerly the vocalist on popular LINC advertisements for such products as Trybutalan XP[1] and Happy Whiskers. They were standing there in the parking lot, frowning at Bob like he was in the wrong, like he was holding things up.

It was quiet on the waterfront. No cars on the Trenton Bridge; not a boat on the river. Nobody wanted to come down here. When you saw the residue of tsunami sludge in the trees, the waterline above all the tunnels, you remembered the time the ocean met the Delaware for a week. Remembered nobody understood how it happened.

Remembered it could happen again at any time, without warning.

Then you didn't care as much about your tuna fish commercial, your dead senator, your threatened secret society.

Eric poked his finger at Bob. "What's the delay?"

"Nothing. With what?"

"Get in the car, then."

"I don't understand why we had to go through this whole commercial sham, Eric." Bob tried for an authoritative assertion of his rights as a member of the team, but he was on the cusp of a whine. He always regretted speaking to Eric when those glacial eyes gleamed in his direction.

"What was *your* idea to solve our little problem, Bob?"

"I'm not saying this is a bad idea, I'm saying—"

"Bob, how long have you been press secretary?"

"I've known these guys for years. Tommy Fletch and I were in college together."

"He's dead, Bob. He died on your watch."

"Why does everybody keep saying that? I'm not a babysitter. I'm the press secretary."

"Right. Now tell me: When's the last time you spoke to the press? Not today. Not yesterday. I don't recall any press conferences the day before."

Bob's face grew heated. "I'm saying I don't know why I had to chew on a man — on *several* men — today. We held our own auditions. We were paying the director, paying the tuna man. When you pay people to do things, you don't have to do anything. That's the whole point."

"Are you questioning my orders? Are you questioning Fletch

Senior? Now's not the time to half-ass our work, Bob. Otherwise we might see a new headline on the LINC Network tomorrow. How about this: '*Illuminati* seek new member at critical time because *amateur dipshit* press secretary allows accidental death'? Maybe you could write that up?"

Bob imagined being Tommy, sitting at their table in the Regency suite, among those prostitutes, in his own overconfident wealth and power. Only to overdose on meph. Whatever the hell that was. He wished he had tried it. He wished he had taken a job selling insurance right out of college. He looked out at the water.

"What are we going to do now?" Bob's voice was shaky. Why would it never produce the desired impact? He slammed his fist into his palm to look more authoritative. Too hard: It hurt his carpal tunnel.

"Now? We're going to train this man to be the next Senator from Nu Jersey. " Eric Smith gestured toward their actor, who ambled over. He didn't look anything like Tom Fletch at any point in Tom's life. He did look drunk though, so that was something. Tom would have been drunk by this time of day, too.

"It's a matter of national security," Eric said to the actor. "You understand, don't you, son?"

The fake Tom Fletch nodded. He must have really needed the job.

"Don't nod when you're the senator, kid. People will think you're weak."

"Yes, sir." Since they'd first met him, the kid was standing up straighter. Why did Eric Smith have that effect on everybody? Everybody except Bob.

"Great," Eric said. "Let's get back to the office and get to work."

---

1. Trybutalan XP must be prescribed by your physician. Do not use Trybutalan XP if you have recently been eating or swimming. Trybutalan XP may cause dizziness, vomiting, excessive fecal production, and other minor side effects. Contact your doctor for more information about Trybutalan XP. Try Trybutalan XP. *For your life!*

9

WORKING, DAY ONE

Working, day one.

"Welcome to Market, Research, Incorporated! How may I direct you?"

"Thanks," Alice said to a disembodied voice in the lobby. She clicked her monoculous down to reveal a hologram — the shimmering, semi-transparent image of a desk receptionist. "New employee orientation."

"This way, please." A virtual LINC arrow flickered, pointed to a hallway on the right. She walked until she was standing on it and a new arrow appeared, this time in a corridor to the left. Alice kept on going, studiously following the monoculous floor arrows until she walked into a man's back.

"Oof," he said, turning around.

"I'm sorry," Alice apologized. "I didn't see you there."

"Are you a new employee?" The man screamed his question as though Alice were on the other side of the room and the room was a warehouse. But it wasn't: He was right next to her.

"Yes," Alice said.

"I'm John." The whole building must have heard. They were corralled in a large open space, like a school auditorium with no chairs. Several of their future coworkers were giving them looks. One young man flipped up his monoculous lens to express to them the full force of his glare for speaking too audibly, then flicked it back down. Aggressive.

"My name is Alice. Why are you shouting?"

Everybody else was occupied on a headset, either staring at the ground or off into the distance through the lone headset eyepiece at a bit of information.

"Hi," another nearby woman said. A few of her coworkers glared up from their headsets. One person screaming was more than they could take; add a second and third in a conversational tone and it violated all the social norms. Alice cringed. She didn't want to make a bunch of enemies on the first day. "Follow me to the silent room," their new addition said.

"Okay," John's voice boomed again over the quiet chatter of headset noises and the silent gesturing of monoculous-image interaction. "Shouldn't we go to the social room? So we can talk?"

"No, *noob*, the social room is for social *networking*. On headset. They'll fire you if you talk out loud in there. I'm Jalia. I'm here to give you the pre-orientation tour. Stop shouting."

"Okay. Thank you." John cut his volume in half.

"I'm not doing this of my own free will," Jalia shrugged. "They're forcing me. It's part of my punishment. Off-location, they said. Not in my cube. Located in a whole other quadrant instead of cuffed and cubed at G-six." She tapped her LINC. "They know where you are all the time. It's for safety. Follow me."

Jalia led them through an airlock. John's eyes widened as though he had never seen one before. Alice wondered where he was from — he looked less fleshy, less headset-attentive than everybody else. Maybe he was from beyond the flood zone. Someplace exotic, like Wisconsin? Couldn't be. Nobody ever came to Nu Jersey from the outside. And anybody who could get out after the Flood had already gone.

"This is the designated eating area. Like I said, it has a social room and a silent room. The social room is for social networking. The silent room is for eating lunch. It's this half of the dodecahedron. You have to enter these vacuum doors following the retina scan."

"Oh." John must have forgotten he didn't need to shout everything he said. "Okay." It boomed around them in the small space.

Jalia turned around. "Hey, stop shouting!"

"I don't know what's appropriate," he said. "It's like this?" John lowered his voice until his lips were moving but made no sound. Alice didn't know how this guy was going to manage conducting headset interviews.

"People can't hear whispering because of HHS, so you have to project your words more and shape your lips while speaking in a low-to-mid-level range. Liiiike thissss," Alice said, drawing out her words into more of a hiss.

"What's HHS?" John asked. Alice gaped at him.

"You don't know about Headset Hearing Syndrome? Where are you from?" Alice's mind reeled at the thought. Everybody knew about it. Could he have come from outside the eastern seaboard levee?

"That's enough small talk. Market, Research, Incorporated doesn't allow it. Keep quiet and follow me," Jalia said. She led them down a hallway in a sea of hallways and into a room where ten other would-be headset interviewers milled around, avoiding each other. Then she cut a hard right, dodged a few drifters, and disappeared. Apparently, the tour was over.

"Good morning," a voice boomed from the front of the room. Alice flicked her monoculous down. It was another hologram. This one was old and burly, wearing a nice-looking, possibly antique suit.

Nobody said anything.

"I said, good morning!"

Somebody coughed in the back.

"Why don't you lift up your monoculous for a change and get a good look at your colleagues," the hologram said. "You'll be relying on each other for survival when the next flood comes."

John and Alice levered up their monoculous and looked at each other. Nobody else moved. The recruit closest to Alice shuffled nervously and then ran out a side door. Taking off your headset wasn't for everybody, even just lifting the monoculous. It was a real test of nerves.

"Great. Glad we got that out of the way without incident," the hologram said. Must have been a recording. It was oblivious to real conditions in the room. "My name is Tom Fletch Senior. I'm the founder of Market, Research, Incorporated, and I welcome you to this exciting step in your career. I'd like you all to pair up and chat with each other. In the pre-Flood days, people did this without wearing a monoculous. Try it now.

"Here at Market, Research, Incorporated, you get paid for conversation. Conversation that extracts information." The hologram winked. "Information we sell." And then it disappeared.

Alice and John turned to each other.

"I guess we already know each other," Alice said. "But I'm Alice. In case you forgot." What a dumb thing to say. She was never going to make any friends.

"I'm still John." John nodded and smiled.

"So. How'd you find this job?"

"I came here to work as a lower-middle manager. It's through the Phase One Post-flood Immigration Pilot Program: POPIPP!" John snapped his fingers when he said this.

"Catchy name," Jalia said, swooping in and breaking back into their pairing. Her tone was glib, but she was staring at John like he'd predicted the next flood, brow creased, eyes full of suspicion. Did they know each other?

"It's a staffing initiative," John said.

"Staffing initiative for what?" Now that he wasn't shouting anymore, Alice noticed his clothes were different. They lacked the sheen of plasticlothes. His arm muscles were more clearly defined than anyone's Alice had ever seen, and they were very noticeable through his fabric shirt. Was it getting hot in here? Then again, she'd never seen any arms outside plasticlothes, except her own.

And her mom's.

Thinking about her mom made her feel like she'd been dumped

into that grave too, like she was trying to go on living under a bulldozer's pile of dirt.

"What was it? I think there was a...*plague* here on the east coast of the United States two decades ago. Right? Isn't that why nobody will live here? So ten years ago they invited young workers to come from West Africa."

"What do you mean, West Africa?" Alice took a half step backwards and folded her arms. West Africa didn't exist anymore.

"I'm from Sierra Leone," John said. Alice waited for him to laugh or otherwise indicate he was kidding, but his face held no trick in it, no joke at all. The punchline didn't come. When she realized he was serious, her heart skipped a beat and her skin buzzed, like a flooder in a puddle hit by a power line.

"Sierra Leone?" Alice, staggered, could only echo the impossible thing John had just said.

Up to that moment, Alice had believed the continent of Africa, along with the rest of the world, had been inundated by the Flood. Per the general consensus.

"It's a country," John said. "In West Africa." Now it was his turn to look shocked. "Sierra Leone? No? Never heard of it?"

"I know it's a country," Alice said. "But we thought—" she fiddled with her monoculous. *What should she say now?* Alice didn't know. How do you explain to a guest that you didn't know he existed?

Jalia broke into their conversation. She always seemed to be hovering nearby.

"Not a plague," Jalia blurted out. "It was a flood. Didn't you hear about it?"

"Oh, perhaps I'd forgotten. We had our own problems back then."

"How'd you get here?" Jalia's tone was conversational. Hadn't she heard John's testimony? That other countries existed, and he was from one of them? Alice's mind was still swirling. Was the whole African continent still above water?

"Our neighbors held a series of fundraisers to send me to this deadly part of America."

"And you came here ten years ago?"

"No, last week. It took four years to get the money for the ticket. Then the work permit took another six."

"Long fundraiser."

"Yes, my neighbors back home are generous. I love them very much."

Alice blushed on hearing the word "love." Applied to people, out loud, in public. It wasn't something you heard much. John was different. He didn't know their ways, like wearing plasticlothes all the time, in case another flood came. It also explained his muscles — didn't look like the people of Sierra Leone were stuck in one primary spot all day due to their vector-based tracking system. For safety.

"If they loved you, they wouldn't have sent you here," Jalia said. She stalked off.

"Ouch," Alice said. "Do you two know each other?" Pretty harsh words from a stranger. Or a new colleague.

John didn't answer the question. He just shrugged.

10

GOOD MORNING

"Good morning!" It was the same hologram from the first day. Tom Fletch Senior.

"Good morning!" Most of the room intoned back this time. They were learning to communicate in public. It didn't come naturally in post-flood America.

"We're going to go over the safety procedures today. Pay attention, everybody!"

Alice followed the hologram's gaze. It had to be a recording, right? But the way it had honed in on Jalia and stared her down hinted otherwise. She returned its stare.

"If there is a flood, and you're in here, and you follow our instructions, you'll survive."

Alice edged her way over. "Who is that guy?" she whispered to Jalia.

"Tom Fletch Senior? The evil overlord who controls us all, that's who."

Alice had some follow-up questions, but the sim-receptionist hologram from the lobby appeared in her monoculous, disrupted their chat with her shrill monologue.

"Welcome to Market, Research, Incorporated! The extra comma is for safety!"

"Doesn't make any stinking sense," Jalia whispered.

"Market, Research, Incorporated will be housing you for four-teen-and-one-third hours a day in a flood-proof workplace deep in the heart of Trenton. Every cubicle is equipped with a LINC-enabled adjustable titanium ankle cuff to achieve full safety."

Alice looked down to see a virtual cuff clamp around her left ankle.

"If you're on location, you can be protected. If you're protected, you can be rescued. The building will emergency pressurize to keep water out and oxygen available until help arrives. This is standard best business practice. ISO-certified. All employees can be accounted for at all times."

"Bullshit," Jalia mumbled. Alice could have sworn she saw the virtual receptionist look at her sharply, but that wasn't possible, was it? It was just a recording, too.

"A small sensor in the cuff will notify the central security system when you are in your cubicle, except for scheduled bathroom breaks. You will receive a twenty-minute unpaid lunch, to be eaten in desig-nated safety areas."

"So humane," Jalia grunted.

"If you are not secured in a known location, you run the risk of being harmed in another apocalyptic catastrophe. I'm talking to you."

Was the sim-receptionist looking at Alice? Nah, couldn't be. It was all an optical illusion.

Jalia sidled up to Alice when lunch break hit. "Excited to be here still?"

"Four hours of emergency procedures isn't my dream day, but if it keeps us safe, I guess it's fine. I need this job."

"What happened? Parents cut your crypto allowance?"

Alice's gut twisted. Should she tell this stranger about her situation? She wanted to. There was a big difference between what Jalia thought her problem was and the truth: a near-constant fear of imminent homelessness. But when she opened her mouth, all she said was:

"What's up with the extra comma?"

"The creators of Market, Research, Incorporated screwed up and named it as though it were a legal firm, with commas between each individual word — as though Market and Research and Incorporated were all partners in the company. Then nobody bothered to change it, so now they incorporate it into their dumb slogans. 'The comma is for safety.' That kind of trash."

"That's so lazy." Alice was immediately scared. She wanted Jalia to like her, but what a mistake. What if her new employer heard her?

"Yeah, it is. You know what they're not lazy about? Making sure you stay off the Hub."

"What's the Hub?"

"It's where all these hallway spokes lead." Jalia pointed to the tower of hallways above and below them at the break dodecahedron. "I got lost and wound up there last week. That's why I'm being punished with this orientation. They've got something going on up there. Something secret."

Alice squinted at a mobile double-lump in the distance: one bigger, one smaller. A man? Carrying a—? "Is that a man carrying a sloth?"

Jalia craned her neck. A buzzer sounded through their headsets. Alice jumped a little, but Jalia leapt completely out of her seat.

"They know," she said.

"They know what? I think that's the break alarm." Alice kept her voice light, but Jalia was scaring her — not with her jump scares, though those were startling, but with her paranoia. Another symptom of HHS. Alice considered suggesting Jalia go get checked for it, but instead she could only manage, "I have to go find John now. To practice our survey."

"Sure. Sure you do. See you later."

Alice passed through the vacuum seal from the social room into the silent room and then into the survey room. What good would it do to survive in one room of one floor of one building in case of additional floods? If the headsets went dead, and the food ran out, and the waters didn't recede, people stuck in a room would kill and eat each other again. It would have seemed extreme before the first flood. Now it seemed inevitable.

John was waiting for her, holding the remnants of a lunch he had packed for himself. Their time together was limited: he was graduating from basic training and moving on to his low-level executive track.

"What was for lunch today? I didn't see you in the break room." Alice had purposefully lurked in there, hoping to see John, but running into Jalia instead. She had so many questions about Sierra Leone and the rest of the world.

And him.

John shook his paper bag. A bag made of paper; who ever saw such a thing? Certainly not flood-proof.

"Same as yesterday. I'm a simple eater. One peanut butter and jelly sandwich, two tiny chocolate doughnuts, and one can of soup. Tomato. Again. My favorites, all of them."

"Where do you get these things?"

"What do you mean? I think they're American. I stocked up before I left home, because I thought food would be too expensive. But I'm sure I can get these things here. Can't I? Your country invented tomato soup in a can."

"I don't think we've had canned soup since before the Flood," Alice tried to remember. "It's not even legal to have cans."

"Oh." John gathered up his bag and furrowed his brow. "I hope they don't arrest me."

"I've only seen these things in five-second clips."

"What's normal to eat in America now?" John asked.

"We've got SnackAttack. There's a big, commercial version of one here in the break room. It's a food printer. Do you have them in Sierra Leone? They had them at college, too. This one gives you instant noodles in a cup, with different flavor packets. Plain. Spicy. Medium.

Seasonal."

"SnackAttack," John said. "Plain. I don't think we have this."

"John, remember when you said you had your own problems?"

"Not specifically."

"Well, you did. What did you mean? What kinds of problems?"

"Oh, lots. One time, militant guerillas came to our house and cut off my mother's hands as a warning to all of us," John said.

Alice was silent for a moment, horrified. Then curiosity overtook her. "What was it about?"

"I don't know," John said. "The economy, I think."

"Oh." Alice thought about her student loans, hospital debt, condo mortgage, and she looked down at her hands. "Did your mom owe them money?"

"No, nobody did. It was a pre-emptive hand-hacking. Maybe the mining corporation sent them. They were upset our village might have been thinking about asking for money. From the mining."

"What was the mine for?"

"Headsets," John said. He tapped his headset. "Minerals for headsets."

"Oh," Alice said. "I didn't know they made these out of minerals. That's terrible."

"Yes, it is terrible." A tear slipped out of the corner of John's eye. He brushed it away with one long finger. "Oh, that's silly," he said to the tear. "Mama always says, we don't cry over lost limbs."

"Did she say it before or after they—"

"I think she said it after. She may have invented the saying."

"Then you came here? Like, to get away from the violence?"

"No, not right away. And not to get away from anything. It was ten years ago when Mama lost her hands."

Alice searched John's face for some sign that sharing all this personal information with her meant they had a special bond. Was this normal in his country? In Nu Jersey, people rarely even spoke to each other in person. She had never heard anybody say a more brutal thing out loud.

"She's a college professor. Five years ago, she got a job as head ethnoarchaeographer to do her research at a site in Mali. And I haven't seen her since."

Alice nodded, though she didn't know what either an ethnoarchaeographer or Mali was. She was worried he'd stop talking to her if he realized how little she understood. She wanted to say something about her own mom, but what if a jumble of lunacy came out?

My mom died, and I buried her body, but I just saw her at home yesterday, hovering on the staircase. Not *on* the stairs. *Above* the stairs.

It wasn't appropriate. Nope. Not good work small talk. Alice wasn't an experienced corporate employee, but she knew enough to know you were supposed to check your problems at the door, so she kept her mouth shut. John was distracted by something behind her, outside the dodecahedron window on the walkway. She followed his gaze. A misshapen lump crawled by.

"Is that a sloth?" John pointed.

It was. The creature looked around. And after it had scanned the area, it stood upright.

And it ran toward the Hub.

"There's something you don't see every day," John said, but his matter-of-fact tone suggested otherwise.

11

LET ME TELL YOU ABOUT

"Let me tell you about headset-based market research," Jalia said.

She leaned in.

Imagine this. An endless list of headset numbers, linking you to random people through your monoculous, connecting, listening, endlessly buzzing; headset messages with pre-recorded announcements, a few unique individuals creating their own personalized greeting or a song.

Do you have to pee? Nobody cares. Wanna stand up and walk away? You can't. Cuffs on. Cuffs always on. They take points off if you're not cubed and cuffed. Then they aggregate the points. And translate those into cryptos.

And they dock your pay.

Nonstop headset buzz. You're cuffed to your cubicle. Did I mention that? There's a slight hum in your ear when you're not reading the script.

And then there's the abuse.

The average Nu Jerseyan posts on headset media one hundred and forty-four times daily. But then they treat *you* like *you're* some kind of floodrat for reaching out to them.

You start to look forward to harassment. At least it breaks up the monotony.

Shit-eating floodrat.

What color are your plastipanties?

What's *your* headset number, so *I* can call *you* when *you're* in the middle of dinner?

"And that's it," Jalia said. "That's what we do here."

John and Alice exchanged the slightest glance, from the corners of the corners of their eyes. Jalia's appearance was growing more disheveled as the week went on.

"Is this the orientation script?" Alice's tone suggested she was walking on eggshells while balancing on a chainsaw.

Jalia flipped up her monoculous so she could show Alice she was rolling both eyes.

The receptionist popped up out of the floor. Alice and John both jumped. It took a lot of getting used to.

"Well, hello there! Thank you for attending orientation! Did you know in the pre-Flood days, you had to receive connects via a stand-alone box in your home glued to the wall? It was called a telephone! Things sure were different back then, weren't they? In those terrible times, the government passed legislation restricting market research calls to those home boxes. Soon after the LINC was invented, a loophole was inserted into the law to allow Internet-based calls through digital headsets and social-media-related technical devices."

The word

Victory!

flashed on Alice's monoculous.

"You may be too young to remember," the hologram said, "but in those early days after the Flood, it was pandemonium."

Dolphins went belly up in an animated montage, floating on a tidal wave that swooped down on the outline of Nu Jersey. Cartoon humans drowned in their homes, their stylized, stick-figure corpses swept into the street. Others cowered on rooftops, then burst into flames.

It didn't seem one hundred percent fact-based to Alice.

The narration continued.

People were too scared to work. They didn't want to die trapped inside the buildings in case of another flood. They thought they could float to the top of the waters to safety, outside.

The narrator chuckled. The same voice as the hologram, Tom Fletch Senior.

Nobody could persuade the American public to go back indoors. The economy ground to a halt. Civilization was on the brink of collapse until the politicians of the northeast corridor and the one remaining insurance company devised a system so secure that people could go back to living and working just as they had before the Flood.

But safer.

The same.

But safer.

Alice couldn't tell whether it was a glitch in the system, or whether the hologram was meant to repeat that line on purpose.

The problem, the hologram narrated, was freedom—the ability of people to wander around undetectable. Couldn't save people in a flood if you didn't know where they washed up, could you?

Cartoon people projected through Alice's monoculous washed under buildings, pounded on windows filled with water, got trapped in short-circuited elevator shafts.

No, the narrator intoned. *We couldn't.*

The answer was simple.

Plasticlothes.

Ankle bracelets.

Getting everybody to sit still indoors instead of roaming around outside.

Keeping people in pressurized, flood-proof buildings all the time.

Stay in your car, house, work.

Especially work. The safest place of all.

The emergence of the headset: A light-weight computer everybody could wear all the time—one earpiece, one eyepiece— to track their whereabouts and link to a global emergency response system: the Logistics Information Network Computer.

Don't remove your LINC or you're gonna sink, the narrator chanted. And chuckled.

Alice's skin broke out in goosebumps, even though the narrator was only describing the facts of her life.

12

ALICE RUBBED HER ANKLE

A lice rubbed her ankle where the safety cuff chafed. Day four on the job. It was starting to smell under there, too, like a congealed noodle cup. When her designated break came, she wanted to try a circulation-restoring stroll upstairs to get the blood back into her foot, but she didn't know where they were, and they weren't allowed anyway— it was company policy to stay in the designated areas where everybody could be accounted for in case of emergency.

The job wasn't fun. In fact, it was terrible, like Jalia had said. If Alice had been living her life thirty years earlier, she might have wished for an apocalypse, a flood to come and wipe it all off the face of the planet, headset infrastructure and all. Unfortunately, that had already happened. The only chance she had of opting out of this tedious economic function was death. And since her mother's hideous funeral, Alice wasn't sure death was the rest-and-relaxation-fest she had always imagined.

That left her with ____.

What, exactly?

Alice's desk cuff sprang open, rousing her from a twenty-second staring session spent minutely examining the empty space in the right corner of her cubicle. An angry red message on her monoculous ignited to warn of her low productivity. Alice swiped the message aside. *There's always lunch.*

She stumbled off the elevator, headed for the social room, and moseyed into a lot of screaming.

"What's happening?" Alice whispered to an onlooker.

"It's G-six. Total meltdown. Slamming her fists into her headset over and over." A small crowd had gathered. Most people were busy recording and up-LINCing the footage. Those still cuffed into their stations craned their heads for a peek while reading scripts.

G-six? That was Jalia. Alice could see her from afar. She'd been at it a while. Her fists were bleeding.

"Do you know why?"

"I dunno, HHS? F-four told me she heard from somebody in Row three that her headset boyfriend broke up with her. But he did it in a way that made her think he's a bot."

"Her headset boyfriend? She never mentioned one."

"Probably embarrassed. I wouldn't mention it either if I couldn't tell the difference between who was real and who was network-generated."

Jalia's efforts to destroy her headset had left it unscathed for the most part, except her monoculous had cracked and sliced open her cheek under her right eye. Alice was gathering all her courage up to step forward and say something to Jalia — she wasn't sure what — when a couple of middle managers came in to lead her away. Jalia struggled. Tensed her arms. Swung her leg up to kick one of the middle managers. They wrestled her hands behind her back.

Alice shrank back and looked away as the men passed by with their burden. Jalia shouted as loud as Alice had ever heard a person get.

"It's the surveys!" She strained towards Alice. "You're next," she spat.

13

SMOOTH STYLE-BRAND REUSABLE

S mooth Style-brand reusable laser razor survey instrument v.5.a

"Hɪ, my name is Alice, and I'm calling you on behalf of Market, Research, Incorporated to ask for your participation in a brief survey. We randomly connected to your headset using our predictive connecting system.

"If it's predictive, it's not random."

Alice wasn't allowed to deviate from the script or respond to comments.

"We're conducting research on laser razor use in households across Nu Jersey. All your answers will be kept strictly confidential and will only be used to improve products of interest to you and your family. Do you mind if I ask you a few questions?"

"Suck a floodrat's dick."

"Great! Let's get started."

"I'm gonna need a beer for this."

"Sure." Alice paused for a few moments and listened for

breathing cues to indicate a settling on the other end of the headset. "I would like to ask you a few questions strictly for demographic purposes. Please let me remind you all your information will be kept strictly confidential. First, are you male, female, or no gender identification?"

"No gender identification."

"What is your zip code?"

"086902."

"Do you live alone or do you share your household with others?"

"Alone."

"Thank you. Next, I want to ask you a few questions about your purchasing habits. In the past ten days, have you purchased a Smooth Style-brand reusable laser razor?"

"Yes."

"Have you purchased this brand previously?"

"Yes."

"How many times have you purchased a Smooth Style-brand reusable laser razor? Would you say it's..."

Alice's monocular teleprompter froze, and although she had memorized the script from reading it day in and day out, it was against the rules to recite from memory. Grounds for dismissal. The headset monitoring technology would know if your eyes didn't align with the text when you spoke the words. She waited for the text to catch up.

"Would I say it's what?" Her respondent shuffled a little and clanked a beverage against the headset microphone.

"...zero to five times, six to 10 times, eleven to twenty times, or more than twenty times you have purchased a Smooth Style-brand reusable laser razor?"

"More than twenty."

"What are you shaving with your Smooth Style-brand reusable laser razor?"

"Excuse me?"

"What are you shaving with your Smooth Style-brand reusable laser razor?"

"I'm not answering that."

"If you care to skip a question, it's perfectly fine, but I would like to remind you that all your answers will be kept strictly confidential."

"I'm still not answering. What do *you* shave with a laser razor?"

"Let's proceed to the next question. Have you used your Smooth Style-brand reusable laser razor for anything other than shaving?"

"Like what? I didn't know you could use those laser razors for anything other than shaving—"

"Have you ever removed the Smooth Style brand reusable laser razors from their disposable casing for purposes of harming yourself?"

"What? No!"

"Have you ever held the Smooth Style brand-reusable laser razor up to a key artery in your own body and considered ending it all?"

"No! What kind of survey is this?"

"When purchasing a Smooth Style-brand reusable laser razor, have you ever thought, 'This is the last laser razor I will ever purchase, because I'm going to end it all with this one'?"

"I was right — you can suck my dick, whether I have one or not." Alice's respondent disconnected. Gathering responses to this survey had proved challenging, even though she was using excellent voice inflection. It was tiring.

She continued connection attempts for the next eight hours, with fifty-seven minutes per hour of connecting and five percent idle time. Ten people submitted to the survey. Of those, three *had* contemplated ending it all with their Smooth Style brand reusable laser razors, and two had used their Smooth Style brand reusable laser razors for some kind of self-harm.

The ankle cuff sprang open. Alice roused herself and kicked feeling back into her numb safety-ankle foot.

Keep up the good work at Market, Research, Incorporated! Thank you and have a safe evening!

Alice's monoculous projected its standard goodbye message. There was a new message underneath.

Can you answer external headset calls regarding company business?

Do you want to be told what to do by your direct superior on a constant basis? Are you ready to staple your way toward a new career of miscellaneous responsibilities and very occasional periods of standing up?

If so, we have the job for you! Inquire on the thirteenth floor today!

Could I answer external headset calls and staple things together?

Alice never had before. Most of the printed words she worked with were purely electronic — text on her one-eyed screen she read out loud into the headset. But she might be able to figure it out. Once feeling had returned to her foot, Alice made her way to the elevators to head home.

The elevator depressurized and the doors opened. Dimly lit inside, was John. He looked awful. Breathing heavily, shirt collar askew. Like he'd gotten dressed in the safety elevator. Every other time she'd seen him, he'd been so put together.

"Hey there, executive." Alice kept her tone light and airy to conceal her concern. "What are you doing here so late? Did they promote you already?"

"I think I'm on my way now," John said. He propped himself up against the elevator's flood-proof frame. Must be that breakneck executive pace—eighteen hours to her fourteen, he'd said? "That's what I was coming to see you about."

"Coming to see me?"

"They advertised a new position today, I think you should apply. The surveys, they — well, never mind. I think it would be a nice change of pace for you. You're so smart."

Alice's face heated. She'd never thought of herself as smart.

"Thanks, John. You too." *You too?* There was a real example of brains.

"Thank you, Alice. It means a lot to me. Will you head up to check out the job now?"

"Sure."

John punched the thirteenth floor button.

"Scary to think about all those people trapped in elevators during the Flood," Alice said as they hummed upward.

"Yes," John said. "It's a good thing we found this job."

Hundreds of thousands of victims trapped in elevator shafts had led to this optimal post-Flood design, they had learned during orientation. The workplace offered the best chance for survival.

The elevator slid into its horizontal cross shaft and depressurized once again.

"This is me," Alice said. "Where are you headed?"

John avoided her gaze. Was he sweating? He was so calm and dry looking in all the previous days. Corporate life was hell. It was obvious.

"Back to work. Good luck, Alice." John patted her on the shoulder. "I hope you get it."

What was John getting?

Alice stepped out of the elevator in search of a potentially better future.

"Thanks, John."

A stale breeze wafted up the elevator shaft and a bandage on John's pinky fluttered ever so slightly. Alice's skin turned icy. Where the tip of his finger ought to be, where the tip of his finger had been two days ago, was now just a bloody stump.

14

BOB LOOPED HIS FAVORITE FIVE-SECOND

Bob looped his favorite five-second ASMR clip into his headset, rested his head on the high back of his executive chair, and let his mouth droop open. After the tenth round of mascara brush scraping across plastic mesh, his palpitating heart calmed enough so he could consider confronting Eric Smith without it exploding.

"Who are you? What are you doing here? What's with these guys in the lab coats? What makes you think you can take my job?" He improvised his monologue while he bit as much of his fingernails as possible, scooping them into a neat little pile on the edge of his desk. When the last fingernail joined the others, he rose from his cushioned chair, still mumbling, burst from his office at a near-run, and ran smack into a plump little urchin standing near Eleanor's former desk.

"Who the hell are you?"

"I'm here to apply for the desk-sitting position."

THE BALD MAN'S chin was housing a ragged fingernail. Was it possible to grow a fingernail on your chin? One time she had seen a news clip about a twin who absorbed its partner in the womb. One human, four arms. This possible case in front of her had involved a lot more digestion, down to the last fingertip.

John's fingertip. What happened?

"Were you the one who advertised the job? It said come to the thirteenth floor."

"Right. It would have been more descriptive, but my secretary quit, so nobody was here to write it. She was a monster. You aren't a monster, are you...?" He whirled his hand in the air.

"Alice."

"Alice. Do you have any qualifications?" He ran his fingers through his sparse scalp. This guy looked stressed. Maybe his mom had unexpectedly died and left him an unaffordable condo without any means to support himself, too.

"Okay, let's see." Alice ticked potential qualifications off on her fingers. "I'm good at sitting, and I can staple things, with...efficiency, very straight, and in multiple positions on the page." Good bluffing. Good use of corporate buzzwords: staple, efficiency, straight, multiple.

"Good, good. That's what we're looking for. We're all plastic-based now for archival purposes. Per flood-proof mandate. Maybe you ought to fill out an application."

"I can—"

Wouldn't that delay the process? Think.

"—but I already work here. Can't you get my information from human and safety resources?"

"If I had a secretary, she could do it for me. What's your usual schedule? What do you do here?"

"I—I'm in the market research interviewing department. I've been there for...some time now. I do headset interviews. I work the usual shift."

"We have an interviewing department?" Her potential future boss threw up his hands. "Great. That's just great. Why should *I* know we're running headset interviews? Why should anybody tell *me* anything around here? Eric Smith sure is good at keeping everything to himself, isn't he?"

The fingernail launched off the man's chin and landed on the carpet. Either it hadn't been attached to begin with, or this weirdo had worked himself into such a frenzy his own misplaced body parts were falling right off his face.

"I don't know who that is." This was better than the interviews. Probably better than the interviews.

"Well, nobody does!" He stumbled over to bang on a vacant desk. Her future desk? "Nobody does."

Alice shifted her feet and peered at the carpet. This guy was volatile, potentially diseased. Maybe the job wasn't worth it. But was she going to stay on the interviews, hating it and afraid of taking a risk, or get out there and begin an exciting new position in stapling? Things couldn't get any worse than they already were. Could they? Maybe if she got fired. Or this job paid even less than she made on the interviews.

Alice took a deep breath. "So. Am I hired?"

The man snapped out of his reverie or five-second clip or whatever was going on with him and seemed to focus. "Yes. You're hired. Report here tomorrow whenever you typically work on the interviews. Let me show you where the staplers are located. As your first order of business, you can get me a printout of your resume from human and safety resources so I can see whether you're qualified for this job."

He lurched down the hallway, mumbling to himself. Alice struggled to keep up with him. Her cuffed foot slowed her down.

"Not a goddamned thing happened around here unless I did it. No fake company created. No article published. Now look."

He pointed into a darkened room on the right. "I think that's where the staplers are, but Eleanor was secretive."

"About staplers?"

"About everything. I have no idea about the staples."

"Sure," Alice said. "Great. I'll start tomorrow."

"Start what?"

"Finding the staplers. And the staples."

"And don't ask me who these guys in the lab coats are." He gestured at two men in lab coats loping down the glass hallway adjacent to theirs. The one on the left called, "Hi, Bob," through the glass pane. The other one waved, then they both disappeared into a side room.

Bob. Was she supposed to call him his name? Bosses usually didn't want you to. They always had some honorific title.

"They seem to know *you*."

"Ridiculous. Maybe you can figure that out, too."

Sir. That's what they wanted you to call them. Like old clips about the military. They wanted you to call them *sir* and they wanted to order you around and they wanted you to run laps or do pushups or staple things over and over.

"Yes, sir. Of course."

Bob's face lit up, and Alice knew she had done the right thing. She could do this. She could figure out *working*.

She made a U-turn and headed toward the elevator. She had to get out of there before this erratic man changed his mind and decided to go through the typical hiring process, probably a six-month ordeal with obstacle courses and electroshock. She'd learn the pay rate and the rest of this stapling career path tomorrow. While she was looking for the staples.

"Thank you so much," she called over her shoulder.

"Don't mention it," her new boss called. "See you tomorrow."

———————————

BOB DUCKED into the restroom to masturbate.

Being called *sir* by a subordinate had:

a. Never happened to him, and

b. Reminded him of his previous day's pornographic material.

He emerged from the bathroom a new man, with one functional subordinate, who he'd just pictured calling him *sir* while he jerked off into the toilet. He didn't care who the hell Eric Smith was. He'd figure it out tomorrow.

Better yet, he'd have his secretary do it.

But when Bob got back to his office, he noticed something that shriveled the remnants of his glorious erection. His pile of chewed-off fingernails was missing.

Stolen.

EVENING COMMUTE. Alice stared listlessly out the window in her old wreck of a car the whole time. It pulled in, slow as ever, and parked next to her mother's inoperable wreck. She made a mental note to get it removed, quickly, or the condo association would fine her.

Dusk streaked the horizon, pink and purple in the east where the ocean had once appeared.

Alice hauled herself out of the car, stomping her useless safety-ankle foot back to life.

"Evening, Mr. Worthington." She waved.

"Morning, Alice."

Mr. Worthington sat on a patch of alterna-grass outside the fifth door from the right, tearing fauxlowers out of the landscaping and eating them. He'd suffered a disastrous but not fatal head injury eight years prior.

"Mr. Worthington, I don't think those are for eating. Well, technically, I guess you could. Faux-glove flowers are made out of a mycelium composite. Where's Mrs. Worthington?"

"Alice, kids nowadays don't even understand what flowers are."

His expendability was obvious: He wasn't on a LINC. There had been a lot of debate about LINC-worthiness during Alice's teenage years. Who gets to live, who dies in the next flood? Prisoners? The mentally ill? The poor? What about the terminally ill? Do you put the LINC on infants? How long do you wait until you give your baby their first headset?

"You're right, Mr. Worthington. We don't."

Alice pulled the door shut behind her and peered around.

"Where the hell have you been?" Alice's mom's ghost shrieked from inside the downstairs closet.

Alice's legs gave out, and she went down like a limp noodle.

"*Fluh*...Mom, what are you doing in there?"

Over the past few days, Alice had caught more and more glimpses of her mom. The reason for the billing clerk's brief mix-up at the hospital had become more and more apparent around the condo. She wasn't alive, but she wasn't quite dead.

But this was the first time her mom had *spoken*.

Alice's mom had been a good mom. Steady. Always reliable. Never held a grudge about the gestational diabetes.

In life.

In death, Alice's mom — never a smoker — had taken up a ghastly smoking habit. It had become impossible to ignore. Clouds of stale-smelling ghost smoke hung about the house, thicker and thicker as the days passed.

She was smoking right now, Alice realized. A ghost cigarette.

The ghost smoke preceded her, a plume that billowed out of the closet. Mom emerged next.

Her dead mom's apparition, there in full view for the first time. It looked like a low-quality image from an old-model monoculous. Alice flipped her own monoculous up and down to make sure the image wasn't coming from her headset. Nope.

"I was looking for my favorite chair and realized you threw it away." When Mom's ghost inhaled, Alice saw the ghost smoke move into ghost lungs and leave a little spot of ghost tar. She was bizarrely made-up, as she had been on the last day Alice had seen her. A beauty queen ghost of a mom.

"Mom, that chair was disintegrating. It wasn't even under the flood-resistant warranty anymore. It could have gotten bugs or rats."

Was it possible to die again after you were dead, of dead person's lung cancer? Was dead-person-cancer a thing?

"Ooh. Listen to Rockefeller here. Thinks she can afford a brand-new chair on *her* salary."

"Mom, you died. You can't even sit on the chair anymore. You're a ghost."

"Just because I'm an apparition doesn't mean you can sass-talk me." Her tone was short in a way Alice had never heard in life. "Look at this." Mom held her arm up, pixelating one moment, blurred the next, alternately translucent and solid. She was still around somehow, though her body was sitting on a flood-proof pallet underground.

"I've got the image resolution of a television from the nineteen eighties and here's my daughter, giving me lip." She inhaled her ghost cigarette.

"You're right, Mom. I'm sorry." This *was* the ghost of the woman who had single-handedly raised her. "What's a Rockefeller?"

"It was this asshole rich family that controlled America back before we were free, before the Flood."

"Oh. Sounds weird. I'm glad we're free these days. I'm gonna go upstairs now. You wanna head up there and...materialize?" Alice couldn't believe the words coming out of her mouth.

"I'll think about it." Alice's ghost mom had been standing inside a hall closet that couldn't have accommodated even the tiniest couch. Dying had addled her mom's brain.

"Okay, Mom. Think about it. Also think about getting out and going for a walk or something. Like maybe toward the light?"

"Oh, ha ha. Very funny. You'd love that, wouldn't you? Always trying to get rid of your mother. I'm surprised you didn't throw a ticker tape parade when I died of my crap lung surgery."

"Yeah, Mom." Alice sighed and rolled her eyes exasperatedly. "I couldn't wait to leave college forever to come home to Nu Jersey so my only living parent could die and leave me all this." She spread her arms to indicate the stacks of moldy newsplastics and books in every nook of the condo.

"You don't have to be sarcastic. There are plenty of people who would be thrilled to have shelter and books and newsplastics. They don't make them anymore."

Her mom's ghost sniffed, but Alice deemed it a manipulation technique or a memory of how to display feelings.

"Why were you standing in our hall closet, anyway?"

"Nothing's in the right spot. Everything's shifted."

"I don't know mom, maybe that's a being dead thing. Everything looks like it's in the right place to me."

Alice snuck a peek at her mom's spectral body. She had considered ending it all after her mom had died because she couldn't picture many opportunities for herself, alone in this world. Now, when she thought of her own ghost living here in the condo too, she felt more hopeful for her life, even the fourteen-hour stapling workday to come.

Alice shifted a stack of newsplastics so she could take the stairs.

"Doooon't—" Mom's ghost appeared next to her. She faded in, gently at first, then with a rush. Her image brightened in the center, fractals of light spinning outward, cubes of image stacking to create the pattern of her mother. It wasn't like the ghosts of clips past — it was weirder. Alice masked her shock with a fake smile in case it was offensive. Hopefully her mom's ghost wouldn't notice it didn't reach her eyes.

Whatever Alice's mom was trying to tell her, it was drawing out. Her voice sounded...digitized. Like it was being beamed through Alice's LINC earpiece on a day of solar flares.

"—you dare throw those away."

"Of course not. We'll wait for the floods to come back and those will do all the work."

"Not funny, young lady. It was a terrible time. A lot of people died."

"I know, I remember the stories." Alice put on her narrator's voice. "Lots of dead people were floating around for a year, until the sea creatures ate them all and got fat. We were beachfront property for a little while here in Trenton, but even though we had a beautiful new ocean view, we were still very sad about the whole thing, and not just because we thought we could be next and had to worry about the ocean coming and killing us all the time."

"Right." Her mom huffed.

"Hey, are there other ghosts with you?" Alice glanced at and around her mom.

"They're not with me, but they're not against me. Didn't see much of anybody in the beginning. Well, I didn't know what was going on, really. Kinda hovered between floors in the hospital for a while. Very loud. Rickety. Thought I was in hell, but it was just the HVAC. I was the only one at first. It figures: They changed the whole administrative process once it's my turn. It's like social security all over again."

"So now there are more like you?"

"I don't want to say I'm a trendsetter, but ever since I didn't die, nobody does. Nobody gets to pass on and enjoy the hereafter anymore, sweetie."

"How come I can't see them?" Alice wanted to know.

"It's not like everybody who ever died came back," her mom said. "Only the recents. The newly dead, like me. I don't know how it works yet, exactly, but it doesn't seem like the living can see a dead person they didn't know when they were alive. When I first got back here, after the funeral, I stood outside the condo awhile, but none of our neighbors talked to me."

"Maybe they were busy on their headsets. Didn't notice."

"Maybe." Ghost mom lit one ghastly cigarette off another.

"Oh Mom, don't do that." Alice went to the kitchen to fix her noodle-cup dinner. "It smells even worse than antique cigarettes. And it reminds me of how your lungs got sick even though you weren't a smoker or anything."

Ghost mom ignored her.

"Hey, can you leave the house or are you trapped here?"

"You're trying to get me out of here so you can loot my things and throw the rest of them in the trash. I'm onto you, missy." Alice's mom waggled her ghost finger. It pixelated and separated from her body image. Unlike in life, when Alice's mom had been capable of a range of emotions, so far her ghost had been either indifferent or highly combative.

"I am *not*." Alice fought a new wave of frustration. "What could I possibly loot in here? Old newsplastic clippings about the Flood? Antique container lids that don't fit on any containers?" She sighed.

"Look, it's just...I'm starting this weird new job tomorrow and I could use your help. I don't know how to do anything. Maybe, since you can be invisible, you can poke around in there for me? Figure out where things are and how to do stuff, so I can be good at my job and not get fired, and we can keep the condo."

"Alright, honey. I'll think about it." Ghost mom tapped her ghost ashes on the floor. Alice looked the other way. She was tired of nagging.

BOB AWOKE with a new sense of purpose: He had an assistant. A real assistant, not the abuse and neglect experience of Eleanor. Eleanor was like part of the office furniture — angry office furniture. This new employee seemed pliable. Naïve. Called him *sir*. Respected him.

He was a *boss*.

A boss of one is still a boss, he chanted to himself, waving on the shower.

A boss of one is still a boss, he chanted in his car, gazing out across the Princeton Strait.

A boss of one is still a boss, he chanted on the elevator ride up to his office.

The elevator doors opened to reveal — Eleanor. Her eyes bulged out of her head and her chest bulged out of her shirt. She reminded Bob of a flood pigeon that had attacked him once, early in the Flood days. He shuddered and pushed his way past.

"Eleanor? Come to steal more office supplies?"

"Real nice, Bob. You little *shit*. I decided this company owes me a lot more than this pittance after I had to view your junk all year."

"How'd you get past the LINC secretary?"

"It's a hologram, moron. I walked through it."

Bob was on the verge of letting Eleanor's surprise appearance shake him when he remembered he was a *boss* now.

He had an idea. Instead of creeping around like a new-shore alley seal, slinking through the trash, he invited Eleanor to discuss the situation with *his* new boss. Eric Smith. She said she'd be glad to. They strode screaming down the hallway.

"Eric will tell you. He's in charge now. You have to file a claim with HR and let it take its course," Bob said.

"*Balls.* Balls outside your pants. That's what I had to see. There is no such thing as HR in this company, Bob, and you know that, you moron."

Bob barged right into Eric's office, Eleanor in tow. He didn't have to stand for this. Eric could—

Be asleep. Asleep sitting up. He wasn't wearing a shirt. His pale, chiseled form made Bob want to throw up. Eric had a glass pipe dangling precariously from the edge of his mouth. The room smelled like sour grapes. An audio clip piped through the room's LINC audio system. Bob could swear it was a recording of the wind blowing across the drainpipe outside his childhood home.

Eric opened his eyes. Eleanor and Bob gasped in unison. He grabbed the pipe out of his mouth.

"We'll give you whatever you want," he said to Eleanor.

"What?" Bob rage-spit on himself. "Do you even know who she is?"

Eleanor left dancing, out of Eric's office and down the hallway.

Eric. What a joke. High on *faux*bacco or some other antiquity. So much for leadership.

Bob stood there, fuming. It was time to put Eric in his place, turn the tables and rake *him* over the coals for a change. His guts churned.

"Why would you start a market research company and not tell me?"

"Good morning, Bob," Eric's voice was monotone. "I didn't start a market research company. Market, Research, Inc. has co-existed along with our headquarters here all along. Tom Fletch Senior started it immediately after Fletch Industries. We're merely contracting with them to work for us. I'm shocked you didn't consider it earlier. How did you ever conduct your political research all these years?"

"It was never a problem before," Bob said, his heart pounding at the prospect of defending years of decisions. Had he even made any decisions? No, when he had met them everything was already set. He had just carried out their fathers' wishes. Fletch Senior issued all the orders. "We never needed it while Tom was alive. Everything went smoothly."

"Sure." Eric sneered at him. "Now we need things to *continue* to go smoothly, Bob. You understand. It's not easy to exchange one senator for another without an election, and we can't risk public awareness, especially when the new senator isn't a senator or even a politician. We're going to have to pave the way with a little bit of research. Why don't you have a seat?"

Eric gestured toward a chair. Bob jumped back a pace and gasped.

There was a man standing in the corner behind Eric. In all his Eleanor rage, he hadn't noticed the man. He wore an elaborate head-piece of...were those bones? His skin looked like a leather coat Bob had owned once when he was young, and he wore only a loincloth, like a caveman. In his weathered hand, he held a glass pipe identical to Eric's. It seeped a plume of purple smoke.

"We have a no-smoking policy, Eric," Bob said. He leaned in and lowered his voice. "Who's this guy?" He shielded his pointing finger with his hand and rolled his eyes to the right.

"Oh, this is my head of research and development. *Bastante, señor,*" Eric said to the man. "*Muchas gracias.*"

Señor nodded without expression and left the room, trailing smoke out the door and into the hallway. He joined a few of the now-ubiquitous men in lab coats and turned the corner. The loincloth was barely doing its job.

"You've exposed our operation to a lot of newcomers, Eric. This actor, this researcher, people in lab coats, a whole market research organization. I'm not sure you're thinking it all through."

"Bob, please, sit." Eric rose, forced Bob down into a painfully hard and tiny chair, then perched on the edge of his desk like a flood vulture.

"I don't really have time for—"

"Stop me if you've heard this one before. Tom Senior may have told it to you — or maybe not. There was a group of primates living on an island chain. They'd started eating these sweet potatoes they found nearby. It was a real windfall for the species. They were borderline starving up until then. Game changing, sweet potatoes. But the sweet potatoes were covered in dirt. I mean, they were *filthy*.

"One day, one of these chimps accidentally drops his sweet potato in the water. Big mistake, right? Wrong. He fishes it out. He eats it. And what does he discover?"

Bob watched a delivery drone pass by outside.

"Sweet potatoes taste better without a handful of dirt on them! One of the other monkeys tries it. And another. And soon...*all* the monkeys are doing it."

"I don't know what you're talking about, Eric. What are you doing with these scientists and these dead-language speakers with their loincloths and their bone hats? Who are these people? Why are they in my office building?"

"There are no dead languages, only dead people." Eric was annoyed at the interruption. "And we're not even doing that anymore."

"Huh?" Bob was totally lost.

"Back to my story. We're getting to the interesting part. The prima-tologists learned it wasn't only the monkeys on the lone island who were washing their sweet potatoes. After a certain number of monkeys learned the benefits, *all* the monkeys learned. On all the islands. Think about it. They didn't even have the LINC. Or a market research corporation."

"I see."

"I'm not sure you do. But we're going to reach our hundredth monkey, and we're going to make sure all the monkeys know how to wash those potatoes. We won't need this governance charade any longer. We won't need to keep the American public in line with all these mechanisms and maneuvers. Everybody will be washing the potatoes."

This guy was nuts.

"Potatoes," Bob said.

"Listen," Eric Smith pressed on. "You've been going through these motions for years: introducing legislation, running commercials, begging for votes, redistricting, faking votes, inventing voters, killing dissenters, protecting this sad little power cult. But it wasn't for nothing. And it's time to wrap this project up."

Eric Smith was having a fit about potatoes being clean. "I think you've got your work cut out for you, Eric. I don't have the time to deal with this."

"Sure you don't, Bob. You have an employee to manage."

He knew. He knew everything. Bob's blood turned cold in his veins. He couldn't let this tyrant see how scared he was. He clapped Eric on the shoulder. Just a couple of bosses here, talking about boss things. Equals. It was like trying to cuddle a floor lamp. His hand was trembling. He pulled it back and shoved it in his pocket. Bob backed out of the office, maintaining eye contact and nodding, only whirling around when he had gotten a few feet away.

"Of course, it's all a metaphor, Bob," Eric called after him. "We can't grow sweet potatoes here anymore. Or any potatoes." His voice echoed down the hallway.

What was he talking about? Can't grow potatoes?

Bob started back toward his office. Maybe he hadn't eaten a potato since college. But what did that have to do with anything?

What did *anything* have to do with anything?

Something happened in Bob's brain, like a hiccup. His thoughts were sharp; he was mulling his way through concepts and phrases to a realization, and then...nothing. They were all over the place, blurred, undone.

The feeling remained, though, and the feeling was fear. *I'm hungry.*

The hunger took over. It was only hunger all along. Hunger replaced all the fear. Time to eat. Time to head back to the old Snack-Attack and have a bite.

Really, this overthinking was ridiculous. Was there any reason to be so afraid?

Halfway down the hallway, he broke into a run.

15

ALICE SAT UNDER THE
FLOODHATCH

Alice sat under the floodhatch in the kitchen. A forlorn wind whistled through the gaps in its shoddy construction.

Sundays were downers — Alice had experienced Sunday depression since puberty. More often than not the sky looked bleak and a light breeze made the condo sound like it was low-level screaming.

It was inexplicable that Sundays should be different, because Sundays were indistinguishable from other days. Time off from work on the weekend had been abolished after the Flood.

Shortly before the Flood there had been talk in America about switching to a four-day workweek so people might kill themselves less. Big buildings could shut off the lights on more days; people would drive to those buildings less often, too, requiring less fuel and resulting in less cursing and traffic shootings. After the Flood, leisure time was out of the question. It was obvious work was the safest option in case of additional floods.

Schools too. For safety.

Productivity soared. The economy quintupled in size. Alice knew all of this had happened because her mom had saved the newsplastic.

There it was, on top of the crate she most often tripped over in the living room. "Economy Quintuples in Size," the headline read.

So here Alice was, working the first job of her life, in a malaise on a Sunday, though it was not the end of a weekend or any other stretch of "free" time. Why?

Genetically inherited end-of-weekend sorrow, she supposed. From a time before the Flood.

She picked up the newsplastic and peered around, expecting her ghost mom to swoop down and hover over it protectively. Alice hoped she would come, so she could verify the concept of a weekend. Alice had heard tales but couldn't remember it herself.

No signs of ghost mom. Alice stared at the floor, her eyes and head blurry. Not even bedtime yet.

Her head was so heavy.

Alice snapped her head up. Had she been dozing? The wind wasn't whistling anymore. The bright spot in the haze indicated the general location of the sun was way over on the other side of the floodhatch. She looked at the time in the upper left corner of her monoculous.

6:22.

She was going to be late for work. Alice remained seated under the floodhatch, the last place she remembered before...

Before what? What had happened? Had she slept sitting up, there in the kitchen?

Just think back on it.

Her day at work had finished. She had commuted home. She had been thinking about dinner.

Right?

What was going on with her?

Alice fumbled around the condo, her mind in a fog. She stumbled one way, then another, beating a careful path through the piles of newsplastics to get to the bathroom. She tripped into a few, sent them skidding.

"Ow," she said out loud, to nobody.

A new text popped up in her monoculous.

. . .

WE NEED TO TALK. -J.

ALICE'S PALMS WENT CLAMMY. She'd seen less and less of John lately, when all she wanted was to see him more and more. Hear his laugh, his stories about home. *Desire* clamminess? Maybe it would have been, but now all she could think about was how awful he'd looked the last time she'd seen him, the bandage on his pinky, what wasn't under it. A whole pinky, that was what. How'd that happen? And after all Jalia's gossip about the Hub, and weird things happening there. Maybe that's what this talk was about.

And what about the sloth? What the hell was a sloth doing inside a market research corporation, and why was it running? More importantly, *how* was it running? Alice had only seen the animals in five-second clips, had only seen most things in five-second clips, but everybody knew sloths were slow.

She tapped the message off screen, shifted on the rainwater release valve for her weekly shower, got under the raintrickle. Now *that* was slow. And cold. And rust colored. Yuck. She probably needed to get the catchment sludge cleared. It was always something with condos.

No time to consider running sloths. She had one goal, and one goal only: to pay this late late mortgage. Not to conduct an investigation. Maybe if she ever got this situation under control, she could save a few extra cryptos each month and after five or six years, get enough together to take a college class. It would have to be on the LINC, not in person, but better than nothing. Back on track.

Alice wrapped her towel around her and tiptoed out of the bathroom, then peeked into the kitchen, the den, and the living room. It was so quiet, so ghost-smoke free. Had her mom walked into the light? There was no way to verify.

Mom. Gone. Alice gulped down her noodle cup, no time to spare, and tried to make the crying happen, if it was going to come.

I'm alone. Again.

She squeezed her eyes. Nothing came out. Maybe she was dehydrated — or maybe it was impossible to mourn a ghost's passing.

Alice lotioned up in order to squeeze into her plastiskirt. After ten minutes of

inhaling small nips of air to suit the restrictive boundaries of her garment, she was in. They'd introduced plasticlothes when she was, what, seven? Tantrum after tantrum. The pain. The suffocation. The sweating. Her mom begging. Pleading. Alice yelling. What a mess.

Now it was normal. She felt naked and afraid without a sweaty, restrictive garment that could allegedly save her life with its buoyancy.

Alice opened the door to face the world. The soupy air greeted her.

Alice sighed. At least she had a job. Time to go to work.

———————————

SHE CHECKED herself out in the elevator doors' metallic reflection. Not bad at all. The weekly shower paired with the weekly scrub-down of her plastic clothes had dramatically improved her appearance. She couldn't believe how professional and competent she looked.

Financially, things were looking up too. She almost had enough cryptos to pay last month's mortgage bill.

And perhaps her mom had gotten closure, had gone to wherever the next place was after life on Earth as a human and then as a ghost.

The elevator announced itself. Its doors creaked open. John.

"John. Where have you been? Seems like a flood-night since the last time I saw you. How's life as a busy executive?"

John sighed. "It's hectic. I barely have time to scrub my clothes with the damp cloth in the morning, and I don't have any time to eat the noodle cups for lunch anymore — much less pack my own lunch. I miss seeing you, though. Maybe we can get together soon?"

"Sure, anytime. You said you wanted to talk?"

John frowned. "Did I?"

"Oh, I thought you texted me." Alice's stomach clenched with disappointment. "I work for Bob these days. That job I interviewed for, I got it. The one you recommended."

"So you're off the surveys?"

Didn't he remember? She was off the surveys because of him. She thought he might have put in a good word for her, but now it didn't seem like it.

Alice transferred her gaze to the bandage on his pinky.

"Yes." She nodded. "I work for Bob now."

"Okay. I don't know him. But — as long as you're not doing the surveys."

"Why not? What's wrong?"

"Uh, I heard they are...boring."

Oh, okay. So, you didn't run into Bob ever? He's some big guy around here." Alice shrugged. "Big enough to have an assistant, anyway. I think he runs Market, Research, Incorporated? Or a division of it. With the help of his assistant. Me."

"Wow. Well, congratulations." John mustered a weak smile. "You always were an excellent lunch partner. If that's any indication of how you work, Bob's very lucky to have you."

"Thanks. I haven't figured out what I do yet, exactly, but I'm sure it'll get clearer. Hey, have you figured out what *you* do? What's it like?" Alice searched John's face for clues and noticed how haggard it had gotten. Should she ask him all the questions whirling around in her mind?

"It's... different. Very different." The elevator chute slid into its designated slot. "This is my stop," John said, "but you take care. Really, really take care in your new job, Alice. I hope to see you soon." He shifted his briefcase to the other hand — *that* hand — and winced as he slipped out the doors.

"Um, you too," Alice said. A chill crept up the back of her head as the elevator continued on its way.

She didn't know anything about her new job. Would they take her fingertip? What was going on at Market, Research, Incorporated?

LATER THAT DAY, Alice was face to sack with Bob's scrotum.

"Could you tell me more about its elasticity?" Bob asked, posed in front of Alice, hands on his hips. "Is it very low, in your experience?" Alice froze her face so it didn't make an expression. She straightened up and tried to move her gaze from ball sack to eyes in the most neutral, non-reactive way possible. She wished she had known this was coming so she could have practiced in a mirror. But who could have predicted *this*?

In many ways, she would have preferred he chop off her fingertip.

"I don't know how many times we're going to cover this. I haven't seen many scrota." Alice gestured at Bob's testicles, keeping her arm short to prevent any accidental graze. "And it was only in clips, so I can't say for sure if those were real or normal or whatever." By the expression on his face she knew she had responded incorrectly.

"I'm not trying to do anything unethical," he had announced to Alice earlier after calling her into his office for a "very important" task. She had sat in the chair across from his desk. He had called her closer.

This is it. The part where I have to perform sex acts.

Bob had delicately lifted his scrotum outside his pants.

To get a third opinion. All he needed, he said, was a third opinion.

The *second* opinion, he explained, had come from a woman he'd been dating for several months who had made a disparaging comment.

Bob danced lightly from one foot to the other.

"Did you see that? The way they bobbled? Is it normal, do you think?"

"Look, Mr. Petri." Alice carefully avoided looking too long at Bob's bobbling balls. "We're a market research company. Why don't we market research ball sacks and see what's out there?"

Bob stopped tapping his feet. "Great idea, Alice. I knew you were going to be a good hire. Draft up a brief research outline this week, would you?" He flopped back into his chair and slumped over, still preoccupied.

"Yeah, fine," Alice responded, seeing herself out to go slump over her own desk. It hadn't been an easy day: John, then a scrotum. This wasn't what she had pictured for herself as a child, or as she was attending college, or dropping out of college, attending her mother's funeral, or sitting around with her ghost mom afterward; she had pictured many things, but she had never, ever pictured herself in an office, staring at a scrotum. Another one of life's surprises.

Alice couldn't face snapping back into her ankle cuff while she wrestled with all these crappy new life experiences, and she couldn't stay at her desk without it, so she turned to another of her fascinating job responsibilities: filing. Scooping up a pile of plastics marked "New Tom" off her desk, she trudged down to the filing room.

She turned the final corner, waved the door open. And then there was a noise.

What was that?

Metal scraping on metal.

A low, droning sound with a high-pitched scrape at the very end.

Getting louder.

Metal on metal.

Scraping. Scratching.

Alice took a step backwards. She could hear her heart pounding.

Nobody else was up here. Right?

Scraping. Scratching.

Ssssscccruuuummmm.

Alice peeked around the corner, crept from aisle to aisle.

"Hello?"

Her voice would have echoed back to her if not for the reinforced concrete and the waterproof vacuum seal on the room. Instead it was swallowed, deadened.

Nothing in the room except files. A whole waterproof room full of waterproof files.

Ssssscccruuuummmm.

The sound again.

And was there a smell?

Tick, tick.

A new sound. What *was* that?

Files shot out of the filing cabinet in front of Alice, and she screamed—

She was face to cigarette with her ghost mom.

Ghost mom chuckled, ghost cigarette tucked into the corner of her ghost mouth.

"FLAMING FLOOD. MOM. *What the hell?*"

"Gotcha."

Alice clutched at her chest, breathing hard. "I don't believe this." She bent over, her breath hitching. "You've turned into such a jackass."

"Hey. Show some respect. When there was a uterus in here, you came out of it. And you gave this ghost pancreas diabetes." Alice's ghost mom showed her the rough anatomical locations of these things with an ephemeral finger.

"Yuck. Spare me. Hey, I thought you couldn't move things. You're a ghost. What gives?" Alice pointed at the hurled files.

"I know, I know. I'm as surprised as you are." Alice's mom shrugged. "When I first got here there was nothing to me, and then after a while in this building: WHAM. It's almost like I'm made of matter again. Very occasionally, if I try hard. I knew I had to use it for something fun."

"Yeah," Alice muttered, "Real fun, Mom. I thought you were dead. What happened?"

"Sweetheart, I *am* dead."

"You know what I mean. Gone into the light."

"Yeah, yeah, the light, the light. Still haven't found it." Alice's mom cocked her head at Alice. "I came here because you told me to, remember?"

"No. I did? I must have forgotten." Alice shook her head, confused. "I was worried about this new job." She looked around. "So...you're living in my workplace?"

"I don't know about living, per se. More or less?" Alice's ghost mom hurled her ghastly cigarette onto the floor and tamped it out with her apparition foot.

"It's funny, now that you mention it. I came here like you asked me to, but I thought I could turn right around and go back to the house." Alice's ghost mom pointed two fingers at her eyes, then at Alice. "I've got to watch you like a hawk or you're going to destroy my beautiful home and all my things. Now I'm stuck here, though. I don't want to say *haunting*, but this is my rightful place. I can feel it in my —" Alice's ghost mom looked down at her absent bones.

"Tell me about it." Alice rolled her eyes. "But I'm here because I work here. I have to keep our damn condo afloat. Why are *you* stuck here?"

"I can't say for sure, but it feels similar to what happened after I died. At first, I was on course for the light. Then there was a sort of *vacuuming* and I got pulled out of joint. The next moment everything was off-kilter."

"Sure. We were all heading to the right place at one time or another. And now here we are." Alice threw up her hands, then crouched down to scoop up the files she had dropped and the ones her mom had flung about, testing the plasticity limits of her clothes.

She glanced through the top couple of plastics. "Notes on the Project," read the headers.

"I don't even know what project these files are from. Perfect. Listen, Mom, I have to clean these up and head back to my boss. He'll be expecting me. You be careful around here. Don't let anybody see you, and don't pull any of this poltergeist crap. On anyone. Including me!"

"Honey, you sure know how to take the fun out of being dead. I don't know whether it will help with your work, but I did see something in here, something very interesting." Alice's mom lowered her voice and looked around. "There's another ghost living under this building."

"Underneath it?"

"Yes. In the foundation. He doesn't know he's a ghost yet, thinks he's in hell. Keeps wailing. Quite annoying. His name's Tom."

"Well, did you try to talk to him?"

"No." Alice's mom sniffed. "I don't want to befriend any old loser simply because we're running in the same dead circles."

"Mom! I need help here. Something is going on at this place. Go talk to this Tom and see what he says. I have to go."

"Busy, busy," Alice's ghost mom said, loaded with attitude, before pixellating out.

Seeing her mom's face cube up and disappear was always a shock, but Alice did notice her own relief at the thought of her mom still being around, mixed with the dread of having to manage her at the office. Relief-dread: another new adult experience.

Her monoculous rang the arrival of a new message. Alice jerked her head right to view.

OUTSIDE. Now. -J.

ALICE'S PULSE SPED UP. She crept back down the hallway. Maybe John didn't feel comfortable talking earlier, or in the elevator.

Bob's office was silent. Should she ask for permission to leave her area? But then maybe he would ask why — and what would she say?

She saw the flicker of his LINC-link projection system through the frosted plastiglass. Hopefully he was busy.

Alice tiptoed past her desk and out the door.

IT WAS SO BRIGHT OUTSIDE, Alice's eyes had difficulty adjusting. She squinted them nearly closed. When was the last time she'd been outside at this hour? Never.

Her heart and stomach pounded as if they were one organ. What was John going to say? Would she get in trouble with Mr. Petri for being away from her desk?

The bushes behind Alice rustled. Before she even had a chance to turn around, a hand clamped down on her arm and hustled her into the foliage.

"Ouch," Alice said. It wasn't the hand hurting her; the grip was nearly as weak as hers. It was the fake plants: they were scratchy. They raked across her arm, held by somebody she couldn't see.

She could tell it wasn't John, though, because all the fingers were intact.

Her eyes adjusted in the shadow of the hedge.

Jalia.

Alice hadn't seen Jalia since the self-punching incident of...last week? No, it was longer than that. Wasn't it? Why couldn't she remember for sure? Why did she think all of her memories had happened last week? What day was this, anyway?

"Did anybody see you?" Jalia peered over the fake bushes. Her monoculous had a piece of dark tape on it, Alice noticed, turning it into more of an eyepatch.

"I don't know," Alice said. She wiped the microdots of blood off her arm where the faux hedge had cut her. "Doesn't everybody see everything? Or somebody sees everything? Everywhere we go?"

Jalia studied Alice. "You're disappointed to see me, aren't you?"

"No," Alice lied. She looked away and grabbed the back of her neck, a one-handed self-hug for support.

"You are. You thought the 'J' was for John. I knew you had a thing for him." Jalia looked like hell. Her punching incident still looked raw. And she had more debris than one fake hedge on her. Jalia looked like she'd been sleeping in the floodplain.

"Do not," Alice said.

"You do. I can tell."

"Maybe *you* have a thing for him."

"No way. Gross."

"What do you mean, gross?"

"Don't worry about it."

"Anyway, do you still even work here? What happened to you?"

Jalia danced around like she was listening to a five-second club clip while Alice was talking.

"What are you—"

Jalia interrupted Alice by yanking off her headset.

"Hey, don't—"

She taped over the monoculous and slapped something like chewing gum over the earpiece. Then she shoved it under the lowest branch of the nearby hedge. She put hers down there, too.

Alice glanced around. There was nobody out there, of course. Outside. Too risky. Having her headset off, though, in the company of somebody completely unstable, could turn out worse for her than the next flood coming in five minutes.

"You don't trust me?" Jalia finished scooping dry dirt over her headset and stood up.

"You punched yourself in the face last week and attacked a bunch of managers. Now you're burying our only lifeline to safety. You shouted some weird message to me on the way out. What do you think?"

"I had to."

"What? Why?"

"It's what they wanted to see." Jalia stood up straight, holding an invisible clipboard and etcher and mimicking the five-second science clip series with Dr. Art Huntington™. "The results they're looking for." She leaned in. "Listen to me. Something wicked is going on in here."

"What does wicked mean?"

"It means bad."

"So now our best chance at survival is buried under a hedge. Great." Alice didn't feel comfortable delivering her usual amount of sarcasm. Something weird was going on, alright, and it was *Jalia*.

Her heart was pounding so hard now that she was off-LINCed she couldn't concentrate on the conversation. She scanned the building entrance for her new boss, racing out to fire her for being away from her desk. She scanned the sky for the tsunami to sweep them all away. She scanned her chest, feeling the heart inside it trying to kill her by pumping faster and faster until it exploded.

"The next flood isn't coming, Alice. You know how I know?

Because the floods—*the* Flood—came from here. Right here, where we work. Market, Research, Incorporated."

Alice couldn't breathe, and she couldn't process any more of Jalia's absurd conspiracy theories.

"Maybe you don't trust me, but you care about your new friend, don't you? Ever wonder why he looks so awful now? I can tell you. Better yet, I can show you."

Jalia's profile cut a menacing image with all those recent facial scabs. If Alice was really scared, though, why was she still out here listening? Something about Jalia — the concern in her eyes, her shabby, sector-five plasticlothes — made Alice feel she could trust her.

Alice sighed. "I know why he's got that bandage. He's missing his fingertip. I just don't know what caused it. Are you saying it happened here?"

Jalia took a step back and looked Alice up and down. "I know you think you're too good for me. Because you're sector one, and I'm sector five. But it takes the grit of a sector five to have uncovered everything I know about this place. Are you gonna come with me or not?"

"Where?"

"Out back. There's something you need to see."

"You mean, *outside* out back? No way."

"Trust me."

Being in sector one during the Flood was an accident. Sectors didn't even exist back then. Getting to stay there was a fluke. Alice was scraping by. Her mom was dead. Sort of. She had nobody and nothing. And now Jalia was going to pull this sector crap? Try and guilt her into doing... what? She didn't even know.

Dig up your headset now and go back to the office.

But John. John's finger. John's full and happy face, turned thin and worn.

Alice pinched the area of her nose between her eyes. Another adult feeling: pain from stress.

"Alright. Fifteen minutes. Then I need to get back to my desk."

"Let's go."

They loped behind the main entrance of Market, Research, Incorporated, past a rattling trailer, past what looked like the guts of the building, past a few other unmarked trailers.

"This way," Jalia said.

Three buildings back now. Alice strained her neck, creaking from long hours of staring straight ahead.

Jalia seized the bottom rung of a ladder to the roof and started to climb. She was already ten rungs up before Alice could heft her body up to the second grip. Everything was quivering: her legs, her arms, her unused ankles. She was going to fall off this maintenance ladder and die for sure. And then where would she be? Haunting the condo?

"Hey," she whispered. Jalia didn't hear her, so she tapped on the ladder, causing sound to reverberate up. Jalia finally stopped and looked down. "I'm a survey interviewer, not an athlete," Alice hissed. "Why don't we use the landing?" She pointed to a series of stairs on the opposite side of the building that ended in the same spot as the ladder, but pointing threw her off balance, and she fell to the ground in a heap, like a sack of dead Flood pigeons. Jalia shot back down the ladder and helped Alice to her feet.

"Okay, okay," she said. "So you're not an athlete: Noted. Maybe next time I'll just tell you things instead of trying to take you on an expedition."

Alice wanted to protest, but she also needed to save her energy, breath, and strength for whatever came next.

What came next was a grueling but lower-stakes climb up nearly five flights of stairs. Then they were outside the Hub.

"Can't... breathe," Alice gasped, crouching and panting for air between words.

Jalia's lips were pursed and her hand was on her hip: no sympathy. Jalia motioned for Alice to follow, and they wound their way around the exterior spiral staircase until they stood outside the collection of hallways that joined to form the Hub. Jalia motioned for Alice to stop, then continued around the corner, out of sight.

Alice couldn't tell how much time passed without her monoculous. Felt like an hour. Probably more like ten seconds. At last, Jalia poked her head out and waved Alice in. "Get up in here and take a look at this."

Alice squeezed into the between-hallways crevasse. Through a tiny reinforced porthole she could barely make out the outline of a door.

There was a plaque that said Art Huntington™ bolted to the windowless metal door. This must be the Science Bureau, always issuing science facts on the LINC. Distributing headsets. For safety. Alice was a little surprised to see it here, in Market, Research, Incorporated. Wasn't it an unbiased government institution, a giant laboratory where they did large-scale...science? This was just one little room.

Jalia pulled Alice back. They crept around until they were on the other side of the Hub. Jalia ducked and peered into a window. Alice followed. Her legs shook. When was the last time she'd stood up for this long? There weren't a whole lot of opportunities for standing. Jalia was right: She wasn't cut out for these kinds of adventures. Adventures in moving around.

This next window exposed the inside of the Art Huntington™ room.

Alice's heart pounded against her ribcage like it wanted out. She wanted out, too.

Inside the Art Huntington™ room, four lab coat-clad employees busied themselves. On the counter, there was a large jar, so big it could fit a person. Though not comfortably.

Alice strained to see what was in the jar.

It was a cloud. There was a cloud inside the jar. And the cloud was raining. Inside the jar.

The lab coats parted to reveal a mass of wires dipping down from the ceiling. They backed off en masse, one holding a cushion.

On the cushion, slender fingers curled to meet a disembodied palm. One of the fingers was a stub.

And in the middle of the room, hooked up to the wires, sat John. His eyes were closed, and his arm was now a stump.

JALIA GRABBED Alice and tore her away from the window. They crept halfway down the steps until Alice couldn't go any further. Shock coupled with two decades of sedentary lifestyle bested her, and she collapsed on the landing.

"Wha, why, wha—" Her voice formed only partial questions.

"You were screaming your head off up there! You're gonna get us killed." Jalia dropped hold of Alice's collar like she was a leftover bag of last week's Flood debris.

"His — his hand," Alice finally stammered out. She couldn't feel her face or her own hands. She clenched her fists.

Jalia's face softened. "You're in shock. Take it easy."

"You could have warned me. How did you find out about all of this?"

Instead of answering, Jalia said, "I have one more thing to show you. Follow me."

Jalia and Alice made their way back down the spiral staircase and crept from building wing to wing until they were out of sight of the Hub. They turned a corner and Jalia stopped short. Alice ran into her, then looked where she was pointing.

It was a field of golden yellow, as far as the eye could see.

"Flowers?" Alice spit out the word in disbelief, like she would have said, *unicorn*? Flowers hadn't grown since the Flood.

"Not any old flowers," Jalia said. She turned to the field. "Hey," she said, and then louder: "HEY."

And each and every flower turned its petals to face her.

Alice sat down right where she was. It was less of a voluntary motion and more of an acquiescence to gravity. She'd had enough surprises for a day.

A week.

A lifetime.

"You know him, don't you?" Alice said from her spot on the ground.

"*Know* is a strong word. I haven't seen him in ten years."

"Did you know they were going to cut off his fingertip?"

"I had an idea, yes." Jalia picked up her foot and gave it a yank. The whole lower half of her leg came off. "John's my brother."

Alice had never seen anybody pull their own fake leg off before. Real flowers, fake legs. It was too much.

"Why didn't you two say so?"

"We can't say anything indoors. With our headsets on. They're always watching."

"Who's always watching?"

"Tom Fletch Senior, for one. He started this company. His son's the Senator of Nu Jersey. They're using us—our body parts—to build a mind-controlling supercomputer." Jalia reattached the lower half of her leg and reached out her hand to help Alice up. Alice took it. "Our mom was prototype one. Then me. Now John."

"For what?" Jalia yanked her to her feet so hard, Alice thought her arm was dislocated.

"I don't know. But I *do* know it's got something to do with the apocalypse." The flowers rippled, a field of bright yellow against the gray of the Nu Jersey haze.

"I gotta get back to work," Alice said. "Before they discover I'm gone."

16

LET'S WELCOME YOUR NEXT SENATOR

"Let's welcome your next senator from the great state of Nu Jersey!"

Scattered and half-hearted applause in the Steinert High School-II auditorium, but they could edit it up a notch later. Bob stepped back from the podium and held out his hand, the tiger tamer introducing his tiger. Bob's tiger was a goddamned commercial actor. Exhausting. This whole fake campaign was draining, his worst yet. They had redrawn Nu Jersey's twelfth Congressional District seventy-two times in the past six weeks. He receded behind the curtain to scan the audience and check off the demographics present.

Eric demanded he target them in the LINfomercials, and there they were, clustered together: well-off elderly singles, impoverished middle-class families, unmarried truck mechanics, divorced headset-coding engineers. It would have seemed a motley crew to anyone present if targeted headset commercials hadn't shaped them to expect this mashup in any American grouping.

The actor strode down from the back of the room and made his way through the audience, shoes gleaming, hair styled — short back and sides with feathered bangs, per the audience test. They had floated hundreds of suit-and-tie combinations in front of their target groups. He was the optimal candidate.

Bob's stomach fluttered. *Operation: Replace Tom* was complete. Something felt wrong. Bob's stomach always felt wrong. Something felt even wronger.

The actor waved and shook the hands of a few of the more attractive voters Bob had handpicked for the front row. Leapt up the stage steps. Approached the podium. The crowd settled in. They'd all been paid. It was impossible to get anybody to leave the house for free these days.

"These have been trying times. Turbulent times." The actor looked at the audience as though he had given birth to them and then watched them overdose on drugs in their formative teenage years, but he forgave them now for ruining their nose, their face, their body. Eric's coaching. "But we're pulling through. You, the people of Nu Jersey, have spoken with your recall of Tom Fletch."

There hadn't actually been a vote. Eric decided they should hide the death. Instead they'd advertised Tom's recall, the snap election. Tom was going to "die of a heart attack" next week, in retirement, once people forgot who he was.

Elections weren't even necessary. Thank you, Post-Flood Government Reduction Act. But Eric wanted to put everybody through this elaborate charade for some reason.

"Now you've entrusted the future of this beautiful state to me, and I couldn't be prouder to call myself the—"

Smile, not too big — don't look especially happy, or like a salesman.

"next—"

Make a non-threatening hand gesture, not a fist. Not a goddamned fist. Close your hand. Gently. Don't squeeze it. Thumb on top. Yes.

"Democratic—"

What? No—

Bob lurched forward, then stopped himself.

"Senator—"

At the opposite end, stage left, Eric stiffened, puffed up his chest.

Made himself even taller, somehow. His expression turned steely. Bob froze.

"...of the great state of Nu Jersey."

The lousy actor had flubbed his line. Bob threw up in his mouth.

The senator was supposed to be a Republican speaking to Republicans. All the faux voters were die-hard Republicans. They'd redrawn the district and modified all the headset ads for Republicans.

Murmurs rippled through the crowd.

Eric scowled at Bob and made a few complicated hand gestures Bob had no hope of interpreting.

Maybe they could fix this with additional headset market-shaping.

Eric touched his lapel and scratched his right cheek. What the hell was he doing over there?

A flash burst from the back of the auditorium. Front-row audience members screamed and bolted. The acting senator of Nu Jersey slumped over the podium. Three rivulets of blood trickled from three laser-sized holes in his body. He tumbled to the floor.

A woman's ponytail caught fire, collateral damage from the laser snipe. If she hadn't been looking left at the time of the assassination, it would have zipped right through her frontal lobe. She screamed. Bob cringed and hid behind the stage curtain, gripped it with both hands. The panic caught on quickly. Part of the mezzanine section craned to look, the middle rows stampeded toward the front.

"Humans take a lot of flak, but is mankind really so bad?"

Bob jumped. Eric had snuck up on him when he wasn't looking.

"Are other species any more majestic?" Eric seized the curtain. Bob was behind it for protection, clenching it in both hands and in his teeth. Unconsciously. "When chimpanzees weren't extinct, they were systematically murdering other primate species. For fun. Do you think they were fulfilling their true purpose on the planet?"

"Uh—" Bob said.

"When a dolphin shoves his penis into another dolphin's blowhole against that dolphin's wishes, do you think either one is rejoicing in the glory of his dolphin life? Are any of the species doing anything worth mentioning?"

Bob couldn't answer a bunch of dumb rhetorical questions at a time like this. He was mesmerized by the woman with the smoking ponytail. She was whipping her head back and forth, smoke billowing around her.

Eric snapped his fingers in Bob's face. "Well, *are they*, Bob?"

Bob stopped watching the demographics trample each other in their rush to get out of the auditorium and turned toward Eric.

Had his eye color changed? From putrid to evil?

"No, Bob. You're right. They're not. But I'm glad you brought up the monkeys. And the potatoes."

"I...didn't." Bob swallowed hard. "I didn't say anything." Eric kept talking, undaunted.

"Last time, we talked about how all the monkeys learned something once the hundredth monkey did. The implication was they weren't together physically."

Eric overenunciated this last word in a way that made Bob feel bad about himself for no obvious reason. He released the curtain.

"Do you think the monkeys adopted the new behavior *exponentially* because of an unseen, species-wide cerebral cortex?"

"Um. I don't know."

"Or is it much simpler?" Eric continued. "Maybe one of those monkeys hitched a ride to the other islands. What do you think? Maybe the hundredth monkey swam around the islands showing the other monkeys how to wash the potatoes. A monkey messiah."

"That woman's hair is on fire. Did you do this, Eric?"

"Well, don't just stand there, Bob. Put her out. Go check on our candidate. Connect to emergency services. Get an ambulance down here. Say something to the people. Console them. They're stampeding."

Eric strode to the other side of the stage. He stopped and turned back.

"One more thing. Put out a press release. The Senator of New

Jersey's just been assassinated. Implicate the Democratic Party of Nu York."

Bob stared at Eric for an eternity. Then he approached the podium, arching his chest to span the distance across the body on the floor.

"Uh, rock the vote," he said into the microphone.

"WE'RE IN A SPOT, Bob. We're in a *fucking* spot."

Sen. Sam Hurst (D-NY) paced to one end of the boardroom, pivoted, and came right back. Why didn't he keep on walking right through that boardroom window? Bob could use the silence.

Why lose only two senators? Why not all of them?

Ever since Eric, he didn't feel like showing up to work anymore. If it weren't for Alice, he'd have nothing there. Nothing at all.

"I know," Bob said. He was expecting a package. He searched the sky for a delivery drone. Did he see the outline of one in the distance? His heart quickened.

"Do you, Bob? Do you? Because every time I come by your office, your balls are outside your pants. You don't appear very concerned about our situation here. We had a senator and then we didn't and then we replaced him and then somebody killed the new one." Sam's voice was hysterical. It wasn't drugs this time; it was real panic. Bob should have been able to feel something too, but no. Maybe he was in shock. After the assassination, he had gone home and slept as though nothing had happened.

"Take it easy."

"Easy? What's easy? Do you think those laser holes sprung up in his vital organs naturally, Bob? I think they're disbanding us. Have you talked to Fletch Senior lately? I haven't. I think we're being forcibly disbanded. Who's next? Me? You? You?" Sam pointed in the faces of the other senators, lounging around the table. They didn't notice or respond. They were too occupied by their headsets to be active participants in the conversation. Ten extra pieces of lumpy, worthless office furniture.

"All I'm saying is, we don't know what happened," Bob sighed.

"But why the hell not? Why *don't* we know what happened? I couldn't be there — I'm a rival. But you were there. You saw the whole thing. How come *you* don't know what happened?" Sam ran his fingers through his hair. It looked like duck feathers in an oil spill. Had he stopped showering? "It's like you're not even working anymore."

"I've been...busy with other things." A light hum from outside grew louder: the delivery drone. It clicked into the room's receiving chute, inserted a package, and took off. He'd put in the order hours ago. Delivery service had gone to shit.

Bob turned his attention to the receiving chute, but not fast enough to intercept Sam.

"What's this? Is it from Fletch Senior?"

"No, never mind, that's for me."

Sam snatched the package out of the hatch like a flood weasel and ripped it open.

"It's a 'ball bra,'" he announced to the boardroom. One of the guys (R-VT) giggled. Nobody else noticed. Bob's face flushed. He grabbed the box out of Sam's hands.

"I said, don't worry about it."

"Oh, I'm not worried about it. I'm not worried about your balls at all. Yours and mine and everybody else's are about to be skewered. What's to worry about? But you're *busy*. With your assistant and your balls and—*and*—who knows what. This place is falling apart. We're losing control."

"We're not losing—" Bob was interrupted by a commotion in the hallway. Sam shot out to investigate.

"What the hell is this?" He shrieked back at Bob. Bob ran to the doorway and peered out, then looked back inside the boardroom. None of the other senators looked up from their headsets.

Two men in lab coats stood there, holding something.

"Afternoon, Bob!" one of the lab coats called. "The Project is moving along. Our new candidate tested perfectly in recent polls like you predicted. We've never seen anything like it."

The lab coats swept into the boardroom. Bob was being shunted backward. Nothing ever went right on Mondays.

"*I* predicted?"

"What are you doing to us, Bob? Does Fletch Senior know about this?" Sam trilled.

"It wasn't me! It was—" Eric.

"The next Senator of Nu Jersey," the lab coat announced.

It was a black-and-white wingtip shoe. On a pillow. Looked sharp. It was the right shoe. It gleamed in the simulated-daylight lamps.

BOB TRUDGED TOWARD HIS OFFICE.

He paused to read a clip on his LINC.

The civil war between Nu York and Nu Jersey was officially announced after Sen. W. T. Shoe (R-NJ) took office.

Constituents agree it is an inherited problem and not a reflection of Shoe's leadership.

Poll numbers for the new senator are relatively high.

ERIC, he sneered. Going over his head and doing the press releases. Again.

He brightened when he saw Alice sitting at her desk, right where she belonged.

"Some war going on, huh, Alice?"

"Yeah." Alice shrugged. "I heard people elected a new guy named 'Shoe'?"

"Uh," Bob said. What he needed right now was a distraction. He tried to recall any of the pornographic clips he'd watched the night before. How had those bosses initiated sex? Yep, that's what he needed for sure. A distraction from all this madness. By having sex. With his secretary. That's what could salvage this week. Before he could figure out how to initiate it, Alice said, "You've got a guest in your office."

Bob edged into his office.

"Morning, Bob," Eric said from the corner.

Bob jumped.

"Hey, could you do me a favor and put yourself on my calendar when you'll be stopping by? I didn't even—"

"We need to talk about the Project."

Bob dropped into his chair, sighing. Eric didn't move, so Bob had to swivel around to face him.

"Look. Eric. You know as much about using the company as I do. Go ahead and do whatever. I don't see why I have to get involved. I already helped with the commercial."

"Yes, you did, Bob. You sure did. And have I told you what a big help you were?"

"No—"

"You *were*, and I forgot to thank you." Eric grinned with dead eyes. "Thank you for your help on the tuna commercial. The actor didn't entirely work out, but it wasn't your fault. You could have done a better job of grooming him, sure, but he was a hopeless case from the beginning. A waste of our time."

Bob eyed Eric. "If it was a waste of time, why'd we go through all that?" Who was he going to deem a waste of time next? He wheeled his chair away from the window in case Eric had a sniper drone pointed at him, too.

"Anyway," Eric said. "We've got a more stable candidate in seat five now, and that's going to work out fine. I need your help with something else."

"Is this about my fingernails?"

"Your what?"

"My fingernails. Normally I leave a small pile on my desk, but lately it's been disappearing every night."

"Bob, you sound like you haven't been getting enough sleep lately. Don't mention your fingernail pile out loud. It's going to destroy your credibility. This isn't about your fingernails. I'm serious: We've got a real situation to deal with here."

Bob stared at Eric, who looked even sterner than usual today. His eyes burned, temples throbbed. Too much thinking.

"Are you okay, Bob?" Eric ran his hand through his hair. It settled about his face even more perfectly than usual. His face was even more chiseled: The *chisel* was chiseled too, his perfect testicle elasticity gently outlined in his pants.

"Yeah, I'm fine." Bob swallowed hard and dragged open his desk drawer to look for his acid reflux pills.

"Good, because we've got a border fire on our hands." Bob shuddered. Men like this didn't belong in politics. Why would Eric even need power? He already commanded it with those ridiculous good looks and properly fitted suits, weird monkey anecdotes that skipped off his silver tongue.

"A what?"

Eric leaned over and punched Bob's headset monitor on with a single commanding finger. Right there, next to the scrotal reconstructive surgery website, was a regional LINCfeed broadcast of the Nu York–Nu Jersey border.

It *was* on fire.

The war had taken off. Quick.

17

ALICE'S CAR PULLED UP

A lice's car pulled up to the memorial Flood re-enactment. She hopped out. Jalia ran up from behind the hologram. She pulled out a roll of thick black tape and they covered their monoculi, then secured their headsets to the outside of the car. When she dove back into the car, Alice banged her head on the roof, hard.

"Ow!" she yelped. "Ow, ow, ow!"

"We've got eight minutes." Jalia said. The look on her face said she had no time for Alice's head injuries, or to express any compassion for those head injuries. They'd been meeting like this every day for a week, on Alice's morning commute. Jalia wasn't working anymore. They'd put her on administrative leave.

Jalia shoved Alice over and climbed in. "Some of your memories aren't real," she said.

"What?" The car started moving forward.

"You were at college, right? Before you came back to Nu Jersey? Do you remember what it was like?"

"Sure," Alice said. "Of course I do. It was just a few months ago."

"Tell me about it."

"Well, it was a lot like this," Alice said. "Flood walls about the same height, the division into sectors."

"No it wasn't."

"What do you mean, 'no it wasn't'? You weren't there."

Jalia tapped Alice on the forehead. "Remember it again," Jalia said. "*Really* remember it."

Alice closed her eyes, scrunched up her forehead, and saw Tampa.

In the cafeteria, she hit the button on the institutional *SnackAttack*

"It was the same," Alice said. "Just like here. Whatever you think I'm supposed to remember, you're wrong."

"I have something that might help," Jalia said. She reached into her plastishirt pocket and pulled out a dark red capsule in a small metal container.

"What is it?" Alice asked.

"Can I be honest with you?"

"So far, you've been brutal. I don't know why you're asking now."

"It's better if you don't know. But it's safe, and effective, and it'll only last for a couple of minutes. Put it on your tongue, and let it dissolve. That's all."

Alice's heart pounded in her chest. Her childhood education had incorporated a certain amount of training in *not* taking a random capsule from a stranger. But she was off the grid here, as far as typical experiences. Should she make an exception?

No.

Yes.

No.

Alice reached out her hand, and Jalia dropped the capsule out of the container and into Alice's palm. Alice stared hard at the capsule, heart in her throat, and then popped it on her tongue.

"Really remember Tampa," Jalia said.

IN THE CAFETERIA, she hit the button on the institutional *SnackAttack*

No.

No, there was no *SnackAttack* Real food. On plates.

Gazing out on the flood walls?

The flood walls disappeared — the horizon, the ocean.

Tampa wasn't flood-adapted.

The girl next to her in class, the teacher at the front of the class-room, no headsets. No floodlines on anything.

A tap on her shoulder, first day of school. "What's that thing you're wearing?"

Alice sitting on the beach, sun in her eyes. Reaching to remove her headset—

The message:

RETURN HOME IMMEDIATELY. YOUR MOM IS IN THE HOSPITAL.

ALICE'S EYES SNAPPED OPEN.

"There's no such thing as the Flood in Tampa," Jalia said, "Because there's no such thing as the Flood outside Nu Jersey and Nu York. It never happened anywhere else. You're not supposed to be able to leave Nu Jersey or Nu York. Your memories of Tampa being like here aren't real. They're headset-generated."

Alice's body shook with a fear from deep inside. If she couldn't trust her own brain, what was left? Maybe *those* newly remembered memories weren't real. How could she tell?

The car stopped at the *Trenton Makes The World Takes* Flood Tunnel to hold for their timed pressure entry.

"Time's up," Jalia said. "Keep checking the files. I'm going to figure out some way to get to John. Have you seen him since...?"

Alice hadn't. Every day in her mind, she saw John's hand on a pillow. "No," she said. "But you can't go back into Market, Research, Incorporated. Won't they kill you?"

"Nah." Jalia said. "They can't. I'm in the biocomputer." She tapped her prosthetic leg. Alice had no idea what she was talking about.

She got out of the car, ripped their headsets off the roof, and tossed Alice hers. She replaced her own and flipped the monoculous down over her eye.

"Jalia, what was in that pill?"

Jalia considered for a moment. "My blood," she said. And she ran off. Alice didn't look in her direction, so Jalia's image wouldn't get picked up on her monoculous.

LINCNOTICE

Minor flood-property-based skirmish on the Nu York/Nu Jersey border, will alert when resolved.

She arrived at Market, Research, Incorporated nine minutes late. Decided to pin it on the civil war traffic.

Alice set to work on her filing. Not much luck. She tried doing keyword searches for their headings — *biomass* and *electromagnetic-field-based mind control* and *hundredth monkey event horizon* — in the company database, but couldn't find anything. They didn't even seem connected to any of the current surveys.

What she really wanted to investigate was everything Jalia had said. Was it true? There were no headsets outside Nu Jersey? Was Market, Research, Incorporated really trying to end the world? Turning people into computers? Growing real flowers? And then somehow giving them consciousness?

What if her boss found out she was snooping around? She couldn't risk losing her job.

He was in his office, yelling into his headset.

"Hi Sam, Bob here. Hey, do you know your state is on fire? Yeah, I saw it online. Sure, hopefully the undesirable parts, ha ha. I know, hell of a thing to have happen on a Tuesday. It's been a cursed day since The Flood. Yeah. Sixty thousand. I read it too. Okay. Won't expect you at the office today. Avoid the riots."

The conversation didn't sound like it had generated any action items. Alice stopped eavesdropping and went back to the files.

Nothing about removing hands. But what did these headings mean, exactly?

biomass and

electromagnetic-field-based mind control and

one-hundredth monkey event horizon

Her mom's ghost sidled up to her.

"Not now, Mom. Bob's in there. I mean, Mr. Petri."

"Oh, is he? Listen, honey, I might be dead, but I can hear him yelling his maniac head off."

"Look, I need some advice." Alice shuffled the plastic sheets over and over again.

"Thought I was supposed to go away?"

"Mom, I need help. I think these files you knocked over are secret. I can't even find them in the database and I don't know how to—"

"Have you tried alphabetical order?"

"Um. What do you mean?" Alice thought her ghost mom had rolled her eyes, but between the low light and the transparency of her image, she couldn't tell for sure.

"This must be the generation gap I always heard about. You can file things according to topic by alphabetical order. I know you know the alphabet, because I taught it to you. A. B. C."

Alice restrained an eye roll. "Uh-huh."

"Libraries used to use a different topic-classification system. It was called the Dewey decimal system. After the Flood, when we switched from paper to plastic, they burned all the old paper books. Trenton was an incineration hub; we could hardly breathe. But it made sense. They had to cut down on the moving debris in case of additional floods. For safety. No more hard copy books."

"Hmmm. Information outside the headset? I can't even imagine."

"It used to be all we had. Then computers. Then phones became computers. Then the headset. Now LINC transmission only. Internet and safety system, combined. Since there's no physical information, we don't need a storage system anymore — even an alphabetical one. But I bet that's how they keep the files. What about the others? Do they say anything at the top?"

"This one starts with 'N'. 'Nervous system.'" Alice flipped to the next plastic. "Oh, look. It's a list, in alphabetical order. All those countries that drowned in the Flood." She kept going. "This one and most of the others say 'The Project' on them. Would they be filed under 'P' or 'T'? I don't know."

Her mom snorted. "Sounds like you don't know much, kiddo. And what you do know is starting to bore me. I'm going to go haunt the break room."

"Mom, no!"

But Alice's mom had already pixelated into nothingness. Her ghost mom had gotten pretty quick, while Alice was getting slower and slower. The brutal work schedule was fogging her brain. What had she been looking for, just now?

She couldn't remember.

THIS WEEK WAS FLYING BY. Since the start of the civil war, Eric had left Bob alone more often. Today, he had woken up punching the air as usual — only this time it was with joy.

He tugged at his new testicle brassiere, pleased as a flood rat on a skyscraper.

Alice's careful research had paid off: The ball bra was *amazing*. Bob looked down at his balls. He was getting a crick in his neck from gazing down, but he didn't care.

I don't think your balls are saggy anymore, Alice had whispered into his ear, breathless with desire.

Say it again, Bob had commanded, giving her orders like a man. Then she had cupped his balls inside their delicate purple underwire and photographed them at his request. He could tell she was eager to do it. She transmitted the images to his headset so he could look at them at eye level.

He'd fallen asleep gazing at their beauty, and he'd awoken to them, too. Perfect. He was looking at them yet again when it became obvious he had woken up for another reason: His headset was buzzing.

Sam.

Bob considered dodging the connect to spend more time looking at his scrotum but thought better of it. Time to do his job like a man with perfect testicles.

"Hey, Sam. How's it going? Any development with the war?"

"Hi, Bob. I hear the whole interstate border is still inflamed, but who knows for sure? It's only Flood refugees out there anyway."

"You still living in the north central post-flood plateau reconstruction area?"

"Yeah. Safe distance away. Listen, I had an interesting exchange with the missus this morning."

"I don't really have time to hear about your marital—"

"You're gonna wanna hear this."

Bob groaned. "Okay. Make it quick." He got out of bed, hit print on his coffee maker.

"I was leaving my house for work, mid-afternoon. The usual. Make the trip to the Capitol building, do a little politicking. Shake hands. Have a drink. You know my routine."

"Sure." The coffee maker failed halfway through the print job. Just a half-cup in there.

"The missus comes out of her room. Walks downstairs. Not all the way. She's holding her headset. Looks angry, like I've been talking about work. You know how she hates it when I talk about work."

"Right," Bob said. "Who doesn't?"

He hit espresso in a last-ditch effort to contain the entirety of his coffee, but it was too late. The coffee overwhelmed his failed cup, which dissolved and spilled off the bedside tray. Only one year old and already obsolete.

I feel you, coffee maker. Except in my case, it was years and years of work.

"She demanded I answer a question! She's never done that before. I mean, in that sense, she's been a good congressional wife. Keeps her mouth shut. Goes to the parties. Hates details. Can't remember shit.

Anyway, she says to me, 'Do you know what those bastards are trying to do?'"

"Harsh," Bob said.

"Yeah. Not like her to say a curse word. I didn't even know she knew any. What she's watching on her headset all day? Not puppies and kitties, like I thought."

"Well, these are tough times. Uncertain."

"Not for her. She's never said anything political to me, ever. Not one opinion. Not even small talk. Nothing. You know. We ran that whole fake campaign out of my house. She ever say anything to you about it?"

"No. She was very pleasant. Kept bringing out cookies."

"Right. Very pleasant. Sometimes, I don't even think she knows I'm a senator. Seventeen terms in office like this. She's consistent."

"So? What *are* those bastards trying to do? And who are the bastards?"

"First, she says she was randomly selected to participate in a market research survey—"

Bob tried the coffee maker again.

"—about the state of the union."

This time, the print button dumped a bunch of loose bioplastics onto its tray.

"Shit," Bob said.

"That's not all. She went on. 'Did you know these riots are happening because those fucking floodrats in Nu York City are trying to saddle us with that statue?'"

"I wasn't—it's my coffee maker. Wait. Did you say a survey?"

"Yes, a survey. Then she used the F-word. That old chestnut. Anybody ever say *fuck* to you? I haven't heard it in, oh I don't know, a decade. But Mrs. H? She's never said it. Never."

"What statue?"

"Don't know. I don't know. I was totally caught off guard, Bob. This woman has never said anything to me about my work. Or anything political. Or the word *fuck*.We've been married for decades. And who the hell even knows why the riots are happening?"

"Nu York City? Is she talking about...the Statue of Liberty?" Bob's coffee maker poured its coffee onto the loose bioplastics. He rubbed his temples and went on, "Hell, I don't know. Why would there be a survey about the Statue of Liberty? It's been ten percent submerged since the Flood. It's not even open. Who would fight about it? Dive tour operators? It doesn't bring in any revenue."

"I know, I know. That's what I said to Mrs. H. I said, 'Who cares? Thing's underwater.'"

"And?"

"And she lost her shit. I mean, lost it. Flood *crazy*. She tore her headset off her head and threw it against the wall so hard the battery panel fell off. Then she screamed at me. 'Who cares about that?' She shouted it twice. 'WHO CARES ABOUT THAT?' Even louder the second time. 'WHAT KIND OF A POLITICIAN ARE YOU? DON'T YOU REPRESENT THIS STATE?' Nuts. I've never seen anything like it, Bob," Sam said. "I was shocked. Scared. She didn't *look* right. Her lipstick was smudged, her wig wasn't on straight. She'd never raised her voice to me before. Never appeared out of full Mrs. Hurst garb. You know. But this time...*this* time. Her old flood sores were out. She hadn't bothered to cover them."

"Yuck," Bob said.

"I know. I was so scared I nearly peed in my pants. I said, 'Sure, sweetheart. Of course I do. I'm going to the office right now to take care of it. I didn't know you cared so much about the Statue of Liberty. We can't have one more partially submerged piece of property to support with our tax dollars. I didn't know you were so fiscally conservative. I'm going to go and fix it right now.'"

"Fix what?"

"I don't know. Something about the Statue of Liberty! Tell me something: How is it that a woman who never expressed a single political opinion in her life started foaming at the mouth about some godforsaken landmark today? A landmark I didn't even *remember* existed?"

"Hmmmm," Bob said.

"*Bob!*" Sam yelled. "What the *hell* is in those surveys?"

Bob's jaw dropped. "It was one of ours?"

"'It was one of ours?'" Sam mimicked with malice. "*Yes*, it was one of ours, you dope. They're *all* ours. I think I'm going to sleep in my office. I'm scared to go home to her."

Bob stared at the dust and mush of his failed cup of coffee.

"I don't know, Sam. I don't know every single survey that gets sent out to the masses. I'll look into it, alright? I gotta go."

"Great. Please. Do that. Look into it." Sam disconnected.

Before he could even look at his testicle pics to clear his head, Bob's headset buzzed again.

Eric.

Bob had barely shrugged to connect when Eric started talking at him.

"Listen, you're going on a business trip."

Bob's balls shriveled inside their purple sheath.

"What business? What trip?"

"I need you to get to South Africa. Today."

"*What*? What do you mean, South Africa?"

Bob tugged at his balls, no longer filling the entirety of their size B undergarment. He opened his curtain and peered out the lone shatterproof ionized porthole-style window of his nautical-themed condo. A drone slipped past.

"South Africa is a country," Eric was saying. *Droning* on. The drone hum faded and Eric's voice became louder. *Is this ball bra making me wittier?*

"Bob, pay attention for once in your life, why don't you?"

"Sure, Eric. Tell me more about this 'South Africa.'" Bob wiggled his fingers in the air, creating incredulous air quotes.

Perhaps he should order a red bra. Purple was the color of royalty, but red was a bold choice too. He'd have to consult Alice.

"Have you never heard of South Africa, Bob? It's a country in Africa. The continent of Africa?"

Now who was the idiot? Africa didn't exist. Everything except America had been wiped out in the Flood. There was no Africa anymore. It had barely existed before the Flood, much less after. Eric

Smith was about to be schooled in a little post-Flood geography lesson.

"I hate to be the one to break this to you, Eric..." Bob muted the microphone so he could snicker. "...but South Africa doesn't exist anymore. It barely even existed *before* the Flood." He made a celebratory leap from his porthole view back to his waterbed. Rode the rolling tide of his mattress. Where was this jerk from, anyway, that he didn't know basic geography?

"Sorry, Bob — *you're* misinformed. South Africa exists, just like it did before the Flood. It wasn't affected. And we have a new market research contract there. You're going to manage it. I'm having a suitcase delivered to your condo. It'll arrive in seven minutes. Pack it and get to the office. Immediately."

Bob's mouth remained open long after Eric disconnected.

BOB STUMBLED across the threshold to the office suite.

Alice looked up from her desk. "New balls dropping your jaw, boss?" She winked. It felt awkward and horrific, but she had been watching clips about influencing people and they had recommended this: say a complementary thing and then close one eye. It didn't make any sense. She'd practiced it dozens of times last night, but she still felt dumb.

Bob swayed over and sat down on her desk, knocking down her magnetic etchers. Alice tried on a more concerned expression, but she could never tell what her face was conveying. She *was* concerned. She had planned on asking him for a payday loan today, now that she had squared away his testicle issue. If she got it, she could make the condo payment on time for once, halt the mortgage-company drone flybys for a month.

Now he appeared to be having a minor stroke.

"Let me ask you something, Alice." Bob scooped together Alice's magnetic etchers, but they repelled each other, scattered to stick to the metal parts of her desk. "Have you ever heard of a place called South Africa?"

Or a *major* stroke.

"Sure. Of course. It's in songs and stuff. It's one of those places underwater now, like Atlantis. Or Timbuktu."

"What if I told you it's a real place? And I have to go there." Bob's head's lolled. He looked like he was going to pass out. His forehead sweat dripped off his nose and landed on her desk. "I mean, who's ever even *heard* of that? Going to a place not here? Everything was destroyed in the Flood! It'll be chaos. I know this is a goddamned set up."

"It's interesting you should mention. I met a guy here in the new employee orientation who said he's from a country in the western part of Africa. Still exists, he said. Not destroyed." Alice searched Bob's face for any inkling that he knew John. Nothing.

"There are probably flood rats everywhere, eating the flood corpses like they did here before the Bureau of Science poisoned them all. I'm going to be sick. Alice, I think I'm going to die there. Eric says there's market research to be done there but I know he's lying to me; he's trying to get me out of the way. He's threatened by me since I got my new confidence." Bob pointed to his testicles.

"Probably," Alice said without looking down. Whoever Eric was, she was pretty sure he didn't care anything about Bob's testicles. Then again, maybe he did. What did she know? "Listen, about my pay—"

"Let's go to my office," Bob whispered. Alice followed him in. He tottered a few steps, swooned and righted himself, then staggered to his desk. Verbally queuing his headset into his speakers, he began streaming the loudest five-second clips Alice had ever heard.

"In case we're bugged," Bob whispered, gesturing around the room as if it could hear him. Alice didn't know what he meant — it sounded like a pre-Flood antiquity, like listening to music, or watching a video for more than five seconds at a time.

"Please have a seat, Alice. I'm going to level with you." Bob gestured at a chair he had lowered as much as possible so he felt more powerful when he had an office guest. Alice plopped down into it and smoothed the plastic ruffle of her buoyskirt.

"I think we should have penetrative sex before I go to South Africa."

Here we go. Time to make some demands.

"Bob, I mean, Mr. Petri, I mean, Sir. I'm going to need a raise. And—"

Alice's heart was pounding so hard, she thought it might crack a rib. She took a deep breath. *Don't stop now.*

"—I'm going to need all my raise money for the year up front. And, third — I can make a presentation about all this, because I know it's a lot — I think penetrative sex was outlawed after all the sex disease outbreaks of the Flood years. You were alive then, weren't you?" Alice smoothed her buoyskirt ruffle again, coughed, and scratched her itch-less nose.

"You weren't alive during the Flood?" A jarring new five-second clip wailed in the background. Alice's heart felt like it was being shredded by the propeller of a mortgage-company drone. He hadn't even heard her financial request. She had rehearsed it once an hour every day for the past week while she was researching a variety of low-hanging testicle solutions.

She struggled to recover. "I was. I was alive then. I was a toddler. My mom and I stayed inside. That's why I don't have the sores and all."

Alice gestured at her face and arms — pale and pudgy from years of noodle cups and restrained sitting, but free of scars from the festering sores that had at one time covered nearly half the post-Flood population.

"The Bureau of Science debunked it," Bob waved his hand. "There weren't any...sex parties...with animals. It was a rumor. Series of rumors. The sores weren't caused by — penetrative sex is perfectly safe, they learned."

"Oh," Alice said.

"It's the logical next step in our working relationship. We've been heading in this direction since you called me 'sir' on day one."

Alice hadn't interpreted calling a superior by a generic term as the pathway to sexual intercourse. And Alice didn't much care for touching other people. But maybe, just maybe, this was that corporate ladder people were always talking about climbing. The lowest rung turned out to be getting cuffed to a cubicle, the one above that was stapling, and then the next one above that, was sex.

But Market, Research, Incorporated had taken a few body parts from her coworkers already, that she knew of. Was this how it started? First you got a raise, then you slept with your boss, then you lost a hand or a leg?

Maybe, but if she lost the condo, she'd have to go live in the floodzone. And then what? Losing a hand was better than that.

She unfastened the top hook on her plasti-suit jacket lapel, and leaned over Bob's desk while trying to press her breasts together. She didn't know what to do with her hands, so she thrust them in front of her, palms up.

She'd seen something like it in an antique movie clip. Was this seduction?

"What about my raise? " Alice leaned in more but lost her balance and had to slam her arms down on the desk to keep from pitching over. "When you hired me, you said there was the potential for performance-based bonuses..." She inched her breasts toward Bob's crotch.

"O-Of course," Bob stuttered, mouth agape. He stood up from his desk and pulled down his pants.

Alice whirled to see if anybody was in the hallway, then waved the door closed. Being discrete wasn't Bob's forte. What *was* his forte? According to the series of professional influence clips she'd watched last night, now she had to say something nice. Bosses liked flattery.

"Somebody sure does have an attractive set of testicles today," Alice said. How did sexual touching work, exactly? Alice took a long time to open her shirt so she could think about it.

18

AT 14:00, AS PROMISED, ERIC

At 14:00, as promised, Eric swept into Bob's office. Alice was long gone by then. Bob had sent her on errands so he could bask alone in the power-hungry glow of completing penetrative sex with his subordinate. He was glad she wasn't around to get mixed up in Eric's charade of pretending to control Bob and the weather and everything under the flood-causing sun and moon.

As far as Bob was concerned, all Eric was responsible for was

stealing piles of fingernails, and

being a dangerous weirdo.

Oh, and maybe

killing a commercial actor

Not to mention

inciting a civil war

And

installing a shoe as the new Senator of Nu Jersey without even holding an election.

But Bob had bigger problems: what was all this, *you're going to South Africa* crap about?

"Here's how it's going to go," Eric said, bursting into Bob's office. "I'll have the car take you to the airport. You'll change planes in

Canada for the flight to Cape Town from there. Start work immediately."

"Canada?"

"We got you a passport. It's linked to your retina scan and fingerprints, but you'll still need a credit card." Eric handed over a tiny
plastic rectangle.

"What's this?" Bob asked.

"It's what the rest of the world uses instead of regional cryptos."

"What do you mean, air...port?" He had a vague sense that
airports used to exist prior to the Flood, but he'd assumed they had
been washed away entirely, and there was no reason to rebuild. The
only civilization left was the United States of America. And even
parts of that were gone.

But *how* did he know? He couldn't remember. It had been on the
evening news, hadn't it? Before the headsets, they had watched
external screens for the news, and that's what they had said. Wasn't
it? Bob could hardly recall his life before the Flood: mother, father,
little house in the suburbs of Nu Jersey, back then, *New* Jersey, little
life — before he became the most powerful man in the world: A press
secretary. For the Illuminati.

"South Africa hasn't had a flood," Eric interrupted Bob's recol-
lections.

"What?"

"Yet. It could happen at any time. It just hasn't yet."

"But I thought everybody—"

"You're going to have to teach them everything you know, Bob.
How to create a corporation safe enough for employees to work in
with this constant threat of imminent death. How to build the special
anti-drowning elevators. How to make sure all employees are
accounted for at all times and movement is limited and tracked. How
to install one pump per room with a vacuum seal and an oxygen-
balancing system in case of full immersion. Noodle cups galore."

"But I don't know *shit* about any of that stuff. I'm a press secretary." Bob swallowed.

"You'll be fine," Eric said. "But you've got to stop mumbling to yourself all the time. You'll frighten the South Africans."

"But where's this airport? In Canada?"

"The second one, yes. The first one is Newark International. In Nu Jersey."

"There's an airport in Nu Jersey?"

"Yes."

"Since when?"

"1928, I believe."

"The Flood destroyed it."

"No, it didn't."

"I haven't seen any airport in Newark."

"When's the last time you went to Newark?"

"..."

"What else don't you know, Bob? Did you know there's a waste isolation pilot project going on behind your condominium complex?"

"Not in my backyard," Bob grumbled under his breath.

BOB SHUFFLED through an airport in Montreal, Canada, newly enlightened to an unfamiliar way of life and utterly broken by it. His heart pounded, and not just from the light exercise. There were no signs of flood-resilience equipment: no contingency plans, no ankle bracelets, no evacuation maps. They weren't even *trying* to survive.

There were no *headsets*. Bob left his on, but it wasn't working. How would they locate him in case of flood?

The rest of the world didn't die in the Flood. The rest of the world was alive. And the rest of the world was suicidal.

Soon, Bob was in an "airplane" taxiing on a runway for the second time in his life.

"How are you?" A lady next to him asked, too close, too loud. She obviously didn't know what was appropriate. At least the flight out of Newark had been so deserted his aisle was empty. Surely he wasn't the only Nu Jerseyan who hadn't known there was still an active airport in Nu Jersey.

Maybe she recognized him, a famous politico from Nu Jersey. Even so, Bob didn't want to suffer this chitchat. He tapped at his headset and pretended to look into his monoculous, though it wasn't working.

"You can't use electronics on the plane until after takeoff," the woman offered brightly. Everything about her was offensive.

"Witch," Bob muttered. He took a pill so he could sleep through her talking.

THERE WAS a tapping on Bob's shoulder. His genitals stirred. Must be Alice, the only woman who had touched him in five years.

Bob opened his eyes to his monstrous flying companion, poking him awake. On this disgusting travel method where everybody was grouped together like a fatal quarantine.

"Time to go," she said cheerily, fluffing her hair. The front of the plane was already empty.

Even with his testicle bra intact, Bob was short-circuiting. The flights had been a challenge; now he was supposed to go do business in a far-off place he hadn't known existed. He picked up his leaden feet and tottered down the narrow, ominous corridor in the center of the plane. The enormity of the land outside, visible through the tiny windows all around him, and the Cape Town sun shining right in his face made him feel like an idiot.

What evidence did you have that everything was gone?

None.

But what evidence did he have that everything existed?

Bob tried to think back to the Flood. He was a senior in high school. That was a couple of decades ago...wasn't it?

Wait.

When did the Flood happen?

Why couldn't he remember?

, Bob. And thanks again for all your hard work." Eric's tone
most cheerful. Then Bob heard the lonely headset hum of
nnection.

* * *

ONE-HANDED, red-shirted man bounded into the Cape Town
minal about an hour later, and stopped, beaming, in front of Bob.

"I can't even get an employee with the usual number of hands,"
ob muttered.

"Come again?" John asked.

"Nothing," Bob said too loudly. "Hi."

"Hi, hello there, boss. I'm your new employee. My name is John."

Bob put his hand out and then yanked it back at the sight of
John's stump. His stomach lurched. He'd nearly touched it. Gross.
Bob froze.

"Don't worry. It's not contagious." John nodded toward his trun-
cated appendage. He extended his left hand. "I promise this one will
stay on."

"I — I'm not worried. You can call me Mr. Petri." Bob shook John's
hand.

Why had Eric sent him this amputee?

John smiled again. "Nice to meet you, Mr. Petri. Shall we retrieve
my luggage?"

"*We love you, South Africa.*"

"*South Africa, South Africa.*"

The welcome quartet was upon them, yammering their gibberish.
John joined in as though he were a part of the routine — jumping left
when they jumped left and twirling right when they twirled right.

"Rainbow nation, South Africa!" John bellowed and clapped,
hand to stump. Bob stood there sweating in his most fashionable
flood-proof suit.

"Sure, sure," Bob said. "Rainbow nation. Okay, let's move it along
now."

* * *

Bob followed his irritating neighbor off the plane. A plane worker
yanked the blanket that she had given Bob at the start of the journey
out of his hands.

"I'm afraid you'll have to return that, sir." She tugged it free. "We
need these for the next customers. Thank you."

Bob glared at her, at that blanket not even made of plastic, and at
her ankles, unmarred by any tracking bracelets. Barbarians.

The hulking metal plane spit Bob out on a staircase that led him
to a strip of asphalt. There wasn't a cloud or a drop of moisture in the
sky. Bob's mouth was dry. The humidity and comfort of Nu Jersey
days was gone. The staff crowded him onto a bus with a bunch of
foreigners. He knew they were foreigners because their horrid cloth
attire brushed his fingertips every now and then. They had no sense
of personal space.

The bus took them all to another building that was as disgusting
as the plane. *Connected to the world!* A sign inside said. Bob couldn't
even tell what it was marketing: Was this company advertising the
entire world? He had never been connected to the world, and he
didn't want to start now.

Bob walked through metal hallway after metal hallway. They
reminded him of the hatches and chutes he was used to — soothing.
Eventually, he emerged into a huge hallway, bustling with people.
Terminal A.

This *situation* was terminal.

Now that he knew there were other continents and ways to reach
them, Bob knew that intercontinental air travel did not suit him. He
peered out the terminal window into the blinding sun. Were those
steering wheels in the cars? Were people driving their own lousy
vehicles out here, wearing these stupid cloth clothes, when a flood
could begin at any moment?

Bob's knees buckled and he went down like a sack of dead floodrats. When he woke up, a dozen people were standing over him,
looking concerned.

Bob rolled onto his side and vomited all over that airport floor. He pushed himself up to a seated position and once again registered the worst-case scenario.

His headset wasn't working.

What was with this place? Why was the sun in full view here, and not shrouded behind a haze, like in Nu Jersey?

His headset wasn't working at all.

Not a single click, buzz, hum, map, or image.

He was all alone.

A WEEK LATER, Bob waited at that same Cape Town airport, not so far from the site of his vomiting. He had come to attribute it to dehydration and an unfortunate twist in his testicle bra rather than the horror of learning he'd been lied to about the existence of the rest of the world for his entire adult life.

The international travelers came and went, dashing around in their non-plastic, non-flood-proof clothes. Bob had tried to wear some after a few days in Cape Town at Eric's insistence via headset — it had started working again shortly after Bob's collapse. Eric buzzed through live, loud, and clear, shouting that things worked differently overseas. South Africa was so far behind they didn't even use headsets yet. Eric could connect directly to Bob to tell him what to do. Bob both resented it and felt relieved.

"Don't you remember what life was like before nanopolymers, Bob? Your skin could breathe. Go on, live it up! You've earned it."

In some ways, Eric was more frightening now than he had been up close. He sometimes acted as though they were long-lost college buddies rather than the master and slave Bob felt them to truly be.

No way, Bob had said. I'm not going to be caught in non-buoyant fabric when the floods come.

The airport singing quartet did a part of their routine Bob had seen on arrival, post-vomit, where they traded places with each other in a half-jog, half-dance twirl. They delivered one last four-part

harmony: "Rainbow nation, South Africa... pherable origin cheered.

"Hey, guy." Bob tapped one of the men... question for you: What's a rainbow?"

"Hello there, friend. Are you feeling better... clapped Bob on the shoulder and shook his hand...

"Oh. Yes, I am. I had never flown before."

"Where are you from?"

"Uh, the United States."

"Ahhhhh, USA. A great country."

"You know about the United States?" Bob asked.

"Of course," the man laughed. "There used to be n... Africans living there before your wartime problems."

"We're not at war."

"Aren't you?"

"Well, now, maybe. War is a strong word. I thought South ... was underwater. You know, from The Flood."

"The Flood?"

"Yeah, The Flood. You know, catastrophic global cataclysm th... destroyed most of the world? Put everything underwater."

"Sorry, boss. Never heard of it. We get a little flooding every here and there, no big deal. Good for the crops."

"Bob." Bob had forgotten about Eric, the voice in his earpiece, still controlling him from afar.

"Hi, Eric. Have you ever heard of a rainbow? Or there being no such thing as The Flood?"

"Like I was saying, go meet John at terminal B and then the General will pick the two of you up."

"Right, right. I've got it. But did you hear what I just said?"

"You'll recognize John because he'll be wearing a red shirt. And he'll be missing his hand." Eric spoke as though this were an everyday circumstance.

"Uh, his what?"

"Hand. Hand! He's missing his hand. He's only got one hand."

"Yuck. Can you send Alice?"

"HOW'D YOU KNOW THAT SONG?" He asked as they stood around the luggage carousel.

"I've heard it at football games," John explained. "I wasn't born near here, though — I'm from a little village in the northwest part of Africa, in a country called Sierra Leone."

"Football?"

"It's a game they play all over the world, except in the United States."

"Oh."

"I don't know why the Americans don't play it," John mused. "It's tremendous fun. Maybe they can't play it in Nu Jersey because there are no fields. And I have never seen anybody run."

"Nah, we stopped running after the Flood, once we realized it couldn't help you get away from anything dangerous. Also, we aren't allowed to move around. When did you come to America?"

"A few months ago. Through the phase one post-flood immigration pilot program. It took years, but it has been a joy to work for your corporation ever since."

"Yeah, sure it has. You can tone it down a bit, John." Bob had never known any amputees before. This one was so happy it made his skin crawl, even under his suit and his layer of buoyancy sweat.

"What have you enjoyed in beautiful Cape Town so far?" John asked. Bob hawk-eyed the luggage carousel.

"Is that your luggage?" He pointed at the next bag to saunter past on the conveyor belt.

"No," John said. "Have you hiked up Table Mountain? Taken the wine tour? Eaten in a fancy restaurant?"

DAY ONE: Bob vomits in the airport; checks into a hotel next to the airport.

Day two: Bob stares at the small corner of ocean he can see from the hotel window, trying to observe any movement that would signify a tsunami.

Day three: Bob, starving, breaks the room's lone SnackAttack (called Keurig in South Africa) and tries to eat the food pouch directly. It tastes like bitter gravel. Cries.

Day four: Bob ventures out and tries to purchase food at a store but is unable to understand the locals, though they claim to be speaking English.

Day five: Bob discovers room service; gorges himself. More vomiting. Bob cries.

Day six: Bob figures out how to turn on the television but finds it difficult to pay attention to an audiovisual clip longer than five seconds.

Day seven: Thinking about Alice. Masturbation. Bob touches clothes made out of cloth for the first time since the Flood, throws up in a department store.

"WORK, MOSTLY," Bob said. "Is that your luggage?"

BOB AND JOHN stood on a street corner outside the airport. Eric beamed instructions to Bob's headset, where they played over and over again, scrolling text and accompanying sound. Bob still didn't understand exactly what he was supposed to be doing in Cape Town.

Once you meet up with John, walk outside Terminal B to the pillar thirty-six taxi stand. Make sure John is visible from the street, and don't leave his side. The General is coming to pick you two up. Whatever you do, stay near John.

Eric had arranged for the message to play back an infinite number of times until the task was accomplished and verified. Bob listened to it a few more times, then turned down the volume.

He felt a twinge in his bladder.

"Stay with John," Eric said softly in his ear.

The twinge amped up to an ache. It doubled, tripled, and quadrupled until it became a massive, stabbing pain.

"Whatever you do, don't move." Bob fluttered his hand and Eric's voice became even softer. He glanced over at John, standing there and smiling at nothing, emanating joy for no reason. Bob pressed his thighs together, then released them when he considered how it might stretch out his testicles.

"John."

"Yes, Mr. Petri."

"What are you smiling about?"

"I'm just happy to be back on my home continent."

"Right. Good for you. Listen, I have to go take a leak. Don't move, alright?"

"Sure thing, boss."

Bob headed back into the terminal to look for the bathroom. He had been in Cape Town for a week now, and he still felt like he was the victim of a global practical joke. In Cape Town, there was no before and no after, no disaster, no sorrow. Just these happy people. Was America the only place that had suffered a deadly tsunami?

During all the years Bob had worked as a press secretary, there had been no sign that the rest of the world existed. Maybe they never said it didn't, but they had never said it *did*, either. Nobody back home seemed to notice one way or the other.

And who was *they*? Bob wondered. Aren't *we* they? Aren't *I* they?

He stepped back out into the blinding Cape Town sunshine in time to see three men approaching John from behind. A van screeched up to the curb. One man put a bag over his head, cinched it tight, and the other two pushed him inside. Slammed the door. Tires pealed.

And then they were gone.

Whatever you do, don't move. Stay with John.

Eric's voice chirped in Bob's ears. The instructions scrolled in his monoculous. And he didn't move. Bob didn't move at all.

19

ALICE PEERED INTO BOB'S

Alice peered into Bob's office. Her mom's ghost had taken it over in his absence, putting her ghost feet up on the desk and using his SnackAttack catchment as her ashtray.

"Mom! Stop smoking your ghost cigarettes in here." Alice tried to waft some of the ghost smoke out of the room. "Hey, take a look at this. What do you think it means?" She held an office plastic out to her mom.

"I don't know." Alice's mom stared through the sheet as though it, not she, were the ghost. "When's your dumb boss getting back?"

"Look, he's not dumb. He just has problems with critical thinking...and talking...and doing. Anyway, if he hadn't given me a raise, we'd be living on the streets. Keep your insults to a minimum."

"That *was* my minimum. What's this?" Alice's mom nodded at the office plastic.

"It's one of the files you knocked over. Some project they worked on here. It's etched, but it *looks* old. Check it out."

The Project

Notes on the crystallization of the biomass frequency

1. Biodiversity interferes with the signal; eliminate to the greatest extent.
2. Achieve brain waves: majority alpha and beta with a minority of theta in the suitable ratios noted in Appendix C; consistent telecommunications networking, audiovisual programming, and other parallel synchronization tactics listed in Appendix E. See geographic coordinates in Appendix F.
3. In the 30-day period leading up to frequency achievement (+/- .01%), construct the biomass synchronizer from the keystone tissue and activate the brain net — do not substitute with alternate or synthetic DNA.
4. Keystone must be trained in gamma wave brain function. Administer the protective elixir after brain net activation to prevent keystone death by radiation.
5. Execute the Project in concordance with the electromagnetic field weakening to produce reduced memory function.
6. Mainline the brain net when the frequency is reached.
7. Minimize any noise to the frequency by slowing the rotation of the earth via placement of large-scale dams.
8. Eliminate disturbance to the frequency by restricting human movement and maintaining consistency of experience; i.e., war, famine, and disease.
9. Engage major dogmatic adherence across the entirety of the globe — eliminate small tribes, hunter–gatherers, non-agricultural societies, and the ungoverned. This will reduce frequency noise.
10. Incite major political violence in as many locations as possible for a 125-year period prior to Project end.
11. Relegate state violence to internment in designated areas to maintain a sufficient magnitude of biological material.
12. Genocide is appropriate in some cases (Appendix G).

ALICE'S MOM YAWNED. "Whole lotta blah blah blah if you ask me."

"Mom, you didn't even read it! What's genocide?"

"It's the murder of a whole kind of people."

"Do you think people's memories have gotten worse over time?"

"Well, of course they have, dear. Everybody's memories are total garbage now."

"Right, because all the info you need is right there in your monoculous and your earpiece anytime. Maybe it's natural. But it says here in order to complete The Project, they're weakening the earth's electromagnetic field. To destroy people's memories."

"Oh, sweetie. You can't worry about retaining memories all the time. We're all less hateful than we used to be. It's better not to remember anything."

"That's not my point," Alice fumed. "I'm saying I think the reason you can't go into the light is right here in Market, Research, Incorporated."

Alice's ghost mom looked nonplussed. "Maybe you should ask somebody." She floated out of Bob's chair to ghost-pace back and forth across the room.

"Do what?"

"Ask somebody. You know, find someone and say, what the hell is going on around here?"

"The only person who tried to tell me anything about this place went nuts and got escorted out. Then she said I was next."

"Dramatic," Alice's ghost mom said.

"It was. And scary."

"Isn't there anyone else you can talk to?"

"I don't know. Mr. Petri's gone. John, I guess." Alice shrugged. "But I haven't seen him around in a while." Alice stopped, involuntarily seeing John's disembodied hand. "There is this one place I want to investigate. It's called the Hub. Employees aren't allowed to go there. But maybe ghosts can. You know, secretly."

"I'm listening." Alice's ghost mom created a space between the image of her ear and the rest of her body—a trick she had recently learned and couldn't get enough of. Alice could have done without it.

"How about I show you where it is, and you ghost around in there? Invisibly? Try to see or hear something?"

"If you say so," Alice's ghost mom said, lighting yet another ghost cigarette. "I don't have anything better to do. Lead the way." A thought struck her. "Hey, we can go talk to Tom's ghost on the way and tell him he's in a building foundation. Not too bright. Keeps shouting 'Bob, *Bob*' all day and night."

"That's Mr. Petri's first name," Alice said. "I wonder if they knew each other."

Alice and her mom's ghost started down the hallway. Alice peered over her shoulder. Her mom's ghost wobbled behind. Her locomotion had gotten more bizarre, more unpredictable lately. Alice rounded a corner, stopped, and looked back: Her mom was gone. Alice retraced her steps and found her mom floating, mouth hanging open, in front of the hallway pictures of the Market, Research, Incorporated board of directors.

"Mom?"

"It's him!" Alice's mom's ghost said.

"Who?" Alice read the caption below the picture. Tom Fletch Senior and family.

"This little boy," Alice's mom pointed at a child clad in ill-fitting shorts. In one hand, he was holding an ice-cream cone; with the other, he grasped the hand of Tom Fletch Senior. Alice recognized him: the hologram from employee orientation. His malevolent eyes stared down the camera while the boy studied his ice cream. "That's Eric," Alice's mom said softly.

"Who's Eric?"

"Oh, don't worry about it. I'll tell you later."

"Looks like he's related to the guy who started this company. Small world."

"Yeah. Small world." Alice's mom poked her finger through the boy's face.

"Well?" Alice prompted. "Shall we?"

Alice's mom lingered in front of the picture.

"Mom? Ready? Let's visit Ghost Tom? Haunt the Science Bureau?"

Her mom's ghost shoulders heaved up and down with a ghastly sigh. Then she followed Alice down the hallway. Alice suspected her mom's ghost knew more than she was letting on.

20

BACK AT THE AIRPORT

Back at the airport. Eric Smith hissing in Bob's ear as usual. Still degrading him from thousands of miles away.

"Rainbow nation, South Africa!" The airport welcome quartet sang in the distance. Bob hated rainbows since he'd learned what they were. Tacky. He missed the comforting haze of the Nu Jersey sky. Bob wished he was listening to an airport goodbye quartet, and getting on a plane, and never coming back to this miserable, oppressive-sunshine-filled land.

"Eric, listen. This guy was a wild card — you don't even know what I went through!"

"You left him outside, didn't you, Bob?" Eric hissed.

"I had to take a piss. What the hell was I supposed to do?"

Bob looked at himself in the airport window's reflection. He looked tired and crumpled, like a shriveled little ball sack that had lost its elasticity, hair plastered to one side of his sweaty, lumpy head.

"Take him with you, you idiot — that's what! The general is coming, and he isn't going to be pleased."

"The general *what*? The general public?"

"No moron, the General. He was your rendezvous!" Eric yelled. "Yours and John's. But now the Illuminati have John and I've got nothing except you and your vacant head. Maybe when this war really gets going, I can use you as a human shield."

"I don't appreciate your tone, Eric. I've been doing the best I can out here. Which I think has been pretty damn good, considering last week I didn't know South Africa existed!"

Something Eric had said was nagging at Bob's insides as he spoke. He sat down on a nearby bench.

The Illuminati. That's what Eric had said. The Illuminati have John.

But *we're* the Illuminati. *We're* the secret society that controls everything.

Bob was about to interrupt Eric to ask what he meant when a huge, camouflaged minivan pulled up to the curb. The window inched down and a cloud of smoke wafted out.

"Get in!" the driver called. He didn't turn. Bob was face to ear — and a third of that ear was missing. The whole top of it was sheared off. Gross.

The van door slid open. Bob peered inside.

"Get in!" the driver yelled again. Bob hauled himself inside. Why was everybody in this corporation missing body parts?

Inside the back of the van, Bob bumped his head on an interior gun rack — holding the first guns Bob had ever seen in real life.

He threw up, and then—

—THERE WAS JESUS. Bob saw Jesus for the very first time. *The* Jesus, from the olden days, before the Flood, when people had all kinds of radical hobbies, absurd beliefs and superstitions. Jesus had long hair and sandals. He wore robes that didn't look very flood-proof. Standing there in front of Bob. Jesus stretched out his hand.

"Bob," Jesus said. Jesus knew his name. Jesus was like the LINC. Full of info. "Bob, always remember. I am the light and the life and the one true way," Jesus said. "And Wednesdays are twenty-nine-cent taco day at Poco Loco."

What's a *taco*?

What's a *cent*?

Bob woke up on the most uncomfortable sleeping device he had ever lain on — more of a torture rack than a bed, with actual metal rods for torture. Bob looked around his immediate area. Not too much to see. It was dark and damp in there, and the walls were loaded with guns. Guns everywhere. At least he was out of the sun.

The General was deep in a one-sided discussion.

"Yep, it's confirmed. Between Jalia, John, and his mom, it could be all we need to finish up the mainframe. Did you add the fingernails? Great. I'll see if there's any effect on Bob. No, no. He passed out when he saw guns. Sure. We'll head up to the Dogon territory right after the extraction to pick her up."

Bob craned his neck to see what the general was doing, but he couldn't see much. He heard some rattling. More guns?

"Sure, but I don't know about keeping him out of Nu Jersey for so long," the General rasped. "Even with Jalia there to amplify the signal, we might lose control. Then what? If we don't escalate the violence, the war'll peter out, just as we've got the headsets in place and the frequency surveys going. The signals are working perfectly through Market, Research, Incorporated. The electromagnetic field is nearly at frequency. Once we get John's mom—"

Bob leaned a little too far and fell off his wire-rack bed. He shrieked.

"I gotta go."

The General's grizzled face dominated Bob's field of vision.

"Look who's awake!" The General winked at Bob. "Good morning, pumpkin! Ready to perform your first extraction?" The general was holding a gun so large Bob could only figure it was one of those Revolutionary War cannons he'd learned about in history class. Bob picked himself up and dusted a filthy, odious powder off his suit jacket.

"I don't know what an extraction is," Bob said.

The General roared with laughter even though nothing funny had happened. He was sitting in front of a large pile of weapons Bob had seen only in five-second clips. He pointed at the digital map in the middle of the table-screen.

"A good, old-fashioned extraction! Bob, you'll enter here," he pointed, "and I'll enter here. There are seven rooms total, plus a basement area. We'll go over the wall to get in, and I've got the dart gun for the dogs."

"What am I entering? I don't agree to any of this."

"The Illuminati have never been the brightest stars shining in the secret-society sky. They're keeping John in a regular house in the suburbs."

What would people even do with seven rooms? How would you flood pressurize?

"But *we're* the Illuminati," Bob said quietly.

"No, Bob, we're not. It's time you learned a few things. We're not the Illuminati. In fact, it's difficult to say what your particular involvement in this secret society is, since you're not in on a single one of its secrets. This is a map, this is a floor plan." The general pointed to the table-screen. "This is a semi-automatic rifle." He held one up. "And this is an Uzi." He set both down on the map.

"I think I'm in on at least one of—"

"You are not now, nor have you ever been, nor will you ever be affiliated with the Illuminati. Right now, we are about to break into one of their compounds to rescue a man of the bloodline we've been protecting for millennia. He's the only reason we exist as an organization."

"We?" John echoed.

"We're the Rosicrucians."

The general handed the Uzi to Bob. He felt a lot of pressure to take it, so he did.

―――――――

Bob and the General sat in a van outside a seven-room home in a suburb of eastern Cape Town.

"He doesn't *act* like a bloodline you've been protecting for millennia," Bob said.

"You've got a bad attitude, you know that?"

"I've been told," Bob said.

"Eric and I tried to develop one of his predecessors, and it didn't go so well."

"What happened? Got kidnapped too?"

"Worse." The general pointed to his own partially-missing ear. "That's a story for another time." He threw his smelly cigarette out the window.

"What *is* the bloodline?" Bob took a bite out of his ration of allotted rusks. The General had started limiting him since he'd crunched his way through the whole first batch.

The General had donned a camouflaged apron and baked them while Bob struggled to gather all the ammunition they would need to kill a bunch of strangers in a rival secret society to Bob's — a secret society Bob had thought he was running until he had been contradicted a few hours ago.

Now he was stress-chewing his way through all the rusks he could find.

The general laughed, a cheerless bark. "You're in a secret society, and you don't even know what the *bloodline* is?" The General searched Bob's face.

Bob just stared and waited for more info.

"John's blood has a DMT content a thousand times any natural occurrence."

"DMT?" Bob maintained his blank expression.

"Di-methyl-tryptamine."

"Never heard of it."

"The spirit molecule?

"Religion's over since The Flood. We stopped congregating."

"You don't know anything? I can't believe this. John's blood is pure DMT. He is the keystone. *The* keystone. The final ingredient in The Project, the primary substance of the biocomputer. When activated, it will transform all human DNA into a portal. Then humankind can ascend into the next dimension."

"Never heard of it."

"John's the biochemical twin of Jesus of Nazareth. The body and blood to end the world."

Bob missed his desk, his office, his little Nu Jersey life so strongly in that moment, his eyes teared up. Maybe he was the most incompetent part of this partnership. Hell, maybe he was the most incompetent part of most partnerships. But these people — Eric, the General — were out of their goddamned minds.

What were his options? He could try to open the door of this antique military vehicle and run out into the night. In a foreign country with nowhere to go, no knowledge of this suburb, and his lone local employee kidnapped by a rival secret society. Or he could continue to assist in the hope that if they succeeded, he would be sent back to his safe life in the United States — to his senators, to his nautical-themed condo, and to satisfactory penetrative sex with his assistant.

"Bob. Bob!"

"Huh?"

"I said, are you ready?" the General grunted.

"Ready for what?"

"It's time to rescue John. Let's lock and load."

"I don't know what that means," Bob quivered.

The General sighed. "I'll get the guns ready for you. All you have to do is pull the trigger. Anybody can do it."

"How is it again," Bob asked nervously, "we're going to murder a bunch of men in a foreign country and not go to prison for the rest of our lives?"

The General laughed and laughed. Again. "We're a secret society, Bob. We don't go to prison."

"Oh," Bob said. That seemed to settle the matter. How, he wasn't sure. The General placed a large gun in his hands.

"When you see other people, pull the trigger," he said.

"Which part is the trigger?"

The General pointed at the trigger.

"That's counterintuitive," Bob said.

"It's really not," he answered. "You'll get it when you're in there. Haven't you seen guns in your five-second clips?"

"I guess so, but it wasn't obvious how it all worked. How do I know if they're good guys or bad guys?" Bob mopped his forehead with his left hand, the gun in his trembling right.

The General beamed. "That's easy. They're all bad." He holstered guns in five different places under his jacket. "Now don't go trigger happy and kill John. And don't move him if he's hooked up to something. Or bleeding. Wait for me."

The General tapped out a powder Bob assumed was weapon-related until he snorted it.

"Need some courage?"

"No. I'm fine without it, thanks."

They got out, and the General stowed the van keys above one of the tires. "If I don't make it back, the keys are here, front left. They're magnetized and I stuck 'em due north."

Bob appeared to be nodding, but he was really trying to hold down his acid reflux.

THEY WALKED for seconds that felt like ages. Bob's heart thudded in his chest. He stopped twice to dry heave. They pressed themselves up against the outer wall of the house, Bob saw a sparkle atop: broken glass shards. He rubbed his baby-soft hands together and shuddered.

"Hey," he whispered. "You know what? Let's do this another time, maybe? What say we go find the entertainment district, hire ourselves the hottest ladies we can find, and have a night on the town?"

"Capital idea," the General winked. "But I'm a moffie."

"A what now?"

"Moffie. It's an old Afrikaans term. Means fairy. Fag. Gay. I'm a red-blooded homosexual through and through. And I'm married."

The General gestured to the blanket he was carrying. "For the broken glass," he whispered. He threw the blanket over the top of the wall and hoisted himself up to perch on it.

Bob reached up to follow suit, but the concrete hurt his hands. Even through the blanket. "Ow!" he cried out.

"Shhhhhh!" The General hissed. He yanked Bob off the ground and heaved him over the wall before Bob could say anything else. Bob landed on his side on the damp ground.

When he could breathe and turn his head again, he saw the General had leapt down off the wall to crouch next to him, dart blowgun in hand. The yard's protection, two massive dogs who looked like they could have eaten Bob in a few bites, were sleeping, small darts in their necks. The General pointed at Bob and then at a door. He held up two hands, then one hand. Bob was too jarred to recall much of their plans, but he thought it might mean go through the door and shoot everybody in fifteen minutes. He nodded stiffly.

Bob missed politics in America. It had been so much easier.

There was only one floor of the house visible, though the General had insisted it was four: three levels below ground and one above. It was silent and dark, except for a faint green glow inside.

The general went racing off into the dark. Why did he have so much energy? Must have been the drugs.

Am I becoming an accomplice to a home invasion led by a raging lunatic?

Surely the judge would see Bob was a victim here too and take pity on him — perhaps commute his sentence or ship him back to the sanctity of Nu Jersey to have conjugal visits with his Alice. He missed her so. He wanted to headset her that very moment, to hear her voice not speaking, listening to him give her orders.

The trees rustled, and a bird that looked like a hummingbird but was too plump to hover chirped a little noise. Bob's overactive bowels threatened to spill liquefied rusks right into his pants.

A repetitive blast from deep inside the house tore through the air. *Rat-tat-tat-tat!*

Bob couldn't breathe.

He held his balls for a minute. Calm down. He pictured Alice visibly swallowing all the desire she felt after he had asked her to lick them and then her licking them.

I'm a man. Could he save a life? Maybe. Sure. He could. He was a press secretary. He was the leader of a secret society — apparently not the Illuminati, whom he was now going to kill, but some other secret society with some other nebulous goal, something to do with a guy's blood.

Dumb. What a dumb idea.

None of this could possibly be true. These men weren't thinking clearly. And Bob was taking orders from them.

The general thrust his head out of the closest window and screamed at Bob, "Now! *Now, you coward!*"

Bob ran to the nearest door and tore it open. There was a shadow moving off to the side. Bob aimed the gun, closed his eyes, and pulled the trigger.

The gun went off and Bob couldn't stop it or control it. He screamed in a falsetto, dropped it on the ground while it fired and fired. Bob darted away as fast as his terrified legs could move. He tore open the closest door and fell headlong down a set of concrete steps.

His third injury of the day was a humdinger. A soft warmth pooled between his head and the sweet, cold concrete. He tried to move, but everything was fading into a green light.

I'm shot. I'm dying. This is what death is.

It's green.

"Hey! Hey boss! You okay?"

Bob woke to John's voice.

"John...have I been shot?" Bob dragged his hand across his face and brought up a mix of fluids: snot, blood, tears.

"It's okay, boss! You're not shot. You fell down the stairs. You're bleeding a little bit out of your head," John reassured him.

"How did I *not* get shot? Guns were firing all around me. What the hell are *you* on...or, in?" Bob asked him.

"Oh, I don't know. Men put me in a van and I woke up like this. I was considering my next move when you fell down the stairs just now." John shrugged his shoulders. He was sitting in a net above a metal platform that hummed and pulsed an unnatural green light. There was a swirl of wires, lights, levers, and tubes surrounding John's body. The net shook a little.

"There's a tube taking your blood out! What are all those flashing lights? Where's the General?"

"Oh, is the other boss here? I haven't seen him yet."

"Ugh." Bob grabbed a corner of the metallic net to pull himself upright. He staggered and pitched towards John's cocoon of tubes and lights, then chose the floor over crashing into that mess. He lay and rested a moment, listening through his blinding, cleaving head pain.

No sounds coming from upstairs. Bob retched partially digested rusks all over the floor.

"Are you alright?" John asked.

"No," Bob said. "I have acid reflux. I gotta get you out of this fishnet lightshow before those men come down and kill us, whoever they are. You can research it for your first task as my employee."

"Okay, boss!" John gave a thumb's up. Bob staggered over and unhooked one end of the wire netting. It turned out to be the wrong thing to do, and they both collapsed to the floor in a heap. It tore a wired, intravenous tube out of John. Blood spattered everywhere. Never one for blood, Bob's vision brightened until—

———

—BOB WOKE up in the back of a van covered in his own sick. John was smiling down at him. He didn't look recently kidnapped at all. He was so stinking resilient, Bob hated him.

"Are you a robot, John? Are you a secret government robot?"

The General exhaled a long, slow puff of smoke into the back of the van. "He's not a robot and he's not part of the government," the General said.

Bob was too weak and broken to move. "You, then. You must be a robot." He tried to point at the General but only managed a twitch of the shoulder. The General chuckled. A man with blood and guts all over his face chuckling was as creepy as Bob would have imagined.

"No, Bob. Nobody's a robot here. I'm good at my job, that's all. And John's just good at rolling with the punches. I know it might seem only mechanically possible to you, but humans *are* capable of achievements and adaptation, too."

"What *is* your job?"

"We discussed this an hour ago. Why can't you remember anything? My job is to secure the bloodline, the prospective keystone individuals our order has protected for millennia. Next, we align the earth's macrobiome to the frequency through the biocomputer. Final step: Ascend into the next dimension."

"You know what?" Bob spat. "I'm sick of all your jargon. I've vomited from head injuries three times today! I'm a press secretary. I write press releases. I want to go home and write press releases."

"We're trying to wrap up a one hundred and thirty thousand-year project here, Bob, and you're going to help. Now, if you follow orders, you can go back to your country, and your assistant, and your senators, all in one piece. And you'll probably have a couple of weeks to live comfortably before all of this winks right out of existence."

21

ALICE COULD SWEAR THEY'D
PASSED

Alice could swear they'd passed by the same faux ficus three times now. They were definitely lost. And her mom was a noticeable wreck. Pixelating far ahead and then lagging behind, mumbling.

"Mom. What's up with you? You've been weird ever since you saw that picture."

Alice's mom, a pace ahead of her, pixelated into a puddle on the floor.

"Come on. Materialize back up here and tell me what's going on."

Her mom's ghost rose and gathered her ghastly entrails until she was slightly taller than Alice.

"I was a girl, seventeen or so. Across the street, old Mister Worthington started having a visitor."

"Mister Worthington? The same old Mister Worthington who's out there eating the fauxlowers every day?"

"Yes. A grandnephew of his came to visit. From Sweden. For a month every summer."

"That boy?"

She nodded, chin trailing through the air. "Eric."

"Were you...friends, or a...*couple*?" Alice had never heard her mom mention him before.

"Oh, I don't know. We were just kids. But he seemed very taken with me. When he saw our home, how we lived. He kept saying, 'All this stuff! All this trash, lying around out in the open.' He said they didn't do things that way in Sweden. And he loved it. Sooner or later, his father put a stop to the visit. And said he couldn't come back."

"Why not?"

"Eric said he and his dad were in America on a fact-finding mission. On behalf of all the Swedes."

"A mission for what?"

"To destroy America."

"Yikes."

"I thought he was talking nonsense, most of the time. But he gave me some advice I never forgot. And for some reason, I followed it. And it saved our lives."

"Yours and his?"

"*Yours* and mine."

"What was it?"

"He said his Uncle Worthington was going to move to a second-floor condominium. And wherever he moved, I should go there too. In fact, I should move as close to him as possible. Because it was just a matter of time, Eric said, before where we were living was going to be completely destroyed."

"How did he know?" Alice stopped in her tracks.

"Honey, I don't know how he knew." Her ghost mom stopped too, and hovered in place.

"How does anybody know if something's going to happen ahead of time? Unless they caused it."

"Is it possible to *cause* a flood? A global flood?"

"I'm not sure it was global, mom. They made us think it was. They manipulated us. Through these headsets. After everything I've seen around here, I think it *could* be possible to cause a flood. And I think they plan to do it again."

Saying the truth out loud was excruciating. Alice's stomach was in knots.

"Let's go see Ghost Tom," her mom said.

THE ELEVATOR SLID into the basement.

"I can't believe my ankle bracelet let me come down here," Alice marveled.

"I think those are for show," Alice's mom's ghost said. "Have you ever gotten shocked?"

"Yeah. Several times," Alice answered. "Back when I was on the interviews, almost every day."

Alice's mom shrugged. A little bit of her shoulder tore off and bounced into the elevator doors. They slid open.

"Weird," Alice said.

"Ol' ghost body ain't what she used to be, ain't what she used to be, ain't what she used to be," her ghost mom sang. "This way."

Alice followed her mom into a boiler room. Her mom flipped upside-down and disappeared head first into the floor.

"Come on up. No, you *can*. You're not in hell. You're *not*. I don't know how many times I have to tell you. You're in the basement of a corporation."

Alice couldn't hear any of Ghost Tom's replies. Her mom floated back up.

"Well, here he is! Finally — took months to get him out of the foundation."

Alice stared. Next to her mom was...nothing.

"I don't see anything," Alice said.

Ghost blood emerged from the walls, thick and viscous. Oozed a path across the ceiling and down the walls until it hit the floor.

"Okay, but do you see that?" Her ghost mom pointed.

"Yeah, I do!" Alice shouted. "Can you tell him to stop?"

"She says stop," Alice's mom called. "No, *stop*! Living people aren't into that kind of thing."

The room's dehumidifier kicked on and Alice jumped. She

couldn't take much more of this supernatural sleuthing. Being in the basement was scary enough. "Let's ask him some questions."

"He's a real chatterbox," her mom answered. "Doesn't shut up."

"Great. What's he saying?"

"He says his dad killed him. Poisoned his SnackAttack. Set it up to look like a drug overdose. He says he's a member of the secret society that controls the northeast corridor. Except, his dad's really a Swede. And he's planning to destroy the United States."

"The United States?"

"Yep," Alice's mom paused. "Whole thing. Actually, the whole world. He says he found out about it from a torso."

"A...torso?"

"A torso?" Alice's mom was turning her head this way and that. Alice imagined Ghost Tom flitting around in there. "Yep, a torso. Person without any arms or legs."

"I know what a torso is!" Alice shot back. "I hope this game of ghost telephone is working. Are you sure he said a *torso*?"

"Sweetheart, he's a ghost, not a foreigner. I understand everything he's saying."

"Okay, okay. So a torso told him about..."

"About the Project. He says it's called the Project. It's going to destroy America...America *first*. Then the world. If we don't stop it. And stop his dad."

"Who's his dad?"

"Who's your dad? Says his dad is Tom Fletch Senior."

"Oh. Right. From the picture. And the hologram. Where's the, uh, torso now?"

Alice's mom cocked her head. "Where's the torso now? He says it's in here. In Market, Research, Incorporated. In disguise."

ALICE and her mom crouched outside the Hub.

"Why are you crouching? Nobody can see you anyway. You're a ghost!"

"I don't want to feel so out in the open," Alice's mom hissed. "We're *sneaking*. Just because I'm dead doesn't mean I ought to be excluded."

"Can you see anything in the window?"

There was a low and ominous sound coming from inside the Science Bureau door — a metallic scraping followed by an electronic pulse that reverberated through the floor, vibrating Alice's feet.

Alice's mom's ghost peered in. "I can't see anything."

"Nothing?"

"Nothing. The blinds are closed."

"Pass through the wall!"

"What? No."

"Why not?"

"I don't know. I'm scared."

"Scared? But you can't die. What's the worst that can happen?"

"I don't want to go in there."

"Okay. You don't have to. Do you think someone is in there?"

"I don't hear anything."

Alice tried the door handle. It was open.

Slowly, she pushed the door open an inch. Peered inside.

Alice retched off the Hub walkway, then clapped her hand to her mouth. A few clumps of vomit fell several stories before landing on another walkway. Alice tried not to move or breathe. No sounds from the hallways after the *splat* of that day's noodle cup. She didn't see anybody below. The walkway above them was empty, too. She peeked back inside.

The room was filled with machinery Alice couldn't identify, clicking and whirring. A body-sized mesh net hung from the ceiling, like a hammock from the future. Wires and cables snaked across the room, connecting everything to everything else. The green pulse of an insidious light glowed.

On the far wall, a seismograph etched its pattern up and down, peaks and valleys over and over again, attached to the middle of the entire enterprise by a pile of wires. There, stretched on a small dais and magnified ten times over, sat the object that had caused Alice to lose her lunch: John's hand.

"Edna?"

Alice jumped.

"Eric!" Before the name escaped her ghost mouth, Alice's mom was sucked inside the door of the Science Bureau, like flood debris running into the sewer.

"Mom!" Alice shouted. She ran inside, stopping short to register a semi-familiar face—an older version of the picture in Market, Research, Incorporated's hallway, *and*—

"You were at the hospital," Alice said. "And on the street. You're...Mr. Petri's boss. Wait. You can see my mom's ghost too?"

He ignored her, staring at the ghost of Alice's mom, being drawn toward a massive glass jug on the table. She was fighting against it but losing, getting pulled into the jar bit by bit, one pixel at a time.

"Every moment of every day, Edna. You never left my mind. How could I live without you? Never touching your face. Never again sitting along your mounds of house trash. Never beholding your fleshy American body."

Alice's mom's ghost lost the battle and disappeared into the jar. Her muffled shouts echoed in the room, cut off after her ghastly visage compressed in on itself.

"What have you done to her?" Alice shouted.

"Nothing, Alice," Eric said. "I care very much about your mom. All of this is for her own good."

Alice scowled. "Yeah, right. Did you remove John's hand for his own good?" Her voice shook.

"We don't have much time. Your mom's safer in there than she is out here, Alice. Trust me."

Alice's mom's ghost was stuffed awkwardly into a jar that had its own weather system. Safer in there than out here? And what did she need to be kept safe from, exactly? She was already dead.

"Why should I?"

"Have you ever read the bible?"

"No. We don't have books anymore. Only inspirational quotes."

"Have you ever heard of the rapture? Revelations? The end times? The apocalypse?"

"We had a flood. Ever hear of that?" Alice knew she should be listening right now, but when she was nervous or scared, or in this case, *both*, retorts came out of her mouth before she could stop them. Like throwing up her morning noodle cup.

"I need you to help Bob. He's in Cape Town. South Africa."

"Why?"

"Bob's in jail. Your first task is to bail him out."

What if she said no? Leave her mom in some mystery jar. Go back to the cubicle. Get the flood cuff on.

Back to the condo. Stay safe. Was that even possible anymore, with this war? Maybe it *was* the apocalypse, whatever that meant.

Go to Cape Town? South Africa? Jail? Like Jalia had said, she wasn't the adventuring type.

"Alright. I'll go." Alice said.

22

HERE, MRS. WOBBLES

"Here, Mrs. Wobbles! There you go, Mrs. Wobbles." The General clucked and crooned while he scattered chicken feed at the feet of a plush chicken, the color of premium noodle cup broth.

"Mrs. Wobbles," he said, "you are one fine-looking chicken." He elbowed Bob in the gut. "Isn't she spectacular?"

"Yes," Bob clutched his side. "Great chicken."

"Not great. *Breathtaking.*"

"Sure. Suffocating."

"Oh, now. Cheer up. Let's have a little talk. Take your hands out of your pockets, man. Are you checking for your *piel*[1] in there? In the army, none of my men were allowed to stow their hands in their pockets. It means you're not ready for action. And we know you're ready for action, don't we?"

Bob sighed and followed the General into the barn, where they sat on a couple of overturned feed buckets. He was *not* ready for action. He was ready for rest, and safety, and a nice peaceful day. Clean his testicle bra, have a good sit at his desk, give Alice orders. He was tired of bleeding, of vomiting. Of farming.

The General picked up a sack the size of Bob without so much as a groan. "I need you to mix up a salt lick for the cattle. Molasses and minerals. Blend them up real slow and careful. First, we shake the mineral mix around, like this." He walked in a circle, shaking the sack's contents onto the ground until it formed a crater.

"Next, we pour in the molasses." He hefted a large pail from the corner of the barn. "Smells good, doesn't it?"

Actually, the sludge smelled like a big mammal took a shit.

"Now, we mix — slowly! Don't collapse a mineral wall and let the molasses out. Here—" He handed Bob a shovel. "Mix. But be careful."

"I'm not really the agricultural type," Bob said. "You know, in America we grow very little anymore. We eat mostly noodle cups."

"Listen, man. I don't care what type you are or what garbage you eat. The cows need a lick. Do it." The General forced the shovel on Bob. He took it with a grimace, checked the handle for splinters, and started mixing. The molasses bubbled and oozed. The mineral walls threatened to crumble.

"Shorter strokes, Bob. Shorter! You're not rowing a boat. I bet you *have* rowed though, huh Bob? How'd you survive those floods?"

"What's it to you?"

"You were a kid, weren't you? Did your parents die?"

The General stared at him until Bob felt so uncomfortable, he had to talk.

"No, they didn't die. We got separated," Bob mumbled. "But we were, uh, reunited later." He stirred so hard he let out an involuntary grunt.

SIXTEEN-YEAR-OLD BOB COULDN'T HIDE ALONE in his home any longer. His parents were most likely dead, and he was on his own now.

"Be back in a few minutes, honey!" Bob's mom had chimed an hour earlier.

Why had they both gone out? Didn't one of them want to stay home and enjoy Bob's company?

Bob was hard at work on a video game. With a television. No headsets back then.

No LINC.

The ground shook.

Teenage Bob

thrown from his couch

under water

drowning inside his house in the suburbs

fighting his way to the surface

crawling up to the second floor

gasping

watching the water rise

alone.

Bob stared at the water roaring through his doorframe as though his parents might float in from their errands and tell him how to survive.

They never did.

THE WATER DRIFTED out after a week. Bob had to go with it if he wanted to stop starving. He found a half-full bag of Cheetos in his room — the only unsoiled food in the house — and vowed to eat no more than three Cheetos a day to survive until help arrived. Then he devoured the whole bag and cried next to his mom's ironing board, perched atop their kitchen island along with some sludge and a few ornamental rocks from the front yard.

Bob peered out the front door, scanned the horizon for another wave. Three of the neighbors' homes were intact. The other three were rubble. Was it the construction, or did the freak tsunami discriminate? The owners were dead. Bob recognized Mr. Ahuja's bloated body trapped inside his SUV, parked in front of his water-logged home.

It smelled like the farts of a thousand undiscovered sea creatures out there.

Bob walked halfway down the block, hallucinating the roar of a tidal wave the entire time until the terror overtook him and he couldn't continue, then ran back into the house. It was quiet. There was no tidal wave. He poked his head out the door again.

He couldn't go out there. He couldn't stay in here.

Bob did a kind of trauma hokey pokey — put his left foot out, then in, then shook. Hours passed. He got all his courage up. Burst out of his house and ran all the way down the block until he couldn't run anymore. Turned around to run back, but his stomach rumbled. He listened for the murderous ocean. They didn't even live close to the ocean.

How the hell had any of this happened?

Bob forced himself to keep going.

The sludge levels in Wawa only reached mid-shelf. It reeked in there, of coffee and gasoline. The lower-shelf items had been swept away in the tsunami. Still a few things up top, potentially edible.

Bob stumbled on an overturned magazine rack and stopped short. His heart clenched and his legs swayed.

Bob's mom stood feet away, holding an open can of soup. She and Bob's dad were crowded around it. Their clothes were worn and their hair was greasy, but they didn't look swampy like Bob did. They'd pulled themselves together. Had some presence of mind. Cleaned up a bit. Checked themselves for wounds. Gotten over the shock.

Before Bob spoke, his mom looked peaceful — at *ease*. Like she had been laughing at a joke. Afterward, she got this look on her face.

He'd seen it before. One time he'd walked into the kitchen after dinner and dessert (one slice of pie each) and saw her hunched over the counter, eating an extra, secret, indulgent slice. She hadn't seen him at first. She was mid-bite, string of saliva connecting fork to lying, hiding-from-Bob mouth.

Mom! Bob had shouted then.

And he did so now.

"You know the floods weren't an accident, Bob."

Bob kept on mixing.

"But you might not know the extent to which your organization was involved. It *caused* the floods. Did you know that, Bob?"

Bob didn't look up. He kept on mixing.

The general sat down on a bucket and took out his rolling papers and tobacco. "I had me a cancer in my armpit about seven years ago now. Inoperable, they said. There was nothing they could do. It was only a matter of time before it would spread and kill me. I stopped going to the doctor. I concentrated all my thinking on my tumor so it would know it wasn't welcome. One morning I woke up, and the tumor was lying on the pillow. Next to me. My brain told my body to get rid of it. And it did. Think of what we could achieve if we could link all the brains in the world."

"I don't know what you're talking about ninety-nine-point-nine-percent of the time." Bob panted. He swirled the molasses around, sweating through his suit, out his forehead, down into the salt lick.

"Now would you look at that. What a beautiful salt lick. You did it right — I'd never know you for a city boy. You're not such a *domkop* after all." Bob's cheeks flushed. He'd never been praised before.

"Let's go take the fence down and rotate the sheep to a new patch of grass, right?" Bob followed the General out into the pastures, long and sweeping fields that made Bob sneeze. Rotating the animals onto new grass was his least favorite part.

"Now," the General said. "Look at the way the levers are turned. Tell me: Is the fence on or off?"

"Off," Bob said.

"Okay," the General had a joyful shine in his eyes. "Now try it!"

Bob grabbed a good, confident hold of the electric fence with both hands. Voltage shot through him. He was going to die.

"Aaaahhh!" Bob collapsed in the dirt, but he didn't die. When he could speak again, he said, "I'm getting out of here, off this deathtrap farm and back to the city, to a travel agent. I'm going to get orders to Alice somehow, to book me a flight home. We got John back. There's nothing left for me to do here. I'm a press secretary, not a farmer."

The General helped Bob to his feet. "Not so fast — we need to lay low. Now that we've hit the Illuminati, the feud is on. No Rosicrucian is safe."

"So, what? We're going to live out the rest of our lives here on your farm?"

"No. We have to go north. There's one other employee we need to pick up."

"If we were going to get another employee anyway, why'd we have to bother getting John back?"

The General shot Bob a look that said, why do I have to bother answering your dumb questions? "Because," he said, "We need them both."

"Who's the other one?"

The General didn't answer for such a long time, Bob thought he might be having a stroke, and considered going to get help. Finally, he said: "It's John's mother."

"We have a policy against hiring family members," Bob said.

---

1. balls (Afrikaans)

23

ON THE THIRD DAY

On the third day of farm captivity, Bob walked back from the kitchen to his living quarters with pilfered rusks in hand. The door was flung wide open and the General stood in the center of his quarters.

"I wouldn't come in here if I were you." The General didn't avert his eyes from the hallway.

"Oh, I just need to drop off these rations before I feed the sheep," Bob said, setting down the rusks on the kitchen table.

"You have a visitor. Get up on the table now. Get up there."

Bob followed the General's line of sight: the largest, brightest yellow snake, and also, the *only* snake he'd ever seen, came slithering down the hallway at him. Bob leapt up onto the table.

"I thought snakes were mythical," Bob said, eyes wide.

The General held a long pole with a hook on the end, Bob now noticed, and he used it to jab at the snake.

"Do you know why they call me the General?"

Bob didn't know if the General was talking to him or the snake. He shook his head without taking his eyes off the man-serpent battle.

"I was a General in the South African army." He edged closer to the snake. "What you're seeing here is a Cape King Cobra." The cobra flared its hood and attacked the pole.

In the previous day's story time, Bob had learned the General was living on a third of his heart's capacity. This guy was obsessed with his own health problems. What a narcissist. When he died of the inevitable snake bite, Bob would be stuck up on the table with that snake on patrol until he starved to death.

"We were dispatched to Lesotho, shooting to kill for days, when one of my men came to me at night.

"He said, 'Sir, what are we doing here?' I didn't know. So I resigned. It was the end of my military career."

The snake and the General continued their fight, each striking in turn. Bob's heart thudded in his throat. Who the hell knew snakes still existed? Weren't they a myth from the bible? Or did they have them in America before the Flood?

Bob's eyes rolled into the back of his head, and back there, deep inside his skull, he recalled another couple of giant yellow snakes he'd somehow forgotten.

"HEY, BUDDY!" Tom kicked his graduation robe and cap across the floor, slammed their door. "Wakey wakey, hands off snakey."

"Huh? What?" Bob sat bolt upright. He had fallen asleep with his apron on after a brief stint at work. Four hours of taking bagel orders from these overprivileged monsters was exhausting.

"You better go get your cap and gown from the bursar's office or they're not gonna let you outta here."

Bob groaned. He just wanted to sleep. If he didn't pick up the outfit, maybe they couldn't force him to leave college. His functional hair follicles had halved and his pimples doubled over the past three-and-a-half years, but life hadn't produced too many other changes, and certainly none in the desired directions of wealth or fame. He still had no idea what to do after college. The mere prospect of gradu-

triker. A paunchy, middle-aged man, Bob
the ...e.
coul...

...an's shoulders, was the head of a giant king
...ed, and he swallowed hard. Bob closed his eyes
cob... was still there. He peered through the haze: a
and ...rate, well-constructed mask. The creepiest he'd
mas...
ever... of our most hallowed superiors, we begin," the
...He raised his arms. Bob's eyes teared up from the
sna...
sm...word!" The man bellowed.
...word," the others echoed.

...valked in a spiral, stalking the group's perimeter and
sha...vder onto the floor. When he reached the center, he set
do...ndle and removed a small pouch from inside his robe,
spi...ontents onto the floor.
...rings, seemingly moving on their own, followed the spiral
un...came to rest, each in front of one man. Tommy and his
fri...the inner circle, their dads on the outer. Bob could make
out shapes enough to see a genetic relevance in the pairs.
...Bob on the outside. Could he sneak back up the cellar steps
and away?

...ss two initiates, step forward."
...s something moving at the snake man's feet?
...b couldn't trust his eyes. They were burning in the acrid smoke.
His ...mach dry heaved.
..."am the word," boomed the snake man.
..."am the word," the room repeated in unison.
..." am the light—" The snake-masked leader knelt and picked up
a sack. He'd stood behind Tommy in the circles. Tommy's dad was
their leader.

Another hood stepped forward. "When Sirius C becomes visible
in the sky—"

And another. "The earth's electromagnetic field will weaken—"

ating filled him with terror. Even on days when he didn't work, Bob chronically napped.

"Whatcha got going on afterward? Me and the guys are gonna have a graduation party. Our dads are throwing it for us. A little gathering. Teensy tiny. Tiny teensy. Nothing major. Wanna come?"

"Uh, okay." A text popped up onto Bob's monoculous. He lowered his chin to brighten the words, superimposed over Tommy's face.

I'M sorry to say we can't make it to graduation, son. Your mother is sick again. They're going to LINC-cast it live. We'll see the whole thing in our little goggles as if we're there! Mom sends her love. We're so proud of you!!! See you at home next month. We'll celebrate!

"BULLSHIT," Bob mumbled. He wouldn't go back there. He couldn't live with them again. He'd stay in Ithaca. Work in the bagel shop until he died in the next flood. He sat up and swung his legs off the bunk's edge.

"Was that a yes? You'll come? Great. Listen, I'm gonna need your help. We still need a place to hold it. Without windows. I was thinking, how about your bagel place? Could we use the cellar? After hours?"

Tommy removed a book from his desk drawer, opened it, and pulled a vial from its hollow. It wasn't a good decoy. Nobody used books anymore. They weren't even legal now. Bob leapt down from his bed and locked the door, something Tom never did, even though vaping indoors was prohibited. What was it like to live a repercussion-free life?

"You guys want to party with your dads in a...bagel-shop cellar?" Bob took off his work apron and stuffed it in his laundry bag.

"Yeah. It'll be different. Bagels! You've got the key to the place, right?"

"Uh, yeah. We'll have to do it after the night shift, and we've gotta be out of there before the bakers arrive. My manager can't know."

"We need to start at a minute before midnight next Tuesday." Tom instructed.

"Um, okay. That's really specific. Sure."

"Yessss. My man."

"Nothing too messy. We have to get it cleaned up by the time the baking crew gets there." Bob knew he'd wind up doing the cleaning. Why was he always working for Tommy and his friends? It was never going to get him anywhere. Tommy wouldn't remember his name the week after they graduated.

"For sure." Tommy sucked on his one-hitter, deep. "No mess," he said, without losing a wisp of vapor from his lungs.

———————————

THEY LEFT their dorm room at ten minutes before midnight, Bob at a near-trot alongside Tommy to keep up as they blew through campus. Tommy had mentioned this graduation party more than anything else in the last three-and-a-half years. He also hadn't smoked weed today.

Bob's whole body was humming with anxiety.

My one chance to impress Tommy's rich dad, all the guys' rich dads.

They climbed the pedestrian walkway at RBG Law Library and descended at the bagel shop exit. It used to be a straight shot from school to Bob's job down on the ground, but a glitch in last fall's Self-Driving Auto FlowCheck Update version thirteen-point-six had torn a student in half when a car knocked her down and K-turned on her spleen. At the time, she was eating an everything bagel with cream cheese Bob had prepared.

The airpaths had appeared a month later, tacking an extra three minutes onto Bob's work commute.

"What's all this construction?" Tommy nodded at the scaffolding below.

"Oh, I dunno, it's like the fifth noodle shop they've built here in the past month. They're trying to force us into an all-noodle diet." Bob's

shrug turned into a shiver. It was
due to the Flood wreaking havoc
had been unaffected. This was typi
it should have been cold and cold wh

"Blech," Tommy said. "I hate noo
Here, take this." He handed Bob a bun
discover the largest hooded sweatshirt h

"What's this for?"

"We ran out of robes."

"Robes?" Bob's stomach clenched, like
ruin any future career he might have at Colle

If you do what they say, maybe one of them w

Each one of Tommy's friends had a pow
There were eleven possible opportunities tonig

"Put it on. And don't say anything. This par
Tommy donned a midnight blue robe and slid the
was covered in shadow.

A silent party? Bob's forehead beaded with sweat
bunch of rich kids and their dads want with a bagel ce
they destroyed any property, the blame would fall on
school expel him the day before graduation? Sure. W
wasn't rich. Could he get thrown in jail? Maybe the own
him work in bagels for the rest of his life to pay back the de

Tommy yanked up the cellar door and ushered Bob
steps, into a wall of smoke that stank of fake grapes.

"What the hell, Tommy?" He hissed. It smelled worse
nonstop marijuana.

"Shhhh!" Tommy whispered. "No talking." Bob stumble
the stairs, tripping over his new sweatshirt. He pulled the hoo
from his eyes, but it did no good once Tommy lowered the ellar
door: The basement was pitch black.

Then someone struck a match and lit a candle. Its light revealed
twenty-one hooded figures standing in two concentric circles. Tommy
added himself to a gap in the inner circle and made it twenty-two. At

"We will use the blood to activate the serpents—"

"And ascend from this world to claim our destiny—"

The sack was wriggling.

"I am the light. And the life—" The snake man dumped its contents onto the floor.

"And the one true way."

A flash of bright yellow on the ground. The cobra hooded immediately. There was a neon yellow snake in Bob's bagel shop. He saw stars. His face felt hot and cold at the same time.

The snake-masked man didn't hesitate. His hand shot forward, candlelight glinting on a blade. The snake's head fell to the floor, blood spraying from its severed body.

Tommy's dad had just beheaded a fucking *cobra* in the basement of Bob's bagel job.

Bob's dinner splattered onto the concrete.

"Oh, gross." Someone said. Sounded like Sammy.

Bob continued to scream-retch all over the basement floor.

"Can somebody turn on a light? Yuck." The basement's lone LED winked on. The snake-man-leader removed his mask, an old version of Tommy underneath, but scarier. And he was heading towards Bob. If Bob hadn't already yarfed his whole stomach onto the ground, now would have been the opportune time to do it.

He avoided eye contact, noticed the bottom of Tommy's dad's robe attracted both the ball bearings *and* the dust he'd sprinkled on the ground. It wasn't magic. It was magnets.

"Is this your friend, Tommy?" Tom Fletch Senior tucked his snake mask under his arm and stepped aside. They had nailed two dead snakes to Bob's bagelboard, where he wrote the bagel of the day every morning. Everything was covered in snake blood.

How many snakes did this party need to kill before they could call it a night?

"What the hell are you doing?" Bob blurted out.

"Yeah, Dad. This is him." There was a beheaded cobra bleeding out on the floor, and yet, the entire room was staring at Bob, covered in his own sick, as though *he* was the problem.

"Have him clean this up. Tell him about the job."

"Okay, Dad." Tommy sighed.

"Tommy, what is that?" Bob asked.

"Those snakes? Oh, nothing."

The snakes formed a double helix.

"Not the snakes, Tommy. But I wouldn't call them nothing. They're something, I don't know what. I meant the jar. That large jar on the floor. Next to my bagelboard."

Was there a cloud inside the jar?

"Oh, that. It's a rainjar, Bob. Don't worry about it. You're such a worrier!" Tommy tousled Bob's hair.

Was it *raining* inside the jar?

"Hey," he said, pointing at Bob's throw-up. "I keep trying to tell you, buddy. You gotta lay off these bagels. You're straight up allergic to gluten."

And that was Bob's Illuminati job interview.

Or were they Rosicrucians?

BOB WOKE to the General's hideous face, fanning him by blowing his rusk breath everywhere.

"Fucking snakes!" Bob shouted.

"It's gone," the General said. "After you fainted, he got tired and curled up in a leg of your pants, on the floor. I jabbed my snake-catching pole through 'em and carried the whole bundle outside. Seen one before, haven't you Bob?"

"How do you know?"

"I'm on your side." The General stepped back and offered Bob his hand.

"I'm a press secretary. I don't have a side." Bob hauled to his feet unassisted. "Why didn't you just kill it?"

"That's not my way," the General said.

THE BACK of John's head. A bunch of splintery logs for chairs. The General's blathering. There was nothing to see or do of any interest out there, in the backyard of the General's farm. Western Cape. Scary. Birds calling a ruckus. Probably snakes everywhere. Was that one now, over there? Who knew what else? Dogs?

What were wild dogs called? Wolverines?

All this open space. Miserable. Bob's stomach was still trying to get used to raw milk, a variety of grains, and a number of other foods that weren't noodle cup. His intestines warbled. It didn't sound like it was going okay.

The General was going on and on, yelling into an antique mobile phone. "I don't think we have any choice! We have to do everything we can to amplify the frequency at this point. I know it's experimental. Yah. I think we'll see a jump. Sure, he'll probably go mad. He's not prepared for any of this." He tamped down his pipe. Probably smoking some panic-inducing shit. "Alright. The Science Bureau is standing by waiting to perform the measurements. We'll see what happens."

"Where've you been?" Bob demanded. He hadn't seen John since the extraction. He looked freshly showered, relaxed as usual, like he was on a goddamned vacation. "Is that a new shirt?"

"I've been around. Doing some reading. Swimming in the pool. Hanging out with the General's mum and pop. It *is* a new shirt, thanks for noticing. The General's mum gave it to me yesterday."

"There's a pool?"

The General rejoined them, snapping his silly little talking device shut, and Bob whirled on him. "Why the hell am I doing all these chores when there's a pool?"

"Here you go, Bob," the General said, sitting down on the stump next to him. "After dinner breath mint." He held open a small metal box of withered old clumps that could have been already-chewed gum from some other century. Then again, the General was right about rusks, so Bob decided to give him the benefit of the doubt. He selected a smaller one and chewed.

Nope. The doubt was deserved. All of it. Ancient gum tasted just as bad as it looked. Bob regretted swallowing. His trusty stomach would send it back up soon.

"Good," the General said. "Now stick out your tongue."

"What? No way."

The General grabbed him by the nose and throat until Bob had to open his mouth to breathe, but he'd be damned if he was going to willingly lose a tongue.

"Nuh-uh," Bob said through clenched teeth.

"You're holding up the works, Bob. Alice is on her way, and all your stalling is just wasted time."

"Alice?" Bob brightened. It was a mistake. As soon as his tongue emerged, ever so slightly, the General flicked a small red pocketknife at it, and slit open the tip.

"Ahhl. 'Ny tongue," Bob said. "'Ut the hell! Ah you kidding 'ne?"

"John?" The General gestured.

John nodded and offered his stump. The general pricked it to draw a drop of blood.

"Ouchie!" John said, smiling through his wince. Idiot.

"The body and the blood," the General said, and before Bob could react, took the knife and smeared John's blood onto Bob's tongue wound. "The book of John. Chapter six. Verse fifty-three. 'Truly, truly, I tell you, unless you eat the flesh and drink the blood of the Son of Man, you have no life in you.'"

Mrs. Wobbles clucked, long and low. And then everything went dark.

———————————

HE WOKE UP SITTING UP, something he'd never done before, another crappy new experience. His clothes were gone. They'd been replaced by a too-small orange fabric shirt and a pair of orange pants. Rough. Made of cloth. His testicle bra was noticeably missing — his balls hung freely in a foreign underwear. Cold. It was cold. He was cold and alone, sitting on a stone slab of a bench, in a...cave? No, not a cave, exactly.

He wanted to take a leak, but the toilet was exposed, out there in the middle of the room. Disgusting.

He didn't have a full grasp on much about himself, including his own name, until a man came to stand outside the bars that separated them, and shouted it: *Bob!* He stood up and called out, "I'm Bob!"

He hadn't known his own name right away. His name was Bob. And he was in a jail cell.

Bob tried to stitch together what had happened, but kept losing track. How many times had day and night passed?

"Where am I?" Bob asked the man on the other side of the bars.

"Cape Town. Five-star jail cell, boss."

Bob rubbed his eyes. "How do I get back to Nu Jersey?"

The man took a sandwich out of a pail and handed it to him through the bars.

"Good luck with that one."

Nonsensical details flashed through his mind, hints of events he couldn't recall in full.

The General. On the farm. Blood on blood. John's on Bob's. Stump blood added to tongue blood.

Yuck.

What had the General said?

This is the light

Bob in the backyard had looked down at his hand. It was sharper and bigger.

and the life

His hand was depth and length and width. But now it had more dimensions.

and the way

Bob's blood and John's blood mingling together. Bob saw the three dimensions, the depth and the length and the width, and he could also see *behind*. Seven others curled up inside. Bob went inside his own *hand*. Bob caught a ride on a couple of snakes in there and floated up into the sky. Two yellow snakes up there, two snakes and Bob too, flying away, not seeing, barely hearing. His tongue was split like the serpent. The serpent and the knowledge.

Welcome to the next step in human evolution, the General said. *Now go see the truth about MRI.*

The truth about MRI?

As soon as those three letters hit Bob's mind, he floated above the old familiar boardroom in Market, Research, Incorporated. The chairs were full. Were the Senators there? No. Their fathers. Fletch Senior at the head of the table. When he spoke, Bob could see the words he said tumble out of his mouth.

"Induction coil magnetometers. A hundred nautical miles off the coast," he said.

The boardroom was oak and mahogany back then: real materials, nothing bolted down, cloth suits, no safety, life before the Flood.

"Nuclear electromagnetic pulse warheads," he said.

Bob floated down off the ceiling to smell the reek on Fletch Senior's evil old breath. The smell of TUNAPHARM© without the synthetic burn. Back then, real fish. Nu Jersey was New Jersey.

"Very little collateral damage. Very little."

Twelve men nodded in unison.

Bob's watchful spirit body floated on Tom Fletch Senior's herring breath, on the words **collateral damage**, which became a solid force that billowed out of his mouth, blasting Bob's body out of the boardroom, into the sky, over old New Jersey before the Flood, over the face of the ocean, floating, flying, out over the waves. Away from Trenton. Ten nautical miles. Fifty. A hundred.

And Bob saw

Platforms stretching across the ocean.

Platforms and platforms full of induction coil magnetometers.

Bob didn't even know what an induction coil magnetometer was, but he knew that's what Fletch Senior's stank old breath had blown him into.

And Bob dove into the waters down to the bottom of the ocean floor, flitting through bleached coral beds and plastic debris to reach an underwater forest of nuclear electromagnetic pulse warheads, row upon row.

And in tiny engraved print on every single warhead:

Property of MRI

When the warheads erupted, Bob rode the tidal wave to shore. This time Bob wasn't just in the Flood. He *was* the Flood. The tsunami hit New Jersey, New Jersey became Nu Jersey, the isolation of the Northeast Corridor took hold, people hid inside, people put on their headsets, people believed the world was underwater, but he saw the whole thing, saw the entire planet all at once, and all its people, and for them, it was true, there was no flood.

Etched on every headset in microscopic print, it said:

Property of MRI

BOB FLOATED BACK into the present time. Still up above. Bob could see himself there in Western Cape valley, staring at John. Bob's body on the ground bolted. The General didn't stop him. Bob on the ground ran off into the night. The part of Bob that hovered in the sky saw everything.

BOB TREMBLED VIOLENTLY on the stone slab in his jail cell until he forced the memories out and didn't think about it anymore. Then the shaking stopped.

"I'm not a thinking kind of person," he said aloud. It echoed off the bare stone walls. Nobody talked back.

Bob ate the sandwich his captor had brought. It was sweet and gummy in a vaguely familiar way, reminiscent of childhood. Outside the cell bars, just another wall. A stranger had drugged him and ruined his mind and now he was stuck in an enclosure in a city right on the water. Their jails had no breathing tubes to save the prisoners in the name of humane captivity, should a tsunami come.

"Help," he rasped. His heart was in his throat, pounding. The water was flooding into his kitchen in the Nu Jersey suburbs. All he had for protection was a half-sandwich.

Was that a low, roaring sound? A flood could come at any time and he would die underwater in there, alone—

A familiar face appeared at the bars.

"Missing something?" Alice reached through, dangled a red testicle bra.

"You're here!" Bob clutched the ball bra and sobbed.

24

THE OCEAN WAS PRETENDING

The ocean was pretending to be calm and not at all murderous. A ruse. Bob refused to turn his back on it. After a moment or two, it lulled him into a false sense of calm that riled up every bit of his anxiety. Bob had thought he would enjoy freedom after the sting of captivity, but he was wrong.

"So you thought you were working for the Illuminati," Alice said to his back.

"Yep." She was leaning up against a poor excuse of a protective wall, the only puny thing separating Cape Town from terror. Tapping her foot like there was no danger at all. Floodennials. So *stupid*.

"But you're not."

"No. We're Rosicrucians, it turns out. Or we are now. Maybe we always were. The General is. I don't know what I am. I'm just the press secretary."

"And this is a secret society designed to protect some guy."

"Right."

"But the first thing that happened when you got here, is, he immediately got kidnapped."

"Wasn't my fault."

"Because everybody wants to use his DNA to make a portal."

"Uh huh."

"And catapult themselves into a new dimension. Which will kill all the rest of the people on the planet." Alice took a seat on a waterfront bench, and pulled a paper sack out of her shoulder bag.

"Allegedly." Bob sighed. "The General's been going on and on about this crap all week."

"I found some files at work, pretty much say the same thing. So then the General, he put this guy's blood in your blood and then you didn't even know who you were or where you were or *when* you were and you woke up in jail."

"That's what happened." Bob knew how it all sounded, but if you can't tell your assistant about your kidnapping problems, your hallucinogenic blood problems, your secret society apocalypse problems, then what was the point of having an assistant at all?

"So now your boss—Eric—"

"Yep, Eric."

"—is still in Nu Jersey controlling all those dumb senators and the war."

"I don't know. He hasn't LINCed me in a while. Since before the farm."

A fragment of Bob's vision hit him like a manufactured tsunami. High on John's blood. Property of MRI. MRI caused the Flood. No, Fletch Senior caused the Flood. The headsets. The lies about the rest of the world being underwater.

"Are you okay?" Alice asked.

"S-sure," Bob stammered. "Why?"

"You just got this weird look on your face. Like you saw a ghost—" Alice abruptly stopped talking and looked away, like *she* had seen a ghost. She pulled a rusk out of the paper sack, and Bob's eyes lit up. "There were all these charges against you. Shoplifting, vandalism, evading arrest."

"What do I do now?" Bob groaned and chomped the rusk he'd swiped. "Do they have lawyers in South Africa? I don't even know what my defense would be. Bad blood? Post-traumatic stress disorder from a counter-kidnapping?"

"Relax," Alice said. "The South African authorities dismissed your case. I had to promise to get you help with these mental health problems you've acquired."

"Mental health problems," Bob snorted. "Yeah, right. It's *bad job* problems."

"They said this crap might fly in the United States but it's not gonna be tolerated in South Africa." Bob rolled his eyes. Alice ignored him and continued. "He didn't meet me when I got here, this General, only left a message at the hotel. He said he and this other guy, this special blood guy you rescued, had to go run errands while you were in jail, so it was up to me to get you out. Then we wait here. Ready to go. Where, I don't know."

"Great," Bob said. "I was thinking my life could use more uncertainty."

"So your secret society had a secret identity?"

"Guess so. Thought I was an Illuminati. Now I'm a Rosicrucian. Allegedly."

"What's the difference?"

"I don't know. They're both secret societies. The General says the Illuminati call themselves that because they have 'illuminated' the true purpose of the Rosicrucians. Who are evil henchmen seeking to enslave the northeast corridor to feed on our energy for their own ascension purposes."

"Ascension to where?"

"I don't know, and I don't think they know. The Illuminati, on the other hand, believe the bloodline needs to be exploited for its powers and then destroyed." Bob etched a diagram in the dirt under the bench.

"Wait. So if you're a Rosicrucian, then you're part of a plot to destroy America?"

"I was surprised, too."

"And the bloodline is just one guy?" Alice said.

"So far. But they say he's got family."

"It's weird to say, we need to exploit this bloodline, and then, it's only one person, don't you think? What's the guy like?"

"Nothing special. You'll see. Kinda weird."

"And this general told you all this while he was electrocuting you on a farm?"

"Yep. It was horrible." Bob shuddered. He forced the memory out, tried to focus on more pleasant things. Alice was looking good. Maybe she'd initiate sex later on.

"Do *you* think you're an ignorant henchman of an evil secret society?" Alice peered at Bob as though evaluating whether he was up to the task.

"I don't know. It's been a rough week."

"These things are called rusks?"

"Yes, rusks."

"Bob, do you ever feel like your brain isn't working right, and you can't pay attention to anything much, so you can't get anywhere with your thinking, and maybe part of your memories are fake?"

"Yeah, every day." Bob shrugged. He thought back to his vision. The headsets. Property of MRI.

"They're pretty good." Alice said. "The rusks. It's nice here."

"I don't care for it," Bob said. "I miss Nu Jersey."

"There's a ghost in the foundation of the building," Alice said. "Named Tom."

"Tom? My Tom?"

"I don't know which Tom is *your* Tom. He says his dad killed him."

"Fletch Senior? Killed his own son?" Bob was getting a piercing headache behind his eyes. He needed his headset to work again. All this staring out at the horizon was harmful.

"Because he found out about this plot. The Project, they call it. And he was going to tell you."

A van pulled up. The General rolled down his window and a cloud of smoke wafted out. "Get in the van, *babbelbekkies!*"

Bob picked up the plastic bag the jail had given him. Alice grabbed her small suitcase.

"This him?" Alice stared down the General.

"That's him," Bob whispered. "My torturer. Everybody calls him the General because he used to be in the South African army. He electrocuted me every day this week with a mobile fence he made me take down and put up so the land didn't get overgrazed. Seemed to really enjoy it. I had to feed his sheep and chickens. And mix a saltlick for his cows."

"Sounds educational."

"He has a nice chicken named Mrs. Wobbles," Bob said, loud enough for the General to hear. They climbed inside the van.

"Mrs. Wobbles *is* a beautiful chicken," the General said.

"I bet! What's a chicken?" Alice asked.

"I'll show you a picture of her. I'm Peter," the General said. "You can call me the General."

"I'm Alice," Alice said, but trailed off when she honed in on the van's only passenger. "John? Is that you?"

"Alice!" John and Alice seized each other in the back of the van.

"Oh, so you know each other," Bob frowned at their embrace. "Is that you?" He muttered under his breath. "No, it's the other amputee we're all forced to work with."

"You didn't tell me the guy who got kidnapped because he's the sole carrier of a fancy bloodline was John! My favorite co-worker."

"Your *favorite* co-worker?" Bob's voice dripped with jealousy.

"John, wow. It's been so long. What happened to your hand?" Alice bluffed.

"Oh, you know. Long story. I'm so happy to see you!" John's only hand was still on Alice's shoulder. Bob would have chopped that one off too, if he'd had his way.

"Me too!" Alice and John gazed into each other's eyes so hard, Bob wanted to throw up.

"No touching," he said, but they ignored him.

"Enough chit-chat," the General said. "There's a price on John's head and Bob's head and my head. It's time to get ourselves out of Illuminati territory. Buckle up!"

"Where are we going?" Alice asked.

The General clamped a cigarette between his teeth and torched it. "Make yourselves comfortable. We're driving to Mali."

OUT OF CAPE TOWN, through the coastal farmlands of South Africa and into Namibia, they drove north. Bob begged the General to stop and let him take a piss. The General convinced him to use a bottle in the back of the van instead. The continent of Africa flew by, barely visible, the General was driving so fast. And Alice had just learned it existed.

"Hey. You know what? There are no evacuation skyways," Alice said aloud, interrupting a few hours of silence following a hurried charging-station stop. The General grumbled about every second they spent not moving.

"There aren't," Bob agreed.

"Don't they have flood code here?"

"No, they don't. They didn't have a flood."

"*What*?" Alice gasped.

"No flood. I asked the receptionist about it at the hotel when I first got here. She didn't even know what I was talking about. Barely knew what floods *are*. Hadn't heard of ours. Joked about how they could use one. They don't have ankle bracelets, or evacuation skyways, or mandatory headsets. You can see the sun on most days. There's no haze. No fauxlowers or things made of mushrooms. Everything is antique, the way things were before."

"I thought the Flood happened everywhere."

"I did, too."

"But you were so *old*. I was only a kid. How did we both get tricked?"

"Old?" Bob turned his face and his entire body away from Alice. He pretended to look out the window, but Alice heard him sniffle. Alice felt a pang of guilt, then a wave of anger. Why was she responsible for his feelings? She couldn't tiptoe around his fragility anymore now that they had to spend all this time in a van together.

John snored, mumbled *Hooray*, woke himself up, itched his nose with his stump, then went back to sleep.

"Hey, Bob?" Alice whispered. "Do you know what happened to John's hand?"

"Hasn't it always been missing?" Bob snarled.

"No, it hasn't. When I met him at work, he had both hands. The next time I saw him, he had a little bandage. Then I didn't see him for a while, I think — but I had left the phones and started working for you."

Alice searched Bob's face for any sign he was behind John's amputation, but his expression was as blank as ever.

"Did you ever go to the Hub at work?"

"Nope," Bob said. "Never heard of it."

"Really? Even though it was in the same building and everything?"

"Yep. Never heard of any hub."

"What happened to John when he got kidnapped?"

"I don't know. They just..." Bob trailed off. "I don't know what those people were doing to him. They had him in a weird metal net. They were draining blood out of him through a tube hooked up to a giant, like, computer, with a bunch of cables and wires. There was this green light on the floor." He shuddered.

"That's what's in the Hub!" Alice said. "In the Science Bureau."

"Since I went to get him in Cape Town a week or two ago, though, he hasn't had his hand," Bob added. "I don't know what happened to it. We can ask him when he wakes up." Alice searched his face, and wondered if he was lying.

THEY HARDLY STOPPED the entire trip except to adjust the solar panels and charge at the solar stations when absolutely necessary. Once Bob found out which side of the car faced the ocean, he stared out the window, looking for it. Could the General out-drive a tsunami? Maybe he could. He was a tough old lunatic. Why was he so afraid of another flood, now that he had proof it wasn't even an accident? The flood fear was always there. Years of headset training ensured it.

If Fletch Senior was behind the Flood, maybe he was going to do it again. Here.

Alice and John jibber-jabbered like best friends. Or worse. Had they slept together? Probably.

Slept her way around the office, same way she seduced me. Should have left him in the kidnapping. His testicle elasticity is probably amazing. The ocean is going to kill us all anyway. There aren't even any flood evacuation routes. How could she let him touch her with that stump?

After nearly a week of non-stop driving, Bob begging to piss in a toilet like a real human being and everyone scraping together meals from snacks in charging stations with no noodle cups in sight, they arrived in Mali.

"This is it," the General announced. "This is the place." He got out, kicked the van's tires, and spat in the dirt. Patted the hood. They all scrambled out of the van.

"The place for *what*?" Bob looked around at nothing. Dirt and cliffs. Scruffy little trees that had never had a proper chance at living big-tree life. No sign of civilization. It couldn't be the place for much.

The General glared. Then he cuffed Bob on the ear. "Next time, *ek gaan jou so 'n harde poesklap gee, jou tanne gaan vibreer vir maande lank.*" Bob didn't know what that gibberish meant. He held his smarting ear and didn't ask any more questions. He'd never been hit so hard before. It was exhilarating. Also, he wanted to cry.

"Come this way," the General said, so Bob did. The others followed. They rounded one rock face only to reveal another one beyond. This cliff had formed into cubes instead of the rocky swoops they'd seen from the van for the past hundred miles.

"Weird looking rocks," Alice said, but the words died in her mouth.

It hadn't *formed*, it was obvious now. It had been carved. Possibly by the hundreds of people who climbed out of their cliff condos to stare at the new arrivals.

25

THE PLACE FOR WHAT

"The place for what?" Bob said again. He'd been saying the same thing day and night since they arrived. No answer. Still. The others ignored him, as usual.

Alice, the General, and Bob sat in the middle of the village, watching the Dogon tribe dance from one side of it to the other. Bob's legs were tired and a little bit twitchy, partially from kicking in his sleep due to the tsunami nightmares, and partially from his proximity to a full-body exercise. Luckily the tribe had provided chairs — maybe the only chairs in the whole village. They weren't even manufactured. Hand-carved. Bob checked first the left arm, and then the right, peering into the wood for splinters before resting his hands.

"How's your hut?" Alice asked.

"Miserable," he replied. "What about yours?" The primitives had sequestered Alice in a woman-only hut, while John, Bob, and the General all shared a guest hut, like animals. He hadn't slept since they arrived thanks to the disgusting sound of their relentless collective breathing.

It had been three days. Bob was still worn out from their exhausting road trip. Not to mention the grating personalities of his travel companions.

"Not bad." Alice was chipper. Probably because of John. They must have been sleeping together on the sly. She was obviously in love with him. Women loved men with a birth defect. Or, in this case, a much-more-recent defect. Bob didn't stand a chance, with his full working limbs.

The tribespeople were screaming some gibberish. *Again*. Absolutely terrifying. They had donned scary masks for the occasion.

I can't tell a stinking thing anybody is saying because nobody ever learned English here.

Bob had tried everything to communicate: talking louder. Yelling. Gesturing. Nothing worked. They still couldn't speak English.

"Really? Not bad? Ours is made of sticks and leaves. Know what that is? Not flood-proof. The *opposite* of flood-proof. Can you sleep, knowing you're gonna die if a flood comes? I can't. I've been waking up every fifteen minutes."

"Well, ours too. But I don't think floods are a problem here." Alice shrugged.

"Yet," Bob said. "Know what they *do* have here, though?"

"What?"

"Roving wild animals. Travelling in gangs. The General made me go on a water run yesterday, and I saw flocks of them. Whole *teams*. Roaming freely. How do you feel about that?"

"Whoa," Alice said.

"Freely! You ever imagine? When's the last time you saw a wild animal back home?"

"I dunno. Never? I think they all died in the Flood."

"Yeah. Better that way. Safer."

"I suppose. I don't know if they're dangerous, though. Animals. Where's John?"

"What's it to you?" She wasn't even trying to hide her affection anymore.

"Jeez. Just making conversation." Alice rolled her eyes. She was so disrespectful.

John was back at the hut now, resting peacefully and comfortably as usual. Bob couldn't tolerate somebody being comfortable right now.

"Quiet down, you two!" The General hissed. He was really into the dancing and screaming. Of course he would be. If there was electrocution involved, he'd probably get an old man boner. Bob shuddered.

"What's happening?" Alice whispered.

"They're commemorating the death of the first ancestor and the time when man acquired the spoken word," the General explained to Alice.

Bob glared at them both. He wasn't finished with his complaints, but there they were, ignoring him again.

Night fell, sudden onset, so quick and dark Bob could barely breathe. He squinted here and there, but he couldn't see a damn thing. The tribe placed torches around their group and at the ceremony platform to light the darkness. Totally ineffective. No electricity. Not even a solar panel in sight besides their own, on top of the van, back there at the village entrance. Useless. Bob heard a noise behind him, but when he jerked around, there was nothing. Only the vacant red land, ominous sandstone condos. Full of savages.

The Dogons had spent the past three days building several altars throughout the village. Bob knew because their work had disturbed every single one of his efforts to nap. Now they were taking turns screaming and singing around the altars, sprinkling offerings of crushed-up noodle cup. They didn't eat noodle cup here, though, so Bob didn't know what it was.

"What's that?" he asked.

"Grain," the General said.

"What's *that*?" Alice asked.

The General knit his eyebrows together. Finally, he said, "You use it to make food."

"Quite a production," Alice said. Just anything impressed her, she was so simple. "This first ancestor must have been something else."

"I'd say so. But this isn't a retrospective," the General said. "First ancestor is reborn again and again — a new body every time, same biochemical composition in the blood, same DNA. He's over there."

Bob and Alice followed the General's gaze. John emerged from his hut, yawning and stretching, led by several tribe members. The Dogons dragged him to the ceremony platform at the center of the spectacle.

Bob braced himself to witness a human sacrifice. John was nothing but trouble. He'd be damned if he was going to save John's life a second time. Next time he saw a guy missing a hand, he'd run in the other direction instead of hitching his cart to that horse.

But the tribesmen stood down, chanted, and swayed. Then the crowd parted, and the largest Dogon yet emerged from the back.

"Who's that?" Alice whispered to the General. "Is it their leader?"

"No. Professor Bangura. Chief Archaeoethnographer of the University of Mali."

"Mama!" John cried.

"Baby!" She bounded onto the platform, clutched John to her chest, and caressed his face by putting her cheek up to his and nuzzling.

"Stumps. They both have freaking stumps. Unbelievable. Must be genetic," Bob murmured to Alice.

Professor Bangura swept over to them.

"It's not genetic, you damn fool! The rebels took my hands years ago. And who did this?" John's mom held his stump up in both of hers and shook it at them.

Alice and Bob looked at the ground.

"I didn't," Bob mumbled.

The General stood up and bowed to John's mom. "Mrs. Bangura—"

"It's *Doctor* Bangura."

"Doctor Bangura, I have some news. And a request."

"I'm listening."

The General stammered under John's mom's gaze. Bob had never seen him nervous before. "We want you to come with us. We need you to, ah, come work for the same company as your son."

"Leave my beautiful work with these nice Dogons? Why?"

"He's been doing a great job, and, we're *very* proud of him. But—"

"Don't patronize me, you son of a bitch! *No tek mi han pul bangga na faya.*"

"What did she say?" Alice whispered to John.

"It's an old saying from our village. 'Don't use my hand to remove palm kernels from the fire.'"

"Why should I help you?" John's mom was getting louder, bigger, and taller, while the General looked smaller and smaller. It was nice not to be the target of humiliation for a change. Bob sat up straighter. "Why should *he* help you? I think we've given you enough, don't you think?"

"Doctor Bangura, we appreciate your family's service—"

"What's the endgame? If you're such a great general, tell me: how do we win this battle?"

Bob leaned closer, to try and hear what the General said next, but then Alice interrupted. She was a terrible assistant.

"What's an archaeoethnographer?" Alice whispered.

"I don't know. Must be some kind of secretary for the tribe."

"It doesn't seem like it," Alice said. The Dogons with weapons inched closer to the General every time John's mom shouted. Were they protecting her from him, or the other way around? "Nobody guards *me*."

"I wish we had other options," the General said to John's mom. "I do. But if you stay here, it's only a matter of time before the Illuminati find you. The time has come. For ascension," the General said, shuffling his feet.

A loud crack erupted, and the sky lit up brighter than Bob had ever seen. It smelled like smoke before he could see the cause: The fuselage of a plane with both its wings torn off soared over the escarpment at their backs, ignited again, and crash-landed on the far side of the village, just beyond the final hut. Bob screamed and curled into a ball behind his loosely-constructed chair.

"Plus, it's starting," The General said. He gestured at the burning husk of a passenger jet, no surprise on his face. Not even an eyebrow arch. For all Bob knew, the General *ordered* the plane crash.

"What's starting?" Alice asked.

And really, the villagers didn't seem too surprised either. What was wrong with everybody? Did they have no reflexes? No survival instinct?

"The end stages of the Project. Earth's electromagnetic field is starting to weaken," The General said.

"That was something else," a voice said from behind them. A voice Bob recognized.

"Tom?" Bob uncurled himself enough to crane his neck.

Floating a foot above the red soil was the ghost of Bob's co-worker and sort-of friend, Tom Fletch Junior.

"Aaaahhh!" Bob screamed, and leapt behind Alice to shield himself. "A ghost!"

"How'd you get out of the building foundation?" Alice asked. "And how come I can see you?"

"Hi, Ghost Tom!" John called from the altar. "Nice to meet you."

"Here we go," The General groaned. "The dead have started rising from their graves already. Early. Now we're in for it."

The fuselage exploded and pumped its thick black cloud into the air over their heads.

"Started? I've been out of my grave for months now," Ghost Tom said. "I've always been a trend setter."

TWO DAYS LATER, Bob threw a cup on the ground and stared at it. "It's too bad this place never developed." He was getting more appalling as time went on.

"Cups don't disintegrate here, Bob. These people aren't here to pick up your trash, you know." Alice scowled at Bob, but he still didn't correct his behavior. He kicked at the cup until she picked it up and threw it in the open window of the van.

"So we're heading back to Cape Town, are we?" Bob ventured.

"Well, no." The General heaved a bag of grain in the back of the van. According to the General, you could make food out of it. It was how Africa and the seven or eight other continents got their nutrients. Alice couldn't picture it.

"We're going to India!" Alice punched Bob's arm and he jumped like he'd forgotten she existed except to pick up his trash.

"What? Why?"

"Because John's mom needs to go there. To work on the market research. Apparently India is an important market. That's what the General said."

Bob started to roll his eyes, then glanced at the General and stopped halfway.

"Am I the only person who thinks it's time to throw out the towel?" Bob twirled around, arms outstretched, like he could beg everybody to get sane.

The General looked puzzled. "Do you mean throw *in* the towel?"

"No," Alice said. "You know, throw out the towel? Like when you're surrounded by the water because you're in the Flood and then you give up and you throw out your towel." Alice mimed throwing your towel into a crushing tsunami.

"That's not the way the expression goes in the rest of the world," John said gently.

"Maybe you both need to get current," Bob muttered. He was trying out a new talking method where he faced away from the General and muttered insulting things, hoping the General couldn't hear and deliver punishment to his permanently red left ear.

"Where would we throw in the towel *to*?" Alice wondered out loud.

The General continued as though she hadn't spoken. "Did you read the pamphlet yet?"

"What pamphlet?" Alice asked.

John joined them and handed pamphlets to Alice and Bob.

"The Dogon tribe got tired of constantly hosting foreigners and explaining the situation to them over and over again, so they published these pamphlets."

"Oh, hell, just sum it up for me, would you? I don't have time to read a whole propaganda piece," Bob said.

To Alice's surprise, the General complied. He didn't even cuff Bob's ear, which Alice had started looking forward to for reasons beyond her conscious understanding.

"The earth is a magnet. There are five static and two mobile electromagnetic pressure points on the planet. With the presence of Sirius C, those pressure points can be activated."

"What's Sirius C?" Ghost Tom hollered from his current hover spot above the van.

"Oh Christ, just read the goddamn pamphlet, would all of you?"

"Alice," Bob whispered. "Could you ask Tom to come down from there? It freaks me out he's not on our level, you know? I know he's supernatural, or whatever, but it would make me feel better—"

"Sure, Bob. I'll try. But he's your friend. Don't you think it'd be better if you talked to him?"

Bob shook his head. He wasn't coping well with the presence of a ghost and was pretending Tom didn't exist.

"No!" Bob turned to the General. He stomped his foot, like a child. "I'll go to a country that doesn't exist, I'll shoot a scary gun. I'll get in a van and go on a deathtrip north into the middle of nowhere. I'll even sleep in a worthless little hut with a bunch of other grown adults, like a prisoner. But I will not, I repeat, WILL NOT READ A PAMPHLET." Bob's screaming brought the village to a standstill. Some of the Dogons removed their masks to stare.

The General sighed and started again. "Sirius A is the brightest star in our sky. Sirius B is its companion star. Then there is a third star in the system, Sirius C, typically not visible from Earth. When it becomes visible again, as it says in the pamphlet, the earth's electromagnetic field will be sufficiently weak."

"Sufficiently weak for what?" Alice asked.

"To produce the proper frequency."

"What do you mean, the proper frequency? For what?"

"For the biomass to activate."

"What's the biomass?"

"The biomass is all the biological material of the Earth, plus the electromagnetic frequency it generates."

"I don't get it," Bob said. He threw his pamphlet on the ground and folded his arms. Alice picked it up and leafed hers open but kept listening to the General.

"When you have the right number of people, whose brains are operating at a certain wavelength, all at once, it creates a vibration. Like a musical note. And that note activates a staircase in our bodies."

"There's no staircase in my body," Bob said.

"There is. A long spiral one. Called DNA."

"Then what?" Alice asked.

"If you hit precisely the right note, by having a certain amount of humans all thinking a particular way, you can turn on the DNA. Like an escalator."

"Then what?" Bob said. "We go up? It's too tiny."

"Yes, like an escalator. An escalator that turns human matter to energy and then evacuates it." The General looked up.

"To what?" Alice asked.

"Someplace else."

"Where are we going?"

"Um," the General muttered.

"What do you mean, 'um'?"

"*We're* not going anywhere."

"We get to stay here?" Alice could tell that wasn't the real story.

"Not entirely."

"Then what?"

"Well..." The General hesitated.

Alice made the universal hand gesture she'd recently learned from him for, 'speed it up.'

"The ascension takes a little more energy than exists now. They plan to use...yours."

"Mine specifically?"

"In the original plan, they were going to use *yours*, as in, the United States. Then, in the revision, also India. So much of American culture was exported there after the tech boom of the early 2000s, there was really no saving them. Their vibration was *kaput*. But now there's a new plan, and it looks like it's not just the United States and India. It's the whole world. Everybody except—"

The General looked around nervously, then he turned to John's mom. "Do you have any protective gear?"

"Of course," she said. She reached into her satchel and distributed a shiny piece of metallic fabric to each one of them.

"What's this?" Alice asked. It was so shiny and pliable.

"It's called tin foil," the General said. "You put it on your head."

"Why?" Bob asked.

"I'll tell you after you put on your tin foil," he said.

Bob stopped scuffing around in the dirt. They all crinkled their tin foil on as best they could.

"What's with this lousy hat?" Bob asked.

"The three Ts of brain net safety," John's mom said. "Tin foil, tunnels, and tiny huts."

Alice could tell Bob was dissatisfied with the answer by his sour expression, but he didn't ask any more questions.

"Swedes," the General said. "Bob, Alice, you're handmaidens to a shitty Swedish horde that's trying to liquefy your country, and the entire planet, in order to escape it."

"I am *not* a handmaiden," Bob said.

Alice leafed through her pamphlet.

THANK you for visiting the Dogon tribe!

We appreciate your interest in our cosmic knowledge.

Please enjoy these easy-to-follow notes on preventing the crystallization of the biomass frequency-

In order to maintain presence on our beautiful planet earth, we recommend you take these easy steps:

1. Biodiversity interferes with the signal; perpetuate to the greatest extent.

2. Achieve the most complex brain waves through a minimum of exposure to consumer electronics.
3. In the 30-day period leading up to frequency achievement, protect the keystone individuals and ensure nobody makes a biocomputer out of their skin and tissue. :(
4. If a keystone individual is identified and limbs removed, seek assistance.
5. Electromagnetic field weakening produces reduced memory function. Avoid!
6. If the brain net is mainlined when the frequency is reached, ascension for some or all humans is inevitable. Avoid!
7. Do not build large-scale dams to stop the flow of water. This would minimize any noise to the frequency by slowing the rotation of the earth.
8. Do not restrict human movement and maintain consistency of experience; i.e., war, famine, and disease.
9. Do not engage major dogmatic adherence across the entirety of the globe — for example, by eliminating small tribes, hunter–gatherers, non-agricultural societies, and the ungoverned. This will reduce frequency noise and presents a danger.
10. Do not incite major political violence in as many locations as possible for a 125-year period prior to the appearance of Sirius C.
11. Do not engage in state violence, such as internment in designated areas to maintain a sufficient magnitude of biological material.
12. Do not commit genocide to prune the biomass and achieve the frequency.

FOR MORE INFORMATION on this and other cosmic topics, please contact your tribal representative to receive additional pamphlets.

. . .

"I've seen this before," Alice said. "Or, the opposite. I saw a plan to do everything this list says not to do."

"Where?" The General asked, but Alice could tell he already knew the answer.

"What the hell are Swedes?" Bob asked.

Ghost Tom floated over. John's mom held a crinkled piece of tin foil around his ghastly skull. "It's true, Bob. MRI caused the Flood. I found out about it. The Project. That's what they call it. Dad killed me so I couldn't tell you."

"But your father is the head of the northeast corridor chapter of the Illuminati," Bob said.

"He's an undercover Swede," Ghost Tom said.

"What is that?" Bob asked again.

"People from Sweden," the General said.

"This is ridiculous," Bob said.

"Wait. Aren't you working for them, too?" Alice asked the General. He drew a circle in the dirt with a stick and put a few amorphous blobs in it that Alice couldn't recognize.

"Sometimes the safest place to hide is in plain sight," the General said. "So you can protect your friends and know your enemies."

"That's not true and also sounds really dumb," Bob said. He winced in anticipation of being struck, but the General didn't budge from his dirt diagram.

"Here's Earth," the General said. "We were originally planning to engage John in North America, here, and his mom in Dogon territory, here." He stabbed a couple of the dirt-diagram blobs with his stick. "We need to cover more ground now. Bob's boss believes that physically grounding the biomass with John's and his mother's DNA rooted in two of the diametrically opposed longitudinal lines is the only way to achieve the brain net frequency."

"Huh?" Bob asked.

Alice was just as confused. "So we're just gonna do what MRI wants us to do?"

"We need to move John's mom to another location. It's not safe here for her anymore. The Illuminati are volatile. Then we have to get John back to the United States."

"But we can't fly," Alice said.

"Why not?" Bob asked.

"There was a plane crash. Remember? Plane falling out of the sky? Just now? Weakened electromagnetic field?"

"It's not the only plane in the world, you know," Bob said.

"Earth's magnetic field weakens five percent every ten years," John's mom said. "Until about three months ago, when it weakened five percent in one day."

"Hey," Alice said. "That's when my mom died."

"I don't know when earth's magnetic poles are going to reverse, but I do know it could happen soon. Flight isn't an option." The General hurled a sack of grain into the van. "We knew this was coming. We didn't know exactly when."

"What do you mean, you didn't know *exactly* when? I was just *in* a plane!"

The General sidestepped Bob to grab another sack.

Ghost Tom tried to swipe a cigarette from the General's stash on the van's dashboard, but his hand passed through it over and over again.

"Shit," he mumbled. The General lit a cigarette. Ghost Tom gleamed with jealousy. *Should have bummed one off my mom.*

"I didn't know your mom died," Bob said.

"Well, you never asked. It happened before I came to work for you. It's *why* I came to work for you. I tried to tell you earlier. Eric put her in the rainjar. In the Hub. Then he made me come here to bail you out."

"Oh," Bob wilted. "I thought you came because you wanted to." He brushed imaginary dirt off his lapel and stared at his fingernails, then chewed on one. Alice ignored his pout.

"She can't get to the other side. She can kind of see the light, I think, but there's a blockage. Same thing with this guy." She pointed at Ghost Tom, imitating a Dogon tribe member's interpretive dance from behind.

"Stop it!" John's mom said. "You're being rude."

"Alright," the General clapped his hands. "Enough. Everybody in! Living or dead, get in the van. It's Dharamsala or bust."

John waved his hand and stump in the air. "Road trip!"

"This is stupid!" Bob huffed and puffed. "What are we going to do, all crammed in here like a noodle cup? We don't *all* have to go to India. Who knows what Eric is doing back in the United States?"

"Don't worry, boss." Alice clapped him on the shoulder. "We'll be back there soon enough."

"Our headsets aren't even working anymore! How are you going to get to India without headset directions?"

"Phone signals and GPS. The stars and the sun," John's mom said. "Street signs. A compass."

"This." The General held up a map. "Asking directions from the locals."

"Ridiculous," Bob fumed.

"We can't fly home for a little while anyway," Alice chimed in. "At least, not until they fix the electromagnetic field issues. Maybe it'll be fun?"

Bob sighed.

"Plus," Alice reminded him, "we have to protect John and his mom from those lunatics who kidnapped John."

"Yeah, right," Bob sighed. "I can't wait."

"Right is right." John's mom said. "*Bad bush no de fo trowe bad pikin.*"

"What does that mean?" Alice whispered to John.

"It's an old saying from the next village over. It means, 'just because you have a bad kid doesn't mean you get to throw him into the bush.'"

"Nice sentiment," Bob said. Then he yanked Alice aside and hissed in her ear. "Has it ever occurred to you that *these* lunatics—" He gestured at the General and Alice and himself "—are *also* kidnapping John and his mom for some unknown purpose?"

"Now that you mention it, no," Alice whispered back. "Obviously, that's why you're the boss. But what choice do we have? We can't get out of here on our own. We may as well go along for now and keep an eye on John and his mom."

"I'm the boss," Bob echoed, as though learning his position for the very first time. "You're right," he said. "Let's get to India. Whatever, wherever *that* is."

———————

A FEW HOURS LATER, they passed Timbuktu. "Oh, wow!" Alice pointed at the sign. "Timbuktu. It's a real place! Now I've seen everything."

———————

BOB SAT in the very back of the van, rolling through a deserted expanse. "Where are we?" His voice had a pleading tone to it, a tremble throughout and a squeak at the start. He needed to start sounding more confident. Like Alice had reminded him, he was the boss. He cleared his throat. "Where are we?" he said, deep, purposeful, like a man. Better.

"Outside the Dogon Plateau," the General said.

He probably outranked the General.

"Still?" he said.

"It's bigger than Nu Jersey," the General said.

Bob had sweated right through his shirt trying to mix some of the grain with water and form it into little pancakes so the General could blowtorch them the next time they stopped.

"I finished making all these little weirdo pancakes." Bob looked around at the crew. Alice was asleep, drooling a little bit in an alluring way. John's mom leafed through some antique book of hers. John was sleeping, head on her shoulder. Ghost Tom was absent, probably floating somewhere above the back bumper. Bob tilted his head so he could see further back. Yep, there he was.

I have to acknowledge Tom's ghost— Bob's mind started, but then he was overwhelmed by thoughts of all his favorite noodle-cup flavors: original, spicy, plain. His mouth watered. If he had known what the future would hold, he would have packed nothing but noodle cups when Eric had first told him South Africa existed.

Now he wasn't even *in* South Africa. Couldn't call up a map on his LINC. It was as if he didn't exist on the Earth at all.

"Tom died because of me," Bob blurted out, to nobody in particular.

The General looked at him through the rearview mirror. "I'm not sure that's exactly the case," he said. "Tom died because his dad killed him. He told us so."

"I knew something was up, though. And I knew he wanted to talk about it. I was avoiding it. Him. I was scared. I'm always scared."

"I'm often scared too," the General said. "Everybody is."

Bob turned towards Tom's ghost again. He waved. Bob waved back. It was a start.

His headset was still only a hum, so he couldn't distract himself with five-second clips anymore or research where exactly India was located and how long it would take to get there.

"What's that?" Bob leaned over the front seat and pointed to a hunk of flaming metal in the middle of the road. "Another plane?"

"Verizon," the General read off the side of the wreckage. He swerved to miss it. "Satellite."

THE CITIZENS of Mali didn't seem to mind the occasional burning plane or satellite in their way. They took it in stride.

Algeria was a different story.

Roads were clogged. Every time they stopped at a recharge station, people were in a panic — screaming, crying, bowing on the ground.

"These people are soft," Bob said. "They haven't been through a flood. They don't know what suffering is."

Everybody turned to look at him like he had said something unpopular. Why should he apologize for being honest?

John's mom cleared her throat. "Everybody knows what suffering is," she said. "There are different kinds. Losing my hands hasn't caused me any suffering. Do I miss them? Sure. But life goes on. I don't think to myself, this shouldn't have happened. But I screamed and cried for a few years to get here. It's called 'processing your emotions.' It's arguing with reality that causes the suffering. And reality always wins."

"How'd you lose your hands?" Alice asked quietly.

"One day, while I was out with John at the market, militants invaded our home. My daughter Susan was never found. We sent my other daughter, Keetah, out of the country soon after. Later that month, they came back, and they hacked off my hands."

"Who did it?" Bob asked.

"Maybe it was the Illuminati?" Alice mused. "Or the Rosicrucians? Or the economy?"

"I couldn't tell at the time," John's mom said. "They don't exactly flash you their ID."

"I'm sorry, Mama," John said. He patted his stump on hers. "Maybe Susan is okay, wherever she is."

"You're a good boy, John. I hope so."

THE SUN GREW low on the horizon. Finally, the General pulled over by the side of the road. They tumbled out of the van.

"Alright," the General said. "Bob, you start up the solar stove. Alice, supervise Bob, so he doesn't ruin dinner."

Bob heaved the stove out of the back of the van.

"Ow! My pinky," he called out, and looked around to see if any assistance would come.

None did.

Ghost Tom was hovering about the van, undulating his shoulders in an interesting way Alice recalled from her own mom's ghost. John and his mom were deep in conversation a few paces away. And the General just stood there, watching Bob make a spectacle out of getting a portable stove ready to use.

He fumbled its tripod, cursed, and slammed it on the ground until it popped open.

Alice couldn't stand to witness the struggle, and she moved forward to help, but the General stopped her with an outstretched hand and a little shake of his head.

She had to wonder, how'd he ever get any job at all? Well, it wasn't like he was a solar stove salesman for a living.

He heaved the stove on top of its stand, shouted at every single step of the process.

unfurl the solar panel [expletive]

plug in the stove casing [expletive]

level out the tripod [expletive]

click the ignite button [expletive]

no ignition [expletive]

[EXPLETIVE]

Was that how he wrote his press releases?

The stove click click click click clicked but wouldn't ignite.

Come to think of it, she'd never seen him write a press release.

"Keep trying," the General encouraged. He heaved their reserve battery out of the van. "You'll get it. I need to go find some rolling papers for my special cigarettes so I don't lose my mind and kill you, then I'm gonna hit the charging station in case our solar panels flop again."

"We'll go collect the water," John's mom said, rejoining the group along with John, their faces drawn, tense. Alice couldn't hear what they'd been talking about, but they'd been quieter since John's mom had told them the story of her missing hands, daughters. Maybe she wasn't supposed to ask about it. It was hard to know how to interact with people in person, minus the headset.

John's mom slipped her antique phone out of her pocket with both stumps, held it up, and commanded, "Open GPS. Map directions from current location to Le Niger."

"Le Niger is a twenty-five minute walk from your current location," the phone said.

It was weird, having a location system not attached to your face.

Alice felt the place where her headset usually rested on her right ear, then rubbed the typical monoculous landing spot on her right eye. Had she ever gone for a walk without hers, back in Nu Jersey?

Had she ever gone for a walk? No, not after the Flood. Nobody did.

"Good luck with dinner." John saluted Bob and Alice with his stump-arm, and then he and his mother set off on their errand. Ghost Tom flitted along behind them until they all disappeared over the horizon.

Alice and Bob were all alone. Alice dripped water into the grain sack, extracted the grain in gritty balls, and smashed it into pancakes. Bob gave up on the stove and began blowtorching them.

"I miss noodle cups," he sighed.

"These pancakes aren't bad," Alice argued, trying to save him from feeling his stove failure. "I like the burned, blowtorched taste. Raw on the inside. Everybody does. It's so much better than even heating." She rolled a couple of pancake balls between her hands. Bob set down the blowtorch and put his hand on her breast. She shrugged him off. "Hey. What if somebody sees?" It felt worse in her new cloth shirt than it had in her old plasticlothes.

"So? What if they do? Are you ashamed of me?"

The first and only time they'd had penetrative sex had seemed more reasonable than this.

"No." *Maybe.* "I just think...it's not proper for a boss to have a sexual relationship with his inferior! Isn't that in the employee handbook?"

"Oh cut the crap, Alice. I know what's going on here. I know you have a *thing* for men without all their limbs. I know John is your *real* love interest. You've treated me differently ever since you bailed me out of jail. Was that a turnoff?"

Alice didn't know what to say, because there had never been a turn-on.

Had she ever felt anything for Bob? He was an opportunity to get out of the interview cubicle. To save the condo. To not be homeless.

Was any of that a turn *on*? Should she want to have sex out of gratitude? Was that a sexy-time feeling?

Alice searched her brain for any sign of what was a turn-off or a turn-on to her, but she was coming up with very little evidence. Then she noticed Bob's face turning hysterical, and she realized she had taken too much time to respond.

This is why people made headsets with a monoculous. At least there was a barrier between you and this kind of crap. She could have covertly searched for the appropriate response and recited it. Conflict avoided.

"No," Alice said. "No, no, of course not."

"You're in love with John," Bob accused.

Maybe she would have been, but they hadn't had the time.

"I'm not," Alice shot back. Her denial stung, told her everything. She could be in love with John.

"Alice, seeing all those pancakes on top of each other is driving me wild." Alice looked down at Bob's mediocre erection, pressed up against his pants.

"Oh, alright," she muttered. Her potential love for John would have to wait. But she did know one thing: *this* wasn't love, and it wasn't affection. What she felt was a sense of obligation. And it didn't feel good. It felt the same as being at work, cuffed and cubed.

She looked around to make sure nobody was coming, then unzipped Bob's fly, took out his penis, and began rubbing it up and down. Bob gasped and shuddered.

Then he made another noise. "Ah! Ouch!" He flinched and pushed her hand away.

"What?"

"You got, like, a grain of sand on your hand. Here," Bob handed her a pancake. "Use this."

Alice tried to view this maneuver as sexual or appealing in any way. Her mind's eye floated above the scene and watched herself give Bob a hand job with a grain pancake. Empty road beyond. Forest behind. A waxing, waning hum the General had explained was due to insects. Lots and lots of bugs. There she was, Alice, in a place she hadn't even known existed. There he was, leaning against the van. Losing control of his legs. They quivered more and more. His scalp broke out in a crimson flush.

Who's the boss now? Alice fantasized about saying it out loud. She knew it would kill his mood, so she settled for thinking it over and over again. *Who's the boss now?*

And there it was, for the first time in her life. Alice was sexually excited, and it wasn't even from sex — it was from power. Soon she was bored with the repetition of it all, so she sped her hand movements up to get the job done.

Up and down his shaft, from the tip to the ball bra, again and again. She started counting the number of times so she had something constructive to focus on.

Bob yelped, and it was over. His semen had somehow exploded sideways, and it was all over his shirt.

Then he burst into tears.

Alice looked away, but that only made him worse. Trying to maintain Bob's functionality was a full-time job, and Alice was living at work. What a nightmare.

"Don't pay any attention to this," Bob sobbed, wiping sperm and tears around his shirt and face. "I haven't been the same since seeing guns. I think I have post-traumatic stress disorder. I've been tearing up at loud noises, too."

"There, there," Alice said, gingerly patting Bob's shoulder with the pancake. "I'm sure it will go away in time — or maybe linger and get worse. Who knows? We're in uncharted territory here. I never thought I would leave Nu Jersey. Look at me now: from Trenton to Timbuktu. Let's finish up the pancakes, huh? It's okay if you cried into them. Tears never ruin the taste of food."

"Alice, do you have feelings for me?" Bob wiped at his eyes, mucus oozing from his nose.

Alice struggled to think about her feelings, but she was distracted by a massive white bird with a black hooked beak flying in loops above.

"Well? Do you?"

The bird landed on the hood of the van, stretched its wings, and made a strange trilling sound. Never in her life had Alice seen a non-domesticated creature so close.

"Sure. Of course I do." Alice was having two major feelings for Bob these days: pity, mixed with an inexplicable loyalty she would have loved to shake. "How about we finish up those pancakes? The others will be back soon."

"Alright," Bob said. "I'll get the hand sanitizer." He zipped up, and lifted the corners of his mouth into a half-smile, though it wore false on his tear-stained face.

26

THIS LOOKS DIFFERENT

"T his looks different," Alice said. The landscape flitting by was closer to pictures of Nu Jersey before the Flood than anything else she'd seen so far — better, actually. Much better. Orderly, thriving. Beautiful, gold embossed buildings with gleaming glass windows. Everything polished.

"What is this place?" John swiveled his head around.

"Egypt." The General coughed his smoker's cough.

"It looks fantastic," Bob said.

"It is now. In the old days? Not so much. A long time ago, the democratically elected government of Egypt was toppled through covert operations."

"Who did it?" Alice asked. "Was it the Swedes?"

"No. It was the United States of America."

"Really?" Alice couldn't believe it. First the rest of the world *existed*, now this.

"Good ol' USA was quite the pisser before the floods. "Nothing but civil war in these parts for decades afterward. Soon the caliphate took over. For the first ten or twenty years, a lot of slaughter. Then, in a real reversal, they got great at public administration."

"Now it looks like wealthy-person heaven," John's mom said.

"America was involved with the rest of the world? When was this?" Alice asked.

"Sure was," the General responded. "Do you remember how America used to be, Bob? In the old days? Before the Flood?"

"I don't. Should I? I was seventeen. Senior year of high school."

Sitting at home alone. Were his parents rotting in the water?

Did they die on impact, or were they fighting for their lives like he was?

Am I an orphan?

Oh God, I'm an orphan!

Sleeping in the wreckage of their house alone, damp with the floodwater.

Drinking the tap water and shitting into their nonfunctional toilet for days.

The smell of rotting, the ironing board on the kitchen island.

Nobody coming to check on him.

Nobody coming to save his life.

Running into his parents a week later in the Wawa.

They were fine.

He wasn't.

Where had they been?

Oh Bobby, we were so worried about you!

Her fake voice for neighbors and extended family.

They didn't come back for him.

He saw it in her eyes.

Were they hiding from him?

He was in the *goddamned house*—!

"Nah, I don't have too many memories about it," Bob lied. "I was pretty far inland. Then I went to college on a post-Flood scholarship they gave to everybody in the Flood areas."

"How about you, Alice?" John's mom asked. "You must have been just a little baby."

"She's not *that* young," Bob frowned.

"Look at her," John's mom said. "Not a line on her face! She's still a child."

Bob's face reddened.

"I don't remember the Flood," Alice said. "I think I laughed when I learned about it. I didn't understand then, and I still don't now. My mom said we used to be a forty-five-minute drive from the ocean. Then one day it was right outside the door. Why did it happen, anyway? Was it climate change? But everybody knew about climate change. Why didn't they do anything to stop it?"

"It's not so easy," Bob argued. "You have to talk about things. It's political."

"What's political about dying in a flood?" Alice asked.

"Everything," the General said. "In the decades leading up to the Flood, a devastating change in Earth's climate was the topic *du jour*. Humans were always debating. Was it getting hotter out, or was that summer rolling around again? If it *was* hotter, was it toxic chemicals' fault, or was it the earth doing its normal thing? Nobody knew."

"We had a flooding problem in our village once," John said, "So the council got together, brainstormed some possibilities, put it to a vote, and then we all pooled our money to finance the winning option. Did you do that in Nu Jersey?"

"No, we didn't," Bob said. "That would never work. That's the dumbest thing I've ever heard. We're not communists. We just kept funding research and then arguing against it. It's called democracy. Read about it. Anyway, it was just a freak accidental tsunami. There's nothing you can do about that."

"Overnight, all at once, the oceans rose up over the land," Alice said. "That's what they told us in history class."

"In one day, the rest of the world was gone," Bob added.

"Almost everything went underwater," Ghost Tom recalled. "Only some of it came back. Everything except the East Coast — all gone overnight."

"Or at least, that's what they wanted you to believe," the General said.

"It didn't affect California right away," Ghost Tom said.

"Yes, it did," Bob argued.

"What do you mean, that's what they want us to believe?" Alice asked over the two men.

"No, it didn't," Ghost Tom snapped.

"Well, I heard it did!" Bob snapped back.

"It didn't affect the rest of the world," John's mom answered Alice, rolling her eyes. "We were fine. There was a saying I heard as a child: 'When the United States gets a sniffle, Sierra Leone gets the flu.' But we didn't get the flu that time. Nothing happened in Sierra Leone. Or anywhere else."

"The Flood didn't happen because of climate change. It was manufactured," the General said. "And the devastation you think happened all over the world? It didn't."

"It didn't even happen in the rest of America," John's mom added. "Only the northeast corridor. Slight effect on Nu York, most of the damage in Nu Jersey."

Bob, Alice, and Ghost Tom fell silent.

THE VAN SPUTTERED TO A STOP.

"Here we are!" the General announced. "New Kabul, Afghanistan."

They stopped at the border between a country called Iran and another called Afghanistan. Two cheerful guards chatted with the General for a few minutes, then scanned all their fingerprints and retinas and waved them through with less of a procedure than crossing the eastern seaboard levee. Very efficient.

They carried on into New Kabul, discussing as much, when the van sputtered to a stop again.

"What are you stopping for?" Bob asked. "Are you going to let us eat outside the van and use a real bathroom for once, like humans?"

The General didn't respond, just hit the ignition button over and over again. He tried holding it down. He hit it with his palm. He whispered something to it. Alice thought he might cry.

"She—" the General said. He stopped, and swallowed hard. His eyes were struck with grief. "The old girl's gone," he said. He stroked her dashboard.

The hood of the van burst into flames.

"Get out. Everybody out. Out now!" the General said. "Here, Bob, take our grain—"

They piled out of the van, snatched up what they could, and ran a short distance away. A cloud of black smoke gathered above and wafted over to hang in the air above them.

"I'll say a few words," the General said. Bob looked at him blankly.

"Bow your heads!" He snarled.

They all bowed their heads.

"She was a good van for sixteen years. In fact, if somebody hadn't loaded her supplementary tanks with a dirty, biodiesel-tainted hydrogen fuel, she'd still be alive today." The general kicked Bob in the shin.

Bob grunted his opposition to the violence. He didn't dare open his eyes.

The van exploded.

"Oof—" Something hit Bob in his back, and he fell to the ground.

"That's my girl!" The general cackled, stooping to pick up the rearview mirror-turned-projectile. "Always done me proud. We'll continue on foot. *Fok voort.*"

Everybody opened their eyes and raised their heads. "Bob, what are you doing down there?" John's mom clicked her tongue in disgust. "You're a real slacker."

They gathered what they could and started off on foot.

"HERE WE ARE AT LAST," The General said. "Dharamsala." A cluster of men dressed in maroon robes passed them on the road. Their uniform crew appraised Bob's motley crew.

One of them nodded. "General," he said.

"Do you know him?" Ghost Tom asked.

"Sure, we've met," the General said.

"I can't believe we made it!" Alice exclaimed.

"Hooray!" John cheered.

"What now? What are these?" Bob dropped the compass to gesture at the monks, and it dangled around his neck. He hadn't understood its purpose the whole time — spinning around crazily, telling him nothing by way of meaningful, headset-style information. Who cared which way was north? How would they ever know to turn left or right?

"Those are called monks. They follow a religion called Buddhism. I'd stand around and lecture more, but we've got to get to safety before we all get murdered."

"Where to? Maybe I can find it on the map." Bob yanked on another lanyard around his neck, this one connected to a series of maps.

"No, I don't think so," the General said. "Not on that map, anyway. It's out there." He pointed into the distance at a row of craggy, snow-covered peaks. "The Himalayan mountain range. We're going to need gear. And sherpas."

"Hoo boy," Ghost Tom sighed. "This road trip sucks."

"What else do you have to do?" Bob asked. "You're dead."

"Ouch," Ghost Tom said. "Rub it in, why don't you?"

"First things first: We need to trade our rolling suitcases for backpacks," the General said.

"Oh!" Alice said.

"Have you heard of them?" John's mom said. "Backpacks?"

"Sure," Alice said. "I had a backpack once."

THE SHINY NEW BACKPACK, black and red, on her bedside table: a gift from Alice's dad, left for her to find after the doctor's visit: vaccinations, standard stuff before she could start school.

The next day, her mom. At the kitchen table. Staring, staring. Out the window, into the parking lot in front of their condo.

"Where's Dad?"

"He hung himself."

No introduction and no conclusion, no interpretation and no tears. Her mom didn't cry, so Alice didn't either. Later on in life, when Alice tried to remember her dad, she couldn't even see his face.

But she could remember the backpack.

So crisp and clean, there in her room, on her bed nestled in the soft, billowy blankets that were typical before pre-flood fabrics were removed. It was such a sunny day, there were sunny days before the Flood. One sharp sunbeam hitting the backpack, shiny zipper, tassle with a pom-pom.

The last sunny day.

Then the Flood.

School didn't start on time.

And the backpack wasn't waterproof, so they had to throw it away.

When school finally did start, it wasn't as good as Alice had always imagined. She never said so to anybody.

"THESE HOTELS SUCK," Bob whined at breakfast, wrapped in five yak-hair blankets. "They don't even have heat. These blankets are itchy. We're going to die of cold up here. I can't walk anymore, Alice. I can't breathe, I can't think. I'm freaking out."

"Don't worry, Bob. I'm sure we're almost there." Alice sipped her yak-butter tea and enjoyed the Himalayan view.

"You don't seem to mind this," Bob snapped.

"I can't breathe up here either, but I don't mind walking every day. Oh, sure, the first few days were a struggle, but after a while the indentation from my flood-safety ankle cuff went away. And, you know, I could get used to this unrestricted outdoor activity...I don't even really miss my headset anymore."

"You're the only one." Bob shivered and huddled into his blankets.

The General approached their table and set down his new and improved smoking pipe. They were getting bigger and more elaborate as the trip progressed.

"We don't have much further to go. Teng Teng! Bring the gear." Their new sherpa Teng Teng heaved five multi-pronged killing devices onto the table with a loud *clang*. *Sherpa* was Himalayan for *assistant*.

"They're crampons, Bob." The General looked at Bob like it was impossible he'd never heard of crap-ons. "Put them on over your shoes. We need them to continue our journey."

John and his mom, Alice, the General, and Teng Teng slipped on their crap-ons. Bob struggled and pulled on the end of one until he nearly passed out. He stopped to rest. John and his mom were doing everything minus the usual number of hands like a couple of awful show-offs as usual, making him look stupid and clumsy.

"I don't know what the hell we're going to do with these." Bob edged forward, clinking with each step. "I can barely walk."

When they were all geared up, the General led the group, a five-person, ten-legged clanging mess, plus one apparition, to the back of the house. Teng Teng pulled on a tassled-rope until a giant velvet curtain slid aside, and revealed an ornately carved door twice Bob's size.

There was an image on the door — one of those Buddhist or Hindu or Christian gods, Bob couldn't remember which it was around here, from a tapestry in the guesthouse. The General had named the whole lot of them off at breakfast. This one was an angry lady with lots of arms spinning around, heads on a necklace around her neck. She was standing on skulls.

Bob had a moment to picture the woman standing on his skull, whirring her hundreds of arms around, before the door was jerked open as though someone had been standing on the other side of it, waiting for a knock.

Bob squealed.

Someone *had* been standing on the other side of it waiting for a knock.

It was a monk.

"Inside," the General said. They all clanged in. The General took a torch from the monk and lit another with it, passing it to Teng Teng.

Bob couldn't see much inside, even with the torchlight. They were gathered on a makeshift wooden platform. *How* makeshift, he didn't know, but when John's mom shifted her weight, the platform let out an ominous creak. Ghost Tom floated above them. At least one of their party weighed nothing.

Teng Teng and the monk began the laborious work of lowering the platform by pulling on ropes from above. The monk on the left heaved slower than Teng Teng, and the platform tilted. Bob gasped and seized Alice's arm. She clung to him, too, just as afraid as he was. *I love you*, he wanted to say just then, his heart beating so hard it might have been a health problem.

"Where are we going now?" Bob was on the verge of tears.

"Down into the mountain," the General said. "And then we have a short hike to drop off John's mother. Believe me, I would leave you here if I could, in this guesthouse, and I want to be clear when I say *you* specifically, Bob, but it's too risky for us to split up now. We might die on this platform, but then again, maybe we won't. On the other hand, if the Illuminati catch up to us, chance of death is a hundred percent."

IT SEEMED LIKE A FLOOD-WEEK, the longest week of anybody's life, before the platform hit the ground with a *thunk*. The General, Teng Teng, and the monk opened a set of doors and stepped out onto a shimmering glacier that filled the cave. Bob followed Alice, both inching along in their crampons, with John and his mother behind them. Ghost Tom brought up the rear from diagonally above and behind.

"What now?" Bob tottered toward the edge, thrown off balance by the darkness and his own shaking legs. Teng Teng yanked first Bob and then Alice back by their climbing harnesses.

"Elevator service is over. Now we go down," the General said. "Teng Teng, let's get the ropes on 'em."

The General and Teng Teng laced everyone's harnesses with rope that didn't look thick enough to hold a human being of any size.

"Could I have an extra rope?" Bob asked. Teng Teng didn't respond.

They journeyed into the chasm, down and down, hitting exhaustion after every few moments, in Bob's case. It could have been a week for all he knew. The sherpa and the General dragged them on.

When they couldn't use their limbs any longer, they napped in hammocks hooked into the wall atop small ledges. While descending on what could have been the seventh or seventieth day, Bob screamed in a higher register than was culturally appropriate for men.

"*What*?" the General snapped. "What is it?"

"I hit the ground," Bob said.

Teng Teng landed next and unloaded the entire party's gear from his back. John and his mother landed minutes later.

Even in the dim light, it was obvious John had been crying. *Must be nice to love your mother.*

"I'm sorry to say this," the General said, "but we need to say our farewells."

A rumbling sound emerged from the torch-lit darkness. Peering in the sickly, faint-green light of the cave, Bob made out the edges of an enormous metal door.

The terrible grinding sound was coming from the other side.

The goddess stepping on the skulls.

The hair on Bob's neck stood up. He tasted metal in his mouth.

The door opened. A man in a white lab coat emerged. Bob clutched at Alice's hand.

John and his mom hugged each other.

"I don't want to leave you, Mama," John said.

I know, baby. You've always been so brave and so cheerful, even though most of the time you're surrounded by complete assholes. Assholes like these." John's mom gestured at Bob and the others. "I couldn't be prouder of you. I don't know when we are going to see each other again, but we have an important job to do. And we're the only people on this stupid planet who can do it. We can and we *will*. Because that's the stuff we're made of. I love you, John."

"I thought he had siblings," Bob whispered to Alice. "What about them?"

"Shush!" Alice hissed back. She was so dismissive.

"I love you, Mama. I'm going to make you proud."

"You already have, just by being my son." Bob rolled his eyes so that Alice could see how unaffected he was, but then an unwanted tear spilled out. He brushed it away as quick as possible before anybody could see.

The man in the lab coat led John's mom inside. The metal door closed, but they could still hear the grinding noise.

John wiped away his tears with his stump. Alice put her arm around him. Bob had cried a tear too, where was she then?

"We'd better go," the General said. "Teng Teng!" He pointed at their bags, and Teng Teng leapt to his feet to strap the baggage of the entire party onto his body again. The rest of them picked up their ropes.

"We have to climb back up?" Bob asked. "You've got to be kidding me. Leave me here to die *too*!"

"Bob," Alice barked, like a rabid dog, and looking pointedly at John, "*nobody* is dying here."

"We're not climbing back up, Bob," the General said. He walked ahead a few paces and dug in the snow bank. "Teng Teng, it's not here."

Teng Teng took the General's trowel, walked four paces left, and dug a small hole in the snow. Then he removed an axe from his utility belt and hammered at the ice repeatedly until they all heard a *clank* that shook the cave walls.

"Aha," The General said. "There you are." He joined Teng Teng, and yanked up a lever. "Like I was saying, we're not going up, Bob. We're going down. Close your eyes, everybody."

Bob didn't close his eyes fast enough. The wall of ice and snow in front of them blasted away, sunshine blinding him. His stomach acid hurtled up his esophagus and exploded out of the cave, off the now-exposed ledge, and fifteen thousand feet straight down.

27

MY CAMEL IS A MESS

"My camel is a mess," Bob groaned. "And he smells like he's dying on the inside." Bob's camel slowed. "Whoa!" He yelled, but the camel had its own ideas, and the beast sank to its knees. Bob's hands gave out — they'd been clutching the sun-cracked edges of the saddle for hours — and he tumbled off into the sand. It clung to his sweaty face.

"I hate Rajasthan," he said. "I hate the desert." Bob's voice was nearing his hysteria pitch. He rolled onto his back and lay where he'd fallen.

His camel belched into the searing air.

"Is anybody else smelling this? It's worse than the decaying dolphins of the afterflood," he called out again.

Alice and her camel stopped short of his head in the sand.

"I love mine," Alice said. "I'm calling him Lumpy. He's the best camel anybody could have. Aren't you, Lumpy? When you squoosh at his head with your hands, it feels like his brain." Alice ignored Bob's sharp glare, and kneaded her camel's fleshy scalp. It wasn't clear if the dromedary appreciated it or not, but unlike Bob, she hadn't been thrown from the saddle yet.

"Click click tsk click." The camel whisperer hit Bob's camel with a stick and heaved Bob to his feet, shouting, *"Apane oont par vaapas jao, tum moorkh!"* [1]

Bob's camel stood up. The protest had ended.

The camel whisperer reached under Bob's crumbling shoe to boost him back on his camel. Nobody's floodproof clothes were holding up well in the desert.

"What's he saying?"

"He says Bob's the best camel jockey he's seen in a long, long time." The General trotted up, reached out a hand to steady Bob, righting him on his camel before he could tumble back onto the sands of the Great Thar Desert. When Bob was as secure as could be under the circumstances, the General pulled an extensive pipe out of the bright orange turban he'd taken to wearing and struck a match on his boot.

"This camel is tearing me in half," Alice said. "I think this is the most painful form of transportation I've ever experienced." Despite the aches and pains of travel, it was still better than being home, cuffed and cubed at work.

"Travelling with you losers is the most painful form of transportation *I've* ever experienced," Ghost Tom announced. He'd taken to materializing either on top of their cargo camel or in the saddle behind Alice, which always made her jump, as now.

"Jeez, Tom, I wish you'd stop doing that," Alice said. "And what's with all the complaints? You don't even have to be here!"

"I shouldn't have to be here, either!" Bob exclaimed. "I should be in my office in Nu Jersey, working in a safe, climate-controlled building. Instead I'm burning alive in this hellhole on some hateful camel on yet another continent where planes don't even work." Alice thought Bob might pass out after his monologue. He was panting hard. The desert really didn't agree with him.

"Planes aren't working on any continent right now. Camels might be painful but they're all we've got. We can't walk the desert," the General grunted, puffing on his pipe and scanning the cloudless horizon. "You'd never make it."

"I'm not going to make it with a camel that sits down every few minutes," Bob said. Alice privately agreed but didn't want to encourage him, so she kept her mouth shut.

"A camel that sits down every few minutes is still doing all the work." The General pointed to Bob and said to their camel whisperer, "*Ganje aadamee jal raha hai.*"[2] The camel whisperer laughed and clucked. Bob's camel stopped in response, and the man climbed its side to wrap a bright orange cloth around Bob's burning scalp.

"Nice hat!" John trotted up beside Bob as though he'd been riding camels all his life, reins in one hand, relaxed. Bob scowled.

"John, you're a natural on camels," Alice said. He looked better than in the early days since they'd left his mom in the Himalayas.

The General moved ahead a few paces. Alice and Lumpy caught up to him around a dune bend, where he paused among the ripples in the sand. She followed his line of sight: Up a distant hill, a tiny hut. The General clicked at his camel to sit down and alighted. Alice tried to do the same, but Lumpy didn't appear to understand her. The camel whisperer rode up beside her and clicked, and Lumpy sat right down.

"I want to learn to speak camel," Alice said. "I can barely walk, though. I don't know if I have a future in camel transit."

"You'll get used to it," the General assured her.

"I don't think so."

"Whether you think so or not, you're right either way," the General said.

The General roped the camels' legs so their transport method could graze without escaping. He didn't wait for the others to catch up. He took off toward the shelter. Behind him, Alice shuffle-limped in pursuit.

"What is this thing?" The hut had a malformed mushroom on top — an advertisement?

"Alice, what do you know about Jesus Christ?"

Alice was thrown. It wasn't the usual corporate small talk. "Uh, not much. My mom said he was big in the eighties."

"Well, there's some interesting stuff about him in the Bible. Where people drank his blood."

Alice thought back to her interaction with Jalia. Remembering the truth about Tampa.

What was it?

My blood.

"Yuck." Alice bluffed, though she'd swallowed a colleague's blood in the not-so-distant past. "Why would anybody do that?" Maybe Jesus put his blood in a capsule too and didn't mention what it was until afterwards. That was a pretty effective move as far as Alice was concerned.

"Well, why does anybody try anything? Maybe they didn't have much to lose. Maybe they did it simply because he asked them to. Maybe they knew they were ready for a change. And it did change them. It changed the way they thought, which, in a way, is the biggest change of all."

"How?"

"John's blood is pure DMT, through and through — the same biochemical composition as the blood of Jesus Christ."

"What's DMT?"

"Di-methyl-tryptamine. The spirit molecule."

Every single thing the General said sparked more and more questions. Alice took a break when they got to the hut. They entered the hut through a short, narrow doorway. In the central space was a small shelf, shaped out of the dirt itself. Alice poked at a broom leaning against the wall. Inside the alcove in the ledge, a small bottle.

"What did we come here for?" She asked.

"This." The General lifted up the bottle, dark and murky, and blew a layer of dust off of it. "It's difficult to explain what it is."

"I'm pretty bright," Alice insisted. "In the past few months, I've gone from burying my mom to conducting headset interviews. It wasn't easy, but I did it. Then I became the assistant of a key executive and now I'm travelling the desert on camelback. I'd say I catch on to things quickly."

"You do," the General conceded. "Okay, have a seat."

Alice brushed the sand on the floor aside to reveal more sand and sat down. The General crouched next to her and pulled his pipe back out of his turban. "So you don't know much about Jesus. Do you know about the Bible?"

"Yeah, sure."

"Did you ever read it?"

"Nah. We didn't really have books in America after the Flood. My mom wasn't religious."

"What about your dad?"

"He was dead."

"Did he die in the Flood?" The General asked.

"Uh, no. He hung himself the year before."

"Oh."

"Mom always said he didn't like hard work, and he probably sensed some was coming." Alice shrugged. The loss didn't bother her anymore.

"I see." The General took a long pause before speaking again. "Well, the Bible was a religious book full of old folklore people told to each other in the Middle East."

"What's folklore mean?" Alice asked.

"Uh, stories," the General said. "It means stories that might be kinda true. One of the passages of the Bible reads as follows: 'In the beginning was the Word, and the Word was with God, and the Word was God.' Do you know what that word was?"

Alice hated it when people asked questions they already knew the answer to. It was one of her biggest pet peeves.

"No," she said.

The General scratched in the sand with his pipe.

A C T G

"ACT-GUH," Alice read. "DNA."

"Yes. DNA is the Word. As we know, the information in DNA is stored as a code, made up of four chemical bases — A, C, T, and G. The order of these bases determines the information for building and maintaining an organism, the way letters of the alphabet appear in a certain order to create words and sentences," the General explained.

"Everything is made of DNA." Alice thought back to her high school biology class to retrieve any other relevant information about DNA and genetics. The only word she could recall was *Mitochondria*. And she couldn't even remember what that was.

"Right." The General struck a match on the sole of his boot and lit his pipe. "But who made DNA?"

"I dunno." Alice traced the letters with her finger. "Doesn't it make itself? There's RNA, which is like DNA, but it builds things, I think. It builds itself."

"Yes, true. DNA is self-replicating." The General tamped out a small fire in his beard from a stray pipe spark. "But it had to start somewhere, didn't it?"

Alice drew a spiral in the sand. "I think it was a meteorite. I remember learning about it in school."

"Yes. It did come from space. But it's more complicated. I need you to suspend your disbelief. Usually when people hear this story they're on psychedelic mushrooms. So it's easier to accept."

Alice cleared her throat. "I don't know what psychedelic mushrooms are, but I think I'm pretty accepting of new things. I'm being haunted by my mom's ghost. Now she's trapped in a jar that rains all on its own for no apparent reason. My boss is the head of a secret society. Last week I went to South Africa, which was not destroyed in the Flood, even though that's what people have been telling me my whole life. Turns out it may only have happened in America. Or just in Nu Jersey. I bailed my boss out of jail because he went nuts after he drank my friend's blood. Swedes exist. And they're trying to kill us. What do you think I'm going to have trouble accepting, exactly?"

John poked his head into the hut with Bob in tow. "Knock knock!" Bob's turban was soaked with sweat.

"Come on in here, you two!" The General waved them in.

"Lounging about, I see." Bob said, and threw himself down on the ground in a huff, but he was too overheated to sustain a forceful expression of anger.

Ghost Tom materialized near the ceiling. It was so cramped he couldn't hover at ground level without occupying one of their bodies to a degree.

"You all smell like camel," he called down.

"At least we can smell." Bob swiped at a ghostly foot.

"Hey!" Alice snapped. "Don't talk to Tom like that, and bisect his apparition. You can't blame him for his own death, anyway. It was a murder."

Bob mumbled something toward the hut wall. Alice decided to consider it an apology.

"This is a tiny hut." John tapped on the glass jar. The General looked scared for a moment in a way Alice hadn't seen before. He picked up the glass jar, then set it back down. He looked pained. Then he continued.

"Yes, never forget the three Ts of safety," he said. "Tin foil, tunnels, tiny huts. These are the places where it's safe to communicate openly from now on. John, I was just telling Alice about your blood. And the blood of Jesus Christ."

"Oh, yeah," John said. "Samesies." He shrugged.

Bob pointed at John's stump. "You think this guy is a Jesus? You must have gotten heatstroke out there. How's he going to preach like that, *disabled*? Heal the sick, or whatever Jesus did that was so great. Don't you think if he had magic healing powers, he'd still have a hand?"

Alice elbowed Bob sharply. "Really, Bob? That's so rude."

"I don't mind," John said. "I'm not sensitive about it, and I don't consider myself disabled. My blood has the same biochemical profile as another guy from thousands of years ago. He wasn't magic, and I'm not either. We're just different. And we don't regrow hands. That's not really how life works anyway. Unless you're a starfish. Then you can. But I'm a human, and I do know one thing. Jesus could be easily weaponized. And so can I," John said. "And that's a big problem."

"Unless we can stop it," the General said. "As I was saying. In the beginning was the Word."

"What's the word?" Tom's ghost called down.

"That Word was A-C-T-G. And the Word was in everything, and it *was* everything. And when there is a critical mass of it, and human brains hit the right frequency, DNA will *activate*. It's all in the Dogon pamphlet."

"Here we go again with that dumb pamphlet," Bob said.

The General ignored him. "That's why Market, Research, Incorporated was created. To move humans toward the right frequency, through the headsets, through the mindscaping surveys, and then, with the biocomputer, activate their collective DNA."

"What will happen?" Alice drew a double helix in the dirt around the A-C-T-G. At least she knew what DNA looked like.

"Humans will ascend from this dimension into the next." The General pointed at the bottom of the double helix and then at the top.

"What's in the next dimension?" Bob unwrapped the cloth of his turban and tried to rewind it, but it only became a loose collection of fabric heaped on his head. The General snatched it off and began rewrapping it correctly.

"Nobody knows. Our creators, maybe? Maybe it's heaven."

"Good luck," Ghost Tom snorted. "I think heaven's closed."

"Maybe it's *hell*," the General said. "We don't know. But we do think this is the purpose of human civilization. If there is somebody on the other side, then whoever they are, they've been cultivating us for this, for hundreds of thousands of years — grooming us to think in a certain way, pruning us to hit the right population and collective thought frequency to activate our DNA and turn it into a gateway."

"Pruning us? We aren't a plant. We're people!" Bob protested. Ghost Tom flitted around his newly turbaned head.

Alice considered John's stump, Jalia's missing leg. What was her role in all this, anyway? And what was up with the ghosts? "Is that why Tom and my mom can't get into the light?" She asked.

The General nodded. "Why ghosts are here, why planes are

falling out of the sky, why our memories are failing. The electromagnetic field of the earth is weakening at an accelerated rate, and it isn't an accident. It's being done on purpose."

"By who?" Bob asked.

"Your boss, for one."

"Oh, so it's *political*," Bob groaned. "I knew it."

"My dad's behind this," Ghost Tom chimed in. "All of it. And I know this much: he's not good. The opposite, actually. He's super evil."

The camel whisperer poked his head in.

"*Prabuddh aa rahe hain!*"[3]

The General stood up. "We'll continue this another time."

The group filed out of the hut and headed back toward the camels.

"John? Did you always know you were the next Jesus?" Alice asked quietly as they walked.

"A little bit, sure I did," he beamed. "My mama always said I was special."

"Everybody's mother says that," Bob sneered. Based on his tone, Alice wasn't so sure.

———————

ALICE WAS the last to mount her camel when a man ran up from behind, shouting. Alice tensed and looked at the camel whisperer to see whether he would click the camels into action, but he and the General stood calmly waiting until the man caught his breath. He spoke in a hushed foreign language to the General, who reported to the group.

"Don't worry, he's a friend. Part of the International Rosicrucian Network."

"Is that Republican or Democrat?" Bob asked.

Alice squeezed Lumpy's head to calm herself. She had a high threshold for Bob's stupidity these days, but she was hitting a limit. The General gestured at Alice and the two men traded more phrases.

"Do you know him?" Alice asked.

"No," the General said. "But I knew his father. All the secret society membership is handed down from generation to generation."

"How?" Alice asked. "Like, just by talking?" She tried to recall what her mother had handed down to her. Some newsplastics. A condo.

"Sometimes by talking. By genetic legacy," the General explained. "From father to son to father to son. Just like the Illuminati. And the Rosicrucians. And the United States government."

"Not too much gender equity in this global plot," Alice mused. "Typical."

"If he knew you were coming back, where was he thirty minutes ago when we were in the shade?" Bob groaned. "It's *hot* out here."

The newcomer spoke and the General translated, "He says when the brain net is activated, we can talk to the whole universe by communicating through our DNA. In order for John — or for *anybody* to survive it, we're going to need this."

The medicine man's son held up the small glass receptacle. The General had forgotten it back in the hut. Its contents glittered in the blazing sun.

"Get that away from my face." Bob leaned so far back he tipped off his camel and landed in the sand for the second time that day. "I'm not drinking any mystery juice! You already put some of that wacky voodoo blood in me."

"*Dhanyavaad*,"[4] the General said, taking the glass bottle. Then their Rosicrucian ally pointed out beyond them, into the desert. The gang squinted out into the distance. He turned around, hopped on Bob's camel, and galloped off.

"Hey!" Bob shouted. "I was using that."

The camel whisperer dug Bob out of the sand and yanked him to his feet.

"Bob, did you see that?" Alice asked.

"What?"

"That man's tongue. It was split in two at the tip. Like a snake's."

"Oh, shit," the General said.

"What? What is it?" Alice asked.

"We just talked outside the tiny hut. No tunnel and no tin foil. They're gonna know. Shit, shit shit shit shit. *Shit!*"

"Who's gonna know?" Bob asked.

"Dad," Tom's ghost said. "And he's gonna kill all of you."

"We've got to get out of here," the General said. "Now."

A small row of dots appeared on the horizon.

---

1. Go back to your camel, you idiot! (Hindi)
2. Bald man is burning. (Hindi)
3. The illuminated ones are coming! (Hindi)
4. Thank you (Hindi)

28

ARE WE ALMOST THERE

"A re we almost there?" Bob poked his head outside the open train door, joining ten or twelve other heads watching India roll by outside.

Idiots. No regard for safety.

But he enjoyed the breeze on his face and kept it out there a little while. It was balmy, more like Nu Jersey weather. The sun was less harsh than it had been in the desert.

"It's tough to say," John called. "We're somewhere." He was playing some dumb game where you chased each other for no reason, as far as Bob could tell, with a plump little kid who was fawning over John just like everybody else — and also for no obvious reason.

John reached out and tapped the boy on the back with his stump. The boy burst into giggles and rushed after John, who darted to the other end of the train car. Bob might have wanted to play too, but they didn't invite him. He sulked at the door.

"We're somewhere," he repeated. "Great." He turned away from the greenery, the fields full of gobs and gobs of plants sweeping by. Unchecked and unsanitary. No carefully groomed fauxlowers. The place was a mess. Alice and the General were ignoring him too.

Bob shouted at them, "I don't get these tied-together cars all going to the same place. They're inefficient. We're so slow."

"It's called a train, you nitwit," the General barked. "This is how everybody gets around all over the world. They used to have them in Nu Jersey too, before the infrastructure advancements of the Post-Flood Agenda shut them down."

They were still fleeing alleged pursuers Bob had never actually seen. Alice said she saw the Illuminati on the horizon too, back in the desert, but she was a little too open to the power of suggestion.

"Give me a self-driving car any day," Bob grumbled.

"We're due to arrive in about an hour. Take it easy. Relax. Our next train down south won't leave for a day or two, so you'll get a break from the horrors of public transportation. We've got to stay put in Varanasi."

"Perfect," Bob said. "Maybe this so-called 'Varanasi' has discovered modern living." Bob turned back to the landscape. An elderly Indian woman hobbled through a field with a load of plants bigger than her strapped to her back. *Unbelievable!* He wanted to say to Alice, but she and the General couldn't get enough of each other.

Neglect. He was going to die of neglect in a country stuffed full of the most people he had ever seen in one spot. "Unbelievable," he murmured to nobody, except for five Indian men still standing in the open train door, pressed together to enjoy the view.

Relax. This, from the guy who had probably hallucinated being pursued by a volatile secret society. Bob stalked off to use the bathroom.

It was a hole in the train floor.

Appalling.

ALICE COULD TELL the General didn't want to talk much around Bob, or John, but she had a sneaking suspicion he might cough up some more details if she could just get him alone.

Once they were both occupied elsewhere on the train, she

plopped herself down to start the interrogation. She made a T with her hands, and the General pulled a couple of pieces of tin foil from his pocket. They unfurled and then re-crumpled the shiny material around their heads. The other passengers mostly ignored them. They were so accepting. In the USA, if your monoculous was bent the wrong way you'd get a talking to, or at least a stern look.

"What was in the bottle?"

Alice got right to the point. She didn't have to call on her intimidation tactics, which was good, because she didn't have any. The General relented immediately.

"Alice, have you heard Bob talk about a man named Eric Smith?" The General asked.

"Oh, only every single day," Alice said. "Bob hates him." Alice studied the General. Bob had said he was working for Eric, but that didn't seem so true anymore.

"Okay." The General sighed. "And did you read the Dogon pamphlet?"

"Yes."

"Good. And you already know about the Project."

"Right. Do the opposite of the pamphlet instructions. Liquify people and the planet, use their DNA to escape."

"Once they've created the biocomputer, it's Eric's job to annihilate the northeastern United States and incite the collective frequency through civil war. That's already under way — but to finish the job, he also needs *this*." The General patted the bottle in his pocket.

"What is it?" Alice asked. "What's in the bottle?"

"It's a key ingredient for the biocomputer — the final phase of the Project."

"What's a biocomputer again?"

"It's the computer Eric is building. It's, ah. Well, it's made out of John."

"*What*?" Alice's reaction escaped from her mouth, too loud, shock and recognition coursing through her all at once. She'd forgotten. Somehow she'd forgotten the worst thing she'd ever seen. It all came rushing back now. First the fingertip gone. Then the whole hand. The wires. The green glow. That's why they were dismembering him. He wasn't being hooked up to the computer. He *was* the computer.

"That's where John's hand went, I'm sure, though I haven't seen it for myself. But I saw the sketches. Years ago." The General shook his head as though banishing an unwanted memory.

"They cut off John's hand. I saw it. I'd forgotten. I don't know how I could forget something like that." Alice stood up. She looked for John, to remember he was okay. For now. Alive. Had most of his limbs. "What does the computer do?" He was being chased by a toddler at the other end of the train car. She sat back down.

"The biocomputer harnesses the biomass, the energy and the frequency of everybody on earth. And then it activates the portal. They're using John's mom's at the station in the Himalayas, and they'll use John in Nu Jersey."

"Why are you — *we* letting this happen?"

"We don't have a choice right now." The General looked around.

"Why not? I can't believe this." Alice was flush with rage. And shame. "Of course we have a choice."

"John is going to be exposed to a lot of radiation when he — when the biocomputer — is activated. That's why we had to get this. Eric's orders." The General patted the glass bottle in his pocket. "Gold, frankincense, myrrh, potassium iodide, succinic acid, Baltic amber, *Laminaria and Saccharina, Fucus, Sargassum muticum*—"

"What's it for?"

"When the biocomputer is activated, and the biomass ignites, according to Dogon legend, it creates a chain reaction in the person...the *people*, I mean—oh, never mind all that. It causes fusion. It turns him into a nuclear weapon. That'll kill him. Unless he drinks this. If John drinks the contents of this bottle, it'll protect his body from the radiation. Keeps him alive longer, until the process is complete. Otherwise he'll die immediately."

"Does it work?"

"Well, we're not entirely sure. This whole thing is one big experiment, isn't it? Eric needs John to drink this potion so he can survive the biomass activation. And I need you to make sure that when the time comes, John doesn't."

"But that will kill him." Wasn't he working for Eric?

"Listen, if John stays alive long enough after the biomass is activated, and our DNA *does* become a portal, and the Swedes *do* ascend to the next dimension, everybody left behind will be torn apart."

"Whose side are you on? How do I know you're not a Swede?" Whose side was anybody on? Maybe there weren't even any sides.

"The earth will be decimated. It's us or him, and I don't mean just you or me. I'm on the side trying to save the planet from total annihilation, Alice, and I need you to get on it."

The General rose and stalked off toward the front of the train.

"There's got to be another way," she called after him, but he didn't look back. John tottered up to Alice with a toddler attached to his leg. "Look at me, Alice! I'm caught." The child giggled.

"I see." Alice forced a smile, trapped tears burning in her eyes.

"WE'RE HERE," the General said. Alice didn't know how much time had passed since she'd learned she was going to be an accessory to murder. Two hours? Four? Without her headset to constantly advertise time, she lost track of the when. The clickety-clack of the train on its tracks was slowing, the farmlands outside replaced by building after building, traffic, crowds of people.

"Let's circle up, everybody." The General ushered the group into a huddle in the middle of the train car. "Keep alert now. We're not out of the woods yet. It's a figure of speech that means *not safe*."

Bob raised his hand. "Is it because woods are deadly?"

"No," the General said. "Woods are not inherently deadly."

"Are you sure?" Bob asked.

"But we do actually seem to be out of the woods," Alice said.

"We're in Varanasi," the General said. "It's a pilgrimage destination for Indian people because of its location next to the Ganges River, which is a sacred site for Hindus. That's a religion, Bob and

Alice. We're going to head to the tourist area and try to blend in for a couple of days. Stay close and stick together, got it?"

Everybody nodded.

BOB NEEDED a break from group living. Alice was always with the General. John was always playing with children. Rather than getting ignored as usual or sitting around staring at Ghost Tom's ghastly poisoned face, Bob decided to venture down by the *Ghats* — so-called holy steps that led to the so-called holy river, according to the General. He'd reluctantly agreed to let Bob go out by himself while the others stayed in and played cards at the guesthouse. Bob wasn't a team player and he'd be damned if he started now.

Bob hated being so close to a body of water, but he snuck a peak at it anyway. What was so holy about it? Bob couldn't tell. Over there, some people were doing their laundry in it. And down the way a little bit, some moms were dipping their children in it. What were the magical properties?

And what was holiness, anyway?

He glanced at the oily water, rainbow colored in patches on the surface, and saw something floating. Pretty big. Was it...vaguely human-shaped? Bob wasn't the only one who had noticed — a small crowd gathered.

It wasn't vaguely human-shaped. It *was* a human.

Floating, lifeless. He remembered scrambling around in his brain for a wisp of belief system when he had thought his parents were dead, but there had been nothing in there to think or do.

Bob's stomach churned. His heart pounded. It was terrifying. Why? What could this body possibly do to him? One of the bystanders poked at the corpse with a stick. They must have never seen a dead body before, either.

The corpse rose out of the water.

Bob gasped and stumbled backward.

It was a horror — gaunt and starved, missing teeth, wearing

nothing more than rags. This man or woman was *definitely* undead. It was the next phase in the end times.

It spoke.

Bob couldn't understand what it was saying. It didn't speak English. Typical.

"What's happening?" Bob shouted at the man who held the life-bringing stick.

"Oh, that's just Akshay. He's our local drunk. We all know him. See him around from time to time. Today he has decided to lie in the holy river until he dies, so he can go right to heaven."

"What are the other people saying?" Bob asked as the crowd's voices rose around them.

"They are trying to lure him out."

"What's he saying?"

"He says no. Let's watch."

After a few moments, Akshay emerged.

"They promised to buy him a lemon water. He decided as long as they uphold the promise, he will go on living," the stick-holder explained.

Bob wanted a lemon water too. The excitement had really upped his heart rate. He turned to the crowd to request one when a woman screamed.

What now?

The woman was pointing at the surface of the river. One fish bobbed to the surface. Then another. And another. Up bobbed a dolphin. All dead. The river creatures were dying.

The mass extinction of the water animals had arrived in India, just as it had come to Nu Jersey's coasts and rivers in the days before the Flood.

We may as well all get in the water and lie down.

Another flood was on its way. Bob climbed the *Ghats* to go find the others.

29

THE GANG SAT OUTSIDE

The gang sat outside the gateway to the Igatpuri International Vipassana Meditation Center. Bob refused to enter.

"The name is too long," Bob said. "It's untrustworthy."

The General sighed. "First of all, it's a nice place to hide from a plethora of attackers."

"This arch is too involved," Bob went on.

"Oh, I don't know, Bob. I like it," John said.

Alice balanced on the curb, and flapped the bottom of her new cloth tunic in the breeze. It caught a little lift, and blew this way and that. She wasn't about to get involved in this battle.

"You *would*," Bob grumbled. "I don't understand why we all have to do this weirdo Rama-krishna-ha-na-ha-ha-ma-pa mumbo jumbo. Another flood is coming!"

"Secondly," the General said, "Pretending to stage another flood is just an intimidation tactic. They're trying to flush us out. But they don't have the guts to follow through. They'd never do anything to jeopardize John's life."

"Except steal all his body parts," Alice interjected.

The General ignored her. "Thirdly, this isn't *mumbo jumbo*. It's meditation. We could all use some of that — especially you. You're a mess. We can't separate. We have no choice. We all go."

"I don't want to meditate," Bob whined. "It freaks me out." He raked his hands back and forth on his scalp and resettled himself into his protest spot on the bench.

John and Alice gave each other a look that said, we're-going-to-be-here-for-a-while, time-for-a-snack, and sat down on the curb to share a samosa.

"So just sit there and think your ridiculous thoughts and keep your dumb mouth shut. It *looks* the *same*." The General chopped the air with his hand so hard to prove his point that he lost hold of his latest pipe, a purple glass spiral. It flew into the bushes. "Now look," he said. He stalked off to retrieve it.

"Why do we have to do this, anyway?" Bob moaned.

"Because John has to, and we're supporting him," Alice said.

"Why does John have to do this?" Bob groaned.

"Yes," John said. "Why does John have to do this?"

"Brain wave training," the General said, returning with his purple pipe in hand and some shrub bits in his beard. "Bob, you don't have to worry about it. I don't even think your brain knows how to wave." The General patted Bob's shoulder and exchanged a pointed glance with John that said, we'll talk later. John nodded.

"Ugh," Bob said. "Meditation makes me anxious."

"I've never tried it," Ghost Tom said. "I don't know if it would be applicable now that my mind is in a grave in Nu Jersey."

"Hmmm, yeah," John said. "That's a tough one."

"I tried it one time, but I couldn't stop thinking about interior decorating," Alice said. "I don't know why. This time I'm not going to be able to stop thinking about this samosa." She licked the crumbs off her fingers.

"Well," the General smiled, "you may as well learn to love the meditation, because we're all doing it for ten days. No speaking, no reading, no writing, no clips, no fraternizing with each other, no contact with the outside world. Meditation all day, every day. Ten days. Enjoy."

Bob's stomach made a terrible noise.

"Want the other samosa?" John offered. He held out the bag of samosas. Bob rose from the bench to hit the bag out of John's hand and into the bushes, where the General's pipe had gone before.

"Let's do this," he said.

"WELL," Alice said, strolling up to Bob, John, and the General, waiting for her outside the main gateway. "How was it?" Ten days later, she couldn't stop smiling. Her skin felt like it was humming, and she didn't quite know why, but she felt great.

"Total garbage," Bob said. "I was a wreck the entire time. I started thinking I had dreamed this whole thing and all of you. This ridiculous trip. South Africa and the rest of the world still existing."

"Sounds to me like you've got anxiety," the General said.

"Anxiety." Bob's laugh was a rabid bark. "Sounds like I have anxiety, he says! I've had anxiety my entire life. When I was a child I had anxiety about being an adult. When I became an adult, I got anxiety about my childhood. I have anxiety today about tomorrow. I had anxiety when I was sitting down about standing up."

"Alright," the General snapped. "That's enough! Anxiety is fear of the unknown, and we've got a lot of knowns to spend our energy on right now."

"I enjoyed the meditating," Ghost Tom said. "It reminded me of the restful few minutes when I believed I was dead of natural, meph-induced causes. Before I found out my dad poisoned me to death."

"That's rough, man," John said. Ghost Tom nodded his agreement. It was.

"Listen up, everybody! I've received intel — that's short for *intelligence*," the General added for Bob's benefit, "that the Illuminati are sweeping the area. We'll be staying the course: hiding nearby at a popular yoga retreat.

"Why don't we get the hell out of here if people are trying to kill us?" Bob was really with it today, getting sassier all the time.

"Yeah," Alice said. But the way the General brandished his own eyebrows took her mutiny down a notch.

"Go to the train station, staffed by the Illuminati? Should we put an ad in the newspaper, too?"

"They still have newspapers in India?" Alice asked.

"Yes, they do."

"Why would we put an ad in them?" Bob asked.

"We wouldn't," the General said, pulling on his own beard so hard, Alice thought he might tear it off. "I think we can stay undiscovered as long as we don't move. Remember, we're tourists and we're here to learn yoga."

Bob groaned. "I *hate* yoga."

"Well, Bob, do you like getting brutally murdered by strangers who won't think twice about pissing in your dead skull?"

"No," Bob said. "I don't like getting murdered. I also don't like yoga. I can not like lots of things."

"Great," sighed the General. "Glad you're on board."

ALICE SAT on the bench just outside her room on the second floor patio at the Pune Yoga Institute. The sky was so blue, she couldn't stop staring up. She breathed in deep and let all her air out. For something so automatic, it was wild how much lessons on how to do it helped. And how much thinking interfered with it.

She'd felt different since the meditation retreat—both more relaxed and *less*. She couldn't stop thinking about John, the elixir, John becoming a computer, John dying of radiation poisoning. Meditation had felt good at the end of it, but it hadn't offered any solutions.

A bird she couldn't see chirped its sharp, repetitive song from inside the trees. Nothing here looked like Nu Jersey.

John bounded up the steps.

"Hey," he said.

"Hey," she said.

"I forgot my hook," he said. The management had loaned him an adaptive prosthetic so he could participate in the full range of yoga poses. "How are you?" he asked. "You look lost in thought."

"I *am* lost in thought," Alice agreed. "I guess I didn't learn anything in the meditation retreat."

"It takes time," he said. "Don't beat yourself up about it." The bird let loose on its raucous song again, soloing like a star. "Wanna come with me? Practice headstand?"

"Sure," Alice said, although she was still working on bending over and touching her toes.

She followed him along the balcony path. The men's quarters were divided from the women's, a tradition they seemed to practice everywhere, Alice had noticed. She wondered what it was like at work. Were there men's jobs and women's jobs? Did everything get separated by gender?

John unlocked the door and Alice followed him into his suite. She noticed a short stack of glossy pamphlets on the desk.

The one on top said

So you think you're the next Jesus? A user's guide
Dogon Collective

John grabbed his hook off the bed and strapped it on his stump. "The yoga room is this way," he said. Alice followed him into the next room, unfurnished except for a few worn yoga mats and a lone picture on the wall—a man with the head of an elephant. Alice made a note to ask the General about it.

"Ganesh," John said, when he noticed Alice staring at it. "That's his name. He's a Hindu god. Ready for yoga?"

"Okay," Alice said. It was a good thing she had managed to trade her plasticlothes for a local outfit back in Varanasi—the tunic and a loose pair of drawstring pants, both made out of cloth, were serving her yoga practice well, or she wouldn't have even been able to bend at the waist without suffocating to death.

She reached for her toes. Reached and reached. A groan escaped her. John threw his body up into a headstand against the wall, balanced on one hand and one hook. Alice found herself gawking at the way every single muscle in his body was visible. She looked down at her own floppy legs.

"Don't worry," he said. "You'll get it eventually."

"I don't know," Alice said. "I don't know about that." So you think you're a Jesus? Alice wondered if Jesus was hyper positive all the time too. Did Jesus have to drop his mom off in a cave laboratory, possibly to die, and then head en route to his own death? If so, what did the people around him do about it? Alice wished she knew more. It was a constant problem.

"What's on your mind?" John asked, like she was broadcasting her thoughts onto a LINC monitor. Alice pulled a couple of pieces of tin foil out of her pocket. John descended from his headstand and they both crumpled the tin foil around their heads.

Why'd we drop your mom off? Do you know they're planning to turn you into a computer? What do we do? What's going to happen to you next? How can I stop it?

All of Alice's questions tied themselves together in her head to make one big problem knot and she burst out crying. "I don't want you to die!"

"Hey," John said softly. "Hey, come on." He took her hand and led her back into the bedroom. "Have a seat," he said, gesturing at a small couch, and Alice sat down hard. Her legs were spent from trying to touch her toes. He disappeared into another room and returned with a glass of water. She readjusted her tin foil hat.

"They're going to turn you into a computer," she said, her voice shaky and thick with tears that still wanted to be cried. "Then you'll die of radiation poisoning if you don't get to drink the contents of that tiny jar we got in the desert. But if you don't, then...I don't know what happens. I think the whole planet explodes."

"I know," he said.

"You—*what?*"

"I know," he said again. "I read the pamphlet." He pointed to the stack of pamphlets on his desk.

"B-but, how come the General told me, like it was a secret?"

"Alice, you know how at the meditation clinic, they told us that meditation activates your pineal gland in your brain?"

"Yeah," she said, even though she didn't remember it.

"It's like *I'm* the pineal gland that can unite the consciousness of all the people in the world."

"Okaaay," Alice said, but drawing out her response didn't lead to better understanding.

"And when that happens, it can be used for good."

"Oh," Alice said. "That's good. Good is good."

"Right," John said. "Or it can be used for evil."

"Oh," Alice said. "Uh-oh."

"Yes," John said. "*Uh-oh* is right. And once that happens, once the brain net is activated, and I'm the motherboard for a computer that unites the whole planet into one cerebral cortex, if you're evil, and you have access to that computer, you can read people's thoughts."

"Like, anybody's thoughts?"

"Anybody's thoughts. From any time. So, if you were an evil Swedish henchman, you would be able to look inside a person's head and see what was in there. All over the world. Which means there's some incentive to feed false information to you. And to Bob."

Alice didn't know what was true anymore. "John, what about Jalia? What about your mom? Are they going to be fed into the computer, too?"

"I hope not," John said, but Alice could tell he wasn't sure.

"And don't you have another sister?"

"Susan," he said, and his eyes turned cloudy. "But she's been missing for years and years now. Since the Illuminati first came for us."

"What about Keetah? The other one who went missing."

"That's Jalia. She took a new name when she got to the states."

"Ohhhhhh," Alice said. "Jalia *is* Keetah. Why the name change?"

"Nobody could prónounce Keetah so she changed it to something easier for Americans."

"Oh," Alice said. "Well, there's got to be something we can do. There's just got to be."

"Alice, the Rosicrucians acquired Bob just for that very purpose, because there *is* nothing he can do. He's a decoy. His mind is just simple enough that whatever he witnesses or hears, it will be available to the Swedes later on, when they're thought-farming the brain net. So the General purposefully feeds him misinformation to try and throw them off."

"So the General isn't working for Eric? He's not part of the evil Swedish plot?"

John pressed his tin foil harder around his head. "No. He's not." Then he took the tin foil off and set it on the desk. "Wanna get back to the yoga?"

"I'll try," Alice said, removing her tin foil and crumpling it into her pocket. She rubbed her tears off with the back of her hand.

"I've got a pamphlet you ought to read," he said. "Not now. Later." He shuffled through the pile on his desk and handed one to Alice.

So You've Been Selected for a Quantum Psychic Entanglement
The Dogon Collective

JOHN LED Alice into his room.

"That hooker," Bob muttered. It was too hot and too bright, and he hated this place. All the other clients stared him down when he screamed while he tried to do the yoga poses. Wealthy Indian people looked down on him just as much as wealthy Americans did. His bed was too soft. The birds were too loud. He couldn't sleep. And his assistant was a total floozy.

He got up from his spot on the bench to go knock on the door and interrupt whatever lewd conduct was going on in there. Not on his watch.

Then the General intercepted him, almost knocked him over.

"Well hello there, Bob. The staff tell me you're having quite the time with yoga." He chuckled to himself. The General seized Bob's arm and dragged him into the yoga hall. "Let's go over a pose or two, shall we?"

"No," Bob said. "I don't wanna."

The General pushed Bob over to an unfurled yoga mat.

"It smells like feet in here," Bob said.

"The smell of feet can't kill you," the General said. "But the brittle decay of your body can. Just try one pose."

"No," Bob said. "I like being brittle."

"Let's try downward-facing dog."

"*You're* a downward-facing dog."

The General gave Bob a look, but the corners of his lips twitched, and Bob couldn't help himself—he broke into a smile. The General burst out laughing and Bob started to giggle too, and the two men laughed and laughed together until their eyes cried.

"Okay," Bob said. "You win."

"Bend in half," the General said. "Like this." He folded his body in two by reaching his hands to the floor and then walked his arms out in front of him, until his body formed a triangle, with his butt up at the top.

How was that even possible for a man of his advanced age and overblown smoking habit?

Bob leaned over, groaning the whole way down, and walked his shaking arms out in front of him, bit by bit, until he could see the wall behind him. Something in his neck cracked. His toes trembled. The backs of his legs were on fire.

"You did it," the General said. "I knew you could. You know, Bob, if you ever stopped glaring and sighing and complaining, and tried smiling once in a while, you could be a very handsome man."

"Don't hit on me," Bob said, from his crooked, trembling, downward-facing dog. "You're married."

The General winked back, upside-down, between his perfect V. "Fine," he said.

_____

"How long have we been on this train?" Bob moaned.

"An hour or two," Alice said. "How come you hate trains so much?"

"I guess I don't like the feeling of motion."

"At all?"

"No," Bob shrugged. "Not at all. I'm a stationary kind of guy."

The General weaved his way over and vultured atop the two of them. He waved John over from his spot by the window.

"I got a couple of things to tell you," he started. "I didn't want to say anything earlier, because I knew this one would throw a grade-A hissy fit" — he pointed at Bob — "but there are still no planes flying. We're getting on a ship back to South Africa, a container vessel leaving today. It's already arranged. We have to be at port by sundown."

"A ship?" Bob's voice betrayed his fear. "What are we going to do trapped on a ship?"

"Second thing," the General continued without answering. "Don't move in any way when I tell you this. Continue to look at me. Keep your expressions relaxed. Right now, on this train, we're being followed."

Bob made a sound much like the blowhole-squeal of a rotting dolphin corpse he stepped on as a teenager at the newly formed Trenton shoreline.

"Don't." The General put his craggy face right up against Bob's. Bob hyperventilated the General's spicy exhale.

"This is what's going to happen. The train is slowing down now. We'll all get up — not all at the same time. Two by two. The order is this: Alice and Bob, then me and John. We'll get out in pairs from two different cars, turn right, and then run down the platform.

"Through all these other people?" John asked.

"Yes," the General said. "As fast as you can. Meet at the far end, there'll be a samosa cart."

"What about me?" Ghost Tom whispered.

"No disrespect, friend, but it doesn't matter when you get out. You can't get killed again."

"Wait! I don't get it," Bob whisper-shrieked. "Could you draw me a small diagram?"

"No," the General whispered, looking over Bob's shoulder. "Because we have to do this right now. Right. Now."

The train heaved its final breath and shuddered to a halt. Alice spotted three men in the next car stand up as a unit, and beat a path towards them, shoving passengers aside.

"Run. Run!" The General growled.

Alice hurled herself out of the train car and down the steps, then took off. Bob tripped and sprawled at the bottom of the stairs, one leg dangling off the platform. Alice ran back and dragged him upright. John and the General erupted from the next car up and started running ahead of them.

An Illuminati attacker sprinting at top speed swiped at John's neck with both hands before suddenly collapsing to the ground, limp. Another trained a gun at the General and fired. Hundreds of train-goers screamed and stampeded. Alice struggled to keep John and the General in view. Bob's panicked breaths matched her own, and they were both slowing down, but they weren't the targets. Yet. Blood sprayed from the General's arm. He was still moving, and up on his feet, John in front of him, dodging a spice vendor's wares. John flung a nearby basket of spice at the pursuers, turning everything and everybody between him and them yellow.

They all tore through the station, John and the General hunted, Alice and Bob trailing behind, past a cow with big pointed horns that faced opposite directions, families reuniting, newspaper stands, food stalls, gift shops, running, running, running.

30

TWO CYCLE RICKSHAWS DROPPED

Two cycle rickshaws dropped them off at port, and the General sat them down in a makeshift waiting room composed of several overturned crates as chairs between two shipping containers.

"Wait here," he said. The General tied off his arm with a strip of cloth he tore from the bottom of his pants.

"It's only a scratch," he grunted. The strip of cloth was soaked with blood before he could finish his sentence. Then he stalked off.

Bob was relieved. He couldn't look at the wound without gagging. He'd had to fix his eyes on a point above the General's left shoulder ever since the train station incident. A giant hook that hung down off one of the port cranes latched and lifted a container, and carried the giant metal box away.

"I don't see Ghost Tom. I wonder if he got...*hurt*? In the attack? Is that possible?" Alice didn't know how to locate a ghost. He could be anywhere. She looked behind their bags, peered around the edge of the container, stared up at the sky.

"I'm sure he's around somewhere," John said.

The container they waited near advertised its features on its exterior.

ECO-FRIENDLY

BAMBOO FLOORING

LIGHT STEEL

"Who cares what kind of floor it has?" Bob grumbled. "Well, he was a ghost already, so..." Bob twirled around, palms to the sky. "He could be anywhere. It's not like anyone can hurt him."

"Yeah, but we can't abandon Ghost Tom in a foreign country."

"I'm over here." Ghost Tom arrived in a whoosh. "But this is the end of the line for me."

"What? Why?" Alice couldn't hide her disappointment. She'd come to rely on his presence as a substitute for her ghost mom. What had become of her, trapped in that rainjar. Was she....? Alive wasn't the right word. Neither was *dead*.

"Dead people can't haunt ships. I don't know why. They'll let any other thing on board. Welcome it, even. Pigeons. Cats. You." Ghost Tom pointed his vapor trails at Bob, John, and Alice. "Ghosts? No way. This is where we part. I'm gonna head back to Market, Research, Incorporated. See you all back home."

Bob nodded stiffly. "Tom," was all he said.

"Bob," Ghost Tom said.

"We'll see you in a bit, then," Alice added. "Be careful getting home. Don't go into the light."

"Don't worry. Still not an option. I'm stuck on this planet with the rest of you saps." Ghost Tom glared at John, Bob, and the General.

"How are you getting home?" Bob asked.

"I'm taking the indigenous tunnels. I'd say it's been a pleasure, but I don't like any of you." And he vanished. Alice missed his ghastly chill in the air immediately.

"Why were you two so weird around each other?" Alice asked Bob.

"I dunno," Bob said. "We just are."

"I thought you two were friends."

"I think he might have been using me, or his dad was using me through him," Bob said. "Then his dad killed him. I'm not sure I have any friends. Real men don't have friends anyway. They just work and look at five-second clips about the news."

Alice shrugged.

Bob shrugged back.

"What do you think indigenous tunnels are?" Alice asked.

Bob shrugged again. "Dunno."

The General returned, tightened his bloody tourniquet and grimaced. He pulled out a little rectangle that lit up on one side.

"What the hell is that thing?" Bob took a step back.

"Do you remember the time before headsets in America? Alice, do you?"

Bob pulled his headset out of his pocket and mournfully donned it out of habit — it was clicking and humming uselessly, as usual.

Alice shrugged. "I don't think so."

"I do," Bob said. "There was something else we used before headsets. I can't remember what."

"Mobile phones," the General said. He held up the rectangle. "*This* is what you used before headsets. Everybody else is still using them. Before headsets, America was on the same telecoms as everybody else. The American headset technology only works in America, on a certain frequency. The same frequency that interferes with your nervous system." He put the antique phone away.

"None of this makes any sense," Alice complained.

"The same frequency that started ruining your memories even before earth's electromagnetic field began to weaken," the General said.

"How come we're using different technology and different measurement systems from everybody else?"

A man in a white uniform stepped into their container corridor and motioned for them to come.

"Who's that?" Bob asked, eyeing him.

The General stood up. He cinched his bandage tighter and winced in pain. "One of the crew. It's time to go."

BOB PEERED INSIDE THE CONTAINER. "We're going to live inside this? You've got to be *flooding* kidding me."

"Shut your trap!" The General snapped. "There are plenty better people than you who have traveled around the world in containers."

Bob tripped over the threshold and listened to the echo. "It's dark!" He wailed. "And stuffy."

"Oh, shut it," the General growled.

"No! Don't shut me in here!" Bob scrabbled his way along the container wall, trying to find the exit.

"Your mouth! Shut your mouth. We only have to get in during port calls. You'll be fine. I'm gonna go get sewn up."

BOB PACED AROUND near the galley. No sign of Rosie, his favorite cook — and the second and third cooks already hated him. He couldn't remember the last time anybody had cooked for him. His mom, probably. Before the Flood. He'd hoped to ask Rosie whether she had any plain noodle cup to soothe his poor spirits.

He was in a bit of a funk. The future was uncertain. There had been a moment when he had seen himself and Alice together, her waiting on him hand and foot all their lives, at work and at home. But the more time they spent together, the less she seemed compelled to do for him. It was a problem.

Bob descended from the galley deck and climbed into his container hammock to take a nap, but John was already inside, in his own hammock, singing a song.

"Oh my darling, oh my darling, oh my darling, Clementine. You are lost and gone forever, dreadful sorry, Clementine." John punctuated every third word by throwing a tennis ball against the side of their container home.

Bob creaked the door shut and waited for his eyes to adjust to their battery-operated lantern, then used his eyes to try and shoot daggers at John. Why couldn't they each have their own container?

"What is that horrible song?"

"I don't know, boss. My mum used to sing it to me. What did your mum sing to you?"

"It wasn't that kind of relationship."

"What? All mums sing to their children." The ship lurched and John used the momentum to rock his hammock. "You know. Rock-abye baby? In the treetop?"

Bob climbed into his hammock. "Hey, could you keep it down? I could use a nap, not a lot of yippity-yap in here."

"Sure thing, boss." John made the universal sign of zipping his lips shut and throwing away the closing mechanism.

"Can you stop rocking, too? I can feel the air disturbance."

"No problem." John stilled his hammock.

"And turn off the light?"

"Of course. Right away." John propelled himself out of his hammock, clicked the lantern off, groped his way back to his hammock in total darkness, and climbed in.

Alice burst in, as much as somebody can burst into a container with a fifty-five-pound metal door. It took ten minutes.

"Guys, I just met a man from Romania. Ever hear of it? He said it's where vampires come from. He said 'Good evening' in his vampire accent. Amazing! I'm gonna try to imitate it. 'Gooood eeeevening.' Kinda like that. Not really. What are you guys doing sitting around in the dark?"

"Napping, until you walked in." Bob thumped the container wall with his fist. "Ever hear of it?"

"Excuuuuuse me. Floodwaters must have drowned *your* puppy. I don't know why you would bother to go on an adventure and not enjoy it. You don't have to put up with this, John. We're going to have a sing-along upstairs in a little bit. One of the crew plays guitar."

"I'm okay, Alice," John answered in the dark. "I'm enjoying this quality time here with the boss."

Bob's effort to get out of his hammock was rewarded with entanglement, shame. When he went to turn the light on he kicked it instead, then pretended he kicked it on purpose for emphasis by yelling.

"I'm not on an adventure, Alice! I'm working. We're all working here. I'm working and you're working and John's working. And these men are working, and this Romanian man you want to sleep with is too busy for that because he's working."

"Hold up, there. I think I must have heard you wrong, because you wouldn't accuse me of wanting to sleep with a member of the crew. And I know you didn't say it in front of another colleague. That would be wrong. And degrading." Alice turned and strode out.

"Women, huh? They don't make any sense at all." Bob strained to push the door closed and climbed back into his hammock.

"I think Alice was very clear," John said. "And made quite a bit of sense."

ALICE skirted the ship's swimming pool, a rectangle-sized hole without any water in it. The second cook had said he'd worked on twelve different ships and never seen a ship's pool with water in it. Still, they kept building in the option. It was nice to have something to aspire toward, Alice guessed.

Another spectacular day on the ocean. She squinted into the horizon, feeling buoyant despite Bob's insulting comments. She didn't know how she would ever sit inside at a desk, day after day, when they got back to Nu Jersey. When she imagined snapping a leg cuff on again and sitting for the rest of her life, her stomach turned over.

Alice was pleased to see Vlad on the bridge, blasting the side of the ship with water.

"Hey, Vlad. Whatcha doing?" Alice screamed so he could hear her, and he turned off the hose.

"Hello Alice. I wash ship before painting. Otherwise, salt will ruin her." Vlad patted the side of the ship like a puppy. "I do this most every day."

"You wash and paint the ship every day?"

"Yes. Lot of ship to wash and paint."

"Oh, wow. How long have you been a ship...guy?"

"I am seaman for 29 years now." Vlad brushed his shoulders off and stood up straighter.

"That's a long time."

"Not for me. I love her," Vlad stroked the ship. "And I hate land."

"What?" Alice couldn't hide her surprise.

"I hate the way it never rolls under your feet. Makes me sick the way it is so...not moving." Vlad clutched his stomach and made a face.

"But aren't you worried about a flood? Or a shipwreck?"

"Sure, things happen. Always things happen. My brother die in wreck. His ship was too old and they do not come back in storm even though they are very close to the land, and he goes down with ship. Ship for cow. He die with cow everywhere all around him. All struggle in the water." Vlad shuddered.

"A ship for *what*?"

"Cow. Ship for cow. I'm speaking English. What? You don't understand? The animal who says, '*Muget*.'[1] You know, animal to make hamburger?"

"Oh, right. The big animal with the tail. We don't have those anymore in the United States. We switched to eating noodle cups. They're made out of other things. Smaller animals, I think. Whatever ones don't need grass or grains." Alice bit her lip and looked out at the ocean. "I bet you miss your brother."

"We never saw each other; always on different ships. I miss to know he is out there on another ship like me." Vlad wiped an imaginary smudge off one gleaming shoe.

"How come you don't wear ankle cuffs?"

"What?"

"Ankle cuffs." Alice clamped her hands around her ankle. "A cuff on your ankle, here. It holds you in one spot." She held herself against the wall of the ship so Vlad got the idea. "We have them at work in America. How come you don't wear those? For safety?"

"On ship, this is not safe at all. We must move around. Is only way for survival."

"They say it's for safety," Alice explained. "In case there's another flood. Maybe it's a land thing." She shrugged.

"I do not think this is safe. You must be able to move to escape from the flood, no?"

"Yeah," Alice conceded. "Seems wrong, now that you mention it. I wonder whether they're *trying* to kill us."

"Ship company try to kill us too by making us work long hour and putting us on bad ship sometime, but they never chain us. This we would not accept. Sailor accept many terrible things, but not this."

Alice looked back out at the ocean. Vlad turned his hose back on and washed salt off the love of his life, whistling.

"I've been conned," she said to the ocean.

---

1. Moo (Romanian)

31

I HAVE A BAD FEELING

"I have a bad feeling about today," the General said.

"But the planes are fixed, right?" Bob turned off the cook stove and their container home went dark. He clicked on the battery-operated lantern. Sweat dripped off his eyebrows and onto the container floor.

"Bob's going to die if he doesn't get to his desk immediately," Alice snapped. "He's allergic to freedom. He needs a headset and a noodle cup right away."

John chuckled, swaying in his hammock. "Get this man a noodle cup!"

The General rapped on the container side, hard. It echoed and they all froze. His face looked pinched. "Listen up. If anything happens to me—"

"—the rest of us are doomed." Bob said. They all laughed because it was true.

But the General didn't laugh.

ALICE LEANED over the railing outside the bridge.

"Stop that." The General poked his head out to yell at her, then pulled his head back in to yell at somebody else. He was in a fit today, Alice mused. Maybe it was the planes. She wondered whether they were able to fly again yet. If not, she'd have two grown-man-tantrums on her hands. She sighed and stepped back from the railing.

"You said we'd be entering at Duncan!" The General was joined on the bridge by the captain and first mate. He pounded on a console with so much force, it was a good thing they could see land and didn't need the navigation equipment anymore. She kept one eye on the bridge and peered over the railing again. Nobody could survive that fall. Vlad's brother had fallen overboard with hundreds of massive animals Americans used to eat before the Flood. And he hadn't made it out alive.

"Ben Schoeman's newly dredged. They rerouted us. There's nothing we can do about it. They're piloting us in that direction already." The captain's voice was casual. Alice pictured the General strangling him. Did a general outrank a captain?

The General scowled his way out of the bridge and descended so quickly she didn't have time to ask him what the big deal was. Alice ran back to the container to get the others. It was almost time for landfall.

THE PORT WAS a flurry of cranes and hooks and sunlight.

One moment the General was in front of Alice, the next he was flying through the air, slamming against a container, and crumpling onto the ground. The freight hook that had torn through his body looped around on its skyway track and disappeared behind a stack of containers.

Bob screamed. They all ran to the General. Alice cradled his head in her arms.

"You'll be safe for a couple of hours," he gasped. "But the enemy will be on the way. Take this —" He slipped a piece of paper into

Alice's hand. "You can get passage on the *Clementine Maersk* in four hours. Keep moving until then."

"Moving where?" Bob cried. "You've got blood everywhere! What the hell just happened?"

"Let's get you to the hospital," Alice said.

"No," the General said. "I'd rather die than be hospitalized."

"That's the silliest thing I've ever heard," John said.

"Medical care isn't for everybody," the General argued. "I don't want to be around to see what's coming anyway. We're all doomed. I'm lucky this freight hook ran straight through me. Probably the best thing that could have happened. This is nothing compared with the lakes of fire you guys will be burning in soon enough."

"Sheesh," Bob said. "Give it a rest, already. Some of us still have to go on living."

"Right," the General gasped the word out, with it erupted a spurt of blood from his gashed midsection. "Sorry. Good luck with the end times."

The General handed the desert elixir to Alice. "Take this," he rasped. "Give it to Eric. But when the time comes, you know what you have to do. I know you want to save him, but you can't." He coughed up a mixture of phlegm and blood and closed his eyes. Alice suspected he was still alive but avoiding any more discussion. She set his head down gently on the ground and took a few steps back, then turned away.

"Let's go," she told the others. They scurried out of the container area, on the alert for errant shipping hooks.

"What the hell does that mean, 'You'll all be burning in a lake of fire soon enough'?" Bob looked incredulous.

"I don't know," Alice shrugged. "Maybe he meant it figuratively."

"He was a nice man," John reflected. "I'm going to miss him."

"He wasn't that nice," Alice said, recalling her orders to withhold radiation protection and kill John. Sure, John thought it was false information to throw off the Swedes, but Alice wasn't so sure. She put her hand on the bottle in her pocket.

"We'd better start running and hiding from the Illuminati so we're not rusty by the time they get here," John urged. "We don't have the General to keep us safe anymore."

"It's up to me now." Bob mopped his own sweaty forehead.

Alice and John burst out laughing.

"Yeah, right," Alice snorted. "Let's head over to the pier, get something to eat, and figure out how to find this new ship." She started up the metal ramp that joined the loading area with the shore.

"On the road again," John sang.

Bob glared at him. "We don't need a sing along now. A man has died."

"I know you think I'm an idiot because I'm smiling all the time," John said casually, wiping the General's blood off his stump and polishing it clean with a napkin.

"John, look—" Bob started, flabbergasted at the confrontation. It was he who should have been telling off John. For sleeping with his secretary.

"In your country, I am often treated as though I must have a developmental disability in order to be smiling. But listen, I'm not happy because I am stupid or ignorant. This is a choice I make. Not to have a look on my face like somebody pissed in my pudding all the time. Not to act like I have less than I ought to have. Think about it, Bob. One of us has all his limbs, and one of us is happy. Isn't it interesting that it's not the same person?"

Bob sneered. "I see the way you look at Alice. Just keep away from her, alright? We're together."

"Oh?"

"Yeah," Bob continued recklessly. "It happened before we even came here. I pounded her."

John winced. "Don't talk about a person like that."

"She didn't seem to mind. No offense, but women like to be held by men who have two arms."

Alice looped back. "Hey, what's the hold up? You guys trying to get us killed, too?"

"Nothing," John said quietly. "No."

"We're coming," Bob smirked.

JOHN, Alice, and Bob sat in a café on the waterfront. Another beautiful Cape Town day, ruined by the death of their leader.

"I don't even know what happened," Bob said, a measure of exasperation in his voice. "Did you see what happened?"

"No, not really. I was saying goodbye to Vlad, and the General was just ahead of me, and then we were all leaving the ship, and all I know is we turned the corner and he was lying there, all torn up." Bob's nostrils flared when Alice said *Vlad*.

"I wonder if it was the Rosicrucians. I mean, Illuminati." Bob brushed at a fleck of blood on his pocket.

"Could have been an accident, with all those hooks dangling around," Alice argued. "In any case, we need to find this guy and get on this boat."

"Are we sure?" Bob asked. "He'd lost a lot of blood when he gave us these instructions."

Alice sipped her latte. "I don't even think he was dying. And he'd already written them out. Who writes out instructions before they get murdered? Maybe he was sick of us."

"A huge hook sliced through his body, Alice!" Bob rolled his eyes. "Do you really think he chose a hook over us?"

"He was a tough old weirdo," Alice said. "I just don't know." Decoy information, Alice thought. Then she thought, *Don't think that without your tin foil! Don't think that either!* But then again, getting sliced open by a shipping crane? If he was willing to go to that trouble just to trick the Swedes—

"I miss him," John said wistfully.

"Yeah, me too," Alice sighed. "He was a real leader. Always knew what to do."

"Okay, I get it!" Bob snapped. "I'm not an alpha male. Look, I can —"

"Shhhh," Alice elbowed Bob, spilling his Rooibos tea all over his lap.

"Ack!" Bob leapt up. Alice peered around him.

The stranger sidled up to their table and joined them by dragging one metal chair, scraping it along the ground from the next table over, to sit and make a party of four again. Much like the General, this man was also missing a small part of his ear. He was around the same age, too.

"Who the hell are you?" Alice blurted.

"Harvan Colehapper." The man said, plopping down in the fourth chair, as if that explained everything.

The three of them kept waiting for more information.

"The General's husband."

Bob blotted his tea-soaked lap.

"Is he okay?" John asked.

"Nope. But right now, I'm more worried about you."

"Me?"

"Yes, John. You. How are *you* doing? You're here to initiate the rapture. The new era in human consciousness. Human evolution. Doesn't happen every day. A man is waiting for you back in the United States of America to turn you into a human supercomputer. How do *you* feel?"

John blinked. Took a sip of his hot chocolate and considered the question. "I appreciate your concern. It *does* sound nerve-wracking."

"Are you with the Illuminati?" Bob sputtered. "Or the Rosicrucians?"

"Oh, Bob." Harvan Colehapper clucked his tongue. "The General must have really enjoyed your company. Listen, forget about the Illuminati and the Rosicrucians for a second: We've got bigger problems on our hands."

"Like what?" Alice asked.

Colehapper leaned in. "Sweden."

"Sweden?" Bob squeaked. "What the hell is that?"

"It's a country in Europe," Harvan Colehapper said.

"No, never heard of it," Bob said.

"Is it new?" Alice asked.

Colehapper distributed the tin foil and donned his last once the group had secured theirs on their heads.

"Where Swedes live."

"Ohhhhh," Alice said. "Yeah, the General told me about them."

"You?" Bob said, his voice escalating. "He didn't tell *me*."

"It's been controlling America for years. It caused the Flood. It created your little cabal. And it's implementing the final stage of The Project. The General told you this already. Don't you remember?"

"Haven't I seen you somewhere?" Bob asked suddenly.

"Yes. The extraction?" Colehapper pulled his spectacles down and batted his eyes.

"I thought so," Bob said. "But that means, you're one of the bad guys! You're trying to kill us, too!" Bob's eyes grew large and he scooted his chair away from Colehapper.

"I don't know *how* you saw me. You had your eyes closed the entire time, Bob."

"You're lucky I didn't shoot you," Bob said.

"The General filled your gun with blanks," Colehapper said. "'Bad' is a meaningless word. We're called the Illuminati because we have *illuminated* the true wisdom of the blood line and what it means for humans. Now we are in a struggle to save humanity from our would-be captors."

"But *I'm* the Illuminati."

"No you're not, Bob. I don't know how many times we're going to have to go through this. We just need you to retain the smallest amount of information for, like, a couple of months."

"That's a long time," John said, sympathetic.

"You and your senators are the Rosicrucians," Colehapper said. "Here to *exploit* the blood line and to serve the Swedish masters."

"I am so sick of everybody thinking they can tell me what secret society I'm in!" Bob cried.

"And what do the Rosicrucians want? And what's the General? Is he an Illuminati too? But...working for the Rosicrucians?" Alice asked. "That makes him a double agent."

Colehapper didn't respond to Alice's line of reasoning. "They want to evolve. Sounds nice, doesn't it? But it's not. Because to do that, they need your bodies. And his." He pointed at John.

"Our bodies?" Bob looked at Alice and then himself.

"Your bodies. Your brains. Your headset-confined, low-level brain-waves. America is ground zero for the apocalypse. And John's blood and body is the final trigger. Just like it said in the pamphlet."

The General's husband pulled out a worn copy of

So you think you're the next Jesus? A user's guide

Dogon Collective

"Oh boy. Here we go again with the pamphlets," Bob said. "Just tell us what we need to know."

"Need to know, need to know," Colehapper said, tapping his head with the pamphlet. "Okay. The whole shebang will cause a massive planetary upheaval, as foretold in the bible — lakes of fire, dead rising, the apocalypse."

"Uh, what do you mean, the apocalypse?" Alice was starting to worry even though she still didn't know what the apocalypse was. It wasn't a reassuring-sounding phrase: *Uh, Pock a Lips.* "We didn't have books in the United States so could you just fill us in on what that is, exactly?"

"Really? You know. The apocalypse. The *end* times. Civilization on earth — *kaput.*" Colehapper paused as though looking for another way to explain it. He started again. "John is the anti-Christ. His blood is here to conclude our world."

"Whoa there, that's a little harsh. John is a nice guy," Alice argued. "Have you met him?"

John hurried a sip of his hot chocolate to wave at Colehapper. "Sure. Nice to see you again!"

"Yes, we've met. Good to see you again too, John. I siphoned off a sample of his blood when we kidnapped him back in Cape Town. We used it to track the event horizon."

"So what's next on the agenda?" Alice asked.

"You have to go back to America."

"But can't we just go into hiding? Protect John from becoming the computer. That's the smart thing to do."

"No, that's the apocalyptic thing to do. The biocomputer and the mind control plot have advanced too far. If we don't get John back to

America by the time Sirius C is visible, the rapture is going to begin anyway, without him. And if that happens, disaster." Harvan Colehapper went *boom* with his hands.

"What kind of disaster?" Alice asked.

"The blood and guts kind. We need him there to hold it all together. If he's gone, total mental and physical implosion. Population-wide. It starts with Nu Jerseyans and Nu Yorkers tearing each other apart. And it ends with people all over the world turning inside out. The earth's poles shift. Then the floods come. And this time, they're not manufactured to hit one state. They'll swallow everything."

"Literally?" Alice asked.

"Literally," Colehapper said. He pointed toward the shipyard. "I'm here to help you board the ship."

"Are you sure the General sent you?" Bob asked. "Why should we believe you, anyway, if you're just a rival secret society? Maybe you're trying to trick us into bringing John back and turning him into a computer."

"Yeah and maybe we're not gonna let that happen," Alice said.

"Thanks, guys," John said. "I appreciate it. I really do. But I don't want people all over the planet to turn inside out. Nobody needs that in their life. I'll go back."

"But I'm still confused, " Bob said.. "Wasn't the General working for Eric?"

"He was, yes. Is. Was." Colehapper looked around, as if they were being listened to.

"Hold up. Are you saying Eric is Swedish?" Bob gripped the arms of his chair. "I need to sit down."

"You are sitting down," John said.

"Does anybody else feel like they're spinning?"

"Yes, Bob, and I've said that multiple times. I even said it plainly to you a few moments ago: Eric is Swedish. What the hell is wrong with you?" Colehapper stared at Bob in amazement.

"In addition to the electromagnetic field problems, the memory problems, and a few other issues, I think we might have a headset-related brain disorder," Alice said. "And malnutrition from noodle cup. We're not good at comprehending or retaining information. It's getting a little better since our headsets died and we started eating real food and doing yoga, but we're still us."

John nodded. "They *are* getting better," he said. "A few months ago they couldn't remember anything for a few minutes."

"Our brains are, how do you say? *Fucked*." Alice knocked on her skull with both fists.

Colehapper sighed. "I see. Makes sense. Well, it's going to take a long time and a lot of hard work, but maybe we can unfuck your brains." He turned back to Bob. "Yes, Bob, Eric is Swedish. He's not Eric from America. He's Erik. From Sweden. He spells his name E-R-I-K."

"Erik with a K." Bob leaned out of his seat to lay down flat on the ground. "E-R-I-K. Erik. A Swede. I guess I never saw it in print," he said to the sky. "I think I'm gonna throw up. So that means Tom Fletch Senior..."

Colehapper nodded. "Is a Swede."

"When is this Sirius C going to become visible, anyway?" Alice turned to Colehapper.

"In one month."

32

THE MAERSK CLEMENTINE
SETS SAIL

"The *Maersk Clementine* sets sail at 3 p.m." Harvan Colehapper nodded toward the port. "We'd better head there now so I can negotiate your passage and get you settled onboard."

Bob, Alice, and Colehapper rose from the café patio and started down the waterfront path to Cape Town's port. They had gotten a few paces when a voice called out from behind.

"No."

They stopped and looked at each other. Alice couldn't see anything from where she was standing. The sun was too bright.

"Who said that?" Bob looked around.

"I did," John answered.

A ship at the dock blasted its foghorn, long and low.

They all looked back. John wasn't with them. He was still sitting at the table.

"What do you mean, *no*?" Colehapper's voice was even, but the look on his face hinted at how little his orders had ever been opposed. Alice wondered how his relationship with the General worked, exactly.

"I mean no," John said. He stayed in place, hot chocolate in front of him at the table, hand pressed down next to it. "I made a mistake. I never should have agreed to leave my mom in the mountain. We have to go back."

"Go back?" Alice repeated.

"It's not even possible," Bob sputtered.

"Your mom is an adult, John," Colehapper added. "She knew what she was getting into."

"Maybe she did," John said, hitting stump to hand for emphasis. "But maybe it's not right for a son to leave his mother alone in a hollowed-out mountain with nobody to check on her. I want to go back."

"We only have a month to get you back to Nu Jersey," Colehapper said.

"I—I'm sure she's fine," Alice stammered.

John looked right through Alice. Could he see the lie? "Probably fine," she amended.

"Seemed like a tough woman, " Bob chimed in. He looked at Alice, too, to avoid eye contact with John. Alice studied her own feet.

The cold, that green glow. The grinding sounds from the recesses of the cave laboratory.

"She *is* a tough woman," John said. "And a tough woman deserves somebody to check on her. We have to go back to the Himalayas. We have to check on my mom."

"You're out of your mind!" Bob's voice was riddled with anguish. "It took us ages to get this far! We need to get to Nu Jersey!" Now he was actually crying. Alice was afraid too, her whole body shuddering at the idea of going back there. But she was also afraid of disappointing John. And afraid of being an accessory to murder.

'I'm not," John argued. "I'm clear. I need to get to my mom." He tapped his index finger on the table to emphasize his point.

Bob, Alice, and Colehapper looked at each other.

"We wouldn't be able to get back there," Alice said, but stopped before she said *in time*. Maybe John's mom was fine. Why were they assuming she was being skinned alive? Well, some secret society or another had already taken her hands, one half-limb each from her daughter and from her son, and kidnapped John for his blood besides.

Colehapper cleared his throat. "That isn't exactly true," he said. "We could get there. Theoretically."

"Theoretically?" Alice echoed.

"Like, *theoretically* we can get there, but *practically* we all die in a plane fire?" Bob asked.

"Not in a plane," Colehapper said. "There's a shortcut. A tunnel."

"A tunnel? What kind of tunnel?" Alice asked.

"The ten forty-three indigenous tunnel from Lesotho to India."

"I knew there would be a way," John said. "There's always a way." Alice and Bob avoided looking at him. Alice let out a breath she'd been holding since John said *no*.

They stood in silence for ages. Alice felt awful. Cowardice versus guilt.

"Let's do it," Bob finally said.

Alice, John, and Colehapper all whirled on him. "What?" They said in unison.

"The guy loves his mom," Bob said. "Let's go check on her."

"What?" Alice said again, with so much force a little spit bubble burst, and its remains glommed onto her lip.

"It's not everybody who has that kind of relationship with their mom," Bob said.

"Well, that was a real reversal," Alice muttered under her breath.

———————————

THE NEXT MORNING, they disembarked from a train in Maseru, Lesotho — a small country completely contained within the boundaries of South Africa.

"The tunnel entrance is twenty minutes' walk from here," Colehapper announced. "Beneath the best Indian restaurant in town."

"Can we stop for snacks?" Bob asked.

"It's not safe out here," Colehapper insisted, yet again. He was like a five-second clip on repeat. Not safe, not safe.

Last night had been rough. Colehapper had convinced them it was too risky to either:

1. appear in public, or

2. think openly about their new plan.

They had been lax about the three Ts of safety, he'd said. They were at risk of being discovered. Even with their tin foil hats on. No talking about official apocalypse business or *Operation: John's Mom* until they got to the tunnel.

Alice, John, and Bob were too tired to argue. They'd slept fitfully, hidden in some bushes down by the waterfront, trying not to think anything too loudly, heads snuggled in their tin foil helmets to guard their brains against sudden intervention by any biocomputer already constructed. *Out of John's mom* was the unspoken horror they tried not to think.

It was a bad night's sleep for everybody.

Today was a beautiful day: partly cloudy, wind at three miles per hour, seventy-seven degrees. And all Alice wanted to do was throw a major tantrum. She was hungry and tired, everybody was. The whole dynamic of the team was off: John had made a decision, Bob had backed it, now Alice was the whiner. It was the worst. She kept her complaints to herself for now, but they threatened to explode forth.

"But we need to eat," Bob whined. "I can't rescue anybody on an empty stomach."

"Alright, Bob. We'll stop for snacks."

ALICE WIPED a dribble of chicken tikka masala sauce off her chin and then licked it before she could stop herself. It was addictive, this food.

"How come we don't have food like this in America?" She asked.

"It's all part of The Project," Colehapper explained. "Taking the biological diversity out of America. It optimizes the biomass for—" He stopped and looked around. "Let's talk about this later."

"So, what's our plan?" Bob mumbled with a mouth stuffed full of naan. "How do we get into a weird mountain lab? Do we need guns? That seems to be how you get people out of places."

"We can't think or talk about that, either," Colehapper snapped. "I don't understand what you don't understand about this. Wait until we get into the tunnel."

The waiter approached their table. He nodded stiffly, restricted by pomp, circumstance, a high collar, a bowtie, a too-tight vest. Colehapper nodded at him. The waiter touched his left shoulder with his right hand. Colehapper did the same, then crouched down and touched the floor. The waiter's eyes widened and he appraised the group. After a pause, he bowed his head. When he raised it again, he motioned for them to follow.

In the Palace of India basement, behind the kitchen, next to the trash room, adjacent to the storage area, underneath a blanket, there was a door. The waiter rapped on it three times.

They waited. Alice shuffled from one leg to the next. She wished they'd had some time for a gulab jamun.

He rapped on the door again, three times.

The door opened inward.

Revealed a man in a robe.

The waiter grabbed headlamps from a dusty shelf and passed them to Alice, Bob, John, and Colehapper. Then he ushered them inside.

And shut it behind them. They heard the lock click shut.

"What the hell is this?" Bob whispered. "I can't see anything. It's dark. It's...hot."

"It smells like someone farted," John added.

"Sulfur," Colehapper said. "It smells like sulfur."

"Actually, I did fart. Just now," Alice admitted. "I could have used a bathroom break before all this. I didn't realize we were starting the tunnel part of the journey so soon."

"We've got to move," Colehapper urged. "You know the old tunnel saying: Descend first. Then talk. Later on, rest. Unless you're in a pocket of toxic gas. Then descend *more*."

"It's not a catchy saying," John said.

The gang continued on in silence. Alice shined her headlamp on the walls from time to time. She saw rough-worn rock at first, but as they descended down the path, the walls became smoother, more polished. Unfortunately for all of Alice's questions, the pace Colehapper was setting made it clear he was serious about descending first and talking later.

And it *was* hot.

Would Alice ever get home and see her ghost mom again? What was she doing down here in a strange tunnel under the earth? Was she even still receiving a paycheck? Were strangers living in her condo by now?

Was she going to crap her pants?

"I don't know why we ever dropped John's mom off in the first place," she said to Harvan Colehapper. Even he had removed his hat and vest by this time.

"We had to drop her off as a decoy, otherwise the enemy knows we're opposing them. It'll blow our deep cover. It goes back to the three Ts of safety," he said, holding up a poorly lit finger for each T. "Tunnels, tiny huts, and tin foil. If we don't have any of those as cover, then the Illuminati know what's happening. They can plug into the brain net and search our thoughts."

"Why don't you just do everything in tunnels, then?" Alice asked, and even though the lighting was terrible, she could see enough from his expression to know he didn't have a good answer. The adults had no idea what they were doing. They hadn't thought anything through. It was terror-inspiring. She wished she hadn't small-talked. She wished she had never even learned how.

THE PATH LEVELED out after a lifetime of descending. Alice noticed Bob staring so hard at the ground just in front of his feet that he ran into John, and they both tumbled forward, out of the lantern light and into a darkness so flat, Alice couldn't make out a single detail.

"Watch where you're going!" Colehapper called. But it was impossible to watch or see anything.

Going reverberated beyond the narrow tunnel, hit a larger space, and echoed back.

Alice ran to catch up. She caught her breath. The air was thick with dust, in her mouth, sticking to her sweat. She couldn't stop *sweating*.

Bob and John lay sprawled out in the entrance to a massive cavern. Alice peered inside.

Alice could make out the corners of a cube on the right, at the mouth of the cavern. She shined her headlamp towards it and revealed a small opening cut out of the front of an entranceway with great precision. Was something etched above it? She couldn't tell.

"Enter here," Colehapper said to Alice. He gestured at the cube, no more than ten paces away. It looked big enough to accommodate only one, maybe two people. *What was it?* She mopped the sweat off her brow and shined her headlamp all around it. It absorbed more light than it reflected back. Alice crept up to the opening, nothing more than a dark abyss. She was too scared to shine her light inside. She looked back at the group.

"Go on," Colehapper said. He wouldn't send her to die, would he? Was this a test?

Alice's heart pounded in her chest, her bowels clenched, her breath came in ragged spurts.

She held her quivering frame together, and stooped to enter, her head darted back and forth, the narrow light from her headlamp whirling around.

It was a bathroom.

33

A WEEK, BOB MOANED

"A week," Bob moaned. "We've been down here for a week." He tripped and nearly fell into a member of the Women's Liberation Army. After Alice's bathroom break, twelve women had emerged from the mouth of the cave to guide them. They were a curious mix of warrior princess gang and battle unit from the future. Alice wanted to know everything about them, but she felt intimidated and didn't want to say anything stupid to embarass herself.

"Not close," Colehapper responded. "Not even a little."

"How long?" Alice asked.

"Not yet twenty-four hours."

"Whoever this leader of the Women's Liberation Army is," Alice said, "I hope she can help us."

"She can," Colehapper assured her. "But I don't know if she *will*."

"I've missed at least sixteen meals," Bob whined, clutching his midsection. "I'm famished."

"You've missed two. Most of that you spent sleeping," Alice returned, jealous. She'd had an awful time trying to sleep.

The tunnel path smoothed and became another cavern. Alice was used to the landscape by now: maze of tunnels, maze of tunnels, giant cavern, maze of tunnels. If their Women's Liberation Army guides abandoned them, Alice would have to abandon hope. Hope of surviving or ever seeing the surface again.

"Is this it?" John whispered. Shouts echoed back to them from inside the next cavernous hall. If those shouts were the leader of the Women's Liberation Army, she didn't sound pleased.

"I have no brother!" A commanding woman's voice bellowed.

"I'd hate to be her brother," Bob whispered to Alice.

"She sounds terrifying," Alice whispered back. Then she worried the woman had heard her somehow. She edged behind Colehapper. It was impossible to see much of anything.

The walls around them ignited. And began to glow.

Lanterns. Hundreds of lanterns. Maybe a thousand.

Held by a multitude of women lining the hall.

The dozen who had led them here joined the women standing at attention, lining the cave's walls. At the far end sat their terrifying leader: a combination of camouflage, weaponry-based fashion accessories, and scars. Alice was reminded of the General's wardrobe.

Which was easy to do, because he was sitting right there. Next to her.

"I should have known that old monster was unkillable," Bob muttered.

"Susan?" John cried out, eyes wide.

"Uh, no, John," Colehapper corrected. "That's Kwa Lele. The creator and leader of the Women's Liberation Army."

"That's Susan!" John shouted.

"Who's Susan?" Bob asked.

"My sister!" John exclaimed. "My sister who died—*went missing*."

"I'm Kwa Lele now," the leader of the Women's Liberation Army said. "Susan *is* dead."

"Is it really you?" John's voice was barely a whisper. Kwa Lele arose from her throne and descended its steps until they were face to face. He walked up to meet her. When he raised his stump to touch her face, she flinched, ever so slightly.

"Just like mom," she said.

"How would you know?" John's face was stricken as soon as the words poured out. "Where have you been all these years, Susan?"

Kwa Lele's eyes blazed. "Good question. Here's another one: Why would our parents leave a child behind, at home alone, when we were *all* in danger, all the time." Her face was cold.

"They didn't know. We looked everywhere for you, all of us. When Dad went back to find you, they killed him, too. Please, Susan. You have to forgive us. You have to forgive mom. She needs our help." John gazed into his sister's eyes. She met his, and she didn't blink.

"I told you: There is no Susan. Only Kwa Lele."

"Kwa Lele. Tell Susan we are sorry."

"You and mom and Keetah decided to make a deal with the devils. They killed our father. They kidnapped me. And then you went to work for them." Alice was starting to doubt this would end well for them.

"We didn't think we had a choice," John said.

"If you don't get along with a hunter in town, don't follow him into the bush. But I'll tell you what. Snails have no blood. None of this is my concern."

"Please. Make it your concern. We need you."

Kwa Lele turned her back on John to address her troops.

"The people who turn their backs when you need them most always return to ask a favor." The rest of the Women's Liberation Army nodded and murmured. One of them took out an old-fashioned paper notebook and pencil and wrote the words down, Alice was surprised to see.

The General joined Alice, Bob and Harvan Colehapper. "Do these belong to you?" Bob asked the General, gesturing at the hundreds of women. Alice elbowed him.

"No," the General laughed. "They belong to themselves, Bob. And you might say, I belong to them." He winked. "I'm a member of the Women's Liberation Army too. Aren't you glad to see me?"

"Thrilled," Bob griped.

"You have a lot to learn," the General said to him. "Though I heard you backed this whole operation. Once you get a taste for extractions, you get hooked, huh? You're not such a *bangbroek* after all."

Bob sighed and shrugged. "I guess not," he said. "Whatever that is."

The General wrapped his arm around Harlan Colehapper's waist and pressed his mouth against his so forcefully, Alice wondered if one of them might have chipped a tooth. Their faces merged, joined by the General's beard, sweat co-mingling. Colehapper caressed the General's damaged ear, ran his finger along its missing top. Then they broke apart and laughed at each other like little kids sharing a secret.

"Ship hook couldn't keep you down, huh?" Colehapper said, grinning.

"You're the only thing I want holding me down," the General returned. "Time for a snack?" He called to Bob and Alice, and steered them into another chamber so John and Kwa Lele could talk.

———————————

"I CAN'T BELIEVE we're going back to those darn Himalayas. It was so cold there!" Bob munched on rusks between complaints. It was true, the closer they got, the colder it got. John had convinced Kwa Lele-Susan to help them extract John's mom after all. She and a team composed of her top fighting squad led Alice, Bob, John, Harvan Colehapper, and the General through the tunnel.

"*I* can't believe you stocked up on those rusks," Alice shot back. "I didn't know we were allowed to take extra. Are you hiding those on your body somewhere?"

"No. There's a nice lady over there who's carrying them for me." Bob pointed to a decorated soldier in the Women's Liberation Army.

"Seems counter to their mission," Alice said quietly.

"What's eating you?" Bob almost sang it out.

Alice glared at him. "Why'd you back John's idea?"

"I thought you'd be happy. You looooove John."

"Yeah, right."

"What are you, scared?" Bob asked.

"No!"

"What's your problem, then?"

"I'm always doing things for other people," Alice mumbled.

"What?" Bob said.

"I said, I'm always doing things for other people!" Alice shouted. "I dropped out of school for my mom. Then I went to work for you. Now I'm hiking through some hot tunnel so John can save his mom. I want to be supportive, but I'm tired. I'm pretending I'm not, but I am. Why am I always pretending to be something I'm not?"

"Sorry, what did you say? I wasn't listening. You were really going on and on."

John interrupted them, walking up alongside Alice. "This is a well-constructed tunnel."

Alice didn't know if he'd heard her complaints, and with any luck it was too dark for him to see her shame for the way she was acting.

"Indigenous tunnel one thousand forty-three," the General said, striding up on Alice's other side.

"Are there one thousand forty-two others?" Bob asked.

"Could be," the General mused, "but that's the year of the tunnel's birth, not a serial number. The Lesotho-Himalaya people of the eleventh century were severe planners. They liked to think a thousand years ahead."

"They did a good job on the arches," John said. "Glad they knew we were coming."

"You," the General corrected. "They knew you were coming."

"I don't even know what I'm going to do next week," Alice groaned.

"Work," Bob said. "That happens every week."

Alice looked back at the woman carrying Bob's rusks.

"Break time," the General announced. It hadn't come too soon for Alice: She only had the energy to plop down against a wall to rest, along with the rest of the crew.

"How did you get involved in this, fool?" Kwa Lele-Susan looked Bob up and down.

"Oh, you know," Bob shrugged.

"No," Kwa Lele-Susan said, "I don't." She laid down her weapons, two extremely large guns, and folded her arms. "If I were the head of an elite militant organization — and I *am* — and I wanted to achieve ultimate victory, I'll tell you, boy: I wouldn't hire *you*." She towered over him by at least a foot. Bob craned his neck to look into her face.

"I think it was random," he said quietly.

"WE'RE HERE," the General called.

"How come you have access to a tunnel that leads right to the bad guys?" Bob wanted to know.

"Don't ask stupid questions, fool," Kwa Lele-Susan spat.

"There are no stupid questions," John countered.

"Of course there are!" Kwa Lele-Susan exclaimed. "As many stupid questions as there are stupid people."

"What do we do now?" Alice tried to redirect the argument.

"Now it is up to us." Kwa Lele-Susan raised her gun in the air. "Hang back until you hear our calls. Then it will be safe for you to enter." Her chosen twelve stood at attention.

"I should come with you," John insisted. "To find Mom."

Kwa Lele's expression was harder than the stone walls around them.

"You won't make it," she said. "Stay here. I'll come for you as soon as I find her." John nodded.

"Are you going in there?" Bob asked the General.

"Kwa Lele?" Alice had never seen the General defer to anybody before.

"No, old man. I don't want your bloody corpse tripping up my soldiers. All of you stay here. We'll come back for you."

"The Women's Liberation Army is so violent," Bob whined. "Whatever happened to nonviolent resistance?"

"How do you intend to nonviolently resist John's mom out of the hands of the enemy?" Kwa Lele loaded her gun. "We are not pacifists. What's our motto?" She shouted to her next-in-command.

"Violence can be the best method of communication," she announced.

"Violence can be the best method of communication," the others intoned in unison. Then they lifted their guns and swarmed down the last stretch of tunnel.

Bob, John, Alice, Colehapper, and the General sat on a ledge and watched them go until the last woman had disappeared into the darkness.

THEIR SHARED dread made them silent. The sounds coming from the end of the tunnel were indecipherable. They had no choice but to wait and wonder.

"You didn't know your sister was alive?" Alice asked John softly.

"No," John answered. "She and my mom had a fight the day it happened. I don't know what about. My parents ordered her to stay home and watch Keetah as punishment. Susan was such a firecracker back then."

"Still is," Alice reflected.

"The rebels came to our village while mom and I were at the market, and we couldn't return for days. My father went back to find my sisters and they killed him." John wiped at his eyes. Alice put her arm around him.

"I used to think it was about the mining," he said. "That's what Mama told me, at first. But she was just trying to protect me from the truth. Now I'm sure they were looking for me. They weren't rebels at all. It was the Rosicrucians, and now they have my mom."

KWA LELE-SUSAN SCRAMBLED up to the alcove where John, Alice, Colehapper, the General, and Bob were waiting.

"Is she alive?" John cried.

"She is," Kwa Lele-Susan panted. "But I couldn't move her. Come with me." She grabbed John's arm.

Alice, Bob, Colehapper, and the General exchanged glances, then heaved themselves off the ledge to follow. John and Kwa Lele-Susan ran up ahead.

THE DEAD LAY all around them — white lab coats everywhere, now bloodied.

"These poor lab workers," Bob said.

"These are the bad guys!" Alice exclaimed.

"I don't know," Bob countered. "Maybe they didn't know. *I'm* not a bad guy. I just didn't do my due diligence before I went to work for the Illuminati or the Rosicrucians or whoever. I just needed a job."

Alice and Bob descended the spiral path until they approached its heart: a tangle of wires deep in the belly of the lab. Each of them stopped as they made the discovery: John's mom lay at the center of it all. She still had her arm stumps and legs, but the skin on the left half of her body was missing from scalp to sole. Even from a distance, it was obvious she was struggling to stay alive. Her breathing came in ragged, staccato gasps. John and Kwa Lele-Susan stood at her side.

"Mom," John whispered. "Mom, I'm here." But she looked beyond him.

"Oh, it's Susan!" She exclaimed.

"I'm not Susan—"

"I knew you would come for me," she gasped.

Kwa Lele-Susan crossed her arms over her chest. "You left me for dead in our house. I was nearly murdered by soldiers."

"Susan, I never stopped looking for you."

Kwa Lele-Susan's face twisted, lit by the green glow of the netting and wires. She turned away.

"What do we do?" Bob hissed to Alice.

"Shush," Alice whispered back.

"Mom, we can get you to safety," John urged his mother.

"Hush, baby. I'm dying."

"No, mom."

"I am. But listen to me. I have something to tell you."

"Is she gonna be a ghost, too?" Bob asked quietly.

"I don't know," Alice hissed. "Shhhhhh."

"It's gonna get crowded," Bob said.

John and his mother spoke in hushed tones Alice couldn't hear. Then her voice choked with pain.

"I know our circumstances weren't the best, but we did what we could with what we had. I know you two are going to change things in this world. For the better." John's mom lay her head down in the nest of wires. And she didn't raise it again.

Kwa Lele-Susan's expression didn't change much, but Alice saw a solitary tear trace down her cheek.

THE WOMEN'S Liberation Army tended each other's wounds at the entrance to the laboratory. Didn't look like the battle had harmed anybody much. One soldier strapped an adhesive bandage to her elbow.

"I bumped it on Sheila's gun," she explained to Alice, when she saw Alice watching her.

"Collateral damage," Sheila said. They high-fived each other.

The General turned to Kwa Lele and John. "It's time," he announced.

Kwa Lele-Susan looked both more and less agitated than she had at the start of the trip.

"Sus–*Kwa Lele*, come with us," John begged. "Please. I don't want to lose you again."

"Little brother, you have a war to fight. And I have my own battles. Maybe we will see each other again someday."

Kwa Lele-Susan took Alice by the arm and steered her away from the others. "I see the way my brother looks at you," she told her.

"Oh, um. I don't. I mean. He, um," Alice's face was on fire despite being surrounded by a cave of ice.

"Like you are the light of his life."

"I don't, uh, know."

"And you, at him. When you think he's not looking at you. The two of you are pathetic. I told him, too. I said, if you make it through this apocalypse, he should ask you to a movie. Or whatever lame bullshit people do in America these days during their leisure time."

"Oh. Thanks." Even though she had just seen a woman skinned alive and was probably going to burn in a fiery, inside-out apocalypse, Alice was grateful. "I wish I'd had more time to prepare myself. Before all this started."

"Prepare yourself for what, Alice?" Kwa Lele asked.

"For what," Alice echoed. "I don't know. Work? Life? Death? Love? The apocalypse?"

"Don't sweat it, little sister," the warrior woman answered. "We're all gonna die anyway. Don't take any crap on the way out." She made a fist, tapped her knuckles against the outside of Alice's hand, and disappeared down the tunnel into the darkness, her squad in tow.

WHAT NOW?" Bob asked. He exhaled forcefully and his breath condensed around him. "I'm freezing," he said.

"We have to get you all on that container ship," Colehapper told him.

"Ugh, we have to travel back through this cold, deathtrap tunnel until it becomes a hot, deathtrap tunnel again?"

"That's right," the General nodded. "Back through this cold, then hot, deathtrap tunnel."

34

BOB STARED OUT AT THE VAST

Bob stared out at the vast ocean around the tiny island of their ship and vomited overboard. It was too damn much. What the hell was under that water? More water. Disgusting.

"I don't know how to do anything about any of this — you know that. I *can't*." He wiped a chunk off his chin. "I'm a press secretary. And I'm not even a good press secretary! Until Eric, I mean, *Erik*, came, I didn't know what was on the other floors of our building. He's so efficient. If he wants to turn Americans into Swedes by making John into a skin computer I don't know how we can stop him."

Alice grabbed the railing to pull herself up from her overturned bucket seat. These days, she was always walking off.

"Bob, we've got to focus. Now that we know what's going on, we can't sit around twiddling our thumbs and let it happen. It makes us as bad as him. Besides, he's not trying to turn us into Swedes — he's trying to turn us into *dead*. This isn't a land invasion. They're invading our bodies. They're invading our DNA. Are we really gonna let that happen?"

She tore her tin foil hat from her head and stalked off.

JOHN, Bob, and Alice were resting in their chamber when a knock echoed through the small space of their shipping container. They looked at each other, nestled in their hammocks, and then at the door. Finally Alice got up and creaked it open, Bob and John behind her.

It was the third mate.

"We make landfall tomorrow afternoon. Nu York and Nu Jersey are still going at it. It might be a little rough. We're on course for Elizabeth. We'll know more when we get closer."

Bob was startled by the sound of another human voice. He and Alice had stared listlessly for days, since Alice had announced they couldn't do anything else until they came up with a plan to stop Erik without killing John. Their inability to even begin a brainstorm had given way to doom, depression. Even John was quiet and subdued. At times he worked on his meditation or hummed quietly to himself and played solitary catch against the container wall.

After the third mate left, Alice walked over to Bob's hammock. "We have to come up with something," she whispered.

"I'm doing the best I can," he whispered back. "I wish the General and Harvan were here."

Alice shook her head. "They can't risk Erik knowing they're alive. Plus, we can't rely on them for everything. We have to be self-sufficient."

"That's not my forte," Bob sighed.

"Maybe we should talk to John about it." She glanced up to see if he'd heard. If he had, he was ignoring her.

"That's awkward. We can't talk to the victim about his own upcoming death."

"I think there's only one thing we can do," Alice continued. "When we get to shore, we have to hide John. Keep him from Erik."

"Where would we hide? We're trapped. Erik controls all the cryptos. We won't even be able to eat if he shuts off our paychecks."

"Look, call the senators together and tell them what's going on.

We don't have to explain *everything*; leave out the Swedish stuff so they don't think we're hallucinating. Most of them are rich. Rich people want to live. They must realize by now that Erik is leading us down a path of war and destruction."

"He's not the one who's really behind this," Bob shivered. "He's only working for Tom's dad. Fletch Senior."

"There's eleven of them. Can't eleven rich politicians do something to stop the apocalypse?"

"I don't know. Maybe they're in on it. Erik will kill us and take John anyway. Then what?"

"We're *all* dead if they take John," Alice said. "Not only you and me. Everybody. The whole planet. We just found out it still exists, and now we're going to let these Swedes kill everybody? We have to stop this! We know there's a window of opportunity to get this thing done. He'll miss it if we keep John away from him for a couple of weeks. It's worth a try."

John balanced a small notebook on his stump, tossed it in the air, and caught it with his hand.

"That's suicide!" Bob hissed. "I think they're in on it, anyway, all of them. We have no choice. We have to deliver John and pretend to go along with Erik's plan, the Project or whatever it's called. It's the only way we're going to stop it."

"You know what?" Alice snapped. "You're a coward. You *want* to turn John over to your dumb boss so he can kill him and use him for parts. You *love* being a loser. You'd rather go back to your stupid life and take orders for a month and then die instead of doing the right thing because you're too lazy to care!"

"You're losing it, Alice," Bob sputtered. Lazy? That was harsh.

"If we stop this plot, what then? You want to go back to work? You want to go back to fake-ruling a dysfunctional secret society? You don't even know what its name is!"

"That's enough." She was really off her rocker now.

"Guess what? Civilization is over. The only point to our whole lives, being born and having jobs and staring into our headsets at five-second clips, was to create this frequency. Now what's our reward? We're going to get all our energy squeezed out into Swedes, and our corpses flushed into the garbage heap of our burning planet." Alice was so angry she'd started hiccuping.

"Take a breath. Calm down."

"*You* calm down! How do I even know you didn't know about all this? Maybe *you're* working for Erik. AND THE ONLY THING YOU HAVE EVER CARED ABOUT IN THIS WORLD IS YOUR OWN SAGGING—"

A DISTANT EXPLOSION, then a close thump that rattled Alice's internal organs. The container floor vibrated, a dull roar. The floor tilted, and Bob, John, and Alice slid into a heap on one side of the container.

"What was that?" Alice untangled herself from the human pile, her heart thumping out of control, hopped up on residual anger, and now fear. She struggled upright, strained to snatch up the elixir from its spot in her hammock pocket, and tucked it into her underwear.

John scrambled up, and pulled John to his feet. They all clung to the side of the container. A loud metal groaning echoed around them.

The floor fell away from Alice and came up hard.

"Ooof," John said, sprawling beside her.

She started to slide. The floor tilt was increasing. She grabbed on to the metal ribbing of the container wall and climbed up, hand over hand. John started up behind her. They reached the top and strained to push open the heavy metal doors until, finally, one swung out and they climbed over the edge.

Bob wasn't with them.

Alice and John looked back into the container to see Bob struggling to right himself near the bottom.

BOOM!

The ship's frame squealed around them, metal on metal.

Outside was smoke and distant shouting, some screams.

"I'll go get him," John yelled in her ear. The smoke was all around and getting thicker by the moment.

"But—" Before Alice could say anything else, John climbed back into the container.

Alice saw the coast of Nu Jersey through a gap in the smoke. It was on fire. The whole thing.

A man ran by her — one of the ship's crew. "Just a mistake!" He yelled. "Friendly fire! We're going down—" The man ducked into a stairwell and was gone.

John threw Bob over the side of the container with his stump, using his arm to pull himself out.

"It's been eight minutes of friendly fire so far," John said. "Doesn't seem very friendly."

"Are we under attack?" Bob's struggle to get to his feet was interrupted by another screech and an explosion. They all clutched the railing.

Another shudder ran through the ship. The metal sounded like it was singing.

Wailing.

John turned to Alice, his eyes shot through with anxiety. "Alice."

The ship's tilt steepened.

"I can't swim."

"But it's mandatory..." Bob started.

"...in America." Alice finished. "It's okay. We just need to get to the lifeboats. I saw one of the crew run that way."

Bob, Alice, and John gripped the railing, sliding and shuffling their way toward the stairwell to the lifeboats.

They arrived in time to see the crew lowering themselves into the water.

Another *crack* and the lifeboat burst into flames.

"This friendly fire sucks!" Alice yelled. "Is this coming from Nu Jersey?"

"I don't know," Bob called back. "I can't see anything. We need to get to the life jackets!"

Another loud blast rocked the ship before they could move. And then John was gone.

"Oopsieeeeeeeee!" His voice called from over the side of the ship.

Alice and Bob exchanged a glance.

"No—" Bob shook his head and his hands shook on their own. "Alice, no way!" Alice kicked off her shoes and dived over the railing.

DESPITE THE TROPICAL humidity of the Nu Jersey coast, the Atlantic Ocean was frigid.

Alice yanked off her pants while treading water. She tied the legs in a knot and blew into the waist. They filled with air.

She spun in the water but couldn't see John. Maybe he had hit his head and sunk immediately? Alice spotted a scrap of red twenty strokes away.

She kicked toward it, holding her pants-life raft.

"John!" Alice saw John's head poke above the water for a moment, spitting and choking, then disappear again. She dove under where he'd gone down. No visibility. The water was a murky nightmare.

Where was he? Burning lifeboat shreds crashed into the water all around Alice. She surfaced.

"John!" A swell overtook her, and she gagged up saltwater. Dove under again. Too much oil and trash around her to open her eyes anymore. Alice clawed at the water again and again until her fingers grazed skin. She seized it, and pulled. John's arm. Her lungs were on fire, she shook with suffocation

I'm gonna die

and then they broke the surface.

Now she'd lost her pants-life raft. Alice couldn't tread water and hold John up, too.

The ship's metal groaned again, and Bob fell screaming into the water next to them. After a few seconds, his head popped back up above the waves. "Help!" he burbled.

"Take off your pants!" Alice shouted. She could barely hear herself over the explosions.

"It's too cold!" Bob flailed, swallowed a mouthful of ocean, and gagged.

"Take off your pants *now*, you moron!"

"Alright, alright!" Bob thrashed around for a few seconds and then held his pants out to Alice, who knotted the legs together and breathed air into them. "Hold the waist closed," she told Bob. "John, grab my shoulders." John grabbed her shoulders. Alice choked more ocean water in and out. When she regained breath, she said, "I need a moment."

But they didn't have a moment. Next to them, a large basket splashed into the water.

"We're saved," Bob cried. "It's the military."

"Climb in," A voice boomed over a loudspeaker from the helicopter.

"I don't think it's the military. Who's there?" Alice shouted.

Between the smoke and the swell of the waves, it was impossible to see. A wave lapped Alice in her open mouth. She choked and gagged and spat.

"It's not safe. We have to swim for it." Alice started swimming towards a small path between an oil slick and a burning pile of rubble with John on her back.

"We're going to die out here," Bob shouted. "We have to climb into the basket."

"No, we don't. You're being lazy." Alice vomited into the ocean. "Bob, I lost the elixir! I lost the fucking jar in the goddamned ocean and if we surrender now, John's going to die!"

A rope ladder descended from the chopper, and Bob scrambled onto it.

"We're going to die if we don't surrender," Bob shouted. "Come on!"

"No—"

"I said, get in," The loudspeaker voice urged.

"It's Erik!" Bob exclaimed.

"We can't! He'll kill John!" Alice swam away from the rope ladder. A net dropped from the helicopter, capturing her and John in one swoop.

Erik climbed down the rope ladder and handed a shiny metal box to Bob. Alice thrashed in the confines of the net, couldn't see what it was.

"Are you going to do something about your employee?" Erik asked.

"I don't think this is really—"

"Do it!" Erik barked.

Bob leaned over to the net, held the tiny contraption up to Alice's skin, and a bolt of lightning ran through her body, numbing her limbs and knocking all the thoughts out of her head. She smelled her own skin burning. Her curses turned into an unsightly mouth foam. Bob startled backward, frightened, and regained his hold on the rope ladder. "Sorry," he mouthed.

Alice gurgled. The net yanked her and John into a painful bundle. She couldn't lift or turn her head.

Erik gave the pilot a signal, and the rope ladder raised Bob and Erik into the helicopter. John and Alice were alone in the net, swaying slightly under the helicopter, net cinched tight around them. The steady *thwak thwak* of the blades beat in Alice's ears.

"I'm sorry," John yelled at the top of his lungs. But there was no reason for him to apologize to her. Alice had failed him, not the other way around.

The lifeboats burned orange smoke into the air. Their ocean home of two months imploded, sinking further into the ocean until all the containers disappeared under the surface along with Alice's hope. When the helicopter turned down the coast toward Trenton, Alice couldn't move her head to watch it go under.

35

ALICE GROANED AWAKE

A lice groaned awake. Her whole body screamed, but at least she could move now. Most of it, anyway. What happened after she'd been tased? They'd flown away. After that, she remembered nothing. It was a big black hole.

She was home, in bed. Under her plastisheets. Back at the condo. As if she'd never left it. Alice heaved her body upright, hobbled over to the SnackAttack and hit print. There it was: a noodle cup. Like she had never left. Like she had never eaten gulab jamun, or a thousand other foods.

She turned her headset on. The day's five-second clips about the Nu York–Nu Jersey war were sandwiched between celebrity news and mortgage notices. Nothing else. Like there wasn't a whole world out there.

Alice sneezed, and one of the clips jumped the queue.

"Senator Shoe and I are confident an end to the conflict can be achieved soon," Sen. Sam Hurst said in front of a backdrop of explosions, next to a shoe on a pillow.

"But it's an actual shoe!" Alice yelled into her headset.

"What's all the fuss?"

"Mom?" Her mom's ghost pixelated into the kitchen, under the emergency flood hatch.

"Hey, sweetie. Welcome back. How was your trip?"

"My trip? Well, let's see. I rode on a camel. Stowed away on a couple of ships. The last one sank. Got hauled out of the ocean in a net against my will. Bob tased me. Turns out he's in on a plot to kill everybody by making us into energy food for Swedes. John's probably a computer by now."

"Well. Better than being a ghost."

Alice sank into a chair at the kitchen table and put her head in her hands. "He's going to die of radiation poisoning from being a human supercomputer because I lost the bottle of antidote in the ocean."

"That's nice, dear. Why aren't you at work?" Her mom asked.

"Wait a second. Why aren't *you* in a rainjar?" Alice countered.

"What do you mean?"

"The rainjar! The whole point to me going and bailing Bob out was because Erik had you hostage in a rainjar."

Alice's mom cocked her head. "I don't know what you're talking about, dear. I'm already dead."

"Wait a minute." Alice eyed her mom's innocent expression suspiciously. "Are you gaslighting me?"

"Come again, sweetie?"

"You are! How'd you get out of the rainjar?"

Alice's mom shrugged. "Wasn't so hard. I unscrewed the lid with my ribs."

"I don't even understand what that means." Alice sighed and shoveled more noodle cup into her mouth. "So you weren't trapped in there?"

"Maybe I was, but I'm not now."

"You see? You're doing it again. I can't get a straight answer out of you. It's been like this my whole life." Alice tossed the rest of her noodle cup into the kitchen sink, then spat her mouthful of noodles out, too. "Bland. The blandest crap I've ever eaten. Is that why you named me Noodle, mom? Because I'm a bland, forgettable nothing?"

"No, hon. In the old days, 'noodle' was slang for brains. I started calling you Noodle because you're sharp as a tack. Always have been. Always using your noodle."

Alice narrowed her eyes. Something in her mind was starting to click. She took her headset off.

"You're in cahoots with Erik, aren't you?"

"Now, now, dear. Three Ts of safety. Don't talk to me without your tin foil on. This house might be tiny, but it's no tiny hut."

BOB'S OFFICE lit up with a flash, then darkened. More explosions. He peeked out his window, then backed away. Sat down again. There was so much soot in the air it looked like twilight, but it was only mid-afternoon. Bob sorted through some newsclips, but before he knew it, he was watching the war again on his LINC monitor. It was so damn compelling. The fight over the Statue of Liberty had gained traction in both Nu York and Nu Jersey in a large-scale, ultra-violent way.

He paged through clip after clip, each bloodier than the one before it.

Average citizens, tearing each other apart.

"Hey, Bobby. When'd you get back?" Sam hung in the doorway, super high but lacking the usual powder around his nose. Instead, this time there was a whole whitish rock sticking out of one nostril.

"Just recently," Bob said.

"You really did it, man. We did it! Is Sweden gonna give you, like, the Nobel Prize?"

"What are you talking about?"

"For finishing their project," Sam said. "The Project, The Project," he chanted. "Snatchface Senior never shut up about it."

"You *knew* about all this?" Bob asked.

Sam sniffed and rubbed his nose. The rock fell off and bounced away into the carpet. "Ha ha, good one. Did I know about it? Yeah! You mean you didn't?"

"No, I didn't!" Bob yelled at him. "I didn't agree to trade all our lives to the Swedes for some dumb apocalypse thing!"

"What did you think you were doing around here all these years?" Sam asked, incredulous.

"I thought I was a press secretary."

Sam laughed until he collapsed against the doorway, fell on the floor. He reached to pull himself up, but only caught the sensor. The door closed on his body, then opened again. He laughed harder.

"Press secretary! Oh shit, that's a good one. That's not who you are!" Blood exploded from his nose with his snort. Showered the carpet.

"You don't know me."

"That's because you're *nobody*. *Nobody* knows you, you *nobody*." Sam got up and wiped his nose with his sleeve. "Anyway, I gotta get in the bunker. That's the tradeoff, right?"

"What bunker?"

"Well, not you." Sam chuckled. "Do you know what your problem is, Bob?"

"That I care too much?"

"No." Sam further wrinkled his wrinkled face in irritation. "That you're a fucking *idiot*. Didn't you ever stop and think about why you were recruited in the first place? It's because we needed somebody even dumber than average to take advantage of. That's why. See you later, Bob. Thanks for your service." He saluted Bob by flicking himself in the nostril, and walked out.

Bob was alone again.

———

AN HOUR LATER, a message flashed into Bob's headset monocle.

COME SEE me at 18:00.

J.

. . .

JUST AFTER DARK, Bob crept into the Hub. John sat in the same metallic netting Bob remembered from a basement in Cape Town, long ago.

It was even darker in the Hub. He could barely make out John's profile in the green glow.

"John?"

"Bob. Come in. Erik has gone to arrange things for the war. He'll be out for a few hours. We have time."

"Oh, god, John." Bob stopped short and covered his mouth with both hands.

John was missing both of his. To the elbows. He was also missing his feet and his legs to the knees.

"I didn't know, John. Alice tried to tell me we had to hide you, but I was too scared. I didn't know they were going to do this…"

"It's okay, Bob. I knew it was coming."

"I made a mistake," Bob said.

"No, you didn't, Bob. Everything's alright." The glow under the metallic netting supporting John's body pulsed faster and brighter.

"How can you say that?"

"I have a plan," John winked. He was so damn charming. It was obvious why everybody loved him.

"Alice was right. We never should have brought you back here. Now she won't even speak to me. And you're a torso." Bob sat down on the edge of the platform under John's net.

"There, there," John said, leaning forward to pat Bob on the shoulder with his stump. "Mama always said, 'Howeva tin trangga tete, I de don.'"

"What does that mean?"

"Bad things don't last. Everything's going to be fine in the end."

"No it's not!" Bob scream-cried. "What do we do now?"

"Well, if it's not fine yet, it's not the end. I told you, I have a plan."

Bob mopped his face with his plasti-tie. "Alright," he sighed. "What is it? Wait, do I need to get the tin foil?"

"No, I'm in the middle of a software update. We're momentarily offline. Your thoughts won't be accessible now. That's why I called you. So listen. Everybody in the northeast corridor has their thought frequency arranged around the statue. And the war is based on it."

"So?"

"So when we get rid of it—"

"Get rid of the Statue of Liberty?" Bob gasped.

"Yes. Nobody wants it. Did you know, people are fighting because they don't want ownership of it?"

"Oh, no. I thought everybody was fighting to control it."

"Nope. It's not a land grab. It's a...a land-reject. When we get rid of the Statue of Liberty, it will depress the brain net frequency. Then you'll use your press secretary skills to make it seem like a goodwill gesture from Nu Jersey to Nu York: a peace offering."

"Goodwill gesture?" Bob asked, as though he didn't know what the words meant.

"You know." John shrugged. "'Nu Jersey recognizes the undue burden statue maintenance will cause to the people of Nu York, and in a goodwill gesture we have decided to lay down our arms and flatten her completely. May we all live in peace.'"

"But nobody *wants* peace!" Bob exclaimed. "Nobody's going to buy that."

John continued as though he hadn't heard him. "Destroying the focal point destroys the war. I'll project my own brain waves out through the headsets on the new message. We can counteract the old brain net frequency with my new one."

"Do what now?"

"Change the frequency enough so the Swedes can't ascend through the DNA and liquidate the whole world in the process."

"But won't it kill you? Alice said you can't live through this without the little jar."

"Maybe. Maybe not." He held up his stumps. "We don't know."

"You'd take that chance? For us?" Bob was awed.

"I will. I'm a badass. I come from a whole family of badasses. It's our way. We just never stop doing badass things with our lives. It's how our mom raised us to be."

They shared a moment of silence, then Bob asked the obvious. "How are we gonna blow up the Statue of Liberty?"

"Not you and me. Me and her." John pointed out the hub's hallway, at a sloth just beyond the second-story walkway.

"With Massachusetts' casino sloth?"

"Uh, right. We just need some supplies and a ride. Can you help?"

"Yes," Bob said. A list of supplies popped up on his headset. "But what about the Swedes? Tom Fletch Senior?"

"First things first," John answered. "We need to keep your thoughts out of the brain net for a few hours. Get over here so I can electrocute you."

"I thought you were in the middle of a software upgrade?"

"Safety first," John said, and then he tased Bob by holding the taser in his stumps and pressing the button with his nose.

Bob gurgled, fell on the floor, and foamed at the mouth.

36

THE CAMERA ZOOMED IN

The camera zoomed in on a small figure climbing the Statue of Liberty. A torso. With magnetic clamps attached to each stump.

"...possibly some form of peace protest or a publicity stunt," the news reporter was saying. But they weren't treating it like a publicity stunt: Troops from Nu York and Nu Jersey were converging upon the statue while helicopters circled and an occasional jet formation cut through the top of the shot.

Another zoom and a focus. John made it to the torch, and when he did, the statue exploded. The flames engulfed a helicopter — one of Nu Jersey's. The right arm of the statue fell intact, crushed a fleeing Nu York platoon.

When the dust cleared, the troops were killing each other.

———

ALICE TRIED to preserve this moment, to mourn the death of her co-worker, her friend, a man she would have loved if they'd had more time. She wanted to absorb the confusion, the chaos, the pain, to remember the dignity of these moments most of his life had lacked.

But she didn't know how. It was soon too late: she'd broadcast that five-second clip into her headset a dozen, a hundred times, and if she had cried the first time, she'd gone numb at the tenth, eaten a noodle cup at the sixtieth, and picked her nose on the hundredth explosion.

By the time she tore off her headset, John's death was as meaningless as the civil war, the genocide, or the job they had shared. John had opted out of all of these, while she was still stuck with all three.

Alice envied him.

But she wasn't going to give up. She'd never stop fighting. She'd do whatever it took.

What would it take?

Alice put down her headset, grabbed the household biodiesel can out of the hallway closet, and her matches, and went outside.

The only solution. To set herself on fire.

TWO HOURS LATER, Alice was still on her doorstep with her gas can and matches. This was it. She stood up and then sat back down again. Two hours like this.

Time to die for the cause.

But first, a brief sit.

She had to end it now or see her energy become an antique, buffet-style meal for a bunch of Swedes.

How had John felt at the end? Heroic? Had he thought he'd saved the world?

Well, maybe he *had*. Maybe Alice ought to do nothing.

Alice flipped through her headset clips, looking for evidence that the crisis was over. But nothing had changed: People were still outside killing each other. Erik didn't even need John alive anymore... that was the only plausible explanation. He must have achieved his critical mass. The brain net was intact, even without John. Was that what was happening? Maybe Bob was dead, too.

The end would be here soon.

"Why the long face, dear?" Alice's mom's ghost materialized next to her on the front step.

"I've got to lead the insurrection against this, Mom. The war isn't the real problem. They're only using the war to control our minds. And they controlled our minds through the headsets to create this war. *And* that's only the start of it. Pretty soon we'll be offered up to Swedes like we're a damn noodle cup."

"Sounds grim."

"It is. I was thinking about setting myself on fire, to try to get media coverage," Alice explained.

"Seems a bit extreme, don't you think?"

"Mom, it's the *apocalypse*. What's more extreme than that? I don't know how to communicate to everybody about the Swedes. People don't even know they exist. I need to get a message into everybody's headsets."

Alice thought for a moment, then continued. "They've started selling weapons at the grocery store, right next to the noodle cup. If I could get a little help, we could go to Market, Research, Incorporated and destroy the computer that's controlling everybody's mind. Then we might have a chance against these Swedes. It might be too late, though. I think Erik let John die because he didn't need him anymore. The apocalypse is already starting."

"Sweetie, are you sure he's dead?" Alice's mom peered at her. "I haven't seen him around ghost-ville."

"It *just* happened."

Nobody was outside the condo complex that day except for old Mr. Worthington, eating his fauxlowers. How could Alice be sure news coverage would come before she burned to death? How could she ensure someone would read her message so people would know what was going on?

What if her note melted while she was on fire?

"This must be what press secretaries are *actually* supposed to do," Alice murmured out loud.

"This plan seems flawed," her ghost mom insisted. "You're not thinking clearly. And don't expect to be able to die properly if you do set yourself on fire or get shot with one of these guns you're so keen on having. You'll wind up right back here with me. And then what?"

Alice stopped thinking. Her mind was in a frenzy. No good ideas would come. She slowed her breathing the way the meditation retreat had taught her.

"What makes you think people want to know about the end of the world, anyway?" Her mom asked.

Mass extinction was the only way to thwart the Project, Alice was sure of it, and she had to kick it off. How do you stop the brain net? Take away the biomass. That was it. The only solution. Her only regret heading into death was that she had spent so much time near Bob's stupid old balls in the end times.

———————

BOB PULLED up at the address listed in her employee file: Alice's condo. If she wouldn't come to work, he'd do the next logical thing— stalk her. The condo was a real switch-up from his nautical palace in the sky. Didn't look safe at all. Even a tide pool could have overtaken it.

No sign of Alice.

There was a man eating ornamental flowers out in the front yard. It gave him something to watch besides headset clips of people killing each other in the street. Helped him pass the time. After about five hours, the lousiest car Bob had ever seen in his life pulled up.

Alice. She struggled to drag a large bag out of the trunk and into her brick shithouse of a condo.

She fiddled with the lock-sensor on her door. Bob leapt out of his car and rushed up to her before she could heave the bag over her doorstep and disappear inside.

"Oh, look!" She stopped yanking and dropped her bag's handle. "If it isn't Benedict Arnold," she sneered.

"Come on Alice, you know I don't know who that is," Bob said.

"Me *either*, but I know he was a *traitor*. Just like you are, you *traitor*."

"I did what I could to keep us all alive. And getting paid. So we can live in shelter." Bob gestured at Alice's hovel. "I'm practical. That's no reason for you to stop seeing me, or coming to work, or giving me very occasional hand jobs. I need you, Alice. We need each other to get through this."

"No, you don't." Alice shook her head. "You don't need me. What *you* need is a soul and a heart and even a tiny little backbone. John's *dead*. His blood and his body parts and I don't know what-all are being used in a computer to control the world. Nu York and Nu Jersey are *killing* each other. *You* let it happen. We could have stopped it. You murdered him and you murdered us and you murdered the United States when we could have saved *all of us*."

Bob waved at the big lumpy bag. "What's this?"

"It's a bag," Alice replied. "Of weapons." She kicked it.

Alice had too much energy, that was the real problem here.

"If you won't stop the Swedes, then I will. Kwa Lele showed us how to do it. 'Violence is the best method of communication.' I'm starting a group of freedom fighters. We're going to free ourselves of you and your disgusting leaders — the senators, that dumb *shoe*. We'll kill any other secret societies that pop up, and we're going to overthrow these Swedes and anybody else. But my gut tells me if we kill all of *you*, we'll be alright."

Alice was staring right through Bob's neck. He'd totally lost her.

"Alice, this is dumb! Have you ever even fired a gun? I tried it. In South Africa. It's terrible. Loud. Bright. You're not going to like it. You're going to get hurt, and you're going to hurt a lot of other people, too. If you come back to work, I know we can figure something out."

"*You're* dumb! More coward talk. Get away from me, coward."

Alice shoved Bob aside, squeezed her bag of guns through her front door, and shut it in his face.

"Alice, this isn't right. Okay. I—I love you," Bob said to the door. "You're the only person I've ever loved. Love is what makes people happy. If we only have a week left on Earth, I want to spend it with you."

There was no sound on the other side. Bob pounded three times. Then he had to stop, because it hurt his hand.

"I know we can work this out! You make me want to be a better man."

The door still didn't open. Bob sat down on the front step and put his head in his hands. Alice's whole neighborhood smelled like it was set on top of a sulfur mine.

"Fine." Bob said. "I get it. You don't care about me. But I know you care about *him*." He knocked on the door one last time.

"Alice!" he shouted. "Watch the clip again. Zoom in on it. Then open this door."

Bob replayed it again in his own headset.

He zoomed in on the five-second clip, too, as he had earlier. It wasn't John's torso on the statue.

It was a sloth.

Ten seconds ticked by.

The door opened.

37

THIS IS A DUMB IDEA

"This is a dumb idea," Alice griped.

"Yes, but all our ideas are dumb. At least in this one nobody gets hurt," Bob said.

"Fine."

"Fine."

Alice used the kitchen emergency-hatch rail to pull herself up from her makeshift seat on a crate of firearms she bought at the Wawa down the street.

Bob tried to load one of the guns, but he dropped all the bullets he held. They rolled around on Alice's kitchen floor. Just another day using the kitchen for warfare instead of cooking. If the United States had any decent food to eat, maybe none of this would have happened.

"This is a lot of work," he panted, stooping to collect them.

"I'm gonna go ask Mr. Worthington to come too," Alice said.

"The guy who eats fauxlowers? What's he gonna do for us?"

"We need more bodies. Mom, you wanna come? You're not a body, really, but — at least you take up some visual space. That could be intimidating." Alice's ghost mom wafted downstairs with her and out the front door.

Mr. Worthington was munching on his fauxlowers in the patch of landscaping in front of his condo, as usual.

"Hey, Mr. Worthington!" Alice called out. "Do you think you could come with me on an errand today?"

"Oh sure, Alice," Mr. Worthington smiled. "Today's not a busy one for me."

"It's never a busy one for him," Alice's ghost mom hissed. "He's *crazy!*"

"Shush, Mom. Nobody uses that word. It's meaningless. Great, Mr. Worthington. Thanks. And, uh, do you think you can hold a semi-automatic rifle?"

"I don't see why not." Mr. Worthington practiced his grip on a fauxlower. Was it appropriate to take advantage of the neurologically atypical during a pending apocalypse? No, probably not. While Alice debated this, the fauxlower moved.

"Did you see that?" Alice asked.

"See what, honey?" Alice's mom's ghost said.

"That fauxlower moved."

"Impossible," Mr. Worthington chimed in.

"And *he's* the damaged one," Alice's mom whispered. "You must really be losing it."

"*You're* damaged," Alice snapped, and stalked back inside. She didn't know how to construct an argument to sway a man with brain damage and a ghost. But she knew that the brain net frequency had started activating the biomass, and like the pamphlets said, dead people walking the earth were soon going to be the least of their problems.

BOB CREPT INTO THE HUB. The light sensor triggered, as did the room's sound system, which started playing a five-second clip of classical music on loop. Bob plucked the sound system's touchpad from its spot on the wall.

"Put that down."

Bob jumped. Erik was sitting in a chair in the corner of the room. Legs crossed, staring at him.

"What have you done to John?" Bob asked.

"He's fine. He's resting." Erik indicated a pulled curtain to his left that shrouded John's spot in the netting.

Erik hadn't seen the statue clip yet. Or was he pretending he hadn't seen it?

Even this *plan* wasn't planned.

Bob stopped breathing and pulled the curtain aside, holding his breath.

John was hooked up to a clump of wires hooked to his skin and joining him to a computer bank behind him, a centrifuge spinning his blood in circles on either side. Wires shoved in each stump. The hum. The green glow. How had he and that sloth blown up the statue? How was he *alive*?

"Don't disturb John. He's busy." Erik didn't rise from his chair.

From behind the curtain, John opened one eye to sneak a glance at Bob. And winked.

Bob struggled to keep his expression neutral. Stall for time. That was his only job. He could do this. He was a man. Stalling for time was one of his many abilities.

"What is that thing?" He asked.

"John is the brain net."

"He's the what?"

"The brain net. It's two words put together: brain and net. The *brain net*."

"Are you saying brainette? Like kitchenette? Like, a tiny brain?"

"No, I'm saying *brain net*. I'll spell it. B-R-A-I-N space N-E-T. John's brain and blood form the cerebral and electromagnetic core that controls the western hemisphere, linked with his mom, who is controlling the eastern hemisphere. Now they control the entire neural biomass across the Earth." Erik sounded triumphant.

Not entirely.

"They are uniting our energy into one mass, and soon, through their DNA, they will provide the dimensional gateway for us to ascend."

"All of us?" Bob knew the answer, but he wanted to see what Erik would say.

"Well, all of Sweden."

"What do you think is going to happen when you ascend?" Bob moved closer to John. What was that green glow, anyway? He should have read the pamphlet.

"I don't know what will be in the next dimension. A kind of heaven, I imagine. Where the gods live. No matter what, it will be better than this. No more military-industrial complex. No more drones. No more eighty-hour workweeks. No more racism. No more sexism. No more murder. No more rape." Erik paused. "You know what? I think we could have achieved that here on Earth. If we had only managed to sink all you Americans in one wave."

"I see how you might think that, but you'll be bored," Bob said. "You'll see."

"It's lonely being a pioneer," Erik sighed. "That's the price you pay for seeing things no human has ever seen. Haven't you ever, just once, gazed up at the sky and wondered where we're from, Bob?"

"No," Bob answered. "Can't say that I have."

Erik shook his head. "Some of us have become so self-actualized, we're going to ascend right off this planet. You, on the other hand— your bodies will tear apart from the inside, and the dead will rise from their graves. Lakes will boil. Fire will rain down. Floods are coming. And you, Bob, you will be one of the very few who understand what a momentous occasion this is. Our time as matter is over."

"I don't know about any of that, Erik," Bob argued, checking the time in his monoculous. "But I *do* know that you *don't* know what life is about any more than I do. Maybe it *is* about eating your own trash and watching five-second clips. What's so bad about that?"

"Either you'll be a walking corpse soon, or you'll be energy, Bob," Erik continued as though he hadn't heard, "to fuel our travel into the next dimension. When the ascension is complete, Earth will be vaporized, and your bodies will be nothing more than space dust."

"How long is this gonna take?" Bob asked. "Sounds painful."

"We don't know for sure, but we're willing to find out. Our true purpose has been prophesied over and over again since the beginning of human civilization, and you're one of the fortunate who will see it. Congratulations."

Bob raised a hand. "Hold up. Did you say, 'the dead will rise from their graves?'" Bob wrinkled his nose.

"At some point, you and anybody else left behind after the ascension will experience a condition that resembles *possession*. We'll be moving up that spiral DNA staircase into the next dimension, and we need to unravel yours for the boost. I think the pamphlet said you'll be able to feel us briefly inhabiting your bodies while you're still alive."

"Complicated," Bob muttered. "Gross, and complicated. Here we go with the pamphlet again."

"The whole purpose of DNA is to replicate until it reaches the critical mass, to become the tool that allows us to ascend through the dimensions. Once we hit the right frequency, with John and his mother in place as our unifying nodes, we will all be one. *Nirvana*."

"That was a band from a while back." Was it him, or was Erik stalling too, with all this blather?

"Not you, of course," Erik continued. "You'll be dead, or getting there. A small group of humans may walk the Earth as living corpses for a time, but there will be no passing on. No reincarnating anymore. This planet and humans have served their purpose, and they're both finished. Isn't that a relief, Bob? All your years of failings are finally coming to a close."

"Erik, go suck on a flood." Bob was getting nettled. This guy was a real piece.

"Watch yourself, Bob." Erik stood up. "You know, I don't need you. I'm allowing you to live out the last week of your life as a courtesy."

"I don't think so," Bob shot back. "You're keeping me alive because you're a slave to these Swedes, and *they* need me. So *you* need me. I think you need each one of us alive because we're close to John. You haven't been able to achieve your stupid world domination because you lost John's radiation juice in the ocean."

Erik's eye twitched.

"That's right. I know about the bottle." It was Bob's turn to be triumphant. "Alice told me. Hey, what if I ended myself right now? What if we all did? What would become of your dumb Project then?"

"Calm down, Bob. Let's leave this room. John needs his sleep."

"I'm not leaving this room." Bob took a step closer to John. "And neither is she."

"She?" Erik asked.

"Yes," Bob said louder. "She. I said, *SHE*." He looked at the door.

Erik looked at the door.

Nothing happened.

"Well, this is embarrassing," Bob sighed.

Alice burst in holding a semi-automatic rifle, with an identically armed Mr. Worthington in tow.

"Where were you?" Bob cried. "I said 'she' like five times." He scooped John out of his metallic net while Alice and Mr. Worthington trained their guns on Erik.

"Uncle Hammy?" Erik said.

John opened his eyes. "I don't know if I wanna work here anymore," he said to Erik.

"Don't worry, John," Alice assured him. "We'll find something else for you to do." She pointed her gun at Bob's face. "Watch it, floodrat," she growled. "Back up."

"Alice? What are you doing? I thought we were gonna—"

"Put John back in the mesh."

"What? Alice, what are you doing?" Bob was agape.

"I said, put him in the mesh."

"But we had a plan!"

"No, *you* had a plan," Alice snarled. "And I had a plan. He has a plan, too." She pointed her gun at Erik. "Turns out they're not the same plan. So put John down now, or I'll shoot you in the face. Get it? That's the *real* plan."

Alice menaced Bob with her gun, and he emitted a tiny, high-pitched whimper. He eased John back into the mesh hammock. The green glow brightened underneath and all around them both.

"Hi, Alice." John smiled at her.

"Hi, John," she said. She took one hand off the gun to pat him on his arm stump. "I thought you were dead. How have you been?"

"Can't complain," he answered. "At least I still have my health benefits and my 401(k)."

"What do you want, Alice?" Erik took a step toward her. "Why are you doing this? *What* are you doing, exactly?"

"Back up!" Alice yelled, jerking the gun back and forth from Bob to Erik. They stumbled backward.

"I was not put on this planet to buy your ballsack accessories, Bob. John was not put on this planet for you to harvest his limbs, Erik. Why is it that you two are giving the orders? When I was outside my house, preparing to set myself on fire, I saw what the *real* right thing to do was."

Erik broke into a slow smirk that didn't reach his eyes and slow-clapped. "Bravo, Alice. Now *that's* ambition."

"Shut up, flood rat. Do you know the Statue of Liberty is gone? Did you even know that happened?"

Erik's face fell. It was Alice's turn to smirk.

"Oh, was that a surprise? Now *this* is happening — Bob, tie him up."

"What?" Bob stared at Alice.

"Tie him up!"

"I'm not great at knots," he whined.

"You know what they say," John said. "If you can't tie knots, just tie lots."

"Who says that?"

"I could look it up on my headset," John offered.

Alice shook her head and turned back to Bob. "Do it!" She snapped. "Now."

Erik sat down in the chair and Bob wound a cable rope around him while Alice oversaw the effort. Then she held out a laser razor out to Bob. He stared at her for a long moment, then picked it up by the tip as though it might slice off his hand.

"What's this for?" He asked.

"To torture him," Alice answered.

"This wasn't what we discussed!" Bob exclaimed.

"Of course it isn't," Alice snorted. "If we discussed it ahead of time, he would hear it through the brain net."

"So you knew about this brain net thing the whole time?" Bob put his hands on his hips.

Before Alice had a chance to answer, the ghost of Tom Fletch Junior floated up through the floor with an accelerated *whoosh*. Bob screamed and flailed. The laser razor in his hand sparked.

Erik's hand hit the floor. Minus Erik.

Erik screamed.

Bob and Alice screamed.

The ghost of Tom Fletch Junior screamed, and disappeared back into the floor.

"Uh-oh," John said.

"What do we do? What do we do?" Bob dropped the laser razor. It went off again, slicing through John's metallic net hammock. It crashed to the ground. John tumbled out.

"Damn it, Bob!" Alice shouted.

"Me?" Bob yelled back. "Did you see that? I didn't expect to see Tom! I didn't even remember he was alive! I mean, dead. I mean, *undead*. And what the *flood* would ever possess you to put me in charge of torture?"

"You weren't supposed to actually torture him!" Alice rolled her eyes in exasperation. "We were just going to intimidate him until he talked so that we knew how to reverse this biomass, brain net frequency rapture apocalypse thing—"

"That's what happens when you don't share the plan!" Bob ranted.

"You *know* everything had to be a surprise. Otherwise, he would have known we weren't really going to do anything and that the Statue of Liberty was already destroyed."

Erik screamed again. Then he bellowed, "Shut up!"

Bob and Alice looked at him.

"There's a blood-clotting kit downstairs, in my office. One of you run and get it. The other one, use this rope to tie off my stump."

"He sure is lucid," Mr. Worthington said. He tapped Erik in the calf with his boot like he was checking a tire.

"Ow! I'm your nephew, you idiot! Why didn't you tell them? I wasn't working against you, you morons," Erik panted and curled into the fetal position. His wrist spurted blood. A bit of tendon lost its grip on his exposed bone and slid off onto the carpet. "I love America! I love eating my own trash and being surrounded by hoarded filth." He turned to Alice. "And I love your *mother*!"

Alice stared at him. "But you killed her! I saw you at the hospital. Then you put her ghost in a rainjar."

"That was for her own good, to protect her from the rapture! Your spirit can't connect with your body once you become an apocalyptic zombie, or you're totally *fucked*!"

"But you were the one who killed her in the first place!"

"She was going to die anyway! She's got CTNNA."

"She's got what?"

"It's a gene. CTNNA. It causes hereditary diffuse gastric cancer. She was already sick. She had lesions in her stomach. The tumors had spread everywhere, including her lungs. We terminated her life early so she could be the first to benefit from the rapture. So she could stay on Earth, with me, until we all ascended. I did it so we could be together. Edna!" Erik called. "Edna, come out here!"

Alice's mom's ghost materialized.

"*We* did it," Alice's mom's ghost corrected.

"I've been trying to save the United States since my uncle first brought me here. I tried to save Tom Fletch Junior, but I was too late."

"He's Erik's step-cousin," Alice's mom said.

"I've been feeding little bits of the worst of your kind into the computer for years to try to stop this thing from working. I've been trying to save you dullards my whole miserable life."

"I knew my fingernail pile was robbed," Bob muttered. He set the laser razor down carefully and stepped away from it.

Alice's mom's ghost wrapped her ghastly trailing arm around Erik's head on the floor. "Honey, we need to talk," she said to Alice. "It's true: Erik was the only thing separating us from the apocalypse."

"The real threat is—" Erik slurred, then passed out and went limp on the floor. A puddle of blood pooled around his new stump, despite the tourniquet Alice cinched on, using a spare biocomputer cable.

"The real danger is Tom Fletch Senior," Alice's mom's ghost finished. "Always has been."

"I wish you'd told me that back at the house," Alice groaned.

"Not the most clever move, dear. Until this little stunt you and your friends pulled, Erik was deep undercover inside this Swedish apocalyptic death society. And so was I."

"Oh," Alice said.

"Tom Fletch Senior is upLINCed to the brain net. If you say it out loud, he knows you know. Even if you think it, he knows. So now *you* know. And now *he* knows. And that's not good. You know?"

38

ALICE WAITED OUTSIDE THE HUB

Alice waited outside the Hub for Bob to return with the blood clotting powder. While she paced back and forth, she spotted a speck of a figure down at the far end of the hallway.

The sloth.

Bob ran up. "I found it," he panted, holding a small packet. "Who the hell keeps blood clotting powder in their desk?"

"Guess it paid off to be prepared," Alice said. "But look." She pointed.

The sloth loped closer and closer.

"I saw you shit during a board meeting," Bob said.

The sloth removed its head.

Jalia.

"Jalia? You're the sloth?" Alice asked.

"I'm not the only sloth. The real sloth is over there." Jalia pointed out the window. There it was, the real sloth, gripping the exposed pipes with its two toes. "We got the real sloth in here first. Then I got this sloth costume so I could sneak around without being detected."

"Keetah," John said. He'd attached his leg blades and joined them outside the office.

"My real name is Keetah." She used her teeth to remove her prosthetic arms and legs, revealing the extent of her own body: a torso. "Around here, they used to call me prototype one."

"I thought you died in the Statue of Liberty explosion," Alice said. "Or, you," Alice said to the real sloth. "Or you," Alice said to John. "One of you."

"I parachuted off the back," she said.

"Great costume," Bob said. "Very realistic."

"Not really," Jalia said. "You can see the seams here and here." She pointed out visible zippers on her disguise. "Luckily people don't look at each other much. Quite a mess here." She nodded at Erik, laying in a pool of blood on the floor of the Hub next to his disembodied hand.

"Yeah," Bob grunted. "Somebody stayed quiet about the plan, and now look. There's blood everywhere."

Alice glared at Bob. "Go put the powder on him so he doesn't bleed out," she said. He gave her a look of resentment before he complied and stalked off.

"There's only one thing you can do now," Jalia-Keetah said.

"What's that?" Alice asked.

"Take John and head out on a goodwill tour of Sweden."

"A *what*?"

"You gotta go to Sweden."

Bob stalked back through them with the bag of blood-clotting powder.

"What's Sweden?" He asked.

"Just put the powder on Erik!" Alice shouted. She turned back to Jalia-Keetah. "Me? Why?"

Erik screamed and revived when the blood-clotting powder hit his stump. Bob jumped back and dropped the bag. Blood-clotting powder flew everywhere. Erik sat up and clutched his stump to his chest.

"Alice, you're one of us," he said.

"No I'm not. One of who?"

"You're *Swedish*."

"I am *not*. Am I?"

"Well, you're not *that* Swedish. I mean, look at your build. Your hair. Your taste in clothes. Your levels of—"

"How Swedish am I?" Alice pressed her fingers gently into her own cheek, as if it was foreign to her. Alice's mom's ghost floated next to Erik.

"One-sixteenth, to be exact," she said.

"Grampy Moofy?"

"No. On your father's side."

"Oh, Grandfather Lars? I didn't know much about him. Dad did say he liked those meat spheres and unvarnished furniture assembly, now that you mention it."

"There you have it," Erik said. "Keetah's right. You have to go to Sweden on a goodwill tour and convince them to avert the apocalypse. Get them to cancel the Project or find a way to ascend without liquidating the whole rest of the world."

"Do we really have time for that?" Bob picked at the seam on Jalia's removed sloth suit.

"I don't know," Jalia-Keetah said.

"Why don't we just take the brain net offline?" Alice asked.

"It's too far along," Erik said. "That's like trying to put a nuclear explosion back in the bomb a millisecond after detonation."

"If we can get the Swedes to stand down, maybe it will deter Tom Fletch Senior. It probably won't work. But I don't expect there's much else to do by now. Better to do something to avert the apocalypse rather than nothing," John said. "Don't you think?" He leaned against the wall, a little taller than the rest of them due to his leg blades.

"Go to Sweden by myself?" Alice would rather take her chances with the civil war and the apocalyptic zombies.

"I'll go with you Alice," John said. "Keetah can take my place in the computer for a few days."

"No more than that though, or—" Jalia-Keetah mimed a slit throat by drawing her stump across her neck. "—that'll be the end of me." John nodded.

"We'll keep it short," Alice said.

"You'll know you went too long," Jalia-Keetah said, "If the Swedes disappear completely."

"I'll stay here," Bob said. "International travel isn't for me."

ALICE AND JOHN sat at their assigned gate in Newark International Airport, Alice in a chair, John in a wheelchair because his leg blades weren't allowed on the plane for no real reason. Alice heard a staccato rat-a-tat-tat every now and then, a reminder of the ongoing civil war, sometimes distant, other times not.

"I'm sorry they won't let you bring your leg blades," Alice said.

"It's just as well," John said. "We don't know what's going on, electromagnetically. They could have turned into projectiles."

GREETINGS, Passenger <u>2489</u>! Your retina view is your waiver. Thank you for flying American! Please accept these robust assurances of minimal risk:

1. The demilitarized zone around the airport has maintained safety procedures for the departure and arrival of planes except in very rare cases. American Airlines is not responsible for lapses in the demilitarized zone. Thank you for flying American!
2. Engineers have realigned our technical capacity to overcome the electromagnetic field disturbance and 98% of planes typically remain in the air as planned (percentages based on 30-60 day average).

WE APPRECIATE YOUR BUSINESS!

. . .

"Did you sign your waiver?" John asked.

"If you mean, did I look at it? Yes. I looked at it. I can't believe we're gonna die trying to get to Sweden."

"Come now, Alice. We're not going to die."

"I can't believe it was part of the plan all along," Alice said glumly. "My mom was a double agent. I'm one-sixteenth Swedish. I don't even understand how much that is."

"It's one-sixteenth," John said.

"How much is that?" Alice asked.

"What do you mean?"

"I'm not a numbers person. We're not mathematical in the United States. Maybe it's a Nu Jersey thing. I don't think in numbers. I only think in words."

"Oh," John said. "Well if you had one thing, and you divided it in half and had two parts, and then you took those two and divided them in half, you would have four. And then you divided all those into two and you would have eight. And then if you split all *those* in half, you would have sixteen. One of those sixteen pieces would be Swedish."

Alice put her head in her hands. "I'm a monster," she said. "I'm a one-sixteenth monster."

"There, there. Don't take it so hard." He strained up from the wheelchair to pat her shoulder.

"I can't believe I'm one-sixteenth Swedish. I've been tricked my whole life!" Alice cried.

"Not your *whole life*," John argued. "It just didn't come up. Only this past year or so."

"You know, you think there are givens in life," she sighed.

"Now that you mention, probably also as a child. With Santa Claus. That's also a trick," John mused. "We didn't have that bullshit in Sierra Leone. If your parents buy you a gift, you damn well know they did."

"I'll go to college, you think. I'll get a job."

"And the Flood. Being created by a corporation instead of a natural event. That's a trick too, when you think about it."

Alice put her head in her hands. "The rest of the world was destroyed in a flood. We can't grow food. My mom won't purposefully kill herself so she can spend the rest of her life as a ghost with a Swedish man who fell in love with her when she was a kid. My mom's ghost won't be a double agent in the apocalypse resistance and fool me by pretending to be trapped in a rainjar. Her Swedish lover won't pretend to try to kill us all but actually be secretly trying to save us from some other guy."

"I know," John nodded. "It's a lot."

"But it's not just that," Alice said. She forced herself to look at John. "You lied too. About Jalia. Or, Keetah. Your sister."

"I know, Alice. I thought it was best. For your protection."

"Nothing that was supposed to keep me safe kept me safe," Alice said.

John lifted his stumps ceiling-ward and shrugged his shoulders.

Now BOARDING Flight to <u>Stockholm</u> AA 1767

"READY?" John asked.

"I don't know," Alice said.

She stood up and wheeled him over to the gate.

39

AN ELEGANT AND MATTE-FACED

An elegant and matte-faced woman strode over.

"Welcome to ReTuna. I'm Lanna Bergström." She stretched out her slender hand. Alice stared at her for a long moment in disbelief at the extent of her cleanliness, then stuck her own hand out. Her icy grip enveloped Alice's pudgy paw.

"Tuna? Is this a faux fish plant?"

Bergström's laugh rang brass out of her long throat. "No, my dear. It's a recycling mall!"

"Don't you throw everything in the trash to biodegrade? Or eat it?"

Bergström's eyes widened the least little bit. "No. No, we don't. You'll see," she explained, and turned to continue the tour.

Only thirty seconds into this goodwill tour and Alice could tell she'd already said something horrifying.

ReTuna was *definitely* not a faux fish factory, it soon became obvious. It was a citadel of wealth, the likes of which Alice had never seen. Chandeliers hung in bunches from the gleaming white rafters. Light sculptures shined. A bounty of plants blazed green in the corridor. *Not* sculpted mushroom synthetics: real live plants.

Bergström led Alice through the mall, pointing out treasures, each a thing of such beauty Alice hadn't known it was possible.

"The group you'll be addressing is this way," Bergström led with a lift of her manicured hand. They entered a coffee shop. The scent of it like life itself. Earthy. Raw. Nothing like the coffee from a SnackAttack. Alice stood to face a small audience of Swedes sitting in chairs, staring expectedly at Alice and Lanna Bergström.

Bergström said a few words in Swedish.

"I'm sorry, will you...translate for me when I talk?" Alice asked, clenching her hands together in all the configurations: right hand on top, left hand on top, fingernails digging into palm. "I don't speak Swedish."

"Oh, they all speak and understand English," Bergström reassured her. "I was starting in Swedish as a formality."

"Oh, okay. That's good." Alice wiped her hands on her pants. She felt like an eighth-day Flood victim. "Hi," she started.

"Hi," the Swedes echoed.

"My name is Alice."

"Hi, Alice!" The Swedes chorused.

"Maybe...you could tell me your names?"

"My name is Anna," the woman closest to her began. Neat. Clean. Legs crossed. Casual. She was wearing the most delicate pair of red, wire-framed eyeglasses. Her shirt looked impossibly soft.

The next Swede and the next Swede and the next Swede introduced themselves. Albin and Ebba and Anna and Åke. Each one impossibly put together, waiting to be convinced.

Alice stood there alone. She wished John was with her. He would have known how to begin.

A few moments passed and she still hadn't said anything.

The Swedes looked uncomfortable.

Alice started to cry. "I can't do this," she sniffed. "I thought when I got here it would be clear that there was some argument for America, but there isn't."

Snot oozed out of Alice's nose, she backhanded it. One of the

Swedes reached a handkerchief out to her, pressed into a perfect triangle.

"We're dirty," Alice moaned, mopping her snot. "We don't have clean water. I guess our food isn't even real."

"Oh, come now," Albin soothed. "You must have some real food and a little clean water. You don't look *that* dirty."

"No, it's true!" Alice cried. "There's no food. There's no pay equity among genders. We don't even have plants anymore since the Flood. I think you *should* liquidate our bodies and energy to ascend into the mystery dimension. Even if we do end up walking corpses, I don't know whether anybody will notice."

The Swedes looked at each other and shifted in their chairs.

"If a woman has a baby, she has to go back to work the very next day," Alice blurted out.

"We heard," Ebba said. "It was one of our rationales for voting in favor of liquidating you: all the crimes against mothers."

"I was supposed to convince you not to liquidate us but now I don't see the puh-huh-hoint," Alice choked.

"But now that you're here, we feel bad," Anna said, uncrossing and re-crossing her lengthy legs. "What do you think about joining us in the ascension, Alice?"

"Doing what?" Alice tried to give the handkerchief back to its owner, but he refused.

"Joining us. In ascending off the planet." Anna lifted one slender finger to the sky.

"Leave America? Forever?" Even the cloth they wiped their noses with was soft. Alice pet the handkerchief as though it were a tamed floodrat.

"Not only the United States: the Earth. Maybe the universe. We don't know. It's an expedition. We can't say exactly where we're ascending to, but we think it's going to be worth a look. You can come with us!"

"America will still be liquidated?" Alice asked.

"Yes, most of the world, now, we think. But *we'll* get to go to the next dimension. Doesn't that sound exciting?"

"I didn't think Americans were eligible."

"Certainly not as a group, no. Just you. We heard you're one-sixteenth Swedish."

"We'd love to have you along," Åke urged.

"The whole point of this tour is for *me* to convince *you*," Alice argued. "Not the other way around."

"Alice, have you ever heard of *fika*?" Ebba rose and wrapped a blanket around Alice's shoulders, guiding her toward the VIMLE sofa with chaise lounge option that Bergström had pointed out earlier in the day, during their IKEA tour.

"No," Alice said. "What's figgy?"

Åke put a steaming hot cup of coffee in Alice's hands and set a small plate with a tiny cookie on the LACK end table next to her.

"*Fika* means 'coffee break,'" Åke explained.

"What's a...coffee break?" Alice asked. The Swedes looked alarmed. She'd said something wrong. Again.

"You know," Bergström said. "A coffee break!"

"No," Alice shook her head. "Never heard of it. Ficus? Is that what you're saying? That's a small tree. In America, it's plastic."

"*Fika*. Coffee break. It came from America!" Ebba exclaimed. "It means, you stop working at some point in the afternoon and have coffee."

"I don't think we have that," Alice told her.

"You used to. We have perfected it, of course, making it a weekly Friday-afternoon occurrence where colleagues can take time out of the day to chat and have a coffee and a treat."

"I've been working for nine months straight," Alice said. "There's been no break. And my company doesn't provide coffee."

Ebba and Åke exchanged a measured look.

"Alice," Åke said. "It's time you had a *fika*."

ALICE'S BRAIN replayed the day's events the way her headset would have if it worked in Sweden.

By the time John had finished his shower, she was huddled in a ball in the middle of the hotel room on her minimalist bed.

She was still surrounded by some of the mysteries of Sweden: for one, a small, blazing-blue dish of chewy red fish made from an unidentifiable gum-like substance.

She saw the images, each more improbable than the one before; experienced the sounds, the smells, the tastes, again and again.

Rolling Swedish countryside

Cities without trash in the streets

They invented the zipper

Fossil-fuel free

Don't forget the red gummy fish

Monarchy since the year nineteen ninety-eight

Swedish meatballs seasoned with gravy, boiled potatoes, and lingonberry jam

Eighty-five percent voter turnout

Corporal punishment is outlawed

Gender equality

Third-highest social spending

Every Swedish resident receives a state pension

Burning a straw goat*what?*

Salty licorice

"ALICE?" John put a stump on her shoulder.

Alice unfurled from her position and sat up. "Eat this!" She thrust a waxy black candy into his hand.

John popped it into his mouth. Chewed and chewed. "Absolutely disgusting," he said. He climbed off the bed and ambled into the bathroom to spit it into the toilet. Alice heard it land in the bowl with a *bloop*.

"People who think that's *good* get to ascend off the planet and see what happens next at the expense of every single person in the rest of the world."

"I know it's hard to handle," John said. "I'll make you a tea."

"John, what do you want?" Alice sat up and watched John busy himself around the tiny kitchenette, turning on something called an electric kettle because they didn't need SnackAttack to 3D-print food out of garbage, sawdust, and addictive flavorings. One of the many hard lessons of Sweden. *Another* of the many hard lessons of Sweden.

"I want to stay in America," John answered. "With you."

"What if America is full of lakes of fire and re-animated corpses?"

He shrugged his stumps. "Nothing's perfect."

"But what if I can get us into Sweden?" Alice asked. "Into the ascension."

"Alice, if you want to stay in Sweden, stay in Sweden. Don't come back to America and die on my account." John tore a sugar packet open with his teeth, then gripped it between his stumps and poured it into her mug. He picked up the spoon with his teeth, tilted his head sideways, and stirred. "But I have to return no matter what. To relieve Keetah from her spot in the biocomputer. Or she'll die."

Alice hated herself for thinking it, and hated herself even more for saying it, but she had to try. "But John, what if Keetah is going to die anyway? And we can live, and...ascend? Together."

"I can't let her die thinking I left her behind, Alice. I would do anything to be with you, but not that."

"What if the Swedes call off the whole thing? Then would you stay with me? In Sweden?"

"I don't think it's even possible to call it off now. Too much has been set in motion," John said. "Plus, nobody ever asked me to be part of the ascension *or* Sweden. Everybody's been pretty focused on me becoming a computer. Am I invited?"

Alice paused. They hadn't mentioned anything about John. Why wouldn't he be invited?

"Sure. Sure you are." Alice wasn't sure. She wasn't sure at all.

They hadn't even mentioned John, now that she thought about it.

ALICE AND JOHN waited at the designated meeting spot, in the middle of Östermalms Saluhall, under the great clock. They'd found a handy device in Sweden called a BabyBjörn® that Alice could strap to herself so John could ride on her back, no wheelchair required.

Alice shifted from one foot to the other, back and forth.

"Am I too heavy?" John asked.

"No, you're perfect. I'm just nervous."

When the clock struck twelve, Lanna Bergström and her entourage streamed in to meet them.

The two parties eyed each other.

"So we're in?" Alice finally broke the silence. "Me and John?"

The Swedes looked at each other. "Alice, we didn't want to say anything earlier. We were hoping you would figure it out."

"Figure what out?"

"We don't really accept, you know—" Bergström looked away.

"I don't know," Alice insisted. "I don't. *What* don't you accept?"

"Amputees," Anna blurted out. "In Sweden." She removed her eyeglasses and tended to a smudge with a chamois from her purse.

"You *what*?" Alice took a step back.

"Sweden is for people with intact limbs," Albin said.

Alice looked in all directions in the market. She hadn't noticed. Total corporeal standardization. They were right: No amputees. Everybody had all their limbs.

"But one of *your* people did this to him. And anyway," she argued. "Who cares what he looks like, or what number of limbs he has? We're going to a place where people don't even have bodies."

"We don't know that for sure. Maybe you get to keep it."

Alice pictured her mom's ghost's perfectly styled hair. It was true....she *had* kept it.

"Let me repeat this back to you. You took a man's limbs for a computer, after you orchestrated genocide for years and years, so you could get people's brains and bodies to vibrate a certain way, so you could use him to unite all that power and propel yourself off the planet into an unknown dimension, and now the one person who helped you achieve all that isn't *fucking invited*?"

"That's not the point," Bergström said.

"What *is* the point, then, Lanna? Tell me. What's the point of having all your limbs and taking other people's and spending all your time wearing soft sweaters and eating spherical foods and assembling furniture based on unclear diagrams? Then one day you blip into another spot where you, what, do the same damn thing? What's the *fucking* point?"

"Take it easy, Alice," John cautioned from his spot in the BabyBjörn®.

"No, I'm not going to take it easy!" Alice yelled back. "I need to know what the point is of excluding everybody else from this thing that's supposed to be so great. If it's so great, why can't everybody have it?"

"We'll talk about this another day, Alice," Ebba said. "You're having a hysterical moment."

The Swedes streamed out and left John and Alice standing in the middle of Östermalms Saluhall. Alice wasn't winning anybody over, and she had no idea what to do next.

THE NEXT MORNING, the Swedish inner circle sent for them to hand down their decision. Alice loaded John into the BabyBjörn® and they set off to ReTuna. It was just a short walk from their hotel.

"I'm sorry you have to carry me everywhere," John apologized. "In the future, I'll have new arms and legs and be more...ambulatory."

"Uh, we're either ascending into another dimension this week or going back to America to die. No need to invest in new body parts. Anyway, you're not a burden to me, John. I like having you around." It *was* nice, being part of a functional team.

"Whatever happens, whatever they decide," John said, "I support you. I'm on your team." Alice held back her tears by looking up at the sky for a few long moments. One escaped, and beat a path down her cheek.

. . .

ALICE STOOD in the same spot at the coffee shop, half *fika*, half Swedish trial, waiting for the verdict. The Swedes huddled in the back near the coffee roasting equipment, speaking in hushed tones for several long minutes.

"What do you think they're saying back there?" John asked.

"Could be anything," Alice replied, with defeat in her voice. "Small talk, chit-chat, ascension plans. Who knows?"

"Could you hand me my latte?" John asked.

"Oh, sure." Alice approached the coffee bar and picked up John's order.

"*Tack!*" John called to the barista.

The Swedes broke their huddle and took their usual seats. Alice couldn't read them at all. Their expressions were unchanged since Alice had made her first disastrous speech.

"We changed our minds," Åke burst out. "We like your plump, shapeless body, the way your people collect useless things for no reason, how you don't know anything about eating good food or the rest of the world. We even accept your amputee friend and his right to exist."

The Swedes burst into a round of applause.

"That's great," Alice said, once it died down. "Now we just need you to stop the brain net."

The Swedes exchanged looks.

"Oh, Alice," Ebba sighed. "We can't do that."

"There's only one way to stop the brain net now that it's all riled up," Bergström added. "Have a seat."

"I'm okay standing, thanks," Alice said.

"Have you seen this pamphlet?" Albin handed a pamphlet each to John and Alice. Alice took John's for him while he sipped his latte.

So YOU'VE BEEN SELECTED for a Quantum Psychic Entanglement
The Dogon Collective

. . .

"BRIEFLY," Alice said. "But that was a long time ago." She showed it to John and he nodded.

"I'll just cover the finer points, then. Once the brain net is activated, there are only two ways out: either you've got to go the ascension-liquidation route, or you need to put together a quantum psychic entanglement."

"What happens?" Alice asked. "In a...?"

"Quantum psychic entanglement." Albin said.

"Yes," Alice said. "That."

"Three individuals go in," Ebba explained. "When the quantum psychic entanglement enters the brain net, the DNA channels a wormhole."

"And it can't be any old trio," Anna interrupted. "It's got to be the one with the blood, plus two who received it. At least one of them had to have it from a while back, so you can't queue it up on the spot. The other one can be more either recent, or had to be exposed to the proxy blood."

"Proxy blood?" Alice echoed, with confusion.

"Keetah," John said. "She's my proxy."

"Oh, well I swallowed some of her blood before we left Nu Jersey. Who else ate your blood?"

"Bob," John said.

"Bob," Alice said. "Well he's never going to agree to this. He doesn't even like *international* travel. He's *never* going to agree to wormhole travel. Anybody else?"

"I don't think so," John said.

"So the DNA opens a wormhole, a tear in the fabric of time and space." Åke punctured his paper napkin to depict. "When the quantum psychic entanglement fuses together in the brain net, it becomes a singularity: a little black hole here on Earth. According to the pamphlet, the universe mirrors this singularity in return. And then, it will swallow the blood." He threw a sugar cube into his coffee and stirred. "The blood gets destroyed, and Earth gets saved. The portal is closed."

"Well that's exactly what we want," Alice said. "It couldn't be more perfect."

"Of the three who enter, only two can emerge," Bergström said.

"Oh. Oh no. That's not good at all," Alice said.

"Which one never comes back?" John asked.

"Not the one with the blood. Only the blood gets destroyed," Albin said.

"I can't live without my blood though, so....that doesn't sound right," John said. "How am I going to come out of this with no blood and do okay?"

"The weakest mind survives," Ebba said with emphasis. "The strongest gets eliminated."

"That means Bob," Alice said. "Bob survives. You and me..."

"Eliminated?" John echoed. "Sounds serious."

"No, no. It's not the weakest mind that survives," Anna said. "It's the strongest. But when it comes back out, it's not the same." The Swedes murmured among themselves. "That's what the pamphlet said."

"We don't totally know how it works," Bergström said, dismissing the debate with a wave of her manicured hand. "It's an experiment. Oh, also, the three people have to love each other. Or they *all* die. *And*, if that happens, not only is the blood not destroyed, and the portal not closed, the whole thing tears the earth apart anyway. Full rapture."

"Lakes of fire," Albin said.

'Blood boiling. Dead people roaming the earth, getting their dirty rotting body parts all over everything." Anna shuddered. "You can see why we'd try to eject into another dimension instead of going through all that. And then the *real* floods come. No chance of surviving those."

John and Alice exchanged glances. "I won't let you get eliminated," he said.

"I don't know how you would stop it," Alice answered. "It sounds like this portal isn't open to discussion. Wait. What did you say? Did you say *love*?"

"Love," Anna said. "The three people have to feel love for one another. Or it doesn't work. That's what it said in the pamphlet."

"You got all this information from the pamphlet?"

The Swedes nodded.

"I don't remember that," Alice said. "Did you read it?"

John nodded his head. "Yes. I gave it to you at the yoga retreat."

Alice shrugged. "No recollection."

"There are only so many pamphlets a person can read and absorb," he said.

"Well, if it's true, we're all gonna die. Because I hate Bob."

"No, you don't. You don't hate Bob," John argued.

"Don't tell me who I hate and who I don't hate," Alice shot back. "I *do* hate him. He took advantage of me. Don't you hate Bob? He took your limbs. And he didn't even know why."

John paused for a long moment, and then he said, "I choose my own fate."

"Really? You planned this?" Alice gestured to John's spot in the backpack, to his four stumps. And then felt like an absolute monster. "I'm sorry, John. I shouldn't have said that."

John ignored her apology.

"*Planned* is a strong word. But I do know that the only person who takes advantage of me is me. I'm choosing to be my best self today. I don't need arms and legs for that."

"But I needed him and he used me. From the very beginning. He used us. He could have helped you get away when we got back to Nu Jersey."

"Alice, maybe he did or maybe he didn't. Either way, that's a thought you tell yourself that makes you feel angry and sad." John put his arm on hers. "We need to feel love now. We need to save America."

"You only like it because you're new," Alice sobbed. "I don't even know what America is. It's been lying to me all my life."

John sighed. "Yes, Alice, the United States is a filthy, lying craphole, but it's *our* filthy, lying craphole."

"I hate to be the rotten herring in the room," Ebba said, clearing her throat, "but there's also Tom Fletch Senior. Without John in the United States, he's replaced the nexus of the brain net with his own mind."

"What about Keetah? Is she okay?" John asked.

"Oh, I don't know about that. From what we understand, it's, ah, what could I say that completely understates the real point? It's a little bit of a mess in America right now. That's why we're telling you all this information that ruins our very own plot. We don't really know what's going to happen next anymore. Things have, ah, gone off the rails, as you say."

"Then we have to take our filthy, lying craphole back from Tom Fletch Senior." John exclaimed.

"He won't go down without a fight," Anna said.

Alice sighed. "Nothing about this is *hygge*."

"Hygge is a Danish word, Alice," Anna said. "We don't associate with those barbarians."

Alice unhooked the backpack to set John down on the sofa, took off her beautiful, soft Swedish sweater, and handed it back to the Swedes.

"I won't need this anymore," she said sadly. "Please return my plasticlothes."

40

BRACE FOR LANDING

"Brace for landing," the flight attendant intoned, with cheer. Alice and John exchanged glances and put their helmets on along with the rest of the passengers and crew.

The Nu Newark airport runway appeared, and their plane dropped into freefall. The hundred or so passengers screamed, including Alice. She gripped John's stump so hard, she might have torn off the rest of the partial limb. They bounced once, then twice, and then settled onto a massive sheet of rubber rolled out for the occasion.

"Was flying always like this?" Alice asked.

"No," John said. "You used to get a drink."

Electromagnetic field glitch planning was a success, but it didn't feel like it.

Alice stepped onto the rubber landing pad with a moderate case of whiplash, carrying John in her arms. They bounced and tumbled a few steps until they rolled off the protective rubber landing and came to rest on the tarmac. It smelled like it was melting. The haze was blazing hot that day.

The cool sunshine of Stockholm was far away. This was America.

"Airport's not looking so hot," John commented. Alice unfolded

John's transit backpack and set John in it, then followed where he pointed with his chin.

Nu Newark Airport didn't look very operational. It was shot up, crumbled to the point of total sky exposure in most of the terminals. Looters had gotten to it, too. Everything was stripped.

"I don't remember what it looked like before the Flood," Alice said.

"I don't know what it looked like before the Flood," John said. "But it didn't look like this when I got here. It didn't even look this bad last week when we flew out."

The pilots descended from the plane on ropes, opened the baggage hatch, and threw all the luggage onto the runway. Alice tried to bounce over to hers, but she couldn't gain her balance and she and John toppled backward, bouncing and jiggling. Looters ran up and intercepted their suitcases, taking off with them.

"Hey!" Alice shouted after them. "That's my Swedish stuff!"

"Don't worry about it, Alice. We can get more..." John trailed off.

No they couldn't. They weren't going to see Sweden again. They'd come to America to die. Alice appraised the ruin around them.

The smell of never-washed plastisocks was all around, suffocating her nostrils. Was it new, or had she never noticed it?

She would have done anything for a *fika*. But it was time to go to work.

ALICE PEERED into Bob's office: The walls were splashed with blood. Tom Fletch Senior sat there at Bob's desk, ancient, wearing skins. Bloody human skins.

"Alice," he said lightly. "I knew you'd come back. There was never any doubt." The skin-monster shifted its weight.

"Where's Bob?"

"Dead, I imagine. Not made of tough stuff. He never was. Probably died in a riot. There have been a few down by his condo this week."

"Oh, okay. Thank you." Alice turned to go.

"Alice?" Tom Fletch Senior called.

She paused.

"I know you have the torso. I don't need him anymore, but I will eat him before this week is through."

Alice backed out of the room. Tom Fletch Senior didn't follow her, though he looked like he was moving — the skins he wore pulsed all on their own, patches of human flesh, layer upon layer. A scalp on his head. A strip of shin on his leg. Extra fingernails trailing from his fingertips.

"There's no stopping this, Alice," he called after her.

His voice echoed down the hallway. Market, Research, Incorporated was covered in blood.

"Gross," Alice mumbled.

SHE UNLOCKED THE DOOR, and hurled herself into the condo. Her mom's ghost screamed. Alice screamed.

"Mom! Why are you screaming? We have to get Bob. Where's Erik?"

"I'm in a panic, that's why," her mom's ghost said, her ephemeral voice huskier than usual. "I don't know where Erik's gone. The brain net made him and everybody else just as rabid as an old Flood raccoon. He ran off."

"He should have come to Sweden."

"He said he didn't want to leave me. Now look. I'm left anyway."

"Maybe he'll come back," Alice suggested. "What if we take the brain net offline?"

"Oh, honey. It's too far along. We've still got the war going. On top of that, people are already starting to turn inside out. You know Sue, across the way? Inside out. Blood and guts all over the place while she was washing the car late last week. And I heard there's a lake of fire in Lambertville already," Her mom said.

"The pamphlet says it's possible to stop it. With the quantum psychic entanglement. I don't know. I have to figure out how to love Bob. While I'm high on John's blood."

"Okay, dear." Her mom chuckled. "If you say so. You sure know how to get yourself into some silly schemes."

Alice bristled at her mom's phrasing, then thought better of it.

"You know, mom, there were a lot of things you did, over the years, and recently too, that I didn't understand. I've been pretty critical of you. Mostly since you died, I guess. But I want you to know you were a good mom."

"Thanks, dear. It was a privilege and my pleasure. Good luck out there." Alice's mom held up her ghastly hand entrails so Alice could high-five them.

John ambled out of the bathroom and climbed halfway up the emergency flood hatch to sink into the backpack strapped to Alice.

Something outside exploded. It lit the condo up and the mushroom cloud rose into the sky. Alice peered out the window.

"Ready?" John asked.

"Ready," Alice nodded.

But she wasn't.

OUTSIDE, the apocalypse was kicking into high gear. A little pond of fire cropped up a few doors down without warning. Alice's neighbors were in the street, scattered. The explosion had leveled the row of condos across from Alice's own.

"Take the torso!" A woman screamed and hurled herself at them. It was Karen, Alice saw, the neighbor on the other side of Mr. Worthington's place. Her face had turned inside out but Alice recognized her by her short blond hair and the way she screamed, "*I want to speak to the manager! THE MANAGER!*"

Alice yanked her headset off, and Karen screamed again, a low, ratchet howl that shook Alice's insides. Karen clutched at her own pulsing face. Then she dropped to the ground, convulsing.

Alice's mom's ghost was right. People were going nuts. The brain net was frying them. Fletch Senior had given them attack orders.

Orders to get John.

"We've got to get to Bob's," John yelled over the din of zombie-esque moans. "*Fast.*" Alice and John ran as a unit for her mom's self-driving car and dove in.

"Bob's house," she announced.

But nothing happened.

"Shit," Alice said. Nothing was working anymore. "Okay, John. Looks like it's fartlek time. Ready to run for it?" They'd practiced running as a unit in Sweden, and now they were about to be tested. John flattened himself against Alice.

"Ready," John said.

"Ready," Alice repeated. "Right arm first." Alice and John dove out of her mom's defunct car onto the ground, dodged a possessed neighbor, rolled, and righted themselves. They sprinted as one, her arms and legs pumping in unison with his stumps, Tom Fletch Senior's growing hoard of mind-controlled attackers trailing and grunting behind.

"I don't know which way to go!" Alice shouted above the grunting din. "I need directions—" Alice slipped her headset on.

TRENTON - NU JERSEY'S Senator held an emergency Cabinet meeting Friday after a night of raging protests that saw demonstrators shut down roads across the state with burning tires in renewed protests spurred by a plunging regional cryptocurrency

GREETINGS, worker 6428! Do you owe money to the government for your condo payment? Come work at Market, Research, Inc.! [Ref. no. 1937]

GREETINGS, citizen 72105! Take the torso! [Ref. no. 00741]

Nu York - The United Nations voiced horror following reports that twelve mass graves had been discovered along the Nu Jersey border in an area recently seized by the unity government after President Swift deployed troops

TAKE THE TORSO

Alice closed her eyes and opened them.

TAKE THE TORSO

Alice turned and raised her hand to John's neck, wrapped her fingers around his jugular—

John hit the headset off her head. "Snap out of it!" He shouted. He slapped her in the face with his stump.

"Oh, jeez. Sorry, John."

"Run," he yelled. "I'll tell you which way to go. Just run!"

Bloody and scorched, they limped up to Bob's condo.

The door was ajar. Alice and John peered in.

Bob was sitting at the table, staring. They entered.

"Take the torso," Bob said. "Take the torso."

"Bob, it's me, Alice! And John. His name isn't *the torso*. It's John."

Bob stood up, eyes still glazed. Not their usual glaze of stupidity and dogged self-concern. Worse. Haggard, bloodshot to the point of a nauseating clumpy clottedness that roped through his pupils. Reached into his brain.

Alice took a step back.

Bob took a shuffling step forward.

She tore his headset off his face.

He screamed and head-butted her.

She punched him in the nose.

"Ow!" Bob cried. "What did you do that for?"

"You head-butted me!"

"Ow!" He repeated, holding his nose. "I'm bleeding."

"You're filthy," Alice said. "And why is the top of your head so soft?"

"Hi, Bob," John chimed in from the backpack.

"Hi, John," Bob said. "Welcome back."

"Thanks," John said. "Glad to see you're not a mind-controlled zombie anymore. Have you seen Keetah? Do you know if she's alive?"

"I haven't been in to the office lately," Bob said. "I haven't been feeling well."

"Bob, listen. We need to attack Tom Fletch Senior."

"What? That old ballsack? Why?"

"Oh, jeez, are you kidding me right now?" Alice rolled her eyes. "He's the brain net! He's sewn John's skin to himself and he's controlling everybody's mind with the LINCs. I don't even think he cares about ascending anymore. Now he's busy being evil. It's pulling in more and more of America, too. It's not just Nu Jersey and Nu York anymore. I saw it on TV in Sweden. But there's something we can do to stop it. We have to get into the brain net."

Bob stared blankly at Alice.

"The three of us," John said.

"It's the only way to stop the Swedes from killing us all," Alice added.

No change in his expression. Totally vacant.

I'm never going to be able to love you. And certainly not in the next few hours.

Come on, Alice. Sure you can, John urged.

"He has no redeeming qualities!" Alice exclaimed. "And now he smells bad, too. We're doomed." She wandered into the kitchen and hit the SnackAttack for a coffee, but nothing happened. Alice sank into a chair and rested her head on a hand. John climbed out of the baby backpack to sit opposite.

"Who smells bad?" Bob asked.

"Wait a second," Alice said. "Did you just talk to me in my head?"

John nodded. "Brain net's going strong," he said.

Alice needed to figure out how to transform the expanding chill in her stomach into action.

"Bob! This is getting totally out of hand," she said. "Let's go. You have to come with us to the office."

"But I don't wanna. I don't want to die!" Bob wailed.

"You probably won't," Alice reassured him. "I'm starting to think I'm the weak link in this group. If I were a mental powerhouse, I would have stayed in Sweden."

41

THEY SET OUT AS A TEAM

They set out as a team for the offices of Market, Research, Incorporated: Alice out front, John in the backpack, and Bob bringing up the rear.

One last commute to work. It was a less eventful walk than John and Alice had experienced earlier, which made Alice suspicious.

Because this is exactly what Fletch Senior wants.

"Look!" John cried. When their workplace came into view, every mycelium composite in the landscaping that surrounded it, every faux blade of grass, every sculpted fauxflower, reached out of the ground towards them.

"The field has activated," Alice said. "Like the pamphlet said."

"I don't know if mushrooms can really save us now," Bob said.

"I don't know if they're on our side or not," Alice said.

"Take the torso," a horde of their coworkers mumbled from inside the building lobby, until their collective mumbles became a roar.

"We can't go that way," John said. "I know *they're* not on our side."

One of their colleagues burst through the entryway doors at full run. An interviewer from Row Q, Alice recalled.

They all turned to flee.

"This way!" A voice called to them from the maintenance alley between the two main research stacks. It was Erik: foil wrapped around his head, two clumps of mycelium composite shoved in his ears, one arm and one stump waving wildly. Erik, and a sloth. The sloth removed its head.

"Keetah!" John exclaimed. His voice broke. "You're alive. I was so worried."

"There's no time," Erik warned. "Fletch Senior's taken over the brain net!"

"We know," Alice told him. "We've been running ever since we got back from Sweden."

The horde rounded the corner, and they all took off running again, Erik leading them inside, through the rubble of Market, Research, Incorporated.

———

THEY CAUGHT their breath in the crumbled ruins of the Hub.

"Is your mom here?" Erik asked, his voice full of cautious hope. His stump had healed awfully. It looked infected. He was filthy and smelled of sewage.

"No," Alice said. "We left her back at the house."

"Oh." Erik was crestfallen. "But if I don't die near her..." He trailed off.

"You won't be able to find each other in ghost-ville?" Alice asked.

"No," Erik said. "I don't think so." He sighed. "I'm here to stop Fletch Senior. If Edna and I are separated—well, I'll find her. Somehow. Let's go."

They crept along in the ruins of their place of employment.

"I hope my 401(k) still pays out," Bob whispered.

"Shush," Alice hissed. They approached Bob's old office — the site of Tom Fletch Senior's current residence, based on the gratuitous splashes of blood along the wall and the chunks of nail, skin, and hair dragged along the corridor, and the new Hub now, too. They could hear the hum, see the glow.

"Maybe he's out," Alice whispered.

Tom Fletch Senior emerged.

"So much for the element of surprise," Bob muttered.

"There are no surprises when you are a god," Tom Fletch Senior boomed. "I've known where you were every step of the way."

"Uncle Tom," Erik said.

"My errant nephew. What a fool you are to get mixed up with these lice."

"You're the fool," Erik spat. "All those years you thought you were grooming me, I loved them."

"You're as insignificant as they are," Tom Fletch Senior sneered. "And you can't protect anybody. Not them, not yourself." But it wasn't a vocalized sentence. His lips hadn't moved. It was a thought planted directly in their brains.

"Now," John murmured. "We have to start."

Alice pulled a knife out of her pocket and nicked John's stump with it.

As a unit, they edged closer to the biocomputer and its tangle of wires, glowing behind Tom Fletch Senior. Mr. Worthington popped out from behind a column. His teeth, his lips, and part of his neck had all been stitched into the biocomputer, married to the wiring and dripping with blood, stretched with skin that extended onto Tom Fletch Senior's patchwork body. Mr. Worthington was armed to the teeth — and missing his.

'Mr. Worthington, you traitor," Alice shouted. "We've been neighbors for decades."

Mr. Worthington's throat spasmed visibly, and he vomited up his own eyeball.

"I don't think it's his fault," John said.

Mr. Worthington pulled the trigger on one of his many guns. The staccato blasts were deafening.

I love Bob. I love that miserable piece of crap who made me look at his balls day in and day out.

Alice shook her head. *Try again.*

Alice cut her arm and Bob's finger with the knife.

"Ouch," he said.

They edged closer to the netting.

"Erik," Tom Fletch Senior intoned, "There's still time for you to join us. Immortality could be yours. Or, hell on earth. Stop them."

"Alice, I know this job hasn't been easy on you," Bob whispered. "I want you to know that, whatever happens, after about a year you get a one-credit-per-hour raise."

Alice squeezed the knife in her hand.

"Subject to adequate performance review, of course."

Don't stab him.

The three of them united the blood on Bob's finger, Alice's arm, and John's stump.

"Grab the wires!" John shouted. Alice grabbed a handful of wires in her other hand. Green light engulfed their bodies. The room shook.

"No!" Tom Fletch Senior lurched forward.

Another of Mr. Worthington's guns went off, but it was a whisper compared to the metallic roar now coming from the net.

A gust of wind blew through the office. Alice strained to see whether the roof had come off, but she couldn't move. It smelled of ozone, like that bloody extraction day in South Africa. Alice's mind merged with Bob's. Bob couldn't breathe. Had he been shot? The air was thick. He couldn't move. His stumps were locked against his body. The quantum psychic entanglement was in full effect.

Their bodies became energy

fused into the singularity

the room around them faded

They looked into the spacetime continuum as one entity.

JOHN AND ALICE and Bob saw this as one, then separated again. Alice floated out of her body, back into her body, folded inside the dark matter inside her body. Alice floated into her heart, one chamber of her heart, a hole in her heart.

The center of the universe. It was a big black hole.

"I can't love him!" Alice yelled into the hole. "I can't love somebody who took advantage of me when I needed help! This is never going to work."

"I don't know what you're talking about," said the hole. "Sometimes love means fusing into a singularity and joining a black hole with a couple of other people because that will save the world. And sometimes love is just being there."

"I can't do it. I want to stop the apocalypse, I really do, but I can't feel love for Bob."

"Hold up," said the hole. "What makes you think this is about love?"

"That's what the Swedes said."

"Well, what do they know? They got that from a bad translation of a Dogon pamphlet they *Columbused*. They don't even let amputees into their country. I'm a fucking abyss in the center of the universe. I say what goes. Apocalypse means *unveiling*. It doesn't mean *the end*."

"Which one of us is the smartest?" Alice asked. "Which one of us doesn't make it out alive?"

"That's not even the point," the hole said. "Stop asking so many questions. I'm the center of this universe, not a personality quiz."

"I can't love Bob. I can't."

"I told you, it's not about that. What makes you think you have to love anybody else? Why not love yourself?" The hole asked. "Plus, what's love mean anyway in a piece-of-shit global capitalist society that commodified everything?"

"Huh?" Alice opened her mouth too wide, and the singularity vivisected her face, pulled her telomeres out of her eyes through long, spider-web-thin strands. Her mind broke and washed out, most of it flooded through her tear ducts, a lesser amount through several of the pores on her chin.

"Nothing," the hole sighed. "Never mind. There's no reasoning with you now. I'm gonna do you a solid."

Alice saw everything from inside the singularity.

The ocean rose up into a tidal wave, a wall of water, rising up and up, cresting around the whole eastern seaboard.

John activated his brain waves at full force to hold off the floods.

Satellites dropped from the sky, one by one.

Fletch Senior was too strong to defeat.

Winds on the surface of Nu Jersey accelerated around Market, Research, Incorporated until they ripped the last comma off the entrance sign.

Alice felt the life drain from John. The universe was taking the blood.

Tom Fletch Senior raised his bloody, skin-covered hand to summon the masses of Market, Research, Incorporated employees.

They swarmed the halls, dragging their bloodied bodies towards the office.

And then they were halted by a tidal wave of bullets.

Beyond them, Kwa Lele and her freedom fighters stood shoulder to shoulder.

Inside the office, Tom Fletch Senior reached into Erik's throat to tear out his heart, interrupted by the butt of Kwa Lele's rifle, hammering into his eyesocket.

The black hole at the center of the universe absorbed the last of the blood from John.

The walls of water lowered.

"No," Tom Fletch Senior gurgled. His skin sizzled and smoked with the dissolution of the brain net.

Mr. Worthington imploded, sprayed the office with his liquified innards.

Erik convulsed on the floor, blood erupting from his throat where Tom Fletch Senior had clawed his way in.

"Edna," he choked, and lay motionless.

WHEN BOB OPENED HIS EYES, he was on the floor, face down. He looked anxiously toward the net. John was in it, covered in sweat, slow trickles of blood running from his eyes and ears, looking awful but alive, breathing hard.

But Alice wasn't there.

"What happened?" John said, after he'd caught his breath. He stared down the net next to him, where the three of them had disappeared, anguish in his eyes, as if a look and a thought could bring Alice back.

"I don't know," Bob said. He felt for his face. "What was that place?"

"The singularity. Alice didn't tell you the whole story," John said. "The Swedes told us. The Dogons told *them*. Three go in, but only two can come out. They didn't know which one would get left behind. They said "maybe, the person who got trapped in there, it would be the one...with the highest capacity to..."

"To *what*?"

"To...reason. They thought it would take my blood, or just my blood's DMT content, and spit me out, and...if one of the two survived, it would be—"

"It would be *who*?"

"It would return...*not* the...smartest."

"So she knew it would keep her and spit me out," Bob cried. "Now what? She's just gonna be trapped in a black hole forever? Why didn't she say something?"

"Because the three people who go into the brain net have to love each other. That was our only chance to stop the ascension, to save the planet from Tom Fletch Senior."

"I do," Bob said. "I do love her. But she didn't love me." A tear escaped his right eye and dripped onto his collar.

By the time the tear had soaked in, Alice reappeared near the ceiling. She dropped into the brain net's mesh netting next to John as though she'd been pole vaulting.

"Huppphhh," Alice grunted.

"Alice!" Bob and John shouted in unison.

"That was some wild shit," she panted. She stopped breathing, her body hitching and convulsing. John patted her on the back with his stump until she coughed out a blob of green goop into the net. It bounced through the mesh and hit the floor.

"What did you see in there?" John asked.

"Everything," Alice said. "The walls of water, you held them back! I saw the past, the future, the present. The center of the universe. It spoke to me."

"What did it say?" John leaned back in the net, and rested his head. The top of his ear was missing. Beyond him, Tom Fletch Senior's skin-clad body lay motionless in a puddle of gore.

"It said it was gonna do us a solid. I think we have a shot at continued existence after all. Americans included."

Kwa Lele stepped out of the smoke and over the crumbled threshold.

"It smells like microwaved horse in here," she said, eyeing Bob.

"You came," John said.

"Not for you, little brother. I wanted to show the girls a good time." She was flanked on either side by her co-commanders, all three covered in blood and green goo. They bumped elbows to celebrate their victory. She smiled and winked at Alice.

"Thank you," Alice said. "We couldn't have survived without you."

Kwa Lele nodded. "I know. Let's get out of here before the police turn up and gun us down, girls." She and her leadership team filed out.

"So. Everything is back to normal," Bob exhaled through a whistle. He gingerly tapped Tom Fletch Senior's body with his toe, jumped back when a flap of skin came off and hit the floor with a *thwap*. "We're gonna need a new board of directors," he said. "You can write the position description up on Monday, Alice. You know, after we get this mess cleaned up." He pointed out a series of bones and small internal organs that had been plastered to the walls. "Maybe we can switch to telework for a week."

Alice tossed Bob her headset. It bounced off his chest and clanged to the floor.

"No way, Bob." She climbed out of the net.

"It's Mr. Petri," Bob said. "I know things between us got a little informal there for a while, but—"

"I'm done with this job." Alice climbed out of the netting. She turned to John. "What about you?"

"Oh, I still need to work here, or my H-1 visa will be revoked. But I do want to take a break now. Maybe get a snack?" John checked Alice's expression to see if she took to the idea.

Alice sighed. "*Fika* time," she said. She heaved John out of the net and boosted him up onto her right hip.

"See you Monday, boss." John waved a stump at Bob. "Have a good weekend."

"See you Monday," Bob answered. "Alice, I'll leave your position open until the end of the week. In case you change your mind."

42

ALICE AND JOHN PICKED

Alice and John picked their way through the wreckage of Market, Research, Incorporated. Parts of the roof had blown off. There were plastics everywhere, pasted to the walls, the ceiling, the mauve office furniture, with a mixture of goo and blood. Ankle-deep green ooze flowed down the hallway, glowing and pulsing with an electromagnetic charge.

When Alice and John hit the corridor, a few straggling, half-hypnotized employees joined, shuffling. Alice stopped and eyed them to be sure they were ignoring John. Electricity hissed and hummed in the air, a smell of lightning striking.

They passed the interview pen. The remaining employees of Market, Research, Incorporated unbuckled their leg cuffs and stumbled out. All but a few still had eyes glazed over from the brain net. One or two cheered. Another approached them. Alice backed away, in case they were still under the magnetic hypnosis of the brain net.

"Didn't you hear?" The interviewer said. She recognized him from her survey pool. Part of his scalp under the headset was shorn, but clotted. One more piece of collateral damage from the electromagnetic winds, the biomass frequency surge? Or maybe Fletch Senior had scalped him. Whatever the cause, he didn't seem to notice. He tapped his headset.

Another coworker limped up. "Did you hear the news?"

"War is over?"

"Oh, no, didn't hear about that. Is there a war?"

"Who cares? We've got the rest of the day off. Fifty-nine minutes of paid leave!"

"Yessss!" They bumped fists and undulated their arms in unison, then ignored each other to scan five-second clips. The celebration of the post-floods.

Alice stared at them. Her scalped fellow interviewer flipped up his monocle and turned to her. "Your ear is smoking." He pointed at John. "Yours, too. And you don't have any arms or legs."

"I hadn't noticed," John said. "Thanks for letting me know."

Alice felt her ear with her free hand. The brain net had shaved off and cauterized a sliver of her left ear. She looked down. Her pants were incinerated up to her knees, her shirt to the elbows. She reeked of ozone.

"What the hell kind of survey they got you on?" Fist-hump took a step backward, as though burning off a chunk of your ear could be contagious.

"Razors," Alice said. "Laser razors."

The interviewers shrugged and exchanged glances, then filed out behind the rest of the bloodied horde.

"What do you think will happen to them?" John asked Alice.

"I think they'll commute around the lakes of fire and you'll see 'em in the office on Monday," Alice said.

Her arms and legs seized with cold. Her whole body shuddered with a chill that intensified and then disappeared. A faint voice rattled the hollows inside her ear. "The light, Alice. It's the light! Erik's here, too! He found me. We're not in the light. We *are* the light."

Alice held a thumb's up to the sky, in case her mom could see her.

"What are *you* going to do?" John asked, ignoring Alice's incoherent mumbling and hand gestures.

"I don't know," Alice said. "But I'll tell you one thing. This corporation is no place for people." She licked her finger and extinguished her smoking ear. "I quit."

The End

STAY CONNECTED, GET A GIFT

Subscribe to my newsletter here www.jrpomerantz.com, and you will be rewarded with *Rats*, the short story prequel to the next installment in the New Espionage Collection, Love in the Time of the Improvised Explosive Device.

YOUR OPINION IS VERY IMPORTANT TO US

Someday I'll have a big, long list of other works, and fans all over the world, but right now nobody knows who the hell I am. Except *you*. Nothing would help me out more than if you'd take a moment to leave me a review: Review this book!

I had a lot of help on this project, and we all did our best. If you see any mistakes, plot holes, misspellings, or anything else that would shame a perfectionist, I'd appreciate it if you'd contact me directly via jr@jrpomerantz.com and let me know.

And don't forget to tell all your friends, family, colleagues, and political enemies about Corporate Torsos Need Not Apply.

JRP.

ACKNOWLEDGMENTS

In the twenty-four years since I first started this book, I "finished" it, we'll say, nine times. Each time, I cried, at least a little. Sometimes, I cried a lot.

When you spend twenty-four years working on something, after it's all done, you can say to yourself, well, that was one thing I worked on among many things that were going on in my life. Or you can say, that was my life's work. If you say the latter, you might cry. If you think about it as the former, your reaction is less emotional.

I don't know why I was crying. I could never figure it out. But I hope it was from gratitude.

I've talked about the book to every single family member and friend I've ever had in those twenty-four years. Writer groups. Colleagues. Dates. Writing classes. Loved ones. Write club. Strangers.

I once stopped dating a man because he made a disparaging comment about the plot. I've never been more pleased with my own loyalty and knowing exactly where it lies.

Writing has been a strange and difficult undertaking, which really surprised me. The entire time. I never became less surprised at how long it took me to write this novel. And I *still* don't know why it took 24 years. I won my first award for writing when I was in grade school, and I thought they'd keep on flowing for decades to come.

They didn't. Because I was just working on this one thing. Writing usually comes easy to me. Writing a novel didn't.

But, every time I spoke to somebody about my novel and the process I was undertaking, whatever they said back, and however that exchange went, it showed me the way.

Everybody helped. *Everybody*. How can I thank *everybody* for their contributions to my efforts over the years? Well, I'll try. If I leave somebody out, there's always the second edition.

I want to thank my first (and only) college writing instructor, Prof. Jack Trujillo, who gave me good, honest feedback about a shorter piece, upon which I lashed out and tried to emotionally manipulate him through guilt because I couldn't handle criticism yet, even though he was absolutely right and I wound up doing everything he suggested.

That story, Vegetables, was published in the University of New Mexico literary journal later that year. It was also my first and only speaking engagement about my published work.

Back up. I need to thank my middle school teacher Mrs. Claire C. Kilbourne, for giving me the most comprehensive set of skills ever conceived in an American public school curriculum. I'm talking about color psychology, handwriting analysis, logic, advertising, how to fake a UFO photo. And, most importantly, creative writing. I have a lot of other teachers to thank, too.

I want to thank my mom for teaching me how to read, saving all my writing, encouraging me, and, for every new job I got, saying something along the lines of, "But I always thought you'd be a *writer*."

I want to thank my dad for the precious financial advice, "Don't quit your day job." This kept my fiction writing independent, unfettered by popular opinion or market.

I want to thank my brother for brainstorming advertising ideas with me a few years before book completion. I do still intend to have the cover art planted in a field and photographed via drone as a publicity stunt.

I want to thank the dozens and dozens of instructors I've had, all the writing classes and seminars I've taken over the past twenty-four years in New Jersey, New York, New Mexico, and the greater DC area. I can't remember them all, there are so many. Gotham Writers Workshop; Lisa Norman, Lori Brown Patrick, and others at the Margie Lawson Writer's Academy; Donald Maass; Kathryn Johnson's

Extreme Novelist courses at The Writer's Center; Maryland Writers' Association, and many, many others.

Thank you to the book coach who swindled me out of a chunk of money in 2018 (I'm working on a screenplay about it, so stay tuned). That was the exact moment I realized I had to start coaching myself through my own damn book.

Thanks to my Write Club, my *real* coaches. The conclusion of this book started with them. They dished out a lot of difficult feedback, but they were right, and I trusted those geniuses enough to listen to them. I'm so glad I did.

I finished the first draft during NaNoWriMo 2015 and I'll always be grateful for that invented month-long holiday. I was at a related event and complaining about my project, some doubts I had, when a young man said to me, "I believe in you." I was so shocked by that unsolicited support that I finished my book draft that month.

Thanks to all the agents who turned me down over the years. I didn't have a computer or a mobile phone when I first started writing it. Since then, self-publishing has risen in a big way, and I'm excited to be a part of the community of independent authors operating outside of mainstream and corporate publishing. I've been getting self-publishing advice and assistance from Mark Dawson's Self-Publishing Formula and from Craig Martelle, et al., via the 20Books-To50K group. They're a treasure.

Thank you to the writing contest Ink & Insights. I entered the first forty pages of Corporate Torsos Need Not Apply in 2017 and 2018. The agent feedback was helpful and encouraging, and I highly recommend it to new authors.

Thank you to my website and book cover designer, Steve Rokitka. I foolishly thought this book would be done in 2017, and I'm so glad I had his images to pull me through these last years to make me feel like I had a book before I had a book.

Thank you to my editor, Mariko Hewer. I post-edited over top of her impeccable job like a monster, so any errors you see are my own and not hers.

Thank you to Luciana Leal. Her commitment to her own artistic endeavors inspired me at a time when I needed it most. Music sparked this story, and her music pulled it through the end of its conception this month.

Thank you to coffee, the love of my life and bringer of cross-pollinated ideas in an intense and severe way.

Thank you to everybody who has ever fought for freedom, and to those who wrote about their struggle. The first time I became aware of them as a group was when I saw a separate ticket window labeled 'freedom fighters' at a train station in India in 2004. I wish I'd learned to know and respect it as an occupation earlier in life.

I started writing a story back in 1996, and in many ways it changed over the years, but in other ways the story stayed the same. I hope I spent my time well, in working on this.

Thanks anyway, though, to you especially, for being here with me now. And thanks for reading my book. If you enjoyed it, even the least little bit, it was worth every hour, every day I ever spent.

- JR Pomerantz
20 June 2020

ALSO BY JR POMERANTZ

Love in the Time of the Improvised Explosive Device